# Vivian Rising

# Vivian Rising

DANIELLA BRODSKY

Downtown Press
*New York London Toronto Sydney*

Downtown Press
A Division of Simon & Schuster, Inc.
1230 Avenue of the Americas
New York, NY 10020

This book is a work of fiction. Names, characters, places, and incidents either are products of the author's imagination or are used fictitiously. Any resemblance to actual events or locales or persons, living or dead, is entirely coincidental.



First Downtown Press trade paperback edition August 2010



Designed by Renata Di Biase

Manufactured in the United States of America

10 9 8 7 6 5 4 3 2 1

Library of Congress Cataloging-in-Publication Data
Brodsky, Daniella.
Vivian rising / Daniella Brodsky.—1st Downtown Press trade paperback ed.
p. cm.
1. Self-realization in women.—Fiction. 2. Young women.—Fiction.
3. Grandmothers.—Death.—Fiction. 4. Astrology.—Fiction. I. Title.
PS3602.R635V58 2010
813'.6.—dc22

2010017236

ISBN 978-1-4391-7202-5
ISBN 978-1-4391-7203-2 (ebook)

*For Roger, whom I do not love for his intellect. Not at all.*

# Vivian Rising

# I.

♈ ♉ ♊ ♋ ♌ ♍ ♎ ♏

*Faith no doubt moves mountains, but not necessarily to where we want them.*

—Mason Cooley

I *can't quite* believe what I'm doing. I should be sitting with my grandma, squeezing her hand while I bravely, physically hold her back from heaven—the two of us beating death together. I should *be* her strength, as she's always been for me. The woman I wish I were would watch like a hawk, offering insightful information about the moments leading to this one, to the team of doctors who've just come screaming into the room. Like a stoic character from the movies, I'd step aside, but never out of view, as they attend to the wild beeping and the terrifying flat green line rolling across her heart monitor.

But I didn't sit alongside in a brilliant display of solidarity as they patted at her purpled legs and, in a stunningly synchronized movement, turned her over, all the while, one of them enunciating questions as if she wasn't dying but was merely from Japan—as if speaking too loudly would help her to understand. As I say, I wasn't there for her at all.

Instead, as soon as they arrived, yanking out steel instruments and prodding at buttons on machines they rolled in, I silently rose from the nubby chair that had come to mold itself to the shape of my butt over these months, and closed myself inside Grams's en suite bathroom. There was no lid over the toilet, and so I just sat down on top of the seat in my jeans and pulled my legs up, curling into myself as deeply as possible.

So I'm sitting here, and I keep focusing on just one detail. I'm trying to wrap my head around—trying to *buy*—the fact that Grams was unable to answer the simple questions, "CAN YOU HEAR ME, MS. SKLAR?" "CAN YOU STAY WITH US, MS. SKLAR?"

This is a woman who always had an answer for everything. A good answer. Like, for instance, the time my mother came storming back into our lives, banging on my grandma's door as if she were running from a murderer, and Grams said, "Thelma, just shut up. You sound like a freaking idiot."

I taught her the "freaking" part back in high school. She really took to it. I don't think she discriminated very well about when it should be used, but thinking back, it really did add a unique flavor to her interactions. The mailman would be distributing catalogs into all the tiny boxes in her lobby and Grams would walk in, and he'd stop what he was doing, gather all of her mail, and hand it right to her. And she would say, "Oh, thank you so freaking much. You are so freaking wonderful to me—thirty-five years you are freaking delivering my mail." She would give him a big kiss right on the mouth, as this is how she greeted everyone, and leave him bewildered, but charmed all the same.

How can this woman be—in all likelihood—dead, on the other side of this door?

"CAN YOU HEAR ME, MS. SKLAR?"

It comes rolling right under the door, as if trying to scold me out. But all I can think is that she *hates* the title *Ms.* She said it was "asinine," another of her cherished words. She once spelled it with two S's so that she could use it in Scrabble to get the bonus points, but whatever. I let her get away with it—sort of. Until the next time we played, and *I* was winning, and she pointed out that my spelling of *sincerly* was incorrect. Which obviously it was, but I thought she'd let me even the score. "What is this freaking 'even the score' bullshit with you?" she liked to ask me. No one needed to teach her *bullshit.*

"It's only fair," I said.

"There's no such thing as fair. You get what you get; that bitch, Mrs. Hirsch, next door, she gets what she gets. I don't know why you never understand this, Viv. There is no point to figuring out why or to wasting your energy being upset about it."

Whatever, *Ms.* All I can do right now is think how unfair this is and ask why the fuck it's happening. I pull myself in tighter, but it's no use, I can't will whatever powers-that-be to shove me back into the womb. All this willing and thinking does absolutely nothing, but honestly, I have a hunch that my mother's womb isn't so cushy anyway.

*Get the hell up and do something!* I keep telling myself. *Don't just let this happen.* But the words fall away like sheets of paper along a swift breeze.

This is even harder to admit than the hiding in the bathroom rather than comforting Grams part, but here it goes: more than anything, I'm pissed off at her. I've been sat down and told that after she'd been here all this time for the anemia (which, by the way, is exponentially worse than the image of wan teenage girls who don't eat enough meat), for the diabetes, for all of that, on top of it, she wound up with a stroke, which took her speech away. But deep down, I can't stop thinking that if she really wanted to, she could just answer, that she could just ring the nurse and say, "I'm freaking hungry! And don't bring me anymore of that green Jell-O crap, or I'm going to freaking flip out."

I did *not* teach her the "flip out" thing. She got that from Kramer on *Seinfeld,* and she does a rather convincing impression—shaking her head and jiggling her hand and everything. Or she *did.* Bruce, my boyfriend, really likes that impression of hers. He's always asking her to do it, when he's around, of course . . . which lately he hasn't often been. But this is certainly not the time to worry about that.

She's being what sounds like unsuccessfully resuscitated out there, and I'm in here pissed off at her. If there was ever a time I should give her a pass, this is certainly it. Didn't she give me a pass when I told her in the fifth grade that I wanted to move in with my best friend, Wendy, because her mother was younger and prettier and it was embarrassing to be seen everywhere with your grandmother? How about when I asked her to stop wearing her "housecoat" out in the street? Didn't she give me a pass when I failed chemistry? In fact, didn't she go up to the school and tell that teacher to just give me a D, who would it hurt; didn't kids with no parents deserve to go to college, and what did she think she was proving by bringing yet another Brooklyn high school student down with the ranks?

Oh, God. My chest is heaving in and out, and yet I can't manage any air. It just got louder out there. I hear someone using their cell phone like a walkie-talkie, asking for something very complicated. I try to work out the syllables, but I can't. I manage to get off the toilet, but only as far as pressing my ear to the door, not so far as emerging from it and facing this.

"We're losing her!" someone yells.

My eyes bulge, but it's like I'm listening to a made-for-TV movie that I can't stand to watch but can't stop commenting on from the next room. Don't they always use that line, *We're losing her!* Couldn't they have come up with something more original for such a pivotal point—the finale—in Gram's life?

This is a woman whose parents put her on a boat to New York—in *diapers*—with a stranger, to escape the Nazis in Poland. Surely with an opener like that, she deserves a stunning ending.

"Get the paddles!" the same voice yells.

The paddles? This is just unacceptable. Don't they always do *this,* too? If I weren't so paralyzed here, wedged in between the sink and the enormous metal garbage pail, I'd go right out there and tell that woman to do a better job. I would go out there and yell my head off at them all—if I could just bring myself to leave this bathroom.

Suddenly I realize there's no talking at all now; it's all hushed silence with syncopated sounds, like something out of Blue Man Group. At least Grams would appreciate that. She called it Blue *Guy* Group, but whatever, she still calls me Vicky sometimes. Or *called* me Vicky. No, that doesn't sound or feel right at all; I refuse to change my tenses.

I hear wheels screech past the bathroom door and then clanging, way too many footsteps, and finally an awful lot of metal scraping against the bedrails. "Get it! Get it!" another voice yells.

My heart is in my throat.

"Don't lose her!" the first voice instructs.

"No pulse. I'm not getting a pulse." This news comes through in a Puerto Rican accent, which I know comes from a bitchy, muscular guy, whom I can picture very clearly.

"No pulse," a softer female voice assents.

Another voice I can't place confirms it.

My eyes are screwed tight. I hate them all. I hate my mother for not being here, for making me not even want her here. I hate my father for dying. I hate my grandmother—how could she just let this freaking happen? And I hate myself. In fact, I hate myself most of all.

There are two minutes of whispery silence, during which I cannot make out any words. I am on the toilet again, this time praying to a God I never seem to make time for except in moments like this. My hands are pressed together, because I'm pretty sure this is the way to do it in crisis. *Please, please, God. Please do not freaking let my grandmother die. She is all I have in this world.*

I squeeze my eyes shut so tightly that colorful geometrics pass beneath my lids. I feel my head wobble a little, like an enormous energy has overtaken me, and I think, I really think that something celestial, something spiritually powerful is happening. I breathe, taking in a wonderful gulp of air for the first time since the monitor began to scream.

*Everything is going to be just fine.* The words come to me, just like that. And there it is, a higher being. *God,* Hashem, as they used to teach me as a little girl in pigtails, has come down to help me and Grams. He understands that I am more culturally Jewish than practicingly so, and he forgives me and this is how he shows me. By giving us another shot.

I open my eyes, stand, place my hand on the doorknob. I draw one last fantastic breath, and prepare to greet a revived Grams with a funny line, something witty that she would appreciate.

"Well, I hope you can get all that over again because the camera wasn't roll—" I look up and see that I had it wrong. God wasn't with me. Grams's eyes are closed, the machines—these things that had been such a part of the landscape of our lives—are already being wheeled out to sit in some storeroom.

Everyone looks up. They hadn't realized I was in there.

"Viv? Viv, I'm so sorry. Your grandmother, Ms. Sklar, has passed on."

I look at this woman, this *doctor,* who had all these fancy tools, and all that training, yet couldn't find a way to do a simple job—to save my grandmother, the person I shared my home, my life with. I feel nothing but hate. God has failed me; this woman has failed me. There is nothing in all this universe, with its designer frozen yogurt, its buses that run on water, and its bottomless supply of items costing only 99 cents, there is nothing, in what I once considered a truly miraculous place, to believe in anymore. “Do NOT call her *Ms.* ever again,” I yell as I climb into bed with Grams, the way I did as a child, the way I still do sometimes, when it’s a rainy Sunday or just a long, lazy day. I put her hand over my head, close my own eyes, and crazy as it sounds, I fall asleep.

# 2.

♈ ♉ ♊ ♋ ♌ ♍ ♎ ♏

*To believe with certainty we must begin by doubting.*

—Stanislaus I of Poland

"Dear, dear." I hear her voice before I open my eyes. I'm half in, half out of a dream state, and my grandmother is trying to wake me up—never an easy task.

Once, after she'd already attempted the "dear" thing several dozen times, I screamed, at her *"Just give me sixty seconds!"* I was one hundred percent serious. Her eyes were saying, "You royal pain in the ass," but her mouth said, "Sure, hon." I don't know why she was so sweet to me when I was being such a royal pain in the ass, but she is being just as nice to me now.

"Thanks, Grams," I say.

I open my eyes just the tiniest bit, fluttery and slow. I try to focus on the window across the way; I have the most wonderful view of both bridges. It's one of the best things about living in Brighton Beach. I can't quite make them out, though. I look a little to the right and a little to the left. But they aren't anywhere. My chest tightens. I sit up with a start.

"What the—?" I ask, swiveling to Grams, who is quite shockingly not my grandma at all but the bitchy male nurse.

Oh, yeah.

Oh, fuck.

I try to ignore him and go right back to sleep. I don't want any part of this new life. If I can just sleep for another thirteen years until I'm forty, I'll feel much better.

"Dear, dear." He's at it again.

"Okay, okay," I hear myself whisper. I am going to be sick. I screw my eyes tightly closed and hope my words will be enough to send him away. I would ask God to help me out, but I remember He failed me miserably—tricked me into thinking He had my back but didn't after all.

There's no one to ask. I have been completely drained of faith, as if the dentist's "Mr. Thirsty" slurped it all up.

The nurse touches my arm and I flinch, yanking it away, and tucking it underneath my other arm.

"I know," he says.

That's all I need. I feel the tears come with a burning at my nose. *We had a deal,* I think. *No crying in front of people.* Before I know it they're unstoppable. I pull the pillow over my face. What's to go home to? I live alone now. There's no one to give me incorrect phone messages when I walk in the door, or to nag me about watching bad TV and then sit in front of it with me for hours on end. There's not a person alive who knows where to get the pickles I like.

How do people bear this? I sit up, coerce my legs over the side of the bed.

"Viv, it's Viv, isn't it? Viv, I'm sorry, dear, but you do have some things to take care of, and unfortunately, you can't stay here—legal issues."

This passes for a bedside manner these days—*legal* issues?

* * *

Don't even ask what you have to do when someone dies. Nobody lets you go home and pass out. Nobody puts the slightest bit of originality into their words of comfort. They all get their sentiments directly out of the pamphlet "How to Cope with Grieving and Loss." I know this because I read the entire thing while I waited forty-five minutes to see the administrator, who walked me through a mountain of paperwork. And just when you think the worst is over, you have to gather all the workaday belongings that look like they will be needed again at any moment—things that belonged to your grandmother, your best friend, your parent. You have to pick up her lovely, tiny, child's hairbrush, with strands of her hair woven in among the bristles, and you have to take that hairbrush, that necklace, that pair of fuzzy pink slippers down a hallway, where someone pulls from a drawer a noisy, flimsy, not exactly clean, plastic bag from the supermarket, for you to put it all in. And you take it onto the subway, like it's just a bunch of groceries you were asked to pick up on your way home from work.

# 3.

♈ ♉ ♊ ♋ ♌ ♍ ♎ ♏

*The problem of synchronicity has puzzled me for a long time, ever since the middle twenties, when I was investigating the phenomena of the collective unconscious and kept on coming across connections which I simply could not explain as chance groupings or "runs." What I found were "coincidences" which were connected so meaningfully that their "chance" concurrence would be incredible.*

—Carl Jung

My mother decided to abandon me the day before I was going to start fifth grade. I had gotten my period the previous day and couldn't stop myself from making the connections. It was repugnant, the way the blood had stained my underwear, the way it smelled like something rotten that hadn't gone all the way down the incinerator chute.

"We're going to spend the day with Grandma!" she'd exclaimed. She was giddy. I should have picked up on that. My mother didn't do giddy. Maybe it was the hormones, but I followed her around the kitchen, riding her wave of exhilaration despite the man who exited her bedroom in nothing but tight orange underwear. Normally I'd say something like, "Who is *that*?" the way someone would handle a dead mouse dangling from a trap. If there was a newspaper or empty wine bottle I'd pick it up and hurl it out the door after them. "You *forgot* this!" I'd yell. But that day I tried to hold my tongue.

This guy was eating breakfast with us, though, which made it difficult to continue to be good. My mother poured out his orange juice slowly, without drips, in a way that bothered me enormously. I always poured my own juice. She'd prepared him scrambled eggs and toast and, only after she had heaped it all into a bowl two sizes too small and set it in front of him, did she ask if I'd like some. But I didn't want to eat eggs made for someone else. I wanted eggs made for me—which they never were. I only ever had two choices: cereal—or, if we were out, no cereal.

"These are delicious. What's in there?" this man asked, smiling more than we were used to around this table since my father died.

"Chopped-up babies," I said matter-of-factly before my mother could answer. I spooned a huge mound of Golden Grahams and crunched too loudly. I squirmed as the blood flowed into the bulky pad stuck into my underwear. *Please, please stop!* I begged my body.

"Vivian," was all my mother said. She gave me the evil eye and I was supposed to know what that meant.

"Well, whatever it is, it's good," Gandhi, the peacekeeper, said.

"There's no accounting for taste," I said. I'd heard that before and liked the sound of it. That summer I said that all the time: mostly after I hurled my mother's boyfriends' jackets and wine bottles and condom foils out the door, but also when Wendy told me she preferred Michael Jackson to Led Zeppelin.

“She’s a spitfire, isn’t she?” the man said, scratching his fluffy hair and rubbing his eye with the heel of his palm all in one movement. Probably I’d been told his name, but I preferred to ignore that information.

“She certainly is,” my mother said. By then, we never spoke in tones you might call friendly.

My mother worked at Alexander’s department store in Manhattan, selling women’s gloves and hats, and she was barely ever home. I wasn’t the only kid whose mother didn’t know where their child was. There were several of us: Shelley Wasserman the Bully and The Incredibly Mature Girls, and a few others. We hung out in the chain-fenced schoolyard when Wendy and the others went in for dinner, shrugging too much and jamming our hands in our pockets like we preferred the freedom to do what we wanted. I was always invited to Wendy’s house, but it made me feel worse sometimes to go there.

“No, thanks, I’m not very hungry,” I’d say.

Her face would redden; she thought I was choosing the others over her. I knew how Wendy measured everything in terms of how uncool her braces made her look. For a whole year she started every piece of advice with, “Well, you remember what my mother told me about braces. She said, ‘Wend, sometimes it hurts to be beautiful.’ And that’s true in this case, too, Viv . . .”

“Please,” I told her once. “*Please* find a new metaphor.” We’d just done metaphors with the cool English teacher who’d played Pink Floyd’s *The Wall* and asked, “Now, what do you think the wall *really* means? Is it just a wall, or something more?” I was tough on Wendy. “If I hear the braces thing again, I’m going to hurl.” I’d hurt her feelings. I could tell by the quiet swallowing thing Wendy did. It’s terrible to say, but sometimes I wanted to hurt her feelings. I wanted her to know what I felt like most of the time. The truth was, these other kids knew this already, and that was a comfort—even if I had to turn a blind eye to an obsession with firecrackers or an excessive attachment to Prince.

The latchkey kids and I pooled our money and shared gooey slices of pizza, wiping the grease on our jeans and refilling our wax cups with fountain Cokes when the counterman wasn't watching. We yelled things in the streets like we were teenagers already; we said, "Yeah, that's what I *thought,*" and "Homework is for suckers." At school we acted like we didn't know one another. I would never tell them that I went home later and did my homework, checking it twice each night after I used the key on my neck to open the building's front door, and the one on my shoe to unlock our apartment on the sixth floor, before I made myself some noodles with butter. I would never tell Wendy how I anticipated her knock, how I cherished the three quick raps of it.

"Pack a bag," my mother said that morning, finishing the last of her eggs. They returned to her bedroom. I sat at the table a long time smelling my body's new odor with no better results. My thoughts went in a circle and in minutes my stomach twisted itself into a tight knot. My cereal had soaked up the milk and softened to pillows. I looked down at those swollen Golden Grahams and made myself listen to every grunt, every moan. I let it sting me like a punishment. How could I allow this to happen when my father had been dead barely three months? My bleeding, I was sure, was my penance.

My mother looked uglier when she emerged from her bedroom. She was showered, smelling of patchouli oil, and wearing a floral dress with a hem that swept the mohair carpet and caught wind when she walked. She'd bought it for a picnic we'd had by the bridge at Fort Hamilton. I remember my father twirling her around and around to "Brown Eyed Girl," while me and Grams played gin rummy and giggled. That dress had great lift.

"All packed?" she asked me, giddy again. Gandhi bumped into her when she stopped short. She was standing beside my summer camp macaroni collage. It had been part of the lesson Mrs. Findler had called our "Introduction to Abstraction." I'd never found my mother, or the Popsicle-stick-framed fusilli castle, more revolting.

"Yeah," I lied. With that lie I wound up taking absolutely nothing to my new life. I hadn't brought my key, but even if I had, I don't think I ever would have gone back to that apartment.

I refused to cry. I knew it was my own fault. Already I'd stained my underwear with blood along the sides of the heavy, hardened pad, and now I'd have to wear it anyway. I didn't have anything to change into. Grams would know I was to blame—for the whole thing.

"Your mother loves you in her own way," Grams said to me on that first night, "but she needs to take care of herself right now." At first she tried to explain the inexplicable. But then she cut herself off. "Who am I kidding? She's an asshole. You're the best daughter in the whole wide world, and she has no idea how to care about anyone but herself. So now I'm going to take care of you—the way you deserve."

I didn't say anything for a long while. My grandmother kept her spare change in the plastic eggs that panty hose came packaged in. She scooped cottage cheese onto her hamburger, a point that my mother and I often poked fun at. "What do you want on your hamburger?" My mom would joke. "Cottage cheese?" I'd squeeze up my face like I'd sucked a lemon. "Ewwww. Gross!" We'd laugh and squeeze out the ketchup like normal people.

"Do you have any questions?" Grams asked. She was thin then and smoked long cigarettes with flowers printed up the sides. When she puffed, her cheeks hollowed out and she looked very old.

I shook my head.

"Why don't you go out on the terrace and watch the sunset? I'll make us some tea," she said.

I did as she suggested. It was humid, but up so high there

was a breeze; it felt like a warm caress, someone rubbing my arms. I sat down on the vinyl-strapped chairs and watched the sun disappear behind the water. It seemed to pick up speed as it sank. "What are *you* looking at?" I said to the person two terraces over. It was Mrs. Kaufman, though I didn't know her yet.

"Well," she said, in the way I'd only seen matronly character actors do on sitcoms. I smiled big at her reaction. It was all I could do.

For weeks I told myself my mother would come back. I called our telephone number and listened to the recording tell me, "This number is no longer in service; please check the number and dial again." I read things into the words, decoded them like a word jumble in the Sunday funnies. For two years, she never even called.

My grandmother explained to me about my period and bought me underwear with the days of the week on them. She taught me how to get the stains out with baking soda.

"You're all right," I told her one night about a year and a half in, giddy on hot chocolate and, maybe for the first time, recognizing that this was really my life now.

She tried not to cry. "You're not so bad yourself," she said, and hugged me, her huge breasts squishing around my sides. *I love you,* I said in my head.

# 4.

♈ ♉ ♊ ♋ ♌ ♍ ♎ ♏

*Once change has forced us to move beyond the confines of known territory, we are instantly confronted with that most chilling prospect, the Unknown. There is no way of knowing what change will mean to our lives and so we shirk the very idea of it. . . . Neptune in the natal chart will describe the individual capacity to believe in self, society and in the Unknown.*

—Cordelia Mansall, *The Astrology Workbook*

*At home, I'm* not ready to tell anyone that Grams is dead.

I approach the two gleaming silver and aqua buildings that make up Seacoast Terrace, trying to look up at the rows of terraces as if I've never been here before. If I could just forget I've ever had this life, then maybe I can begin a new one.

But my eye travels up to our terrace on the nineteenth floor. I have an internal homing device for it, even though they're all identical. It helps that we have a giant statue of an eagle leaning out over the terrace railing. This was Grams's idea for scaring away pigeons. She detests—*detested*—pigeons. They've been waging war for decades now. Mostly, the pigeons win, *won*. Whatever.

I give one last look at the empty sky, the sky that supposedly holds the God that I no longer believe in. I descend the four marble steps and follow the grooved, scrubby carpets meant to prevent the old people here from falling and suing the building, which has happened many times. You wouldn't believe the proliferation of Jacuzzi tubs that resulted. The automatic glass door slides open to let me pass.

"How's Sandra today?" Jameson the doorman asks. I do my best to walk tall and cheery past his desk.

"She's doing great," I say. But it must have none of the truth I attempt.

"You're lying." His face drops.

"No. No, I'm not lying."

"Now, I've known your grandmother for forty-eight years—met her on the Fourth of July. I says, 'Who the hell decides to move on the Fourth of July?' There's a huge fireworks display over there by the boardwalk, blasting every two seconds, traffic as far as the eye can see, and there's this little lady—a real looker she was in a pillbox hat, pretty shoes. I had a little crush on her, you know . . ." And he goes into the spiel he's given so many times I can recite it myself. But this time, instead of picturing Grams and Jameson on a cute date at the Chinese restaurant down the block, splitting chow mein and Peking duck out of chafing dishes, my heart aches. Something in my face tips him off.

"She's gone," he says, stopping right in the middle.

I gulp. I will not cry in front of Jameson. He'll just start crying, and then someone else will come by—believe me, there's always someone else coming by around here.

"No, no. She's not," I say, as much for his benefit as mine. I shake my head back and forth, shut my eyes, willing it to be true. *By the time I open my eyes again, she'll be back.* I haven't done this since my mother left. I can remember sitting in this very lobby, saying the exact same thing. It didn't work then, either.

When I open up all I see is Jameson. His shoulders are shaking, up and down, as if he were a passenger on a bumpy train. I hate the way strong people can look so young, so helpless when they cry. It makes the whole world seem hopeless.

"I can't believe it; I can't believe it." He says this over and over as we comfort each other—hand in hand.

"Can't believe what?" The shrill voice belongs to Rachel Valmay in 12K. She always comes down about now to walk her cat. The sight of Rachel and the cat brings on a stabbing pain in my abdomen. Grams and I have spent hours making up stories about Rachel Valmay and that cat of hers. Grams's favorite was that the cat was Rachel's husband, and when he wouldn't eat her "mock chopped suey," which she is always pushing on everyone in the building, she placed a hex on him and turned him into a cat. Grams elbows me whenever Rachel Valmay walks by with the cat. "Just look, the cat's got the same walk as Ira, exactly the same walk."

"Grams didn't pull through," I try to say, my chin shaking so much the words are barely decipherable. Pretty soon there are four seniors in florals, and one giant blond Russian woman named Irena assembled by the sofa and three armchairs, off to the left of Jameson's desk. We're across from the decorative waterfall, which, against the rules, I often splashed around in as a child. Everyone's crying and hugging and saying things like "I'll order in knishes from Mrs. Stahl's for the shiva," and "You'll need to have the funeral at Moishe's. It's the nicest." Everyone's nodding their heads in agreement, for the moment grounded in the comfort of duty, until grief pokes its head in again.

"Sandra is always saying how lovely they do things over at Moishe's." Mrs. Kaufman doesn't mean to say it; it is just such a natural thing to say.

No one knows what to say to that. We all sit, looking at one another, palpably aware that someone—an incredibly vital someone—is missing. I stand, wanting to give everyone time to let this sink in.

"You know where to find me," I say, smile as best as I can, and mechanically, check the mail. From the stack on the shelf in front of the mailboxes I grab the newspaper with our name on it. I walk the mirrored corridor to the elevator bank, clutching the flimsy plastic bag of Grams's things tightly to my chest. I'm not even going to attempt to convey how empty I feel as I open the door to the apartment, filled to the brim with the treasures Grams spent a lifetime collecting—the pretty bowl of seashells, the grouping of impressionist cityscapes in gold bamboo frames over the couch, the colorful Chinese bowls of relics from her life: incense we bought at a street fair, dried flowerheads from birthday bouquets, pennies from all fifty states, and real glass marbles she played with on stoops not too far from here.

I kick my shoes off, then straighten them out snug along the wall, though she isn't here to yell at me if I don't. I slug some of the liquor Grams kept in a crystal bottle on her pretty mirrored bar my entire life, and plop myself on the couch. Rather than face anything just yet, I once again fall very, very deep asleep.

I dream of the first time Grams took me to temple. Shul, she called it. My parents were atheists and so was I. We thought organized religion was for chumps. We preferred free love and believed in the Beatles and in hyphenating your daughter's last name no matter how many people might give her a hard time for it. When John Lennon was shot, we didn't know what to believe in anymore. Unfortunately, the name was a keeper. Vivian Sklar-Singleton was my socially responsible cross to bear.

In the dream, Rabbi Menachem comes up to me and says, "Do you have any questions?" the way he had in real life.

Instead of the answer I really gave—"Only one: where do babies come from?"—I say, "Why does God abandon you?" He begins, "God is . . ." but he fades to black. I look to Grams, who'd been holding my hand, and she's gone, too. I realize it's not the two of them who've disappeared; it's me. I've gone hurtling down the rabbit hole Grams had read to me about so many times. I free-fall for what seems like an eternity and land with a painful thud on sharp grass blades. All around me, Mad Hatters laugh hysterically. I always despised the Mad Hatter. I think it was the teeth. I cover my ears but it's no use at all.

# 5.

♈ ♉ ♊ ♋ ♌ ♍ ♎ ♏

*Sweeping away tracks makes traces, all the more evident the more you try to hide.*

—Zen proverb

This time, when I wake, there's no fooling myself. In the dim morning light, I know she's gone. I feel it along every inch of my skin, like a rash. I take it into the shower with me, along with one of the pretty little oyster shell soaps that Grams kept from her flight attendant days, collected from hotels all over the world. It feels like the right time to finally use one. I slide my finger beneath the round seal in the back. It gives easily after so many decades, and this finally sends me into an unstoppable, throat-shredding cry.

An hour later, I'm clean but angry as hell. My throat is raw, but somehow I like the idea of this; there should be some physical symptoms of the hurricane raging inside of me.

I pull on a little tank top, and over it one of Grams's housecoats. I can't help myself. I dab some of her Shalimar behind my ears and slip a picture of us underneath the snug tank so it sits at my heart, and I set to work.

First I call Moishe's. *Moishe's.* My grandmother is having her funeral at a place whose name we made fun of in our everyday vernacular. Each time we walked by she'd say, "What kind of a name is Moishe's?" We'd try to rhyme it: "Koishe's? Stoishe's? Deutsche's? Froishe's?" And eventually we started to call it Froishe's, because we'd liked that one best. When we couldn't think of a word, instead of asking "Where's that 'thingamajig" or "Whatchamacallit?" we would say, "Where's that goddamned *froishe's*?" Every single thing in this apartment has probably been a *froishe's* at one time or another.

"How can I *'elp* you ease through your pain and suffering?" This is how the beyond-Jewish-sounding man answers the phone. You don't know from this kind of Jewish-sounding unless you've spent considerable time around first-generation Brooklyn Jews. To me, it is the most comforting sound in the world. All the emphasis: "oy" and "you should never know," and *"gevalt"*; "forget about it," "over my dead body," "he should rot," "I don't believe it;" "an ass like that! And she walks around in those clothes!" It's music to my ears.

I can picture this man from memory: he is of medium height and very thin except for an extraordinary belly that stretches his shirt.

I have to stop myself from saying, "Froishe." "Moishe," I say, "it's Viv Sklar-Singleton."

"Oy gevalt. I don't believe it. Those doctors. They should rot."

I close my eyes to soak in the comfort. I'll take what I can get. "You come in and go over everything, but Sandra already picked out the jazzy mahogany model—had me carve something real nice into it."

I sob silently. There is no other place I could possibly have this funeral.

I call the cemetery to let them know we'll be cashing in on the plot my grandmother bought from the Teamsters' Union fund-raiser all those years ago. Next is the job I've been dreading: I call everyone we know and tell them the funeral is the day after tomorrow.

"Do you need anything?" each asks.

"No, no. I'm fine," I say. That pizza-eating girl with her thumbs hooked through dirty jeans settles back in my skin before I know it.

She's just in time, because the last person left to track down is my mother. The woman who refuses to own a cell phone. This would be too practical for a person who is never in the same place for more than a few months.

I flip through to her page in Grams's black book, which serves as information central in our family. Whenever I needed to check a birthday or a phone number, I'd say, "I've got to put a request in to information central." Now I flip the pages like they're my own; it feels sneaky, like going through someone's underwear drawer.

My mother's entry is seven pages long—front and back. There are places listed in America and abroad; places in Kansas and Oklahoma, Scottsdale, and on the coast of Spain—each one has peculiar instructions drawn in Grams's pristine cursive, like: "Ask for Giorgianne," or "When Juan answers tell him you know Stephan's friend." My mother has lived everywhere, yet I have never seen her in even one of these places. I used to pick up the extension and listen in to Grams's entreaties: "Just invite her for a few days, just *a few days*!"

"I just can't," she'd say. *I don't care,* I'd tell myself. *I couldn't give a crap.*

When I picture my mother, it's right here on our couch. There's a slumped look to her mouth, and her eyes are glued to the carpet. She's only half sitting, as if she's ready to bolt the moment a cross word is said. I'm not saying she doesn't deserve sympathy; I'm just saying that she makes it so difficult to feel bad for her. When a person makes the same mistakes over and over again, blames the past for all of it, and tosses everyone to the side like collateral damage—you wish they would just get over it. But she's not expected to do that; that's everyone else's job.

First I try the last entry in the book, which notes, "Call on Tuesdays after seven p.m." It's a number in an area code I don't recognize. A gruff voice comes through on the other end. "Go for it."

I'm not sure what the proper response to that is. "Ummm, is Sheila there?" I try, after an initial pause.

"Oh, *that* one," he says, laughing in a way that makes my skin crawl. I can practically see him shake his head on the other end.

He doesn't say anything for a while.

I worry he might hang up, so I try again. "Is she there?"

Again, a painfully long pause. "Nah, she's *long* gone from *here,*" he says, his dramatic emphases such a perfect fit for my mother, I'm surprised she left.

"Yeah? How long?" I try.

"At least . . . three days." This is like pulling teeth. And believe me, I'm in no mood for pulling teeth.

"Do you know where she went?" I ask.

"I think that's a question you'd better ask her, doll." I don't like the way he calls me "doll," and this is just the impetus I need to go over the deep end.

"Listen, *guy,*" I say, "I need to speak with my mother, okay? Now, you'd better freaking tell me where she is, or I'm going to freaking come down there and yank every single one of your teeth out just the same way you're making me drag this information out of you, got it?"

"Whoa, there, Nelly," he says.

I'm embarrassed for him. I don't know where my mother finds these men who quote Roy Rogers in their daily speech.

"Listen, are you gonna tell me, or am I going to have to bring the cops down there?" I try to deliver this threateningly. I have no idea what the cops would have to do with it, but I'm sure he's in trouble for something; there's always something.

“There’s no need to get nuts, okay?” he says. “She went off with this ice cream truck driver; probably ringing his bell right now.”

This is the last kind of shit I feel like hearing. This is my mother. She thinks she’s gonna be something fantastic. She never settles because her opportunity might be right around the corner. She’s running, probably from the realization that she lost her husband, and now she’s a single mother. Only, she’s been doing this for so long that she’s not a single mother any longer. I try to stay on track. I’m just engaging in a simple transaction of information. I need to think how I can extract it. “Do you happen to know the name of this man?”

“Jim something.”

“Jim something,” I repeat, and take a deep breath. “Do you think there’s anything more inside your head that you can give me before I go all female hormonal on you?” These guys panic as soon as you mention the H word.

“I don’t.”

I’m not going to be able to invite the woman to her own mother’s funeral. Maybe it’s better this way. But I know that my grandmother would never have it. She loved my mother, though she was mortally disappointed in her. She wanted me to learn to love her, too.

“I do have his phone number, though. She gave it to me so’s I can call her up when the hot fudge delivery arrives.”

Hallelujah.

# 6.

♈ ♉ ♊ ♋ ♌ ♍ ♎ ♏

*In one test, 21 UK astrologers chosen at random were asked whether they had noticed affinities with their clients: 16 said yes.*

*Affinity effects seem to manifest in three main ways:*

1. *Clients tend to have the same outer planet(s) prominent as the astrologer. Thus astrologers with a dominant Neptune or Uranus tend to attract Neptunian or Uranian subjects respectively.*

2. *Clients arriving over a period tend to exhibit the same kind of transits or progressions or to be experiencing the same personal problems as the astrologer.*

3. *Clients often tend to arrive in groups of predominantly one Sun sign or another.*

—RECENT ADVANCES IN NATAL ASTROLOGY

How *I wind* up in Manhattan after that is a little difficult to explain.

I call Wendy at our office. She's been working with me at *Skylar Good Foods Journal* for two years, ever since she came back from Turkey, where she went after Japan. "I can't think of a fucking thing to say," she tells me.

"That's fine. Nobody knows what to say," I assure her. "Listen, these are really hard times," I add. "For everyone. Just do my columns. That's more than enough."

"I don't believe this," she says. "You're the one in mourning, and you're comforting *me.* I'm not getting off the phone with you until I think of a good piece of advice."

"We might be here awhile. Remember the Pacific Seafood Extravaganza debacle?" I say, recalling the day I was out sick and Wendy stayed at the office until midnight thinking up a good rhyme for *flounder.*

"Right," she says. "I still don't know how your grandmother came up with 'grab a pounder of flounder.'" I can see Wendy waving her pen. She believes this helps her think. I'm pretty sure after that night Grams might disagree.

"Let me check our horoscopes." When the pen waving fails, this is Wendy's second line of attack.

"That's like trusting your fate to a fortune cookie," I say.

"I know, I know. We all have vices, Miss Perfect, okay?" This banter nearly makes me forget why I'm not right there, sitting on a stack of papers in Wendy's cube, while she pulls up our horoscopes on Google. "Okay, me first. Cancer: *The day will come when your efforts will be rewarded. Do not worry.*"

"Oooh, that sounds important," I say, rolling my eyes.

"You know, I can't remember why we're friends," she says.

"I bring you coffee in the morning."

"That's right," she says. "*Pisces: Keep your eyes open for signs. Today they will be very, very important.*"

"Thank God you read that to me. Could you imagine what kind of disastrous thing might happen to me if I missed a *sign*?"

"One day you'll thank me," she says.

"Thank you," I say. "Can I go now?" I ask, though this exchange is so normal I am loath to hang up.

"No, you can't. I'm still thinking of my piece of wisdom."

"I'll just get comfortable then." I look over at the Seacoast Terrace calendar's July page, its rainbow-over-the-beach photo. Mrs. Kaufman took that back in 1979 from the sixteenth floor after one of the biggest storms on record. Inside tomorrow's July 20th square Grams had written, "Donate $50 to the Humane Society." We have many, many kitten-playing-with-a-ball-of-yarn address stickers.

We are silent; I hear the light background of conversation from Wendy's end. I can't believe there are people there on Sunday. I think how much I've taken for granted in that safe haven of humming fluorescents.

"Got it," she says. "Go do something your grandmother loved to do, but rarely got around to. I bet you she'd like that."

Wendy's advice sticks with me as I boil water for tea. I look at the calendar and know just what to do for Grams: I should go into Manhattan and order a falafel sandwich with extra tahini and tomatoes at Rainbow Falafel. And the second I bite into it, just as she always did, I should complain there isn't enough tahini and tomatoes. And then twenty minutes later I should say, *That was the best falafel in the world—just the perfect amount of tahini and tomatoes. This* she would find the perfect tribute.

I grab my keys and some money and shove it all into the little red leather pouch Grams always keep things in; it's the perfect size for the pocket of her housecoat—which is probably why Grams walked around with it nestled in there for the past decade, pulling from it tissues, change for the ice cream man, scraps she'd clipped from the paper.

I leave the apartment happy to look as ridiculous as I feel. The train screeches to a halt at the platform as I approach. I enter and sit directly across from the doors spreading my arms wide over the back of the empty, molded orange seats.

The gritty Brooklyn skyline floats by, with its endless billboards and brick facades, and then the water along the bridge, and then I'm ensconced in tunnel blackness. It's a long ride. I emerge at Union Square Station feeling both more alone and more connected to Grams than I ever have.

I turn left onto Seventeenth Street, my lip curling into my grandmother's ornery expression. I'm getting excited to eat the thing; this is the way Jews fill holes, with food. I walk quickly, thinking maybe the falafel will jerk me back to my old self. Stranger things have happened: a patient at Mercy Hospital in Springfield, Massachusetts, claimed to see the Virgin Mary on a dirty window pane and thousands of people came. Why can't my epiphany arrive in the form of pulverized chickpeas?

At the door, with its hopeful rainbow decal, I can nearly taste the rich spice of cumin and the cool, creamy tahini. I reach out eagerly for the door, but my wrist wrenches when the handle won't budge. The place is closed. All the lights are off and when I shade my eyes to peer through, all I see is a bunch of cardboard boxes folded inside one large one. Everything looks used up.

I didn't really think a falafel would save me. Even that Virgin Mary was explained away by glass experts: minerals caused a chemical reaction. It's obvious that I could go anywhere else and eat something she might like right now. Or I could eat nothing at all and go home. But I don't do either. I look around with no idea how to find my emotional true north.

I turn toward the street. Now, I know this sounds like something Wendy would do, but I'm looking for a sign, like that horoscope said—something, anything to tell me what to do.

Cars pass, leisurely, with the windows open, and music spills out in a cacophony of tunes, in a way unique to summer. A couple passes. They appear intensely connected—not in a new, sensual, way, but in a time-worn patina of meaningful silence. I watch them cross to a bar—a little wine place I hadn't noticed before. They disappear inside, and my eye travels up to the windows above the bar. There's a neon sign illuminated, and it's in the shape of a *pigeon,* of all things. I laugh. Grams would get a kick out of this. I've never seen this pleasant little light before, but I'm drawn to it. I cross the street to the door that would ostensibly lead me to the second floor, where the bird light is. "Ha ha, Wendy," I say aloud, "You're still a kook." I inspect the row of bells with their green label.

1A: Copy Brothers
1B: Sandra's Hairstyles
2A: Pigeon Astrology
2B: Brooklyn Design

It's all so surreal and comforting that I ring the bell for 2A without thinking. It's as if the universe has invited me here. Or I really need to go back to bed.

"Come in, darling." A woman's voice, Spanish or Italian, sails through the speaker vents.

Can she see me? Clutching my elbows, I take the stairs two at a time and find myself face-to-face with a formidable woman. She's tall—at least six inches taller than my five feet, five inches, and she has enormous wavy black hair, the kind that might have Matchbox cars, cheeseburgers, birds—anything—concealed in its masses.

I just stand and stare.

"I've been waiting for you," she says. "There you are—finally."

"I bet you say that to all the girls," I say.

She doesn't see the humor. Her seriousness puts me at ease. Though I'm the kind of skeptical person who once asked a Girl Scout, "Are you *sure* these are really *ten dollars* a box?" I actually find myself believing that I was meant to come here. The tears get out their armor.

The woman puts her hand on my shoulder, and I can't help myself, I let the comfort ooze through me. She leads me to a small table covered with a fringed black cloth. It looks like a shawl, embroidered with flowers and swirled flourishes in every color of the rainbow. Its silky fringes brush the tops of my bare knees as I slip into the chair she pulls out for me.

"I'm Kavia," she says. "Kavia Leona."

The name echoes in my mind, as if I've heard it down a long hallway. The reverberations are soothing, my heart slows to a bearable cadence.

"Close your eyes," she says.

I've heard about these Gypsies, how you aren't supposed to trust them, but I'm markedly unconcerned. She feels for my right hand with a grandmotherly touch, and her safe, strong caress chokes me with reminiscence.

# 7.

♈ ♉ ♊ ♋ ♌ ♍ ♎ ♏

*People consult an astrologer when they are searching for answers and solutions to their life issues, dynamics, and concerns. Their birth charts show both the things that come easily in life and those areas where they get stuck. Often we don't move forward past our stuck places—not because we don't want to—but because we don't know how. The birth chart is a symbolic map of the psyche or personality and provides a view of the many possible roads in that map. It is the astrologer's job to help the client to see those roads and also, importantly, to validate and to bring illumination to the individual's experiences.*

—AMANDA OWEN, ASTROLOGICAL CONSULTANT, LECTURER, AND TEACHER

W*hen were you* born, dear?" Kavia asks.

I think about this fact of my birth and it seems like someone else's life I'm recalling. "February twenty-fifth, nineteen seventy-nine," I say.

"At what time?"

"Nine in the morning," I say. It was a very warm day; this is the one story I remember my father telling me: "Balmy—in *February*!" He got a real kick out of you, my grandmother used to say. I always liked that image of him: grinning unabashedly over something adorable I'd done.

I could probably open my eyes now, but I am enjoying the delicious sensation too much. The idea that I could imagine Kavia as someone else is indulgent, childish, but I give in to it just the same.

There is some noisy fumbling and I know she could be grabbing for anything—cyanide, a light saber—but I trust this woman; she would not steer me wrong. In my head we're picnicking on tuna fish sandwiches at the beach, guessing at the cruise ship destinations just like Grams and I did.

"You are Pisces," she says. I can hear her pull out a book, flutter through the pages. "I want you to look at this. Open your eyes, for God's sake—what is your name?"

"It's Viv," I say, sounding pathetic and hollow.

"Viv. Good name, Viv. Means 'alive.'"

*"Really?"* I never heard that before. I let the idea of it marinate, my eyes still closed, while I listen to the sounds of Kavia jotting something down. "No, I'm lying," she says, deadpan.

I open my eyes to the sight of a hand-painted circular chart, divided into sections. It's a little creepy, like I shouldn't be looking at it, and in each section is an image of each of the different zodiac signs. I've seen them all before, but never like this. Here they look prophetic, important, with warning eyes, like something from a witch's spell book. I'm a little frightened, but intrigued, too—as if there is something here in these incomprehensible symbols that might help me.

"*Zodiac* means Circle of Animals and it is a belt in the universe along which all the planets move. It is the ecliptic, so called because this is the only region where the moon can experience eclipses." I picture it, as Kavia describes it in her hoarse voice, just a tick above a whisper—a mass of blackness, so peaceful and enormous, it could swallow a person's worries up without a trace.

"The sky is divided up into a dozen pie pieces and each of the twelve degree pieces is a birth sign." She points to the illustration, where, in between the sun and the ring of painted symbols—the ram and the crab and the Gemini twins reaching out like faceless droids to one another—is a ring of precisely drawn lines intersecting like an intricate cat's cradle. Their outermost angles form sharp points, looking from afar like the pentagram stars in horror films, the kind drawn in bat's blood.

When I turn my head a bit, I can see that some of the lines are blue while others are black, and if I pivot just slightly, the star appears to twinkle, as if hovering in the night sky. One ring beyond the signs are symbols, almost like hieroglyphics; somehow they are more intriguing than even the zodiac signs themselves. And beyond these, along the outermost edge, are numbers. All of these numbers and symbols look so authoritative and sure, so exactly what I am looking for.

I recognize the symbol for my sign, and the one she'd referred to as Capricorn, its marriage of a line-graph dip and an Arabic letter squiggle. I am breathless for her to decipher it all for me so I can leave here completely fixed.

"Your sign," she says, looking up from the chart now, "is the twelfth sign of the zodiac." She points to the Pisces symbol, and it amazes me that somehow *I* am on this page. "The twelve signs are further divided into four elemental groupings, which are also sometimes called 'triplicities' because there are three birth signs in each. Fire signs Aries, Leo, and Sagittarius are full of adventure, always looking for the next opportunity. Earth signs are, as you might imagine, more grounded and practical; they are Taurus, Virgo, and Capricorn. We also have air signs—Gemini, Libra, and Aquarius, who reflect the symbolic qualities of air—they have the unique ability to see things from all angles, and remove themselves from the thick of things to see what's really going on. As a water sign, Pisces, like Cancer and Scorpio, is changeable and communicative, with flowing feelings that play a managerial role in their lives. You are creative, deeper than you appear, like the water itself; you are very sensitive and can be prone to melancholy and vulnerability."

She explains to me that these groupings can be further divided by "qualities" or "quadruplicities" (three groups of four): the cardinal signs are Aries, Cancer, Libra, and Capricorn, and these are malleable and active; fixed Taurus, Leo, Scorpio, and Aquarius are just the opposite; and mutable Pisces, Gemini, Virgo, and Sagittarius not only *can* change but *constantly* reinvent themselves.

"Each sign is naturally aligned with a planet," she explains. "And Pisces is where Jupiter resides. This positioning gives you a thirst for knowledge and understanding, as well as a lucky streak," she tells me.

I can't help but nod my head in agreement: didn't I already say I was lucky? "Lucky ducky," I say with a grimace, riding the line between skepticism and a yearning to believe.

She ignores me and continues on with the gumball machine generalities: "You aren't much for rules, you are in love with love, compassionate, idealistic; you have a tendency to sacrifice yourself for love. Your intuitions are reliable; you can even tend to be psychic. You are a chameleon and adapt to whatever situation you find yourself in." Sure, this is all true, but that's the kind of vague stuff they say about all the "water signs," isn't it? *This is dumb,* I think. I'm waiting for her—at any second—to disprove the shreds of hope I have for possibly having stumbled upon something to believe in. Still, I can't help but tease out some profound truths in her observations. I stayed with Bruce for way, way longer than I should have—years longer, because I loved the *idea* of him; Grams used to say that. It must have been true, because I really didn't see him all that much. And when we *were* together, and he wanted to do things that I couldn't stand, like play video games for hours while I watched the moves he'd mastered. I would convince myself that I enjoyed this, too, that there was something poetic in a digitized Tony Hawk carving the perfect bowl.

"You've got a Neptune influence, which encourages your sensitive and spiritual side, but it can also make you vulnerable to deception." Kavia points to a yellow orb, painted with plump legs and wings, "Here, at the center, is the sun. The sun is the key to the zodiac signs—a birth sign actually represents where the sun was in relation to the planets at the time you were born. Its placement determines the lessons you have to learn in life."

For Pisces, she tells me, this is a big emotional ordeal. "You need to learn to discriminate between ideas that can be made into reality, and those that can never be. You spend your time thinking in a very concrete way of the things that you *want* to happen: you picture what a person will smell like, what they'll be wearing, what flowers they'll arrive with, and that they'll do exactly what they ought to. But sometimes, we must realize, things will not work out the way we imagine them."

*You said it, sister.* I don't have to tell you that *this* is no cookie-cutter BS; this is *me* she's describing, it's me exactly. I nod my head tightly, noticing that she doesn't use phrases like "people believe" or "some think that." Why should she? Look at all those numbers, symbols, boxes—all that *work*—proof of the science that went into this. Kavia presents it all as fact, and though I want to keep up the skepticism, there is something welcome and convincing in her manner, which makes me accept the whole *schpiel* as if she's a Doctor of Astrology, the head of the medical astrology unit at Mount Sinai Hospital.

"This positioning here is responsible for your character traits, the basic elements of who you are and who you can be." She traces with her finger, the line from the sun to the mermaid that in this chart represents Pisces. "Once a Pisces learns these lessons, and I mean, really understands what they mean, you can truly be who you are and feel totally comfortable in that. We can then be mindful and understanding of those who don't share our depth of emotional understanding."

"We?" I say before I realize.

"Yes, I, too, am Pisces."

"You are?"

She nods her head.

I feel instantly more convinced of her authenticity, as if this affinity of ours means something, must be more than coincidence.

"There are many benefits to a Pisces sun. In my case, it's helped me to work out my relationship with my mother over the years."

I swallow. I can only pray that I will one day appreciate my mother in a way that will give me something other than indigestion.

"I have a *great* relationship with my mother," I say, testing this Kavia with her enormous hair and enormous ideas.

"Sure you do," she says, with a tone that could pass for sarcasm as easily as it could be taken seriously.

I wrinkle my face up like a California raisin, but she doesn't pay me the slightest attention. She turns back to the book, an inscrutable expression on her face, pointing to the ornate drawings of three planets. "The simplest kind of reading has to do with only the sun, the moon, and Saturn," she says. She swings her finger around the wheel. "The position of the moon in your chart determines your emotional approach based on *past* experience. *Your* moon is in Capricorn, which is opposite the natural position of Cancer for the moon. This can present difficulties." Kavia pulls a photocopy of that page from her endless series of pockets. On it, she begins writing with a pen she'd liberated from her hair.

She raises her head "You *know* what I meant before when I mentioned my mother. You, too, have had a difficult mother, who was a weak figure or completely absent; she was busy with other things and didn't nurture you properly. So now you doubt yourself and neglect your emotional care. As a result, you choose romantic partners with whom you never have to really let go, people with whom you can just risk the minimum. This aspect means you are very focused on duty and responsibility. But, you'll see, later in life you'll get to experience that childhood you never had."

This simply cannot be happening. Those laughing Mad Hatters actually showing up at my apartment would be easier to swallow than this woman ticking off my most intimate challenges and concerns, things I don't share with anyone. The sensation is as off-putting as it is soothing: like someone introducing you to yourself without blinking an eye, as if you've obviously never met. "All right," I say. "Who told you all this?"

Kavia isn't sure if she should be insulted or complimented. "Your ephemeris," she says, finally, with a fair amount of bravado.

I'm picturing a cross between a spleen and a small intestine, but try as I might, I can't get myself to imagine it speaking, much less spilling my darkest secrets to this curt woman, with her clumpy mascara and pearly eye shadow. "My *what*?"

"Ephemeris." Kavia pinches a chunk of pages from the bottom corner. There must be two thousand of them with their shiny red edges. She flips them, landing on the exact page she's after. She smoothes the open pages with her palms as if this is a Dead Sea Scroll she's gotten a hold of, and skims through several dozen pages, all of which look identical to me—like mathematical tables, or tide charts. She looks up at me with a knowing smile: "*This,* my dear, is the ephemeris."

From what I can gather, it is *not* something that aids in digestion but an endless series of figures in boxes, hand-drawn, and from the looks of it, several hundred years old. Each of its tiny squares contains a number—negative or positive—which, she explains, represents the longitude of the sun or a planet that is significant to me. How could any planet be significant to someone like me, a gazillion miles away? Yet, Kavia explains, our connection is so precise that even the slightest shift in latitude, say if I were born in Queens instead of Brooklyn, would alter its effect entirely. It matters whether you're born at midnight or noon. And even then "birth twins" born at the same exact moment but in different parts of the world, will have a different forecast, a different life blueprint.

The amount of labor involved in this pursuit is astounding. Kavia explains it all as she deciphers these numbers and symbols, scratching out calculations that even Bill Gates would grapple with. I'm finding it difficult to maintain my skeptical gaze, much less follow her words, when inside I'm so dazzled.

"How do you figure this all out from *that*?" I ask.

"It's very complicated," she says. "But I'll try to put it in layman's terms for you." I cock my head, puppy dog–style, as she explains her method: "Convert the time into local mean time, then find the equivalent sidereal time, which increases at approximately four minutes every day, and varies slightly year to year. The numbers are logarithms, where each number in the units place is zero plus a decimal, the tens is one plus a decimal, and in the hundreds is two plus a decimal . . ."

I realize I am way out of my league once she says. "To calculate the revolutions of Venus versus those of the earth, add 24 hours in a day to 60 minutes in an hour, to 60 seconds in a minute and we get 19,366, which corresponds to 8,641, right here on the chart. The 'characteristic' being 1, we get 86'41." It reminds me of when I was about twelve, and got it into my head, after watching *Pretty in Pink,* I only wanted to wear clothing I made myself. The moment I realized you couldn't even think of starting to actually make anything until you first worked out dozens of measurements and completed hours of meticulous cutting and pinning, I was through with fashion and on to painting by numbers, where it was perfectly clear where everything went, and the results were immediate.

All this time Wendy has been reading me my daily horoscope I pictured some guy in a peaked wizard's hat, his legs propped on a desk while he spins a mobile of the universe with a Superpencil, deciding which stereotype to focus on that day. I had no idea. All this precision and detail, and all the while she's recording it on a rickety old tape recorder, leaning close to the speaker perforations now and again.

"This is just a taste, you understand. There are still the houses, the very important rising sign, and the nodes. There are the aspects that measure angles between planets—accounting for subtle personality differences between people. There's your very important ascendant, or rising sign, and your descendent, and of course, what we're all interested in: the progression, or where the planets are right now. But we'll get to all that at some other time."

When she closes the ephemeris and swings back to the picture of the zodiac, I feel like someone's switched the lights out. *Stop it,* I tell myself. *You're just desperate, the perfect downtrodden victim. It's probably all bullshit anyhow.*

Still, I can't help but think that all these years have passed, and I had absolutely no idea those planets meant anything at all to me. Missed opportunities, needless heartache. Wild relief floods me and my internal lights flicker on; it's as if I'm realizing how to do this life thing for the first time.

I say as much to Kavia, and she immediately drops her gaze, in pure disgust. When she finally looks at me, it's with all the affection she would show a maggot in her salad.

I sit very still, praying she won't tell me to get the hell out—not with all that insight bottled up inside of her, waiting to be tapped. I swallow.

"Don't you know the laws of the universe?" She asks this as if I must be the stupidest person alive.

"You mean, like relativity and gravity—that kind of stuff?"

"No, not that kind of stuff," she says. There is a complete lack of inflection to her tone. I can't decide if this lends more or less emphasis to what she says. "Not that kind of stuff at all." She sighs, pulls a Diet Coke from some hidden pocket in her dress, and takes a long sip. *"Unus Mundus,"* she says, and lets it hang there as she walks to a messy bookcase. Kavia picks through the titles to assemble a pile, which she hands to me before returning to her seat.

*Unus Mundus?* Has she been watching too much *Harry Potter*? I tighten my lips and my grip on my purse.

"*Unus Mundus* means 'one world,' that everything is unified, returning to and coming from the same source. And though it was coined back in the sixteenth century by Paracelsus, an alchemist, it was Carl Gustav Jung who made it popular. Jung used the word *synchronicity* for 'meaningful coincidence,' which he said was a concept possible only because an observer and connected event are products of the same source. For instance, you might have heard of the Butterfly Effect. If a butterfly flaps its wings, this can have a ripple effect on the entire universe: he makes a little wind, this turns a bird's head, the bird finds a worm, eats it, and so on and so on. So you see, we are all connected—you, me, that bitch next door."

"What did you just say?" I nearly yell, my fists contracting.

She repeats herself.

It's as if Grams herself has endorsed this woman, this fantastic find at the helm of a fluorescent pigeon. I'm sold.

"Did you think it was all just meaningless?" she asks, calming my worst fears in a flash.

It's comforting to think that no matter where Grams is, no matter how far apart we are, eventually we will make it back to each other again; that we are from the same place, and somehow still affect each other. I imagine this *Unus Mundus* to encompass everything—the planets and beyond, things I should have paid more attention to on that eighth grade class trip to the planetarium—and it offers me a sense of stability, if only for a moment, to think I am not just Viv, but Viv and the Universe, whether the universe likes it or not.

"It is also sometimes referred to as the Journey of Wholeness," Kavia says. She pulls out another book, flips the pages by licking her finger and then jabbing at each one. I like this phrase, too; it's precisely what I need to be—whole. I need to be whole again.

For the next forty minutes this "taste" of Kavia's insight zings me over and over again.

“Let’s get a quick peek at what’s going on in your chart right now,” she says, plucking a book from another pile. This one is fatter than it is tall, and has a gold fabric cover with no title, as if the people who’d be looking for it would recognize it, no name necessary. “Get the gold book,” they’d say.

Kavia refers to another enormous chart with lots of color and neat notes written in random boxes, things like, “Very troublesome” and “Watch for this!”

She drags her finger across the page nearly to the far right margin, and then, abruptly, she stops. Her nail digs a little into the tiny box where there is a –5 written.

When I turn to her for an explanation, there is alarm in her eyes; the white shadow only exaggerates it like a French street mime doing “Shock.” I get panicky. If this woman can read the map of me, and she’s looking at me like that, it can’t be good.

“Is this for real?” I ask.

“Of course,” she says. I sense she wants me to understand that she knows exactly what I need to do.

My mind frantically backpedals: I wish I had met her before that final day in the hospital. Maybe Grams would be here right now.

I have never had less faith in myself—not even on the first day of junior high, when I held the post of the bus stop with a death grip, swearing they’d *never* unglue me, not until my mother came back. I struggle to convey this to Kavia, to beg her to tell me what to do; what emerges is a hoarse croak.

“I know,” she says. It really seems she does.

There are footfalls down the stairwell, a pigeon alights on the windowsill. It gives a single *coo* and darts its head forward, liquidly, then flies off.

“What does it say?” I ask when I can’t stand it any longer.

“Next time,” she says, clapping the book shut with both palms.

“Please, just one thing. Tell me one thing.” I hate the sound of my own voice. How can I possibly care what this woman—who allows bristly hairs to grow from the mole on her chin to unspeakable lengths—how can I care what *she* thinks?

Kavia meets my gaze. "You will meet a young man in your building. He will be very important to you right now. Get his sign, and don't forget the time of his birth."

My heart sinks. Clearly she has never been to my building, and it's obviously misrepresented on that chart of hers, if it's even there in the first place. At Seacoast Terrace, I am one of exactly three people who don't get the senior discount on the bus. I must have been out of my mind to believe in this malarkey. But I'm glad it's happened, I've always wanted to use the word *malarkey*; besides, there are plenty of people who haven't got an ounce of faith. What makes me think I've got to be different than the guy on Forty-fifth Street who grumbles at the traffic, wearing the "God Is Dead" T-shirt?

I was completely out of my mind. That's what made me think it.

Sure, there have been a few *coincidences*—Wendy's horoscope, her stupid falafel idea, the pigeon, my grandmother's name, her *exact words*—but even a broken clock is right twice a day, isn't it?

"That can't be correct," I say. "Are you sure there isn't something else? You looked very concerned. And that doesn't sound so bad, even if it's completely out of the realm of possibility."

"I'll double-check," she says, which seems very out of character for her. She reopens the book, ruffles through a few pages to another chart, and this time slides her finger across very close to the top and stops swiftly again. She tries to play down the horror this time by shading her face with her palm. Just when I think she'll speak, Kavia slaps the book shut and says, "That's enough."

There's something ominous she's seen in there. And try as I might, I simply cannot write it off as bullshit.

"Please tell me what you see," I say.

“Oh, you don’t want to know this, believe me, you don’t.”

“I can take it,” I say, though I’m not so sure myself. She doesn’t budge.

“*Oh,* I get it. I’ll come back and pay you some more money again, so you don’t need to worry about that. I’m hooked by your cliff-hanger. Well done, well done.”

She squeezes her eyes in distaste. “No, distrusting girl. This is not about money. I don’t like to tell bad things.”

My heart drops.

She hands me the tape of our session—*a tape*! I think again with mockery—as if her lack of technical savvy is reason enough to distrust everything she’s said.

“Come back Tuesday. One thirty.”

Nine whole days away.

“Sixty-five dollars,” she says, jabbing out her hand. With inordinate hostility she accepts a hundred-dollar bill and makes change—handing me a wad of crinkled bills and eight quarters.

When I’m at the door, I can’t help but plead once more. “Please tell me what you’ve seen.”

Something in my features persuades her, because she sighs in preparation, as if making way for something substantial to emerge—a watermelon, or an atom bomb.

My fingernails dig into my palms.

“Has anyone ever told you that you can be a real pain in the butt?” she says.

“*No,* as a matter of fact.” Grams must have said that to me three times a day but I won’t give Kavia the satisfaction of saying so.

“I see death. Someone very important to you is dead.”

If I had doubts, she’s cleared them, like faith’s Zamboni.

Kavia looks at her watch and shoves me out the door with a nudge and the pile of books to read. I tell myself I am no more frightened, no lonelier than I was before. Yet, when the door hushes closed, it’s as if everything is fresh again, only the cuts are deeper, because now I know there are any number of dangers lurking—all written out in those boxes, ready to blow at any moment—and I know I've only been given the *tiniest* taste of what they are.

How? How could she look into those tables and know that Grams was meant to go?

Outside, it's grown dark. The smell of soured trash permeates. Someone leans out an apartment window to yell down at a throbbing car alarm, "Fuck you!"

*Exactly,* I think. I'm frozen on the stoop.

"Hey! Hey!" someone yells from just above my head.

I look up.

It's Kavia.

Her hair waves down the brick facade like garden snakes. "Don't take the train!"

"Why?" I scream back up.

But she's already slammed down her window. I press at the buzzer, the one suddenly so dear. Finally resigned that she's not going to answer, I descend the three steps and turn left toward the park. Just as I step over a giant crack, one shaped like a mountain range, Kavia's voice comes screaming across the intercom: "Next week!" she yells.

I run back, my heart racing with anticipation. "Hello? Hello? Kavia!" I press the button, shaky.

She doesn't pick up.

# 8.

♈ ♉ ♊ ♋ ♌ ♍ ♎ ♏

*Some astrologers have ESP at least some of the time. They often get a perfect answer but hardly know where it comes from.*

—Dal Lee

At *my college* orientation, I was the one laughing as the hip guy in the sweater vest and yellow suede Pumas picked at his "O hell, my name is . . . Mike" tag and recounted an urban legend about a naive couple victimized by an ATM scam. I laughed and picked out the Midwestern freshmen by the sheer terror on their faces.

I would never be described as gullible. I'm from *Brooklyn*—the borough that invented street smarts. Our sign says, "Welcome to Brooklyn, Fughedaboudit," for crying out loud. You wouldn't see that anywhere else. Just try to imagine it in the Berkshires, or Sweden, or Saint Rémy-de-Provence.

So, when Kavia's words of warning reverberate through me, I instinctively ignore the nagging about scams and bullshit and do as she said. Though I've never traveled any other way, I don't take the subway home.

Paired with her knowledge of Grams's death, it just seems that Kavia *knows* I should avoid the train. And though I feel one step away from a Psychic Hotline addiction, I go to the nearest cash machine, take out a wad of cash—enough to last me several weeks, just in case (though I'm not sure of what case)—and I hop into a cab.

I am so spent I forget to use the Brooklynite's trick of coercing unwilling cabbies into the long ride; that is, I don't say, "Take Broadway," and then, only once we've gone three blocks or so, finish delivering the rest of the route: "to the Manhattan Bridge, to the BQE to the Belt Parkway, to the Knapp Street exit."

"Brighton Beach," I say instead. "Brooklyn"—and either taxi drivers are becoming unprecedentedly soft, or I must look just desperate enough for him to do as he's told.

At home, I avoid Jameson's eye. I pretend to glance his way by turning my face, but I pick the waterfall as my focal point. I offer up a small wave and go right up to our apartment. Out of respect for Grams, I fold and neatly put away all my clothes before falling into bed.

I am *not* a pain in the ass, I say to the dark.

# 9.

♈ ♉ ♊ ♋ ♌ ♍ ♎ ♏

*To most modern scientists, the idea of significant cosmic influence upon human behavior seems implausible. The matter is made worse when no concrete mechanisms are suggested by which such effects are obtained, and made worse still when the explanations offered are couched in language reminiscent of supernaturalism and occultism. Those concerned about the absence of mechanisms seem to overlook similar opposition to Newton's theory of gravity, with its action at a distance, once seen by critics as occult; and some have suggested that Newton may have been untroubled by the action-at-a-distance problem, largely because of his own involvement with astrology.*

—Marcello Truzzi, 1935–2003

T*he kitchen is* already warm from the sun the next morning when I turn the radio dial up real loud the way Grams likes. I could have never guessed that the sound of public radio is different alone—tinnier, a tad more authoritative.

I run the tap and fill Grams's old kettle with water for tea. It's already over a flame before I realize I've put in enough for the both of us.

"The Q train hasn't had an accident in five years," says Lakshme Kressly, the morning announcer with the British accent we love, with an air of suspicion.

The words go through me as I take my seat at the table, the one facing the window. I give the sky a good looking-over before I realize—with a jolt—what Lakshme's talking about.

I reach for the radio—next to the collection of takeout chopsticks we'll never use—and turn it up.

"Ten passengers sustained critical injuries. They were all riding in the first car as the train collided head-on with a sitting train at Brighton Beach station last night at exactly five forty-five."

My chest knots. That's exactly when I would have been on the train. And that's the car I take, the one that platforms just at the staircase here. I'm looking out at the train right now, and what she's saying must be true because there are plywood boards blocking off that end of the platform, and yellow police tape is draped all around.

*Don't take the train!* Kavia had yelled.

I run to the window, shivering, and shade my eyes from the sun's glare to get a better look. How can this *be*? This is *astrology* we're talking about—the stuff of *Cosmo* magazine and gumball machines at the A&P. It's not real. It can't be.

And yet two cross-armed cops are camped out at the scene as if to prove to me that it certainly can be real. Not only that, but it clearly *is*.

The teapot whistle scares the crap out of me. I jerk my head into the windowpane. "What the fuck?" I ask of the window, of Kavia, Grams, Lakshmi, even of Mrs. Hirsch, who I know is listening with a glass against her door.

I follow the story all morning. I turn on CNN and there

it is. CNBC, New York 1. On the *Today* show, Matt Lauer bumbles his way through unscripted questions to injured passengers. "So, umm, how do you *feel*?" he asks via satellite to someone so bandaged up you can barely see his eyes through the slits in the cotton gauze.

I'm trying to convince myself that there's no way Kavia could have predicted this train accident. It goes against every fiber of my being to put my faith in astrology. But how can you deny evidence when it crashes right in front of your face?

So I feel only slightly embarrassed when I log onto the Internet to check my horoscope for the day.

"Believe. Give over your skepticism and realize that sometimes the impossible really is possible."

If the universe is going to all this trouble to tell me something, the very least I can do is listen.

And so I try. Rather than rush right into calling my mother at the ice cream man's place, I allow myself a moment of pause out on the terrace. I reach out and start petting the "feathers" of that wood-carved eagle statue we have hanging over the railing. It's a thing I used to do for Grams, and she would say, "Umm, you know that's freaking fake, right?", real snotty-like, and I'd give her the evil eye, which I happen to be very good at. But there's no one here to give the evil eye to, so I'm just stuck petting the damned thing over and over again, like a broken record, which no one's around to set back on track.

A memory is stoked from the ashes. Right after my dad died I kept wishing for a sister. I'd come to understand that babies came from big bellies, and so I encouraged my mother to eat more, assuming the rounder her belly grew, the better the chances of my scoring a little sister.

"I don't understand why you keep feeding me macaroni and cheese at seven o'clock in the morning," she said one day, the third in a row that I'd brought her a bowl of the Day-Glo orange Kraft dinner.

"Because I have to be at school at seven forty-five," I explained.

My mother ate the pasta in heaped, hungry bites. Each morning I carried it into the bathroom and carefully placed it and the fork she liked—with the shell handle—along the back of the vanity, in between her makeup bottles and pots. I took great care shifting each one just a tiny bit to make room, while the bowl burned my hands. My mother would flip out if any of them fell over.

"I'm flipping out," she'd say, and, with the heel of a palm at her brow bone, my mother would stare at the spilled crush of blue powder, with its mesmerizing shimmer, as sad as if it was my father himself. If I squinted into the makeup spill, I could almost make out the silhouette of a head, a pair of arms, a receding hairline camouflaged by a long ponytail. Even then, I knew this was just wishful thinking.

"I. Am. Flipping. *Ouuut.*" She'd say it slower the second time and she'd crouch down to wipe up the mess with sheets of crumpled toilet paper. I'd showed her more than once what Grams had taught me, to sweep up with two squares of white cardboard she kept from panty hose packs. If we got to this point, it meant I would be late for school.

She would call into work, and I'd bang on her door, but she wouldn't answer. I'd disguise my voice and tell the woman in the main office that my daughter, Vivian, wouldn't be making it to school today, on account of athlete's foot, or lice, or conjunctivitis.

In the bathroom, there were always a few splodges of midnight blue left behind like bread crumbs along the path to the pink swan-shaped garbage pail, which matched the decals on our shower door and the nubby traction pads inside the tub—all of which my mother hated. When she'd found the trash can, shopping with my father and me at a department store in Long Island, they'd laughed until big sighs slipped out, and I laughed, too, though I didn't know why.

At the time, we didn't know that my mother would be

crying over blue eye shadow splodges that might or might not resemble the curve of my father's potato chip belly. In all those weeks coaxing my mother to scarf down Kraft dinner for breakfast, things were generally calm on her end. George Harrison sang the parts that made me laugh: "Hare Krishna, Krishna, Krishna," from the hi-fi in the living room.

"Mmmm, mmmmm, delicious," she'd say, in between mascara wand shimmies over her long lashes. She sounded nearly content, scooping up sticky forkfuls that looked like tiny sculptures to me. After a month of this, my mother came home one night from her job at Alexander's, giving me the evil eye, which *she* is also excellent at. She pulled from a paper bag a six-pack of Tab, some huge pumpkin muffins, a half dozen bagels, a tub of fat-free vegetable cream cheese, and a pint of Frusen Gladje. "I've gained too much weight," she said. "I'm *officially* taking up a low-fat diet."

I needed a new strategy.

While I tried to work it out, my mother got real good at opening up her mouth wide to get her teeth around those muffins, which obscured her entire face. Finally I settled on something I thought could just about work. I began to scissor out pictures from the Sunday paper's advertisement inserts—photos of babies and baby dolls, with and without coupon perforations across their lips. I clipped many, many pictures of Betsy Wetsy, and real baby accessories I hoped would get the point across: bottles, enormous soft packs of diapers, tubes of rash ointment. I arranged them into collages by color or shape.

This plan didn't pan out, either. The most attention I attracted was one afternoon while my mother watched *One Day at a Time.* She got up from her seahorse curl during a commercial break. With a yawn she sauntered into the kitchen for a Tab and gummy bears. Through the wall cut-out, she looked over my shoulder at what I was working on. "*Hmmm,* I like your use of color, very Degas." It was all the pink that made her say that. We'd become acquainted with the ballerina painter before my father died. He would drop us off in Manhattan nearly every Saturday before he went to work, and we always seemed to find ourselves in front of the spining tutus in the quiet of the Met. Degas was our favorite, followed by Tiffany, who did the glass near the wishing fountain, and then Manet, whose girl in the blue velvet coat we could look at for hours—or at least a good three minutes. Even then, those perfect museum afternoons seemed like something from a movie I'd seen long ago.

Two weeks later, on the second night of Hanukkah, I unwrapped, from a sheet of primary-colored dreidel paper, a creepy porcelain baby doll, with plush fabric arms and legs but hard, molded fingers and lifelike eyes, with lashes and lids that rolled when you tilted the head. Or threw it on the floor. Or hung it out the window.

"I saw those pictures you were cutting out," she said. "I knew just what you were trying to tell me."

Wendy and I named her Carrie, after the horror picture we'd once watched between splayed fingers. One day, after hanging Carrie out more and still more precariously from our window—first by merely tilting her over the sill, then completely upside-down, then by slamming her shapeless knee under the window—I made Wendy, in the courtyard below, laugh so hard that she became Betsy Wetsy herself.

But I'd taken it too far and frightened Wendy when the only anchor between window and ground was one of Carrie's single banana ringlets. Wendy took one look at the doll's eyes rolled all the way back and ran inside. "It was just a joke!" I yelled.

For three months, I carefully, lovingly even, rolled that doll around in her pink nylon stroller, gently "fed" her saltines, and diapered her with real cloth and pins like Grams showed me. I bathed her and fluffed her shiny hair.

My mother never caught on. Eventually, Carrie lost her right arm, and this freaked me and Wendy out so much that I stuffed her down the incinerator while Wendy watched. I pulled the chute door open to make sure she'd gone down, and told my mother someone had stolen her at the park. Between the red cheeks, the fake tears, and Wendy's nodding, it worked. Carrie, and with her the whole baby venture, was officially in the trash. My mother shed the extra macaroni weight and then some. I found out where babies really came from, and I was horrified to think what this meant about the men filing through my mother's bedroom door.

It's been a while since I thought of this. I feel strange, as I'm face-to-face with the eagle statue, alone.

I shake my head, drape an arm over the eagle, and look over the railing. The waves way down below caress the sand tenderly, like someone who's been away a long time. I have not bothered to call Bruce. Mindlessly, I start to pet the eagle. I look down at the boardwalk, to the point where Bruce and I first met—five summers ago, right around the time Wendy moved to Japan from Turkey. It's not all that surprising that I haven't called him, or for that matter, that he hasn't called me. Ever since Grams started to get sick, his presence began to diminish. It was subtle at first—our weekend dates would end a couple of hours early, then he was busy on Friday, then he didn't come around for dinner. Before I knew it, he wasn't returning my phone calls until five days after the fact, even if the message said something like, "The doctor said Grams's white cells are so low she can't get her treatment today."

And when he finally would call back, he'd ask, "How's it hanging?"

"Some people put up a wall when disaster strikes," Wendy had said. "But when you smack yourself up against it enough times, you should probably make a new plan."

But now, the idea of being alone is so overwhelming that I pull my cell phone out of the back pocket of my jeans, which I am wearing beneath the housecoat. I'll pull out all the stops—cry hysterically, whatever it takes, to not sleep alone again.

Slowly, I scroll down to his name; I already know he isn't

going to pick up, so I'm drawing the whole process out, holding onto the possibility for as long as I can.

As I wait for the call to connect, there's a long, piercing screech from the adjoining terrace. It's odd to hear anything from that side. I give a little jump. My muscles contract. I can't see what it was because the bamboo shade "Officer" Richter's divided his terrace off with is pulled all the way down. The nails-on-the-chalkboard effect subsides, and I tiptoe closer, trying to peer through the shade. But I can't see more than a shadow. The slats are too narrowly spaced. As far as I know, Richter hasn't been out there in twenty-eight years—since his crossing guard days that earned him his nickname.

Bruce's phone rings.

"Richter?" I sing out. It is so strange to hear someone on that terrace that the little hairs on the back of my neck prick up. *You're overreacting because that Gypsy woman freaked you out. Stop it.*

Nobody answers. But I can still hear movement—box-shuffling or something.

Now I hear what sounds like metal-on-metal scraping—chairs or a table, maybe. On the cell, Bruce's phone is still ringing.

His voice mail clicks on: "Hey, you've reached your destiny. Make the most of it." He says this is a joke and a guy would have to be a real idiot to mean something like that, but I have my doubts. Like, for instance, for a joke, it isn't exactly funny. The message ends and there's the woman telling me to wait for the beep, even though it's self-explanatory. As the beep sounds, the noise next door evolves into a distinct bang, and "Officer" Richter yelps.

"Richter?" I call, louder this time.

I experience a rush of vertigo. I want to hang up the phone, but my brain won't cooperate with my body, which has wrapped itself around the eagle statue. I have no idea why. It's not so weird, really; this eagle is the closest thing to a person I've got here.

My arms are hugging it so tightly I can feel the splintery bits cutting into my arm. I don't know if I'm really scared, or if it's more of a hangover from Kavia's frightening suggestions. Other than that Carrie incident, I don't normally scare easily. I've got the phone tucked insecurely between my cheek and shoulder, and a protective impulse kicks in: I yell out, just as Bruce's voice-mail recorder beeps to an end, "Hello! Are you okay, Richter?" I picture his whiskery cheeks sprinkled with the white and gray hairs that he never seems to find with the razor, the way he used to look in his crossing guard uniform.

"Hello?" A voice that is so clearly not "Officer" Richter's sails my way. All I can think of are those rows of boxes on Kavia's charts, the secret dangers woven between the numbers. I can hear but can't see whoever it is struggling to raise the precariously rolled bamboo. I'm torn between running inside and staying put to see if I'll need to go all Peter Parker on this guy.

"Shit," the voice says, and I assume from the way the shade is jolting to the left and right, but not one centimeter vertically, that he is having some trouble.

Finally the thing gives way. I struggle to connect this new face with the disembodied voice. It isn't Richter, and he doesn't look like a burglar or someone here to service the air-conditioning unit.

In fact, he looks like a movie star—the unlikely kind that I always prefer, like Joaquim Phoenix. Only he has puffs underneath his eyes like he hasn't slept in weeks. He is clean-cut in the immaculately groomed way boys from this neighborhood always are: that smell of intense cologne and freshly applied deodorant packs a punch. He has dark, nearly black hair, cut nice and short, like a mowed lawn.

He's looking at me strangely, and that's when I realize I'm still clinging to the eagle. I back off suddenly, throw my hands up in surrender, and the phone slips from its dangle at my jaw and proceeds to fall over the railing. We both run to our parallel railings to watch the thing sail down nineteen stories, crash onto the steel mesh park bench below, and finally split into pieces, which bump and bounce with considerable velocity before disappearing into the shrubs.

I gulp. The knobs of my throat roll against the cool steel of the railing.

"Can you hear me *now*?" the guy says, and I have to hold myself back from smiling. I don't do that anymore.

I'm just happy I haven't whacked Mrs. Regan in the head—she usually sits out there reading the entire paper, even the sports section, about now. But for some amazing reason she isn't there today.

"Good thing that woman with the purple hair isn't out there," this vision in freshly laundered cotton says, as if he, too, knows her habits. He has this slow, very confident way of talking that calms my questions about his motives.

With the answer I come up with, you'd think his presence the most natural thing in the world. "It's magenta," I say. "Very popular with the over-fifty crowd. They think it adds color to their skin." I'm always defending old people. "It's like you're chugging cocktails of Maalox and Zynthroid from pill boxes yourself," Wendy says. That's what this kind of environment will do to you after twenty years.

"Right," he says, "magenta." He repeats the word as if it's from an obscure aboriginal dialect. "That's like fuchsia's cousin, isn't it?"

"How do you know about fuchsia?" I say, my fists uncurling a little. He doesn't exactly look the hot pink type. More important, I can't understand how he would know about Mrs. Regan. I have never *seen* him here before. And I would recognize him, believe me. As I say this to myself my thoughts are raked back toward Kavia's prophecy about meeting a man at Seacoast.

*Wait a minute. Wait just a cotton-pickin' minute.*

"Oh, I know about fuchsia," he says, like it's an unpublished-password bar on the Lower East Side. "Isn't that on the Lower East Side?" he says just as I think it. I've heard the cliché, but it really happens now: my heart stops. I've only just met him, but I'm looking into his eyes like I've been there many, many times. At the same time it's so novel, I can't tear myself away. My mind starts whirring and just as quickly, that stops, too.

"Nolita," I say, with a knowing head shake, though I can't remember if that's the neighborhood under the Brooklyn Bridge or the one by Chinatown. Could Kavia actually have "known" I would meet this person? *He will be important to you.* Instead of sounding like something I might find inside a stale cookie at Fortune Wok, these words sound prophetic, each one requiring a space of contemplative silence. Could she have seen him somewhere amidst the numbers and figures, making his way toward me? Can I actually be that important? Can this astrology stuff actually *work*?

In all likelihood he'll just saunter away, back to wherever it is this kind of gorgeous man emerges onto neighboring terraces from, and I'll never see him again. I'll think of him, from time to time, when my disappointing husband picks his teeth in public, or forgets my birthday. "Nolita, now which one is that?" he says. "The one under the Brooklyn Bridge?"

It's as if my brain is repelling the possibility that this could actually be happening, that he could be saying the private things that pop into my brain like destiny was real, rather than a brilliantly marketed name for cheap coral blush. Actually, if I really think logically, it's possible he might be dangerous. Bad guys come in all kinds of packages, even freshly buzz-cut neighborhood boys with good senses of humor and the appearance of kismet.

I try to work it out. He was delivering some food to Richter—a pizza, or a meatball sub with a side of marinara—and he was waiting for Richter to count out the quarters from that giant milk glass vase he keeps them in to treat himself with takeout every other week, an excruciating process. As he looked around Richter's place, he recognized a great opportunity; he thought, maybe this is one of those rich guys who shelters his money in discreet things that don't necessarily *look* valuable. How could he know that Richter, like Grams, is not a millionaire the way the new Russian tenants are—with their endless streams of cash for marble countertops, Jacuzzi tubs, and floor-length furs. That folks like Richter are holdouts from the old rent control days? And now he's scouring the terrace for something of value and here I've gotten in his way. Well, good. People think they can get away with anything these days.

But not this guy. I know this goes right along with all those girls who wind up abducted on Caribbean vacations by romantic-looking Rastas, with their generous, relaxed smiles and free pot, but no matter how creative I get, I simply cannot picture a criminal who irons his jeans. I look down at them now, their creaseless silhouette, and shake my head.

"See something you like?" he asks when he catches me staring; this is the vernacular of my school days, the dialect of Brooklyn kids, the kind of thing you have to know your audience to say, the kind of thing that brings you back to sneaking cigarette drags behind the superette on Avenue U. This stranger, somehow, isn't really a stranger at all.

"Why, you offering?" I deliver my line with a flirty sideward glance, the way Wendy and I worked out all those years ago that the line is best executed.

"Only if the right girl comes along."

It's nice to know I've still got it.

Still, when he gives the final line of this famous exchange, it seems too on-point, too heavy for someone I haven't been introduced to yet. I fidget. He smiles. I fidget some more. He smiles bigger and clears his throat. He's looking at me with something like . . . *amusement.*

"So, how do you know about that woman with the *magenta* hair?" I ask. I don't know what I'm worried about. It isn't difficult to tell this is the kind of person who helps little old ladies to cross the street past gypsy cabs aiming to mow them down. His eyes smile first. Even in my disbelief, I realize it's an amazing thing to watch. "Oh, I've seen how things work around here." It's like he's decided to be mysterious. Through the mystery, nostalgia's coming across loud and clear. It's the Drakkar Noir cologne he's bathed in; it smells like moss, amber, wood, a warm body, escapism, the hallway of my junior high, or—if you chose to go the Kavia route—destiny. I chalk it up to escapism, with a side of reminiscence for days I didn't appreciate when I had them.

"Oh, you have, have you?" In light of our exchange, I now glance at Richter's rusty, torn beach chairs and grimy metal table and think how ridiculous my worries were.

"Sure. It isn't that complex."

"Mmmm-hmmm," I say, lowering my eyes. Who the hell *is* this guy? And why—though we're talking about nothing important at all—can't I stop from feeling like it's one of the most significant exchanges of my life?

"Except there is that one woman with the cat," he says, making a gesture that indicates, to anyone who'd know, the pushed-in fluffy face of Rachel Valmay's cat. "I have no idea what to make of her."

"You pass," I say.

He smiles.

"Glad to appease you," he says, simultaneously mouthy and sincere.

His eyes are enormous. And clearly fatigued.

I look closer and I can see that the eyes of this man I was supposedly destined to meet are ridiculously sensual, coming to liquid points at the outer corners, and they are such a deep brown that they look chocolate dipped. He's one of these people who doesn't look *at* you; he's looks right *through* you. I feel naked, like my skin's transparent, and he can see all my organs, my heart beating hard in my rib cage.

The smile spreads down to his nose, which creases at the sides really sweetly, and finally, his mouth lifts up at the edges—slightly, but enough to make his entire face one big smile. It's impossible not to smile back.

He doesn't say anything, so I start to babble. "So what are you doing here?" I blurt out. "I know you don't belong here, because only 'Officer' Richter lives there. And no one visits him! Ever! Not in twenty-eight years." Out of habit, I do the little air quotes that Grams and I always do around his title, because, though he was really only a crossing guard before he retired twenty years ago, Richter introduces himself as an officer. Nothing against crossing guards. It's just that no matter which way you look at it, this is not the same thing as a police officer.

But instead of laughing the way Grams always does when I do the air quotes, the smile flies off his face. It's like all the life has drained from him in one swoop. "No one?" he asks, sounding hopeless.

His tone resonates. Why do I feel as if we've plowed through more complex emotions in five minutes than most people go through in five years?

"Well, not *no one,* precisely." I really want to find someone to point out to him. I want to comfort him the way I've wanted to be comforted. I need to find one measly person, to make that smile reappear. My stomach wrenches watching this beautiful man look so lost. And my memory stumbles upon the exact right answer. The memory of our old life burns a warm spot inside, the pleasant routine Grams and I used to have—and Richter was a regular part of it. I smack myself on the forehead and shake my head really exaggeratedly, for effect. "What was I *thinking*?" I say.

There is a twinkle of hope in his eyes and I put it there. It's beyond reason, it's purely chemical, my urge to please this person. I am probably displacing all of my urges for closeness onto him, but I stand up real straight and puff my chest out like a blue jay all the same. "My grandmother and I have dinner with him every Thursday, and then we watch *Lost.*"

His twinkle gives way to that fantastic eye smile, rolls into the nose crinkle, then the actual smile itself—bigger this time around. I nearly fall over the railing. He walks over my way, to the metal divider between our balconies and extends his hand.

"I'm Len," he says. " 'Officer' Richter's son." He imitates my air quotes, but tempers the awkwardness with a comical, shocked look, and then a sexy smirk. I laugh. Amazingly, somewhere, the embers of happiness still smolder.

"Viv," I say, slipping my hand in his.

"Very nice to meet you, Viv. Very nice." And though many people have said this to me before, it's never been quite as meaningful. "So what do you think? Should we go down and see if we can find that phone?"

*Right. The phone.* I can feel my cheeks heat; thank God I'm not a blusher. Well, not God—I'm off that guy. Thank—well, thank *the stars*. Yeah, that feels right. At least we needn't be concerned with *their* existence. "Sure, I'll meet you on the other side," I say.

But when I walk past the sofa, Grams's crocheting, eternally unfinished in the willow basket on the floor, I know I can't do it. I'm not ready to go back out into that world. I stand with my ear against the door and wait to hear Len emerge from the next apartment. I don't unlock the chain, just pull the door open as much as I can with it still latched, and stick my nose out. "I'm sorry," I say. "I forgot I have something I need to do."

His eyes aren't good at concealing his disappointment. Maybe Len needs a break. I know that "Officer" Richter is pretty sick, which is probably why Len is here; and since I've never seen him here before, they must have some kind of complicated relationship.

"Hey, no problem," he says, digging his hands in his pockets. His dark jeans pull just far enough down from his faded NYU T-shirt to reveal some skin. I must be pretty sick to get so hot and bothered after my grandmother just kicked the bucket, but maybe this is my heart's way of saying it needs a distraction.

Len gives a friendly wave and turns toward the elevator. I envy him his bravery, but there's no way I'm going out there.

I watch his back as he slumps a little on the way to the elevator, and somehow all the pain is magnified. As I shuffle over to snuggle up shamelessly with the crocheting, I'm not sure if I've made him up altogether.

# IO.

♈ ♉ ♊ ♋ ♌ ♍ ♎ ♏

*The fluttering of a butterfly's wings can effect climate changes on the other side of the planet.*

—PAUL ERLICH, EMINENT AMERICAN BIOLOGIST

M*rs. Kaufman comes* by a few minutes later with some food. Actually, it is *so much* food, which comes from so much effort to quell the grieving, that it deserves a proper inventory.

This woman, with her thoughtful chin stroking and her knobby fingers and shockingly beautiful hair, which she twists up into a loose, elegant bun every morning, and brushes out the old-fashioned way—one hundred times—each night, is as proud of her culinary bounty as she is of her long hair. So proud that no one would dare tell her that quantity does not necessarily equal quality. Nor would they mention that it's a good thing she married Mr. Kaufman, because from the looks of his belly, he's the only one who can stomach it. So here we go.

*Mrs. Kaufman's Menu of "Delights"*

1. Roast chicken with lemon and herbs (2.5 birds; Mr. Kaufman ate half of the third and caught hell for it).
2. Kasha varnishkes (2 lbs.)
3. Groats (3 lbs.)
4. Mashed potatoes with margarine and ground black pepper (1.5 lbs. from original 2.5; Mr. Kaufman, *again*)
5. Noodle kugel (5 lbs.)
6. Brisket with carrots, celery, and onion (7 lbs.; apparently Mr. Kaufman won't touch this with a ten-foot pole).

"Darling, just get it over with," Mrs. Kaufman says when I explain the predicament about calling my mother. "Do you want me to do it for you?" she asks, fingers tapping against the dainty flowered teacup she prefers. Clink-clink-*clink,* Clink-clink-*clink*. I zone out to the rhythm of it.

Mrs. Kaufman has been my grandmother's best friend since they were both married. Their ceremonies were two days apart, mind you, and they wore the same rented dress, holding the identical bouquet, at the same shul. They delivered their children within twenty-five days of each other, quit smoking together, quit their part-time jobs together, quit complex carbohydrates, spicy foods, trashy romance novels together. They fell off the complex carb and trashy romance wagons together, too. Mrs. Kaufman knows everything there is to know about my mother, and she knows a hell of a lot about my grandmother, but not nearly as much as I do. I can't help but experience a thrill in the knowledge that Grams was always waiting until Mrs. Kaufman was out the door and safely in the elevator bank to say something hysterical for my ears only. "Did you see what she was *wearing*? It looked like a peacock was murdered." "What?" Grams would say when I raised a brow. "You don't think she's downstairs with Morty saying the same things about me? It's what we do."

"No, no. I have to do this myself." I smile as I take in Mrs. Kaufman's blouse—it's purple, green, orange, blue with paisleys, and stars.

"You don't owe that horse's ass of a girl *anything*," Mrs. Kaufman says, piling the deep tin trays into our fridge and jolting me out of my reverie.

Unease ricochets off my chest as I glimpse Grams's nail polishes along the fridge door. I've told her that no one does that anymore, that keeping them cold helps them to "stay" is an old wives' tale. "So what?" she'd say with an enormous shrug. "If I had a husband still, I'd *be* an old wife." How do you get over losing a woman like this?

You start by taking it out on the inadequate women you are now left with. "Hello?" My mother actually answers on the first ring. She must be waiting for someone else to call. Someone for whom she doesn't have a lick of responsibility. Someone who might do something for her.

Mrs. Kaufman is trying to act like she's not listening, but she fit all the trays inside the fridge several minutes ago, and there is no reason in the world she'd still be here when *General Hospital* has already started, other than to make sure my mother comes to the funeral. She believes my grandmother deserves to have her only daughter present. And she's right. She's absolutely right.

"Well, finally!" I say, sounding like a Jewish grandmother myself. "Where have you been?"

"Busy," she says. "Actually I have to—"

I cut her off before she hangs up and doesn't answer for another two weeks. "What? Go on a tour of the neighborhood with the ice cream man?" I'm not letting her get the upper hand today. Normally, she hangs up and I'm left wondering what the hell I was thinking, to try with her.

Mrs. Kaufman stops pretending she's rearranging the trays, closes the fridge door, and creaks to a standing position, inspecting the calendar, probably as a ruse. But I can tell by the way her shoulders sag suddenly that she must have seen the little box where tomorrow, on the day of Grams's funeral, it said, *Buy present for Edie Kaufman's anniversary.*

"What? How do you know about that?" My mother says. "What are you—checking up on me now? You are *not* my mother, you know." My chest goes cold. My face is flash-flooded in hot tears. I wasn't prepared for this reaction—especially in front of Mrs. Kaufman.

I don't know what I expected. I guess I expected, like a freaking idiot, that my grandmother would take the phone from me, the way she always does, and say, "Sheila, stop acting like a freaking horse's ass. Come home for your daughter's . . . birthday/college graduation/prom night" . . . the list goes on and on, really.

But of course, she isn't going to say, "Come home for my funeral." I'm so mad at this realization that I don't know what to do. I'm silent so long, I can't believe my mother hasn't hung up. This is the longest conversation we've had in five years.

"No. Mom, listen. You have to come home."

Mrs. Kaufman starts mouthing something. I cover the speaker with my hand and whisper, "What?"

She mouths back, with a whoosh of hushed, emphatic words: "Give me that damned phone. Give it to me!"

I shake my head. I appreciate where she's coming from. But now that I've jumped in, I feel chivalrous for my grandmother. I want to, I *need* to do this for her.

Mrs. Kaufman must get it, because she tucks her arms in, and with a *hmmpph* loud enough for my mother to hear, sinks into "her" kitchen chair, the one between Grams's and mine.

I carefully chose my words when describing my grandmother's condition the few times my mother reached out to us in the past year; I had short sound bites ready, and edited out words like "leukocytes" and "staph infection" to get as much in before the line went dead. But how do I know whether she even allowed herself to believe any of it, or if she completely dumped it out of her head?

The last thing I should be concerned with is her feelings, but I realize, instinctively, maybe for the first time, that my mother loves my grandmother, too, even if she never did know how to show it. The idea angers me: how *dare* she get to love that fantastic woman? Where does she get off?

"I'm sorry, Viv. I just can't right now. I've got"— Let me just tell you how much it kills me not to mimic what she is about to say: *I've got a lot going on.* But I manage not to say it. —"a lot going on," she finishes with a sharp exhale, as if I don't know the half of it.

"Mmm-hmm," I say, reminding myself to breathe. I glance over at Mrs. Kaufman, who looks childlike and tired, as if age is no rival for grief, She rolls her palm and bugs her eyes for me to get going.

She needn't have. I've used up my patience reserves. All I want to do now is throw the phone and ask Mrs. Kaufman to go ahead and tell her that Grams is dead, but I know I can't do that. "Mom, listen, I have to tell you something. Grams—well, we, she's—"

I'm lost. I don't have the words.

All the inadequate euphemisms storm through my head: "with the big guy," "in that place in the sky." They seem like phrases for a walk in a sunny meadow compared with the breadth of loss. I can't bring myself to use any of them. I clear my throat, a stall for time before I miss my chance completely.

I draw a breath and zero directly in on the milky cataract of Mrs. Kaufman's blue eye for gravity. "Grams has passed away." I say these insufficient words as quickly as possible. My voice is surprisingly steady, I realize in the banging silence following. It's as if I *have to* be strong—for someone else, for my mother.

My mother is silent for a long while. "Well, if the funeral is this week, I just can't make it, I'm afraid. I've just got so much going on."

I want to scream, I want to invent a Wii game to smack her over the telephone. I'm prepared with five different curse words, but what comes out instead is staggeringly mature. My mother can't help but play this game. All I need to do is go along with it—though it is completely the opposite of what I'm rightfully entitled to—and she'll come.

"I know, Mom," I say. "I know you've got this project right now. It's bad timing for everyone. But we've just got to do it. We're doing it all exactly as Grams wanted."

Somehow, that does it. She's coming. She doesn't ask how Grams died, how I'm handling it, what I'm going to do with my life now, or whether I'm frightened. I freaking hate her for it. But she's coming. And somehow, I'm once again swimming in tears, this time out of gratitude for this one tiny blessing.

Mrs. Kaufman stays for tea. I entertain her with one-liners she doesn't get the way Grams would. She's here to support me, as much for my benefit as for Grams's. I come to see there are things that *she* is now floundering over an outlet for. The most obvious of these is gossip. While acting as if nothing were more disturbing than the burden of discussing someone else's business, Mrs. Kaufman and Grams loved to one-up each other by securing the inside scoop first under the flimsy guise of community public service. "The people need to know." *Yeah, right.*

"So, I hear you've met *Mr. Richter's son*," she says slowly, nodding her head to emphasize each word and then jutting out her chin in expectation.

"Mr. Richter has a son?" I ask. "Young people" in this building are here for the entertainment value. I find it satisfying; already I have missed it dearly. Curling around the edges, though, is a haunting peculiarity: wonderful as Mrs. Kaufman is, with her powdery smell and her intimate knowledge of all the teeth I've ever lost, she is no Grams.

"Well, if you want to play that game, fine. I don't like to concern myself with this kind of gossip. But I have it from a credible source that you had a rendezvous on the terrace. For another day," she says, her outstretched palm halting to a stop with perfectly feigned nonchalance.

In a second, she takes another tack. "Oy." She shakes her head so I'm sure to get the full extent of her expression; she's pretty good at this. "What I really must tell you is, you should never know from the kind of strain between these two—Richter and his son. I cannot say I blame the boy, his father abandoning him so young like that. I think he was only two. They all lived here for a couple of years—yes, before you came to stay—and then Richter, you know, ran off to Acapulco of all places, with a teacher from the elementary school on Brighton Fifth." Her hands work out all the emphases. If you plug your ears and watch her gestures, it's as powerful as Italian opera.

I think of the distress on Len's face earlier when I stuck my foot in my mouth and mentioned his father being alone. My stomach twists up like those long mozzarella braids at the gourmet store that Grams always says are too expensive to try. "What if you don't like it? Then we're out seven dollars; think of what you could do with seven dollars."

We're both quiet because this is when Grams would inject a wonderful insight about the subtle but complicated ways in which Len and Richter must love each other even if they can't quite meet on common ground. She's excellent at reading people—*was* excellent. Oy.

I don't want to hear anything more. This kind of information should come from Len himself. Still, I can't help but listen. I can't help but feel concerned. As I said, this is the kind of guy you want to go out of your way for, and besides, if destiny *has* brought us together, shouldn't I be trying to help?

Mrs. Kaufman lifts her cup to her lips, her eyes darting down over it, and says, "Now you didn't hear this from me."

"Of course," I say, crossing my fingers behind my back, just in case I'm ever against a wall and have to divulge. If I've learned anything, it's that you never say never.

"I don't know exactly what happened, but soon after Richter came home from the trip with that hussy from the school, Anita—that was Richter's wife's name—and Len moved out. They lived in Brooklyn for a while, and then I think they moved to San Francisco."

San Francisco—that's why his accent is so nicely tempered. I immediately picture him there, fatherless but never acting like it; the only place I know over there is the Golden Gate Bridge, so I watch him in my mind walking right across it, his shoulders square and strong, no cars in sight, the sunshine a halo around him. It's ridiculous, the clarity of these images. I barely know him. *Fate, schmate,* I tell myself. And yet, whether it's desperation, the idea of misery loving company, or something equally escapist—like clinging to Kavia's prediction—I can't help but feel I do *know* him. I can see him saying something like I would, something like, *Look, I don't need anyone,* just because he's afraid of what happens if he admits he might.

Mrs. Kaufman's fingers creep to her mouth and lightly rub her chin. "In the end, Richter didn't wind up with the woman from the school. As far as I know, he wasn't in contact with Len and Anita. *I* certainly never heard him speak a word about them. So sad; *very, very* sad." She pinches her left cheek, feels around at the papery skin there. She peers at the chunk of sky out our window, over my shoulder. "I don't know what was in Richter's head to do this; he was much older than Anita, certainly. *I* think, and this is just from my gut you understand, that something happened to him before he even moved to Seacoast, something that screwed him up."

You don't know about these gut feelings; these two women, my grandmother and Mrs. Kaufman, they have guts that should be in the Smithsonian, that should be studied under a microscope for accuracy. These guts could star in a very popular reality television show.

*My* gut, on the other hand, is churning. It seems like the entire world is lost. It seems like a wonderful time to shut the door behind Mrs. Kaufman and never, never open it again.

# II.

♈ ♉ ♊ ♋ ♌ ♍ ♎ ♏

*The irony of life is that we do not necessarily appreciate that which we have and only become aware of certain needs or attributes when they are withheld or denied. To acquire belief in self means that it is necessary to experience that lack of belief which most of us are familiar with as lack of self-confidence.*

—CORDELIA MANSALL

I *have no such* luck. Instead, it's a long day of phone calls and visits from neighbors. I'm not keeping score here, but I read my horoscope, and it said: "Visitors will come; push your luck in work situations."

I stretched the words like taffy, balled them up, and stretched them once more before rolling them neatly to swallow down.

It paid off. In the hubbub, I had completely forgotten to call into work. At *Skylar* the phone rings once, not even a full ring before my boss, Stan Hedger answers. Smarmy as always, he tells me, with no attempt at sounding convincing, that he feels badly for my "problem"—as if Grams was a puppy piddling on the carpet each time I leave the house. But if I want to keep my job, he says, I'd better be back on Thursday. I can hear him paging through the *New York Post,* as he does when he's on the phone with someone he couldn't give a toss about.

*He's an asshole,* Grams says in my head the way she did when I recounted the day over graham crackers and applesauce. I tell her to shut the hell up, that's my boss she's talking about. Only this time she doesn't throw the paper towel roll at me and ask, "How did you get so fresh?"

"Oh, Vie," Stan says. I've corrected him thousands of times. "Oh, oh, oh." These are meant as sighs of empathy, but I can tell he's rolling his eyes and, from the creak of his chair, that he's turned from the paper to his e-mail. *Push your luck in work situations.*

"Life and death, it's all yesterday's sourdough boule, isn't it?"

"Yeah, especially working for a dim-wit like you," I say. This is the kind of stuff we are always getting away with in the Grocery, Frozen, and Perishables section, because Stan doesn't listen to a word anyone says, unless it has to do with saving his own ass—and I'm not going to lie, it gives me a little lift to get away with this now. I've always said that cursing my boss right to his face is hands down the best part of my job.

"All crap," he says, without skipping a beat.

"You should think about getting into grief counseling," I say.

"Yes, yes," he says as filler. I can hear him peck-typing. "Now, I want you to take your time tomorrow *and* Wednesday." He delivers this as if it comes from a deep generosity, but this is merely our company's minimum policy on family deaths—most supervisors give a week under the "any more is at supervisor's discretion" clause. Not Stan. "But you must be back on Thursday morning, otherwise all of the newsletters that you're exclusively subscribed to will be stored up in your e-mail box, and we don't want any 'information silos.'"

As soon as he says "information silos," you know you're in major trouble, about to be bombarded with business terms he collects from his Middle Managers of America meetings every third Friday at Applebees. This is the kind of guy I'm dealing with—a person to whom Pick'N Pair Lunch Combos is an example of flexibility in action.



I throw my hands in the air just the way I did in gym class when Mr. Gridlow would yell, "Sklar-Single-I'm-too-important-to-have-just-one-name-like-everyone-else, get in your usual position: outfield."

I am so *not* in the mood for Stan.

"We need to be on the cutting edge; you *know* how the taxonomy of this corporate structure works. If *Skylar Good Foods Daily Journal* wants to continue as the market leader in knowledge sharing and database *resale,* we need to uphold our corporate *responsibility*—and Grocery, Frozen, and Perishables is the most important section in the magazine. Our sector counts for eighty-five percent of the entire grocery *market.*"

He really does care about this. That's the amazing thing. Wendy and I—who, after much collusion with the facilities manager "happen" to be cubicle neighbors—expend a lot of energy whispering into our shared wall and exchanging electronic greeting cards that say, "Happy Red Meat Month! I've come to suck your blood," or "It's Cheese Day! Do you know where your mold is?" While we are doing that, Stan has got his head in his hands, and he's cursing the rising price of Danish Jarlsberg. If he wasn't so downright mean, I'd really respect the guy's dedication. "The difference between the *chickpea* and the *garbanzo, Vie,*" he said once, "is subtle but *absolutely* important. It's the difference between being common and being a *nom de cuisine.* Which do *you* want to be, Vie?" All the while I'm supposed to be picking one of those that I'd rather be, I was thinking instead, how many italics did he abuse *this* time?

"Publications *cannot* make it these days by being mediocre. *Writers* cannot make it by being mediocre." He pauses and I whisper into the phone, “Asshole.” I think better of it and say, “No, make that *ass-hole*.”

I cannot tell you how much at this moment I despise Stan and his italics and his soft cheese fetish. I have every reason to trust my horoscope, to stand my ground. And so I say, “I’ll be back on Friday; I have to sit Shiva for three days.” Even though the name sours on my tongue, I say, “God says so.”

But Stan’s talking over me, already off and running about our duty to be cutting edge in pitted olives and the expanding pickle relish category, and I’m not sure he’s heard me. I’m pushing my luck and for once, I’d like to see where it takes me.

He’s saying something about dried dates when I replace the phone on its princess receiver and make my way to the sofa. “Let him fire me,” I say. I pull something from the bottom of Grams’s crocheting basket and wrap it around my neck like a scarf—though I know it’s meant to be a teapot cozy. I quell my worries: Stan certainly won’t miss a “chickpea” writer like me.

At four o’clock, the buzzer goes off and I race to the intercom, my feet slapping on the vinyl tile. I’m sure it’s Wendy, and my spirit lifts just thinking of something funny she might say, anything at all.

“Viv, I’ve got a package for you. From a *secret admirer,*” Jameson says.

I hear another other voice whisper, “*No!* I told you not to say that!”

I’m crushed it’s not Wendy, and I’m not buying Jameson’s and some neighbor’s attempt to get me out of the apartment.

“Whoever comes up to our floor next, can you have them bring it up to me?” I ask. It’s what we always do. Jameson is not technically allowed to do this in these days of plastic explosives forged from beauty supplies, but this group of residents isn’t exactly what you’d call a security risk. At least not since the cold war ended.

"Nope."

I'm just about to hang up when I realize what he's said. "Excuse me?" I ask.

"Your *secret admirer* says you have to come down and get it yourself." Again I hear that other voice—definitely male, not exactly identifiable—and now I'm not so sure it's one of the over-55s after all. There's muffling, as if someone has wrapped their hand over the mouthpiece. Then Jameson's back. "And he says you must do it within forty-five seconds, or the eagle dies."

*Len?* "All right; tell him ha-ha, I get it. Now could he just bring the phone up, since he lives right next door?"

I hear Jameson repeat this, just as I said it. Then I don't hear anything but crackling. I have to pull the handset away. When I replace it, there's more murmuring. Jameson is a heavy breather, so I know when he's back. "No," he says. Then he hangs up.

This is ridiculous. I make my way to the door.

Obviously, I want to see Len. I look at the door that leads to the hallway, which leads to the elevator, which leads to the lobby, and the neighborhood, and the world, which I'm not sure of any longer. I don't feel the courage I need to get to the other side, where there are people walking around and doing normal things like picking out the firmest Lebanese cucumbers and waiting in line to select fillets of salmon from icy freezer cases. I know that once I see them doing all these things Grams used to do, that I won't be able to convince myself she's coming home any minute. That she'll walk in from her watercolor class with something under her arm—that could either be an orangutan or a collapsing beach cottage—to hang in our bathroom.

Still, something propels me to take Len's directive seriously. I'm not proud of this, but, before I go downstairs to get whatever Len's got waiting for me, I try Bruce's phone once more. I can feel, pulsing through my blood vessels, how lonely

I am, and it terrifies me. I am tempted to pretend that Kavia is right: that Len is destined to be someone I can depend on in an Unus Mundus way, and in pretending that, I might be tempted to get real close to him by jumping his bones and having him spend the night.

And just because I'm so pissed at what I'm about to do, so pissed that I need someone to blame, someone to hold on to, I do something even more pathetic. I leave a horrible message, and I use tons of Stan italics, too: "I just thought you *might* want to know that my grandmother *died*, not as if *you care*." I hate myself just a little more.

Bruce's unresponsiveness allows me to justify the fact that, if my initial frisson gives way to more, and if that more is reciprocated, then I am about to have sex with "Officer" Richter's long-lost son.

After all, I am my mother's daughter.

And I'm more than a little curious about Kavia's prediction.

The keys weigh heavy in my hand as I lock the door and walk the hallway. I drag my fingers along the wooden molding, alert to its imperfections, its indentations and nodules, the whole way to the elevator. Here, on the other side of the door, the whole world is different. I don't know the survival tactics. Each step toward the elevator deflates me.

I'm standing, waiting, and my shoulders sag. I don't know what I was thinking. I feel like I'm cutting class—going to meet a boy! My grandmother is dead and I just want to get laid! I am just going to turn around and duck back under the covers. I retreat, but after only two steps toward my door, I get a strange feeling, like the universe has got my back, like I'm *not* alone, not with all those numbers and lines and symbols that represent everything and everyone; I get the feeling that they have woven a safety web for me. Everything will be fine. I force a smile, but it fades. The elevator door opens. It's Len.

He doesn't seem surprised to see me there. He's carrying a box with a plump checked bow tied around it perfectly, professionally. The thick ribbon ends are intentionally frayed and then crimped, and the overall effect has a subtle punk-rock flair.

I'm impressed.

He holds it out to me. "I wasn't going to let you change your mind," he says, pushing the elevator door aside when it begins to slide between us. His hand holds it back firmly, in a take-no-bullshit way, which, I'm not going to lie, completely turns me on.

I'm caught; his eyes are all over me, and that shimmery feeling moves along my skin. It's wonderful and terrible. A second ago I was shut down, and now I'm zinging and zipping. I want to trap this moment in a room, and slam myself inside of it. So what if I am devoid of morals, ethics, and the values that good people who've just lost loved ones are supposed to have? It's destiny, I tell that nagging in my head. *So shut up.*

Len extends his hand, inviting me into the elevator. I don't think it over. This is just what I need; it must be because it's a wonderful feeling—structure, clarity. I'm euphoric, just from standing near him. I may never go back to that apartment. I may never leave this elevator if this feeling would only last.

Neither of us speaks on the way down. The mirrored car jerks back and forth, cables squeal, but neither of us seems to mind. It's crazy how our eyes lock. I hope that if fate brought us together, then we are something more than two desperate people displacing emotions in a way too destructive to fathom. Sure, we're *fated.* I've watched enough public-television screenings of British soap operas to recognize it's the kind of scenario that could only end horribly.

Still, it feels wonderful, and I think, well, well . . . *maybe.*

The car comes to a stop on six. The elevator door opens, and there's Rachel Valmay, with her pumpkin hair in a great shellacked upward sweep, her cat chewing on its pink rhinestone leash.

Len does the best thing—it's like we already have our own insider joke, just how me and Grams did. But instead of saying, "Wow, am I thirsty!" the way Grams or I would whenever we saw Rachel Valmay with the cat on its leash, Len's "cuckoo" code is, "It's certainly a *fabulous* day today!" He stretches his arms as if taking the entire world inside them and gulps hard, so his Adam's apple rises and falls. Somehow, I know exactly what this means.

Rachel Valmay smiles big, shaking her head vigorously. I'm so thankful for a person to share an inside joke with, I could kiss that cat, which has taken to rubbing its head in the knobby crook of Rachel Valmay's wrist.

I once told Bruce about the way Grams and I scream "thirsty" around the cat with her cockamamie leash. He said, "That's wonderful, Viv. Next you'll be making fun of crippled people in wheelchairs. That is really hysterical, Viv. I can't stop laughing. Really."

Rachel Valmay asks, "How are you doing, Viv?"

My legs shake. I've no desire to play the melodramatic Italian widow. I prefer private grieving: me, a mini bottle of rum, and a bed will do just fine, thank you.

Len's hand brush my knuckles on the brass bar behind us before pressing firmly on mine. Sensation floods me in a giant rush. I imagine it's like being told your plane is going to crash, going through all that terror, only to be told, we've found a safe place to land after all.

*Hallelujah!*

He doesn't let my hand go as we descend through the final floors. And Rachel Valmay notices. It's clear from the way her eyebrows have disappeared beneath the curl of her orange hair. "What's with the orange hair, *heh*?" Grams liked to say . . . sometimes before we were safely out of earshot.

The elevator car wobbles to a stop. The door shuffles open.

Rachel Valmay steps out first. "I'll see you tomorrow, dear," she says. The cat, with its dainty jaunt, leads her down the corridor and around past the furniture we all sat in when I came home from the hospital, the first time we gathered without Grams.

Len's hand is still on mine as we watch Rachel Valmay scoop up her cat and wave its paw at Jameson. In a falsetto kitty voice she asks, "And how is Mister Jameson the *doowman* today? We *wuv* to say hello to nice Mister Jameson, don't we?"

Len shoots me a sideward glance. We both smile, our hands strange and fantastic, one inside the other. I can't even remember the last time Bruce held my hand.

I don't ask where we're going. I don't ask what's in the box, securely sandwiched between his right thumb and fingers. I merely follow in a kind of delicious numbness that is so welcome I simply let it wash over me in rhythm with the tide ahead. We walk to a bench—not the first or second from the stairwell, but the third; Len picks this one as if it's *his* bench. I like the idea of him sitting here, looking out at the waves, listening to the seagulls and the Russian conversations from passsersby.

"Sit," he says, bending in an exaggerated bow, the box tucked behind him. It makes me smile.

He sits, too, and looks at me with that same amused expression he wore when I thought he might be a burglar. "Aren't you the least bit curious what's inside this box?" he asks. His voice is nice and gravelly, but only with just the right amount of coarseness to give it a nice texture, like he's been around; like maybe he knows something we don't. He's working the local accent, but it's refined around the edges. Obviously, he's been away for a long time.

I shrug my shoulders as if I couldn't care less, as if beautiful men bestow generous gifts upon me every day. "No." But I do want to know. I want to know so that we can become that much closer, and then we can have sex. And I can show that Kavia whatshername that this man is not going to be "important to me," merely a one-night stand and, if I'm lucky, a couple of orgasms.

"No? You couldn't care less?" He squeezes his eyes against the sun.

The sky is bright, like it doesn't give a shit that the world as

I know it has come to an end. There're only two fluffy clouds across the entire bird's-egg blue expanse of it, and they are reflected pristinely in the water, in between a tanker and a gleaming cruise ship. Grams and I used to guess the destinations. We'd conjure up somewhere exotic, with a lot of syllables, like Mykonos, Maravagi, or, Kalamazoo; we said we'd go one day (not to Kalamazoo).

"Not a lick," I say.

A pigeon flies overhead, cooing. My grandmother would have yelled something sassy and Biblical-sounding like, "Go to hell, you cockroach of the sky!" I shrug at Len's question and try not to make too much of the pigeon, or the memory, as the hair on my arms stands on end. But seeing as the entire reason for the eagle statue is to scare away the pigeons, and since I was bonding with it when I met Len, and it was Kavia's pigeon light that attracted me to her and her prediction about my having been "supposed to" meet Len, it's kind of remarkable that a pigeon is yelling its annoying little head off at us right now.

"All right, fine then. I'll just keep it for myself." Len places the box, which looks about the size of a perfume gift set, or a kosher salami, gently upon his lap and steeples his hands between his thighs, his fingers pointed to the weathered boards beneath our feet.

I try to act like I don't care if I never see inside the red paper, but I can't pull it off. I've always been impatient for surprises. I once broke my grandmother's favorite chair balancing to reach the very back of her closet for my Hanukkah gifts. I grab for the present with a snap. But he's faster than me and snatches it just out of reach—holding it up high. "What do you say?" he asks, batting his eyelashes.

"Gimmie it."

Len clucks his tongue three times, like a schoolteacher. "I'm sure you were taught better manners than that by your 'Grams.'" He says her name just like I did earlier, when I mentioned us watching *Lost* with his father. It shouldn't get to me, but it does. *He doesn't know*. He thinks she's *alive*. I'm about to open my mouth and correct him when I realize something fantastic: I don't have to. With him, I can act like she's alive. With him, things can remain just as they were.

It's such a relief. I almost feel like my old self again. I wonder if it is as simple as this, what Kavia meant by Len being important.

In a spike of bravado, I catch him off-guard and grab the box from his hand.

"Fine," he says, so familiarly it's frightening.

I tug impatiently at the ribbon and it gives way easily. It's an old-fashioned box, made of heavy cardboard, with separate top and bottom pieces. I pull the top off and hand it to Len, and our hands brush. I look up and he's gazing at me with those enormous eyes. I don't ever remember a simple look with Bruce being so purely enjoyable. With Bruce, I'm always thinking of things we can do—take the train to Coney Island, eat dim sum in Chinatown, check out a music festival (not that he ever wants to do those things), because I always feel like we have to be *doing* something. But this—this is something different. We're not *doing* anything, and yet, I feel I could sit here all day.

I pick through layers and layers of gold tissue. I'm told I'm a difficult giftee, but I never thought so. With me it's merely about sentiment; I think the best gifts are meaningful between that person and me. Grams got it right every time. Except for the "modern art sculpture," which she—fair enough—mistook for a flower instead of a woman's breast. I can name off every birthday gift she's given me for twenty-eight years. I still have them all: a slim volume of e. e. cummings's poetry, a night-time reading lamp, the soundtrack to *The Sound of Music* (don't laugh; it's good), a perfect straw beach hat, and yes, even the ceramic-with-feathers breast. With the exception of what we've grown in the habit of calling "the boob," these are things that show you know the person you've bought it for. I could never part with even the wrapping they came in.

Inside the layers of gold tissue is another box, a much smaller one, covered in deep red glossy paper that looks like patent leather. I lift the lid on this one and inside is, at last, the gift. It's a cell phone. Only, this one's not the free Nokia that comes with a two-year agreement, but a top-of-the-line iPhone. I've been drooling over it for months.

"Open it," Len says, his gaze darting around my face like an infrared laser, gauging my response.

I do as I'm told, and I can tell right away that the thing has been opened before. For one, it's got this great grafitti'd skin over it that says "Brooklyn" in a really cool way, with a backward R and a stylized K like all the guys in our school used to do on the brick façades along Coney Island Avenue. It makes me think of the little paper sketches they'd draw for me instead of doing work in class. I collected dozens of these over the years; still have some, probably.

"Wow," I say. "You shouldn't have. It's too much. And besides, I already have a phone."

"Really?" he asks, a mischievous crease at his eyes. "It wouldn't happen to be this phone, would it?"

Len pulls something out from behind his back that used to be my phone but is now a cracked key pad and the shell of a battery. I can tell it's mine because on Bring Your Daughter to Work Day, the receptionist's daughter stuck a flower sticker on my 9 button. There is literally nothing else.

"That's it?" I ask.

He looks down at the splintered plastic pieces in his palm with a nodding head, but then stops, mid-nod. "Oh, wait, there's more."

There. I knew it couldn't be that bad.

Len digs into his pocket and pulls out a perforated sliver of metal that must have been the microphone.

"Right," I say, worrying it through my fingers. I can feel his gaze as I inspect the remains.

A second later I catch his eye just where I'd felt it, and

we're in hysterics. I'm thrilled to make him laugh; it's extraordinarily empowering.

Suddenly, we both stop, look at each other, and move closer, a centimeter at a time, until our bottom lips touch—just barely. A series of tremors reverberates down my spine to my toes. He tugs my lip between his, and anchors it gently, but purposefully, with his tooth. My back is arched so that my chest touches his; I'm as concave back there as I can be, and our tongues haven't even made contact yet.

And then they do. And our hands explore each other's hair, ears, necks, shoulders. He feels so good, so solid, so *alive*. We can't seem to stop; there's always another angle, another lock of hair. It's everything and nothing, swirling and standing still. *Could it possibly be?*

Who knows how much later it is that we come up for air and the sounds restart, people reappear around us. I don't care how long it's been, who's seen. I want this day before Grams's funeral, before we seal everything away for good, to last forever, to never, ever end.

"Scroll through the menus," he says, and though our mouths have parted momentarily, I can feel something changed in the way mine sits upon my face. I don't think it can ever be the same now that it has been used in this way.

As we sit, we're still connected. One of his hands is splayed over my shoulder, and the fingers of the other are tangled in my hair, gently feeling around at the base of my neck. It's heaven.

I'm not sure how to turn the phone on, so I fumble around. Len watches my fingers, which makes them slow, clumsy, until finally he shows me where the button is hidden.

He presses down on a strip of steel I hadn't noticed along the top, and the screen blinks to life. I see the cheery Apple logo spring onto the center of the screen and my heartbeat kicks up a notch. I have a fancy-schmancy iPhone—one of those things I'd always want but never get for myself. Sure, I'll miss out on complaining how inferior my crap phone is in comparison, but I'm pretty sure I can live with that.

Len shows me how I can use my phone to get the weather, as an alarm clock, to get my horoscope, and to show Grams hers. "So she can tell you it's a load of crap," he says.

My stomach lurches. I am never going to get used to her being gone. Len's hand guides mine, showing me how to tap the screen when my finger freezes over the temperature in Miami. How is it I am able to enjoy *anything* when my grandmother is dead? When she is being made up—probably to look nothing like herself, despite Froishe's best efforts—in the purple sparkly dress she loved so much, the one Froishe came himself to pick up earlier, with a tear in his eye. Everyone was sweet on Grams. Everyone.

"You don't like it," he says, a blank expression hovering over his face—like maybe he believes this and maybe he doesn't.

"No, it isn't that. It's—" I'm about to tell him. I really am. I mean, I can't just *pretend.* I know that. This isn't kindergarten. Or L.A.

His eyes open wide in expectation, his hand on my shoulder tightens and his chest puffs, as if bearing up to take in whatever I'm about to say.

"—It's just that this is such a wonderful gift," I say, cursing the estuary that's sprung from my tear ducts. I've been known to call crying a waste of water. But apparently I'm no longer the boss in this relationship.

"Hey, hey," Len says, so tenderly the tears accelerate. I can feel the neck of my shirt growing wet. Which makes me think of the old, smelly clothes I'm wearing—a T-shirt I've slept in for the past ten years or so, and some pilled gray yoga pants—and now I really want to cry.

"I'm not crying," I say.

"I know," he says, and swivels me in, and when he bears his other arm around my back, and doesn't rub, the way I hate, but holds real nice and strong, it's the most natural thing in the world—like I was always meant to have those hands around me, and I only now realized it.

* * *

Len doesn't say anything. He's just pressing me and smelling fantastic. I can't remember ever being so incredibly low and at the same time so incredibly high. And there's no way to turn it off.

When my breathing has slowed at last, my nose, which has been grazing the skin along Len's neck on and off the whole time, drags itself up all the way to his earlobe, and then I'm right back where we started. I'm kissing his ear, and he moans.

Len doesn't wait for me to come around gently to his mouth. He grabs my face with his hands and pulls me to his lips. This time there is no long, lingering touch; it's starving kisses. It's a Picasso painting—all unruly angles, but with a striking beauty at each one.

"Let's go up to your apartment," he says, breathy, right into my mouth.

I don't have to answer.

Len gathers up the box, replaces the lid, and crumples up the paper, ready to toss it in the mesh can just a couple of feet from us.

I surprise myself by stopping him. "No. Let me keep that," I say. "I want to keep it."

Len nods his head, those generous almond eyes fluttering slightly, and he smooths the paper before tucking it under his arm with the box.

We retrace the length of the boardwalk, descend the steps, and retreat along the cracked sidewalk to the jammed parking lot behind our building. Len leads me by the waist, and I find myself glancing at passersby, proud to be held by him.

Thankfully, we don't see anyone I know as we stand in front of the hot wind of the Downy-scented laundry vent. Len thumbs through his keys. He finds the right one and twists the lock, shuffling me inside with his arm. The hallway is empty as we hoof it to the elevator bank. But I know Jameson is watching the hallway on the security camera. He sees everything—renegade squirrels, termites, Mr. and Mrs. Regan twice going to second base by the recycling bins.

Out of respect for normal people who don't behave this way when they're grieving, I pull away as Len leans in to kiss me. But as soon as the elevator door opens and we file in, I cover the camera lens with my hand and bury myself back in that taste of his lips, his tongue, the feel of his ear.

I am out of breath and dizzy when we stumble our way to my apartment. Inside the door, I can barely focus to work up an excuse for where Grams is.

"Grams is in Florida," I finally manage. It comes out muffled beneath the shirt he's yanking over my head. Len inclines his head, maybe too vigorously. His eyes are screwed shut so I can't tell if he believes me.

When I undo the fly of his jeans, I am bolder than I ever was with Bruce. I allow myself to feel around his waist, to tuck my hand down the back of his jeans, to experience the warmth of his skin there. It feels like everything with Bruce was a trial run, leading me to this moment, that maybe, I should *thank* him for deserting me. We had our moments, but mostly it all seems to me as if we were playing the roles of two people who were supposed to be passionate about each other—trying to get the gestures and facial expressions right.

We are in my room and I close us inside, as this is the only place in the apartment untouched by Grams's "vacation to Florida."

When he unsnaps my bra, Len lets out another groan, the way he did when I kissed his ear. Encouraged, I tear into him again. Soon he's got me on my bed, kissing the life into me, his excitement rigid against my panties. I'm rolling along skies; I'm a jetliner, or a bumblebee on the lam—free and far, far, away. What ensues is the kind of thing I've never allowed myself to believe in.

What follows is excruciating.

Len must leave the warmed, rumpled bed to tend to his father's evening needs. He leaves me with the special "comfy" headphones on my ears, to listen, in the appropriate order, to a bunch of songs he's loaded on the iPhone for me. I picture him the entire time he's gone, shuttling over the mulberry shag carpet with tablets and tonics, stoic and helpful—his feelings safe in a pile here in my room, between the oscillating fan and my pelvic bone. I think of the way his feet looked bare—perfect in their thinness, their asymetrical toe pattern, their sprigs of dark hair like miniature Brillo pads.

Even while I'm smiling madly, running my tongue over parched lips with an ate-the-canary grin, I'm sure he will never come back, that I've made him up to keep me company. It would make perfect sense; I've never done anything like this before.

It will be a painful descent back down to earth.

I chew my nails. I pull off my split ends.

Three hours later Len knocks. I know this sounds crazy, but I sense it's his knock. Through the peephole, the white of Len's eye is veined with red.

I swing the door open and drape my body around it loosey-goosy. "Hey, there," I say, emboldened by what we've shared, clinging a little too tightly because it's been prophesied. My eyes go to his mouth and I crane around the dead bolt to kiss him, allowing myself to linger. I revel in the aftershocks. When I open my eyes, though, he's pulling away.

Something collapses in my chest.

"Hey, I just wanted to say that I should probably stay at home tonight."

"Is your dad okay?" I ask.

"Yeah, yeah. He's fine. But I, you know—just would like to sleep in my own bed. You know?"

Sure. Except your bed is in San Francisco. And that's two "you know's" there, guy. No need to pull out the full-body Kevlar. I've made a sophomoric error. I've allowed myself to heap clumps of faith, like so many gum wads under a school desk, onto the first intense guy who shot a "How you doin'?"

in my direction. "Sure, doesn't make a difference to me," I say, tossing up my palm. I watch him swivel and take the two steps back to his open door. I can't see anything but the mulberry shag and Richter's coat tree, shaped like an actual tree. The door shuffles to a close. How stupid I was. As if a new life could fall into place, just like that.

Only, against all odds, he comes back. And with the slightest measure of awkwardness, the right amount for people who've seen each other naked and now realize they barely know each other, we proceed to pick at Mrs. Kaufman's noodle kugel. In between coaxed-down bites, we swig shots from each of the novelty liqueurs Grams has been saving all these years. I tell him she won't mind. She encourages sexual freedom and boozing—especially mixed together.

"Sounds like quite a gal," he says, clinking his American Airlines shot glass against mine for what must be the sixth time in fifteen minutes. The liqueurs have done their job and we are once again mostly at ease.

"If she were here," I tell him, "she'd say, 'That Len Richter, he's a real eligible young mensch.' That's her favorite term: 'Viv, I've met a real eligible young mensch,' she'd say to me." I catch myself when I stare off into the memory of her for too long.

Len's smile gradually straightens. "Well, if she weren't drinking Maalox mai-tais at the early bird special"—he shoots me a sideways glance—"I would tell Grams that maybe she shouldn't trust Len 'Officer' Richter, Junior. If you took a poll among the burnt ladies of California, you'd agree. Running's in my genetic makeup." We're laughing so hard over the air quotes that I pretend not to feel terrified at what he's said. Maybe this *is* kindergarten after all.

"I'll take my chances," I say, swabbing at my eyes as Len sighs away the laughter. My stomach swirls to the tune of *slow down, Viv; slow the fuck down.*

But the tune hasn't got a chance. Len's got the iPhone playing through some tiny speakers, and the room is spinning, and we start laughing when Len says "Psychedelic Furs" only it sounds like "Furgs," which is probably only funny when you've just added an empty bottle of crème de menthe to the seven or so empties that you are carefully trying to balance into a castle. The structure collapses.

"Ooops," I say, my hand to my mouth.

"Ooops," Len says and leans in, sweeping my hand away, and kissing me. Hard.

"Ooops," he says again, when he pulls away.

My eyes stay closed a beat too long. My internal alarm blends with the sound of The Psychedelic Furs singing "Love My Way," and Len leans in to kiss me once more, and somehow we do it all again—clothes everywhere, chair broken to choking giggles—only even better, and certainly drunker, this time. And when I fall asleep, my head is on his smooth, muscled, but not too muscled chest, and his arms are tight around me. His fingers rest at the jut of my hipbone, and I am close to sure that nothing will hurt me again.

# 12.

♈ ♉ ♊ ♋ ♌ ♍ ♎ ♏

*For you to have been conceived—everything—and I mean EVERYTHING—had to happen exactly the way it did. If your father had started ¼ second earlier or later, had the temperature been ½ degree warmer, had any random noise occurred other than the random noises that did happen—even change of what your parents were thinking about—and you cease to exist.*

*. . . For any of us to have been born, everything at the moment of conception had to happen exactly the way it did or we wouldn't be here. And it also applies to all our ancestors. My parents, their parents, all the way back to the beginning of life on Earth. If any event happened differently than it did—no one who is alive today would exist.*

—"Papa" Sid, retired clinical social worker

T*hat night,* I dream pure memories. They aren't of my life with Grams, but of my life before that—with my parents. I dream my entire collection of them, and even in the dream, I can't help but wonder what this means.

My father was a quiet man with a trusting face. He rode an enormous motorcycle with a flame-lick decal. When he was alive, my mother laughed in a tinkling way, especially when she explained how everyone liked to chitchat with him because he didn't ever actually say anything. "He could be silent for three hours easy, just nod his head, and no one would be the wiser," she'd say, biting back her enormous, gleaming smile. It had something to do with his eyes, she said. They were wonderful. "Everyone's best friend." She'd flit her eyes toward him, looking absurdly happy.

My father was the kind of man who blushed and grabbed for the mini hotdogs when his wife said these things over a coffee table.

Our years together were dotted with biker parties in the park, where everything smelled like leather and mayonnaise-based salads. On Fridays, even though we didn't believe in it, we observed the Sabbath with my father's parents and acted like we bought it all—even the part about not using electricity. We made a big show of wearing naturally wavy hair instead of smoothing it out with hot rollers, and bringing food that didn't require cooking, like pillowy challah breads from the bakery, or three-bean salad with Italian seasoning sprinkled over the top.

In the shadowy dark of my grandparents old Rockaway Parkway minty green row house, my mother would hold my hands and swish the candle smoke toward my face. She looked lovely doing this, really natural. My father would have his hair combed back and gleaming with Brylcreem for his mother's benefit.

On this night before my Grams, whom my mother called my "real" grandmother, on the night before she is to be buried in a box and never seen again, I dream these beautiful, perfect evenings back into life before reality wends itself into the picture.

In the dream we leave my father's garage loaded up with the O rings we wore as "Madonna bracelets." We're half-jogging, singing off-key the theme to *One Day at a Time*. The bells at the door linger a few beats too long. On the other side of the door, we aren't on Bell Boulevard in Bayside anymore. We're back in our apartment, and my mother forgets me in my bedroom coloring in Smurfette's shoes, lips, and hair in my favorite shades of pink and red, trying not to get any Magic Marker on my Holly Hobby comforter. When I realize that day has turned to night and day again, I run to her bedroom door and knock, but she won't answer.

I'm frightened and I'm hungry. I'm concerned about a burning smell coming from behind my mother's door. It's the day of the cigarette fire; I have dreamed this event back into life so many times. In the end, there wasn't much physical damage, only a small, hardened hole in her daisy print bedspread. But it was the beginning of the end. And this is where I wake—at the beginning of the end.

After what I put my body through last night, it is no small miracle that I wake at all. My eyes flutter. In a matter of seconds, I'll remember this memory fog, this hazed descent into reality, as the last blissful dregs of disorientation. But for now I half expect to see my father pad down the hallway, engrossed in that same worried forehead rub I've frozen on him all these years. I focus on my desk chair—an old spindly thing I found at a tag sale and re-covered with fish-pattern fabric.

Instantly, nauseatingly, the chair, with its cheerful take on dead fish scales and tackle boxes, grounds me. Slow to switch gears, though, I focus on an imperfection on the seat.

*I love this chair.* "It makes you smile," Grams said. "It's worth it. It was a godawful pain in the ass to fix up, but it's worth it." She'd swapped smoking for orange Tic-Tacs by then, and she smelled like a whole mouthful of them as she leaned in to kiss my nose.

I shut my eyes again. In a moment, they reopen and I see the chair once more, this time noticing a lot of clothes hung over the back. Normally, I take very nice care of my things. Otherwise Grams goes through them, and this has ended badly more than once. As I'm in the habit of putting them away immediately, I am thrown by the mess.

Upon further inspection it becomes clear that I do not recognize these garments at all—a faded orange T-shirt and a pair of men's jeans. *Men's jeans!* Bruce must finally have come around; he used the spare key we keep with Jameson, and here he is.

"Good morning, Sunshine," Bruce says.

Only it's not Bruce.

Panic rolls from my chest to my fingers and back again. It stretches around my back and shoots up my spine. I sit up like a dart, shielding my nakedness with the floral top sheet. And there he is.

Oh. *Oh. Ooooooh—wooooooaaahhhh.* I spin back toward the wall with a start. My head pounds. Everything goes fuzzy. I remember the shots. *I drank Grams's liqueurs—even the pharaoh head and the one with the worm in it. Boy, is she gonna be pissed. She is saving those for when Yanni answers her fan letter and finally comes over to try her salmon croquettes.*

Something isn't right. Oh. Oh, yeah. There isn't going to be any Yanni or salmon croquettes. I honestly cannot believe it smacks me just as hard as it did in the hospital room. Oh, fuck. Fuck. Fuck.

I steady myself with a hand on my end table, and for the first time I concentrate on the beautiful man who happens to be lying in my bed. Pleasure lingers lazily beside grief for a delicious second. This fabulous boy, without a lick of clothing on, the sheet draped diagonally over his chest like it was arranged by a professional painter for a sitting, places his massive hand on the top of my head and pulls me close to him until our foreheads touch and we're looking at the whites of each other's eyes. His lashes sweep mine. My eyes stay wide open as he kisses me, his own closing languidly.

My grandmother's funeral. It's today. I pull back and grab my fancy iPhone carefully, like it belongs to someone else, and take a look at the time. The funeral starts in twenty minutes. Shit. Holy shit. This is bad. I mean really bad. The woman who carefully picked carrot bits out of my chicken pot pies for the better part of a decade is being buried—and I can't even muster up enough appreciation to be punctual for the occasion.

I jump up. "Look, I have to—" I'm just about to make up some excuse about why he needs to leave right now, something about an emergency trip to Alcoholics Anonymous maybe, when I hear the front door creak.

I'm half standing, half kneeling on the bed, a deer in headlights, holding my iPhone like a Fabergé egg over my nakedness, as if that is going to do anything. Oh, please don't let it be Bruce. Not now . . . though it *would* be just like him to do absolutely nothing to help and then arrive out of nowhere holding up a jumbo packet of Skittles, as if tasting the rainbow just might fix everything. And it would be just at the perfect time to completely sabotage whatever this crazy thing is that's happened here with Len and my clothes and this galvanizing thing we keep doing with our eyes, and the way that the worst week of my life is burnt through with a gleaming, fiery ball of light.

# 13.

♈ ♉ ♊ ♋ ♌ ♍ ♎ ♏

*When people grieve they are coming to terms with what has changed in their lives. Following loss the grieving person has to relearn the world and themselves because everything has changed. Grief is not an illness. We don't "get over" profound grief because we are changed both by our love and by the loss of our loved one. But life will eventually have meaning again, although our loss will always be part of us.*

—Australian Centre for Grief and Bereavement

"Vivian!"

I don't even make it to my bedroom door before the voice rips through the air, a flame over a line of gasoline.

There is only one person who calls me Vivian, and the reason behind her doing so is that she chose that name out of thousands of others, like Susan and Margaret and Annemarie, which were too plain, and she "detested" when everyone shortened it to Viv, which she thought sounded like a cream for pimples. *This* is what mattered to my mother—that her daughter might not be confused on a list with Oxy—not whether she celebrated my birthdays, or, say, *lived* with me.

"Oh, boy," Len says, as if he senses this might be to my distaste.

"You don't know from oh boy," I whisper and then clap a hand over my face, hoping I might disappear down a rabbit hole or through one of those tesseracts I always thought might come in handy. I can feel my eyes bulge. Adrenaline races through my body, its interaction with the twenty or so miniature bottles of liqueur making me sweat profusely. I can hear her footsteps on the linoleum.

"Hey," Len says in a whisper, his mouth in my ear. Even in the chaos, I can appreciate how the sheet slides off his body. Jesus, he is an *actual* man. "Everything is going to be okay," he says, in precisely the way you might want someone to when you need it most. He squeezes my hands in his.

My eyes dart back and forth, inspecting him—this fantastical male force of calm and comfort, Clint Eastwood in *The Bridges of Madison County*—and something crazy happens: I believe him.

He winks at me. "I'll only come out when it's safe," he says, and hides himself in the tiny half bathroom off my bedroom. He pops his head out and throws his T-shirt my way before snugging himself back inside and clicking the lock into place. I pull the shirt on just as my mom ducks her head in.

"Vivian!" She throws herself onto my bed like she's Sandy in *Grease,* and I'm the experienced Pink Lady, the one who might be pregnant but is too stoic to tell the boy who did it. This is my mother.

I'm as stunned by her presence as ever. It's much easier to hate her from afar than when you are reminded in person of how childlike she is. It's kind of difficult to hate a helpless fawn. The thing is, sometimes *I* want to be the helpless fawn.

*Stop worrying over what's fair already, hah?* It's outstanding that Grams has the time to help me on the day of her own funeral. But I shouldn't be surprised.

My mother starts in about traffic on the Van Wyck and construction patterns in the Midtown Tunnel, and I tune her out to get ready as quickly as possible. I try my best not to be distracted by Len on the other side of that flimsy door. I begin rummaging through drawers for underwear and a bra and, for some reason, stockings, even though I never wear them. I'm so nervous, I don't know what I'm doing.

"You have *no idea* how difficult this is for me," she says, picking at a loose stitch on the blanket. "I feel like I have no one now. I'm all alone, you know." The thread snaps. Probably the whole thing will come undone now.

I know, believe me, I know how clueless and egomaniacal she sounds, but she's crying already, and her shoulders are shaking. And I can't help but feel bad for her. The thing is, I know how difficult it is to lose Grams; I'm feeling the same way myself, though I've done a pretty good job of avoiding it so far.

We're already late, but it seems more important to comfort my mother—comfort is mostly what this day is about anyhow. It's okay if we're a little late, I decide; it's not as if they'll start without us. So, I go over to the bed, the black underwear, and real garter stockings crumpled in my hand, still covered only by the delicious softness of Len's T-shirt, the smell of him all over me. My mother won't notice; I once cut my bangs to a quarter inch of my scalp and it took her a week to realize. "You look like Ish Kabibble," she said, and turned back to folding the laundry.

She's turned over on her stomach, propped up on her elbows, her legs bent back at the knees. Ankles crossed, she swings her legs like crazy; her curly dark hair seems like it's everywhere. I rub her back in the little circles she likes. She shuts her eyes. "Mmmmmh. I miss that." This, she misses.

"It's a terrible feeling to have no parents, to be an orphan. I don't know how I am going to go on from here. I mean, what am I going to *do*?"

That last bit is an excellent question. I have been asking it myself—over and over and over again. Somewhere inside me, a sage I've been harboring knows the answer. "We're going to continue to wake up each day, and do what we have to do. Though things won't ever be the same, eventually things will be better, somehow. Grams wouldn't want us to stop living. She was all about the living, you know that."

And this is when it hits me—I told Len that Grams was in Florida.

"That's what Grams would want," I say, my voice barely able to carry the sentence in its entirety.

My mother inclines her head, gravely, as if truly considering the weight of this statement. In her moment of introspection, I take the opportunity to grab my peep-toe heels and black silky sheath. I can't help but remember when Grams and I bought the dress at Loehmann's. It reminded us of something Audrey Hepburn wore in *Roman Holiday* in that wonderful bicycle scene that we couldn't get enough of. I hoof it to the bathroom but it's locked. My mother doesn't notice that the door unlocks from the inside. Len twists the knob open and I slip inside quickly. My whole life seems to be taking place in the bathroom these days.

My mother's talking the whole time and I toss out "mmmm-hmm" and "yeah" every now and then to keep up appearances.

Len is sitting on the side of the tub with my copy of *Fascinating Geographical Trivia* in his hands. "Did you know that in New Caledonia there are twenty-three languages, and *forty* in the Solomons?" he says in a voice just a tick above a whisper. He looks up with a supportive smile. I'm surprised at how *un*mad he is about the lying thing. "I knew already," he says by way of explanation, and closes his finger in the book.

"Why didn't you say anything?" I whisper back.

"I thought I'd let you feel it out on your own. That's how I would've wanted to handle it if the tables were turned."

Logic. What a refreshing idea. And he's exactly right. It was the best thing he could have done.

"Where did you come from?" I ask, feeling at the crossroads of conflicted and enamored.

"From Brooklyn. Where else?" He exaggerates his accent, making me smile. This guy could only come from this particular place in the world; it strikes me as something rare and valuable. It's the same place I'm from, and it's a remarkable thing.

How could I simultaneously feel so wonderful and terrible?

"Mmmm-hmm," I say, loud enough for my mother's benefit. I can hear her talking. Len pulls me down onto the side of the tub. His hand applies just enough pressure on my arm to reintroduce that delicious security he blanketed me with earlier. He kisses me soft and slow, watching me protectively, but I can tell that the chemistry is still darting around between us. "Yeah," I say to mom. Len and I smile. It's incredibly comfortable and intimate.

I shake my head; I have nothing else.

"You just do what you need to do." He's looking into my eyes and his enormous pupils dilate quickly.

Again my head bobs. I stand, lift the T-shirt up and off, suddenly conscious of my body. I pull on the panties, hook the bra behind. His eyes are on me the whole time. I slide the sheer black stockings over my legs and clasp the garter to attach each one. They are very pretty. I'm glad I decided to wear them. Len seems very glad, too. I hope, if Grams is with us today, she doesn't see this part.

"I know you're going to a funeral and all, but those are very hot," Len whispers.

I can't help but smile at his reflection in the mirror. He looks very nice wearing bedroom eyes on the edge of my tub, even if I *am* wearing my funeral lingerie.

He places his hand on the back of my thigh, just high

enough to send an enormous rush through me. I wish I could put him in my purse and take him along to hold onto my thigh like that the whole time. I would feel a little stronger with him clamped there.

I step into my dress and twist my arm around my back to yank at the zipper. But Len's quick on his feet, and he's suddenly behind me, a head taller. He pulls the zipper up slowly, tooth by tooth, all the way to my neck. Then he leans around and pulls my hair to one side. He hovers behind my ear, and kisses me there. I nearly fall over.

Tearing myself away, I swivel around to face him. "Listen, I'm sorry, but can you just stay here until we leave?" I don't know how else to put it. I hand him my key ring, the apartment key sticking up from the lot. "Lock up, and then you can just leave them with whoever's covering for Jameson." I don't want to think about the gossip this will generate after the whole secret admirer thing, but I see myself as having little choice.

"No problem," he says. His look is difficult to read. "I'm here," he says after a second. My stomach churns. I've floated luxuriously on him all night, a buoyant raft cutting me across a choppy ocean. And now I have to swim alone. And there's a shark circling.

"Vivian!" she yells, on cue.

"Thanks, really," I say to Len "Officer" Richter, Junior, a man I won't forget anytime soon. I squeeze his hand. And then I twist the knob and steel myself to face whatever will present itself on the other side of that door, outside, at Froishe's Jewish Faith Funeral Parlor—even though I'm not ready. Not ready at all.

# 14.

♈ ♉ ♊ ♋ ♌ ♍ ♎ ♏

*A few minutes before the funeral begins, the first formal act of mourning,* kriah, *the tearing of one's garment or a ribbon, takes place. Kriah is a centuries old symbol of inner grief and mourning. Mourners stand as they perform it, showing we face grief directly and that we will survive, even without our beloved departed. Before the cut is made, mourners say the words of Job, "The Lord has given and the Lord has taken, blessed be the Name of the Lord," and recite a brakha which is a reaffirmation of faith.*

—USJC.ORG

(UNITED SYNAGOGUE OF CONSERVATIVE JUDAISM)

M*y mother and* I take a car service to Froishe's. The livery driver is off-the-boat Russian and doesn't speak a word of English except for "Cash, cash," which he repeats until I say, "Okay, I got it."

My mother, who speaks fluent Russian, is turned on by

this, apparently, and decides to flirt with him. I have no idea what they're saying but her inflection betrays the tone of the conversation. This is one of the worst things about seeing her: I'm nine years old again, feeling unlovable and wanting to hock a loogie into her boyfriend's cereal bowl.

How could she think about flirting right now, I muse for a half second before I think, *Okay, Pot, who's calling who black?* She tosses her head back, hooks her ankle behind her calf. I inspect her as if through a geneticist's microscope—reading significance into each speck of her iris—and suppose I'm looking at myself in twenty years.

*Don't cry; I'm warning you.* I tell this to myself as we turn the corner and slow down in front of Froishe's. I have no desire to become the center of attention. I won't be screaming "Mama mia!" and throwing myself emphatically over the coffin. I would prefer to maintain my dignity, my shoulders erect, looking as indestructible as one of those Smart Lid food containers that elephants can't squash on infomercials. I'll fall apart when I get home. Alone. And with French fries.

But my eyes tingle as the driver slams the old-fashioned steering column shifter into park and repeats his refrain: "Cash, cash." Tears collect at the corners of my eyes, ready to pour down the sides of my nose.

It isn't any better when my mother grabs for my hand; she's all squirming fingers and knuckle grips as we walk beneath the domed entryway to Froishe's, a place I've been to many times, but never with such a leaden feeling to my bones.

I don't even know this hand of my mother's. Mine goes limp in hers the way it might on an awkward first date. Everything's happening in slow motion. We're met with a sea of shaking heads, and I recognize them all, but can't place them without reaching deep into the pits—Josephine Dephano from . . . the bridge club; Anna Schwartz from . . . Suzanna's Hairdos. It's everyone Grams has ever known, the ones whom we haven't memorialized here before, anyway. Her brother's kids are here and a couple of his grandkids, too—all looking very much like the dozens of pictures plastered over our fridge, only with nervous, tight mouths. There're all the people from every restaurant we've frequented over the years, my old teachers, people who work at the pharmacy, nearly every occupant of our building—the list goes on and on. There are literally no seats. Someone I can just make out but can't place from this distance, stands in the front row; this tall and as yet faceless man motions with an open palm for my blinky mother and me to take two seats.

When I realize who it is I don't believe my own eyes. At the same time, my brain responds, *Of course; of course it's Len.* He doesn't wait for us to walk the long center aisle; he swiftly approaches as people grab our hands, shaking their heads, their pity as uncomfortable for me as it is for them. Meanwhile, my mother seems to relax amid the attention. Her grip around my fingers loosens.

I avoid the looks as courteously as possible, inspecting ceiling beams, windows, while my mother begins a long, loud wail I haven't heard since my father died.

Len looks fantastic, in a dark, navy suit with a crisp pink shirt and boldly striped tie. He takes each of our hands in one of his as if it's the most natural thing in the world. My mother must think he works here, or want to take him home for dessert, because she doesn't bat an eye as he passes us mini packages of tissues. I shoot him a funny look, as if to ask, *Where the hell did you get these, and by the way, what are you doing here?* He winks at me and a dam gives way in my chest.

When we reach the front row, Len gently eases my mother into her seat. He squeezes my hand and I take the seat next to her. He seems to understand that I wouldn't want the same kind of coddling that she does.

It's not something I'm proud of, but the sight of him walking off to stand against the wall at the end of our row makes me feel stronger. It reminds me that I just might be able to do this—or at least that I have no other choice.

The rabbi takes the podium and begins the service. He's in the same kind of shabby suit he's been wearing for decades, a mode of dress that endeared him to Grams. "The schlocky thing is humbling," she'd say.

My ears prickle at the sound of her name on his lips. "Sandra was not the kind of woman a person could easily forget," he says. The words hang there over everyone. "She was a real firecracker—a mother, a grandmother, and a friend besides." His pace picks up, as if she's here and he's excited to introduce her. "She was a member of my congregation for over sixty years—when she wanted to be. You couldn't make her come when she didn't want to. This is a woman who said we should raise money for a family who couldn't afford dues and then went out and in twenty-four hours came back with all the money. In cash."

I can't decide if the laughs make it more bearable or more painful.

Each time I turn to Len, standing against that wall as if he were always meant to be there, he has such a look of compassion, it fills me with hope.

The rabbi speaks at length. The anecdotes continue to get laughs and sniffles. I realize that my mother has not been to this rabbi's temple since my father died. It must be difficult for her, burying her mother in the same cemetery. I can't help but draw parallels: Did my mother lose her faith, too?

The rabbi turns serious and then smiles big. "Without fail, I give this prayer in Hebrew, but Sandra made me promise to also do it in English today, so that her granddaughter, her Viv, as she called her, would understand, since—and these are Sandra's words, Viv—'she didn't bother to finish learning Hebrew.'"

The crowd laughs and for a moment it's like she's actually here. I let the Hebrew wash over me; I've always liked the sound of it, even if I never could be bothered to finish learning it. The way I only vaguely know what's being said leaves me with something like condensed broth after a long, slow boil: the rich essence. The difference is that now not even this does it for me. All the chicken soup in the world isn't going to bring back my faith, and finally that's one thing I can say I am glad Grams isn't here to see.

Then he delivers the English: "Source of all, You who governs all things with infinite wisdom and mercy, and who guides the destinies of all. As a parent You love us, and shower Your blessings on us. Therefore we shall not murmur even when sorrow befalls us, but with humility and unfaltering trust accept Your decrees. In joy and in sorrow alike, we praise Your goodness and acknowledge Your justice. We remember that we are strangers on earth. Like a shadow our life flees away. . . ." The final lines send a shiver through me. "Though we walk in the valley of the shadow of death, we shall fear no evil, for You are with us. Praised are You, Sovereign of all space and time in all Your dispensations, and may your name be sanctified for ever and ever."

There's a tug at my heart. I *want* to believe. I want to raise my shoulders to their full height and fear no evil. I am that kind of person. The kind who looks at evil and tells it to go to hell. I hunt down the bright side. Even in the weeks after my mother left, I looked out the window for her curly hair, listened for the clack of her Candie's sandals on the pavement.

But now I can't. I just can't anymore. What kind of God wants to shred the fabric of love to bits? What kind of God lets you think everything will be okay and then says, ha ha! Just kidding!

Only after she's gone do I see what Grams was, that she was light-years better than any traditional parent could have been. Only now do I fully appreciate that what I had in her was a blessing, a gift, even if it sometimes made me eat Brussels sprouts.

In the strangest of ways, I have my mother to thank for it. Say she'd tried her hardest, stuck around and droned her way through my elementary school years, junior high, my rebellious high school period; there's no way she could have measured up to the kind of "mother" that Grams was.

"Now her daughter, Sheila, would like to say something."

My mother, who always has something to say, had called on her way back to Brooklyn to demand they make room for her on the schedule of events because she's the daughter. But now she clams up so tight she crosses her arms, her fingers, shakes her head back and forth—no; she can't do it.

I squeeze her hand to let her know this is okay. Where my wisdom has sprouted from I won't claim to know.

Rabbi Menachem doesn't miss a beat. He clears his throat and says, "Then we'll move right along to her granddaughter, Viv."

I hear my name, but I can barely connect it to myself. Instead I think, *I've heard that name before, haven't I?* I don't belong here, with all this mourning and loss. I should be out on the terrace begrudgingly surrendering to Grams sips of my peppermint tea, complaining about her lipstick along the rim and asking why she's drinking it if she says it's gross whenever I want some at the Key Food?

My toes point, but that's as far as my body seems to want to go. It's like starring in a horrible movie biopic, but no one remembered to tell you it was being filmed, and you're unprepared. But it's too late; the spotlight's already blinding and everyone's waiting.

I swivel and take Len in—his tall, lean, athletic build—but it seems like there is a mountain between us, which I have to hike over to reach the podium. When I get there and unfold my paper, I'm sure I've lost my footing. My heartbeat thumps in my ears, at my throat, around the back of my head. My mouth feels as if someone has swabbed it dry with cotton.

My voice cracks, but works its way into something intelligible: "Grandma Sandra—Grams—was an unbelievable woman—full of zest and humor and chutzpa. She loved her daughter; she loved her brother and granddaughter; she loved her nieces and nephews in a way that reinvented love, really. To call her a grandmother, to me, was never enough. She was a parent, a best friend, a shrink, a confidant, a person to stay huddled up against in a snowstorm, someone to coach me through recipes and to brainstorm ideas for books that she always hoped I'd write, someone with whom I was forced to share peppermint tea that she claimed not to like. She was the giver of sour pickles and cabbage knishes. Sandra was the lender of books, the writer of letters, the donator of scarves, the lover of elephants, and all things from another time, things that had enjoyed many lives before they came our way. She loved to eat out and to recommend that everyone order the salmon burger. She loved to eat French fries and deny it afterward. She didn't love change, yet she would surprise you every once in awhile by signing up for cable television or having an amazon.com order shipped to the apartment. She was the first person I'd ever heard propose the time-travel theory on *Lost.*"

I can't help it. I look up when the laughter rolls along the rows, and I turn instinctively to Len; he's trying to hide his tears, fisting them away as they appear. I remember what I told him about his dad watching *Lost* with us. "Of course, other people had very good theories, too," I add.

This gets some strange looks. Len smiles.

"What did she say?" an older man I recognize from the congregation asks in a loud voice.

"Huh? What has she lost?" someone else whispers.

"Turn up your hearing aid, Morty," the woman next to him yells with a jab to his ribs.

"Ouch," he says. "That was really hard."

My little cousins giggle. In my nervousness, I follow their lead. In a wave, the crowd follows, slowly, softly, using poor Morty Schlessinger for some levity.

I can tell Len's smile is fueled by pride. I instantly feel proud, too. It's a new emotion for me, this pride, and it comes in handy as a booster.

Locked in our extended gaze, it occurs to me that Len may not have such a laundry list of things to say about his relationship with his father. Wendy always tells me that what I have with my grandmother is even better than having a parent, that in most cases, people never have something as special, as close. It doesn't make me feel better now she's gone. What it makes me feel is frozen—an iridescent salmon at the fish shop on Brighton, wide-eyed with terror. But I have to get through this speech.

I've paused too long and people start to squirm. I look across the room, to the very back, by the door. And that's when I see Bruce. He's standing by the Tree of Life, with its branches of dead people that lead to other branches of dead people, and he's looking as slick and self-contained as always. His hair is freshly cut and his hands hang confidently at his sides, as if he attends funerals every day. He acknowledges me with a dip of his chin. It's easy and obvious and makes me want to smack him.

Two men; two sets of risks. There's no right answer, I think. Just as quickly, I realize my error. There *is* a right answer. And I know just where to find it, don't I? It doesn't seem so crazy now. In fact, it seems like common sense. What *else* would I do but refer to my horoscope, just waiting there to light my way?

Somehow I stumble through the rest of the eulogy. I accomplish this by ignoring both of them and focusing instead on Morty Schlessinger with what I hope is a warm, gentle smile. Inside I'm wooden. "She never let you leave her home empty-handed. She liked to make vegetable soup . . . and freeze it in takeout containers from the Chinese restaurant. She preferred dark-meat chicken and she always kept the wish-bone. You may not know that she liked to drink Corona with lime. She was a card shark and the world's greatest Scrabble player . . . though she sometimes cheated. She wrote down the seven-letter words to prove it. She liked four-letter words and she wasn't afraid to use them." I don't recognize the words on my own paper, though they're in my own handwriting—the plump, loopy G's and H's I spent hours perfecting for Mrs. Templeton's approval for that important third-grade switch to pen. "Now just take a look at that beautiful penmanship, would you?" Grams had said, when I brought home the official document, on which I wrote ten times in my neatest cursive: "I will mind the lines and I won't lift my pen."

I take a breath and prepare to finish. "She could surprise you by learning something profound even after all of her experience. She loved leopard prints and buying extraordinary gifts. She rarely splurged on herself. She was very proud of me, of all of us." I pause and look at my mother. I feel so much anger it knocks me, and I have to grasp the edge of the podium. Mostly, I'm angry at my compulsion to comfort her, after all this time, though she would never do the same for me. When she looks to me with her fraught fawn eyes, my stomach shudders.

"Grandma Sandra, for any of you who don't know, is also an adjective. It describes a particular object cherished by her family and many, many friends: A Grandma Sandra Blanket. And today, I would like to give her name a second meaning."

I'm near the end, but I'm losing steam now. I can't look at Len and I can't look at Bruce, and Morty Schlessinger is starting to give me the eye. I can't allow myself to be swallowed up by my mother's desperation. I would normally look to Grams at a moment like this. It is so obvious how truly gone she is.

"A Grandma Sandra," I say in this great void, "is what I'd call anyone who can ignite and maintain a love so overwhelmingly huge, that it encompasses every one of us in this room. I think that type of accomplishment should be known as 'a Grandma Sandra.'"

"Hear, hear," Morty Schlessinger says.

"There will be a hole always in my life where Grams kept her place. But over time I hope to fill it with good deeds, and long talks and generosity, and a real, tangible kind of love for my own family, children, and grandchildren one day, in the manner I was taught by my Grandma Sandra." I hear this now and barely remember writing it. I fold the paper, descend the stairs, and take the seat next to my mother.

I can't even begin to try and explain why I do what I do next.

# 15.

♈ ♉ ♊ ♋ ♌ ♍ ♎ ♏

*Every life has a measure of sorrow, and sometimes this is what awakens us.*

—Steven Tyler

S*omeone must have* vacated the seat on my other side and in their place sits Bruce. I'm not sure if I should be relieved or angry that he doesn't grab for my hand. After a few minutes, I nearly convince myself that we are sitting somewhere innocuous, like in a booth at Roll N Roaster, and that right after we are done dipping our last French fry in horseradish sauce, I will go home and Grams will be nagging me about how I'm going to get fat if I keep eating there, and why didn't I bring her back anything, don't I know how she likes the sweet potato with butter and cinnamon?

It's that tempting to swing back to something familiar, and so I do my best not to look at Bruce for the rest of the service. I continue to avoid Len. I refuse to make another catastrophic mistake, if I've been given the tools to avoid doing so. I need to see my horoscope, and everything will be alright.

It's not that difficult to avoid their stares, really. I weep silently into my lap, covering my face with my hair. My mother is holding onto my hand as if it's that floating door Kate won't share with Leo at the end of *Titanic*—and together, we withdraw into our own bubble of misery.

"We will all proceed to the Mount Ararat Cemetery, in Farmingdale, Long Island," the rabbi says, closing the service and his prayer book with a sharp echo through the microphone.

My chest bumps. I introduce Bruce to my mother.

"I need to use the bathroom," my mother says a moment later. I'm thrilled for the excuse to escape. I am ashamed, but there is nothing I can do but check my horoscope in the funeral restroom stall. I tell myself this "innocent check-in with the stars" is like sucking down a piece of dark chocolate after a salad: a reward for being strong. I'll just see what it says; what's the harm? Besides, I'm sure there's no way this will work again, and once it all turns out disastrously, I can get right back to being a faithless adult like everyone else.

I guide my mother by her elbow. My grandmother would blow a gasket about how badly she needs moisturizing cream. She was a stickler for smooth elbows. My mother closes herself inside one of the stalls and I close myself in the other. I sit down in a heap and I experience a certain amount of déjà vu. I really don't know what it is with me and bathrooms lately.

I slide the iPhone out of my pocket nervously, perform my search, and watch the navigation tool load, rushing it along in my mind. But that halo of loading indictor lines just goes around and around and can't seem to get where it's trying to go. I hear my mother fumble with the toilet paper roll. I'm running out of time. I try to reload it by jamming my finger on the hopeful curved arrow. I wait. A tiny sliver of blue begins to sprout on the status bar. Relief floods me. I watch, imagining micro-movements, but soon enough, it becomes clear nothing more is happening. The page isn't loading. I close out and reopen the browser and type in "Pisces daily horoscope" a second time.

My mother flushes the toilet. I listen anxiously as she reloads her shoulder with her giant leather bag. Items collide and shuffle around inside it. She unhinges the stall lock with a bang and makes her way to the sink.

She sighs. "Oh, Vivian, I don't know how I'll survive this," she says.

"I know, Mom," I say, staring at the screen. Why won't this damned thing work? The thing is, I don't know how to survive this either and I'm trying to find out from someone who does, but for some reason I just can't make contact. *I.* (Calming breath.) *Can't.* (Calming breath.) *Make.* (Calming breath.) *Contact.*

"Honey," she says, just as the hopeful blue strip begins to make its way successfully across the navigation bar.

It's loading. *It's loading!* Slowly as hell, but there appears to be a transformation taking place; the navigation screen morphs to black and a tiny blue Q*bert cube pops smack onto the middle of the screen where an image is loading.

"Honey, what are you doing in there? Come on, we've got to go. What do you think, the whole world is going to stand around and wait for you to do your business?"

My mother thinks I'm being selfish for what she thinks I'm doing in here: going to the bathroom. Only *she* is allowed to do her business while we all stand around and wait. I'm gripping the device, hoping through clenched fingers that this damned cube will give way to some cheesy celestial imagery, and that I'm about to see my destiny, a path carved out specifically for me in the deep brush cover between Bruce and Len. My knuckles going white, I realize something. I *am* being selfish: not to my mother, but to my grandmother. This is her day, and I am behaving like my mother. I'm closing myself off from pain when I can't deal with it, turtling. I owe it to Grams to set this right, now. If she and I had one thing in common it was our distaste of exactly this kind of behavior.

Though my heart thuds, I press the screen back into blackness. I say to my mother the kind of thing my grandmother was always begging me to. I unscrew my lipstick tube, hold it poised over my lips, and I say, "You are absolutely right. For a second there, I was acting just like you." I don't listen to the guilt that wiggles its way around my heart, or the misgivings about poor timing. I just pucker up, and blindly roll some Kiss Me Coral over my mouth. Grams always said I looked much lovelier in lipstick.

I pull the stall latch free and open the door so I'm face-to-face with my mother. She is quiet, and looks a little hurt. She turns her eyes to the floor and tongues the inside of her cheek.

I take her hand. She looks up.

"Mom, let's be there for each other today. Okay?"

This seems to do the trick. She gestures assent, her dense hair immovable, and returns the squeeze I apply to her fingers.

By the time we're rounding the driveway of the cemetery I tell myself it was all for the best. I didn't really need to see my horoscope. Astrology is ridiculous; it's no better than pinning your hopes on an ice cream man scheme; it's no better than pinning your hopes on a wet-eyed boy who happens to be next door when you need someone to fill you up. I don't believe any of this for a second.

When I see him at the cemetery, Len is all the way at the back. Bruce is as close by my side as he ever gets—a few feet and an emotional mile away. It's as if I'd imagined everything that happened yesterday—the iPhone, the hands on my bottom, right down to Len's slight nocturnal nose whistle. Who was I kidding anyway? I've piled all kinds of wonderful traits onto Len that probably aren't there at all; I needed those things for comfort so I imagined a one-night fairy tale in which I got them. The end.

In fact, I'm not even so sure, looking at him now, that he really exists at all. That guy back there could be anyone—an Impressionist take on *Funeral Guest, Far in Back,* all swirls and squiggles, pallette knife jabs in magnificent relief. Only, now there is a tangible, sticky something between us, a Hubba Bubba dangle of goo connecting the hurt between us. And that is undeniably real.

I have absolutely no idea why I'm holding on to Bruce's dead-fish hand. I feel the dense knot of it the entire time: this is all wrong. It's backward, a mirror image of what should be in every sense of the word—the open grave, my hand smoothing little circles over my mother's back, Len far off while Bruce marks his territory. Maybe I've used up my last stores of desperate activity, because I can't bring myself to correct my course. Maybe I'm simply drowning in an overflow of it: if this one last thing, my relationship with Bruce, stays the same, then maybe Gram's death won't hurt as bad.

We stand before Grams's open grave, the dirt piled on either side. This cannot be happening.

And yet. My heels are sinking into the grass, my mother is sobbing uncontrollably, yelling "My mom, my mom," and as a plane drowns out Rabbi Menachem's voice, my heart breaks in two.

I'm stuck with my mother and my careless boyfriend and if these are the best decisions that I can make, then this is my destiny. End of story. There is no Unus Mundus; there is no synchronicity. There is a prayer I can't understand in Hebrew; there is Jameson; bent over like his back is broken, there is my five-year-old second cousin bawling her eyes out as she picks up on the communal mood. If I squint my eyes sharply enough, turn my face just the right way, I might find a pattern in anything—those trees, that grouping of people making their way to an orange Ford Focus—couldn't I?

When I get the nod, I place a pristine yellow rose on the coffin. It's stunning and thorny and difficult to handle without destroying it or hurting myself. I hold my mother's hand while she does the same—only slower and with more deliberation, shedding petals all over, as if this is her show and she wants us all to know it. My mother is first in line to shovel dirt onto the lowered casket. When it's my turn, I hesitate, fidget with the hem of my dress. The rabbi says: "This act symbolizes our trust in God; we trust Him enough to turn our dead over to Him with our own hands. This is the final act of caring for those who have cared for us." I trip over a distant cousin's shoe on the way back to my spot. I've always been a terrible liar.

Through my weeping, Bruce's flaccid hand rests limply on the most uncomfortable part of my back. I can't imagine laughing over the word *dungarees* ever again. I cannot imagine laughing over anything really, ever, ever again.

*"Yitgadal v'yitkadash, sh'mei raba b'alma div'ra chirutei."*

"Happy Livestock Week!" Wendy mouths when I turn back to see her. She wants me to laugh, to remind myself I'm alive. But like most everything, this joke is a relic from another life.

The prayer is a relic, too: *God is great; may he bring us peace.* Though the syncopation of the words accelerates my heart, the sentiment is completely hollow. If I ever believed it, I certainly don't now.

I walk back to the waiting car, and the three of us—my mother, Bruce, and myself—are ushered into the backseat. I'm the only one who sees that it is Len and not the flirty Russian driver holding open the door this time around. Of course, nobody else knows him. He's done this—despite what I'm doing to him. This might be my chance to make it right. I take one look at him, and realize my error. His body has stiffened. Each tense movement is jammed with significance.

As he disappears down the road, among its row of parked cars, mourning headlights shining at the ready, I tell myself this thing with Len wasn't much different from the spectacle of a funeral procession. It was a customary, age-old way to deal with grief—messy and imperfect, and with someone always getting lost along the way. Still, as I glance back toward the cars diligently following, looking as deflated as their occupants, one thought permeates: What if it *isn't* merely that? What if it just happens I am destined for something more?

Inside the car, Bruce is completely silent, his gaze out the window, his body language casual; he might be going off to happy hour at a sports bar. He's leaning as far into the window as possible without winding it down and jumping out. I try to work out how many words besides "I think it's a left here," he's said today. My head pounds; I'm finally catching my breath from the frenetic pace of sobbing, which thankfully cut off in one quick flash at the on ramp to the Belt Parkway. The skin under my eyes stings. My mother's head is down. She's lying over my lap with her legs curled up, her high heels piercing the door's leather upholstery. Her back jumps every few seconds as she cries loudly into my thigh.

"Shah, shah," I soothe, the way Grams always did for me. In the leathery, stale back of this car, everything is exhausted—the mangled, burnt metal of the ashtrays, the cracked plastic of the door handle, the masking tape over the torn seat. The sounds of traffic are hushed by my mother's wails, by the closed windows, the hum of the air-conditioning, and the motor. I should have ordered a Lincoln. But Grams liked this car service, the one with all the sevens in the phone number. I called without thinking.

My mother suddenly sits up, her face turned toward the divider. "Bruce, you'll be my son-in-law one day. You're a good boyfriend. I know you're very good to my Vivian." This is her way of feeling sorry for herself, of showing me how much better off I am than she is; she's done me so many favors to lead me to this. *That's right, Mother, I'm fine. I'm just fucking dandy.*

I try to remember the way Grams and I navigated the Korean greengrocer's for our week's supply of veggies and fruits—how she'd head straight for the least ripe bananas, and I'd inspect the Kirby cukes for the firmest in the pyramid. We'd meet at the register within seconds of each other, without so much as one redundant green pepper, without missing a beat. Why didn't I ever realize how beautiful this was?

My mother falls asleep as we crawl, in clankety starts and squealing stops, by Starett City, the giant depressing apartment complex that was probably, in its day, a dream come true for aspiring architects. Far enough away to pique the interest of a body language expert, Bruce is snug against the window, engaged in text messaging, his brows tugged in concentration. I watch the familiar landmarks, wanting to hold on to this final bit of my life with Grams, wanting to make it last and last. But something keeps poking in the way. No matter how I nudge away the image of Len and me—our gaze long and steely, before we fell asleep last night—it holds strong.

I see a sign that sent Grams and me into peals of snorty laughter: "This mile of highway sponsored by Esther's Dressy Dresses." Only someone has crossed out *Dressy* and written in *Ugly.* We've loved this ever since it appeared ten years ago; we never understood why we loved it so.

"It's so stupid," Grams would say, trying to catch her breath as we drove alongside the giant Canarsie garbage heaps. "Maybe it's funny because it's so dumb."

Only just now do I understand the allure: it's simple, innocent humor; there isn't one drop of complication to it. And sometimes in life—despite its murky lure of Lens and star maps, its astonishing thud of dirt clumps on pine, and its stunning finality—simplicity is just what you need.

"Turn left here," Bruce says a few streets before our building, at a short cut. I fight the urge to slap him, and scratch the back of my hand really hard instead, leaving two pink, stinging trails that cross my veins in resolute arcs. I pull my iPhone out and with great hope ready myself to soothe regrets, which are mounting. I resume the attempt to check my horoscope.

The screen goes blank. Horizontal lines manifest from the top down.

Despite the logic I've clung to at this funeral, on this death day, this paltry attempt to honor someone whose honor is too big for honoring, I'm terrified of what I might see on that screen.

"Mercury retrograde in Aquarius approaching Jupiter.

Glimpses of the future are here. Do not, whatever you do, miss your opportunity with Mr. New. Looking backward would be the biggest mistake in the world."

"Ha!" I say out loud before I realize, and clap my hand over my mouth. My mother stirs but doesn't open her eyes. I feel a burst of her breath on those scratches at the back of my hand. It was a Ha! of horror, and it echoes in my ears. I'm that same Viv holding out, refusing to dance even a single kick ball change until her mother shows up at her recital. Nobody's eating even a crumb of my cake until I've bored myself with denial and I'm good and ready to move on to the next grief stage.

"What?" asks Bruce, finally looking up. He puts his cell phone away and slings a wooden arm around me.

To my suprise, relaxation surges through my limbs like whiskey. In the haze where familiarity, contempt, and lassitude converge, there's only one interpretation I zero in on: the horoscope was wrong. Best of all, it turns out I didn't need faith in anything after all. What a relief. From here on out, I can simply continue on, satisfied with merely existing.

"Nothing," I say. "Nothing at all." For the rest of the ride, I let my mother's breath soothe me. That and the rhythm of cellophane from a funeral parlor mint rolling between Bruce's fingers. I let these sounds syncopate the air coming in and out of my lungs, and concentrating, like this, on the most basic block of life, I fall asleep.

To his credit, at least Bruce waits until my mother is once again snoring—this time in Grams's bed, with her mouth open and little pops of air breaking through—to break up with me. I've just tucked the afghan tight under her shoulders and closed her inside the bedroom. There are ten people still sitting shiva in the living room, creaking on all the chairs we never sit on, the ones with shaky legs and loose springs. The crowd has whittled down from the seventy or so who stopped by earlier. They're hovering over macaroons arranged on foil trays, dolled up for the occasion with black paper doilies. *It's a shiva! Pull out the black paper doilies!* I imagine the ornery lady with the mustache yelling when she takes orders at the Kosher-Style Deli.

In the exhausted energy of our apartment, all hunched shoulders and buckled-over bellies swollen with corned beef, sugary coleslaw, and smoked salmon, thoughts of the past, told with nostalgia and despair, drift over to my bedroom along with the smells of onion bagels and cabbage knishes. "I think we both know this isn't working out," Bruce says, fiddling with that same square of cellophane. We've closed ourselves in here because Bruce suggested we take a little break. Clearly, it's really a big break. "You used to be so strong," he tells the fish scales on my flea market chair.

Even as my mouth stretches to an enormous O, I know I'm not really as shocked as I'm allowing myself to believe.

Just like that, he's gone. He forgets his flashy business card holder, which he *told me* he wanted for his birthday three years ago, which I have always hated, but bought all the same, thinking there is something very, very wrong between us. But I told myself, Viv, it's only a tacky business card holder, not the end of the world.

I slip out and walk the hallway, the one Grams won't ever walk again, not in that rickety old body of hers anyhow, and I throw the card case down the trash chute, listening to it bounce down nineteen stories to the basement, where it will be incinerated down to nothing.

I'm pretty sure I hear Grams say, "Good girl," the way she used to when I was three and had spelled my name out properly. *Good girl.* I can't make it all the way back to the apartment. My legs collapse at the knees and I slide down against the wall, taking a loose scrap of wallpaper down with me. I sob silently, my chest aching, my hand smoothing the wallpaper. I get up, smack some life into my cheeks, and go back to my company.

It only takes two minutes with the coffee drinkers and the

knee bouncers to realize that—even if it *is* as irrational as betting my future on Franklin Mint collectible plates—it *feels* right to heed Kavia's advice, and besides, there's no denying it any longer: my horoscope was spot-on once again.

It takes two minutes *plus two seconds* for me to assuage my sanity by calling Wendy to double check. "It isn't crazy; it's survival," she says. "We do what we have to do."

"Isn't that from a Sarah MacLachlan song?" I ask.

"Don't get smart with me," she says.

"But isn't it?" I hang up on the tail of my joke so she'll think I'm okay.

There are two more days of shiva. Wendy sails in and brings a load of horoscopes from publications around the world—even the ones from Australia that are for tomorrow. "Look, we'll all go down together," she says, her fingers scraping her bulky auburn hair from her face.

"Now, I *know* that's from a song. Billy Joel."

When she escapes back to work I feel a tug; part of me aches for my regular life. "Take me with you!" I want to yell, knowing exactly how her dog feels when she closes the door on him. But I smile and say, "Get outta here before I start singing." She plugs her ears and winks her way out the door.

My mother picks through the shiva rules like fancy flavored jelly beans: she wears her torn ribbon like a badge of honor, even to bed, where she refused to fall asleep to reruns of *L.A. Law* because we aren't supposed to watch TV. But when she woke up, she showered and then spent hours in front of the mirror coaxing her hair into soft waves, like Carly Simon circa 1982. All this while listening to Linda Rondstadt's version of "Desperado" on a continuous repeat. She sang along in a way that could tear your heart in two. I never could do sad as compellingly as my mother.

I spend most of my time trying to keep my smile up, getting

shooed out of the kitchen by neighbors for trying to help, and when I'm barred from doing anything that might occupy my mind for even a few minutes, I take to mindlessly palming pistachios into my mouth from a bowl I don't recognize, placed on a surface where we'd never put food.

My mother's been scavenging Grams's closets for black dresses, and managed to find all these gorgeous little numbers I never would have thought to give a second look. She jazzed them up like only she could, with brooches and scarves, until they looked like something from Madison Avenue that needed a toy poodle to match.

On the second night, when everyone leaves, I find her in there, clothes in a minor promontory on the floor. The few dresses still on the rod are pulled half off their hangers, dangling precariously. I cringe; Grams would have a fit.

"Speak your mind," was a common thread in most of the horoscopes Wendy read to me earlier that afternoon. We went through all of them, disregarding the parts about success in long-term investments, since I don't have any of those, and the part about favorable conditions for gambling. It was a way to speak to each other that didn't require awkward, polite sentiments about being sorry for things that aren't anyone's fault, which nothing could be done about anyhow.

"Hey, do you mind cleaning up after yourself?" I say to my mother, following my horoscope's advice. Grams is probably flying about on her fluffy angel wings, *tsk*ing and saying, "Unbelievable. You don't listen to a word I say for thirty years going, and now you do exactly what strangers tell you just because they claim to see it in the stars? Gee, I'm honored, Miss Shirley MacLaine, Junior." I bend over and lift a crocheted dress from the top of the mound.

I laugh but my mother misses it, shimmying out of a crushed-velvet number with an empire waistline. I get a whiff of Grams's perfume as Mom tosses it on the bed like something to send to the Salvation Army.

“Sorry, sorry,” she says, surprising me, leaning over to follow my lead.



On the third day she wears the dress she tried on after that exchange—a triangular floor-sweeping thing in a thick Chinese silk that has a certain timelessness. It has a long V neckline and she’s wearing it with big gray ceramic beads, glazed so they catch the overhead globe light when she drifts over in perfectly postured steps like a silver-screen siren, to the food table—which she makes sure to do once every ten minutes.

I’m in the middle of counting how many times someone has complained about the heat when Len comes by with four trays of mini knishes—two potato, one cabbage, and one kasha, exactly the mix I would choose if pressed—and a plate of pastrami and rye bread garnished with a star of pickle spears and one black olive sprouting from the center. Immediately, I flush. “Does anyone think it’s hot in here?” I ask no one in particular.

Len smiles, but there is that disconnect still wedged between us. He wears the demeanor of a soldier on duty—compassionate but restrained; the food trays like armor; he’s here with Kosher-Style Deli because it is what he must do. I ask after his father, and before I get the whole question out, he says, “He’s good. Good.” My heart squeezes like a fist.

When he leaves I wish he wouldn’t, but I don’t dare say so. The coffee drinkers and knee bouncers watch, their eyes darting back and forth, like a line of Kit-Cat wall clocks.

Later that night, I watch the sky darken slowly and then suddenly, the bridge and cityscape lights illuminate like so much magic determined to continue on. Mrs. Regan’s washing dishes again. Rachel Valmay is talking about her cat’s gallbladder, something about mushing up rice and steamed tempeh. “Tem *wha*?” Mr. Regan keeps yelling. “I can’t hear you. My hearing aid is going in and out.” It sounds like a good time to sneak out for a breather. I sink into my bed as if I weigh a million pounds. It feels fantastic. Like this, I reread the new pile of horoscopes Wendy slipped beneath my door this morning. "Go out and cheer up someone ill" seems to be a common theme.

Back with the company, I snack on chocolate macaroons and then I put together a black-doilied tray of pastrami, rye bread, spicy mustard, and pickled tomatoes for Richter. This has nothing to do with Len, I tell myself.

I knock on the door loudly, twice.

Len answers, surprised to see me. He's in navy sport shorts with white stripes down the sides. "Hello," he says, not unkindly. But it's not what anyone would mistake for intimate, either. He opens his eyes wide, waiting for me to explain my presence. Suddenly I feel like coughing up my mistake the way Rachel Valmay's cat did with that green marble earlier.

"I've got appetizing," I say, which is the most positive thing I can think of.

On the other side of this wall, my mother is holding up my grandmother's cocktail rings to the light, the ones eight-year-old me and Grams would stack on our fingers playing Desert Queen, which mainly involved hanging a sheet between a dining chair and one end of the sofa, bedecked in jewelry and scarves.

When I left, my mother was saying things like "This alone must be worth several thousand. Don't you think?" while she shooed the cat away from licking them.

Right now I really need for there to be a bright side; I need to believe there's something positive I might set off in the universe by presenting this fatty-meats tray to the lovely sick man in the next apartment and his intriguing son.

"I thought nobody used that word anymore," Len says.

"Appetizing? Yeah, well, around here they do." I dump the tray into his hand and try my best to look sane.

"You've no idea how much I like the idea of a girl like

you bringing me a pastrami sandwich," Richter says from his perch on the woolly La-Z-Boy; a walker rests on all fours a few inches from him. I could put those crazy tennis balls on the bottom for him the way all the old folks do in these parts. Len doesn't know the ropes yet. I hope he stays but not to learn anything like that. He shouldn't have to know a thing like that.

I happen to know Richter doesn't like to eat alone. No matter how hungry he is, he'll leave the thing sitting there until you have something yourself. So I've brought enough for myself and Len, too. The three of us sit with the big, fat sandwiches, reaching for pickles and napkins, watching a rerun of *M*A*S*H*. We talk at the commercial breaks in an easy, lighthearted way that feels so wonderful I know I can't be the only one enjoying it. By the end, Richter's eyes are fluttering as he fights off sleep. His skin is ashen. What hair he had seems to have diminished to a gentle, cotton fluff at the very front of his head.

Before I leave, Richter officially dozes off. I pause at the door, my heart racing, I don't turn around, but manage to say to Len, who's followed me out, "I'm sorry about Bruce; I—"

Len cuts me off with a hand on my shoulder. "Please, don't. It's not that. I was actually glad to see him there. You need someone right now, and like I said, I'm not the sticking around sort. You're much better off with Bruce." There's something leaden to his voice, something in his eyes saying the exact opposite. I sense that's not nearly close to the whole story, but there is no arguing with him. His tone makes that clear.

If there's more concrete proof that you shouldn't fuck with whatever the universe has got planned for you, I can't imagine what it might be. Still, I have all night to do it, while the stubborn feel of his hand insists on sticking around; it sits there right along the bone of my left shoulder and won't dissipate. Not even when my mother wails so loudly I have to run in and hold her hand while she squeezes, asking over and over until dawn, "Why do they all die? Why do they all have to go and leave us, Vivian?"

I assume it's rhetorical and, instead of answering, just do the little circles with my free hand, while the other loses feeling inside her intense grip.

# 16.

♈ ♉ ♊ ♋ ♌ ♍ ♎ ♏

*Love is a gross exaggeration of the difference between one person and everybody else.*

—George Bernard Shaw

Before I know it, it's Tuesday morning. My mother left before I woke, off to pursue riches in the ice cream truck industry, I guess. There is no note. When my eyes open, I'm hunched over against Grams's headboard. My lower back is on fire. Mom's taken my favorite photo of Grams from the side table, along with all of her jewelry except for one charm bracelet, which I wound up with because it has no monetary value and "looks childish." She handed it over to me, as if it was a huge favor she was doing me. I've also managed to hold on to the Hebrew name plate Grams wore every day, but only because I hid it in the bills basket, a place I knew my mother would never look. *It's just a photo, it's just jewelry,* I tell myself as I fill the kettle.

I splash cold water on my face from the kitchen tap. "Use

the bathroom!" Grams scolds in my head. She really had a thing for the long strands of my hair winding up everywhere.

"Don't you have anything better to do than *noodge* me?" I ask to no one at all, sipping my tea loudly the way Grams hated. I cannot believe I actually miss my mother. I cannot believe I actually have to go back to work. People should have a year off, minimum, after something like this. I finish the tea quietly, my forehead on the window. Dozens of seagulls conduct a noisy meeting on a couple of arched lampposts over the boardwalk like it's any old day. One of them lets go of its bowels just as a bald man walks beneath. "Shit!" he yells when he's hit. *Exactly*, I think.

# 17.

♈ ♉ ♊ ♋ ♌ ♍ ♎ ♏

*With Taurus rising, you are likely to take a slow and steady approach to life. You will most likely prefer to deal with things in a methodical, careful and systematic way. Your approach could be considered both pragmatic and realistic. This sign is not known for its love of change, and with Taurus on the Ascendant, you may tend to avoid trying the new and untested until you absolutely must. With Taurus Rising, life is best approached as a series of steps to be taken one by one, with plenty of rests along the way. This can be problematic when your preferred pace does not really match the situation at hand."*

—Star Signs Australia

I *can hear Grams* with her whole "You get what you get; that bitch next door she gets what she gets" shtick, but I can't help thinking I *deserve* a better forecast for the day I have to return to work.

"Expect the unexpected today. Take life slowly; don't jump in headfirst," I read to Wendy. I'm at Grams's desk, drinking a second cup of tea next to an empty armchair that's got thirty years of someone's butt print sunk into it. "Good morning, empty armchair. Good morning, ass print," I've taken to saying.

I've got a whole new vocabulary for this life. There is also the phrase "my little problem," which I've taken to using for this astrology obsession of mine. And there aren't many people who'd get the privelige of this information. But Wendy seems to think I'm perfectly normal. Partially, I go to her because she's always been a loyal devotee of these kinds of esoteric things. She's always hunting out magic luck charms. In her cube there's a "Buenos Suertes" gnome from our Barcelona trip, a three-legged Chanchito pig from Chile, two copper horseshoes, ten mass cards, and an amulet she claims found *her* at an antiques fair in Sicily. She's always telling me not to buy a computer right now because Mercury's in retrograde, or to wait until Jupiter turns direct to tackle big projects, like breaking up with Bruce, if I'm finally going to do it. Normally I say, "Uh-huh," roll my eyes, flop my tongue, and throw myself on the floor to prove someone *could* actually die of ridiculousness.

"Yes, yes, you have finally mastered a decent imitation of 'spider gets the bug spray.' I'll give you that," she says, because her convictions *cannot* be dented. Say what you want about their validity, but they are completely indestructible. And this is more than I can say for most people.

"Look, I would take this seriously," she says now, "but you *have* to come in to work. As a matter of fact, Stan thought you were coming back yesterday. So bring a lot of cotton."

"What? Cotton? What the hell are you talking about?"

"For your ears. Cotton to shove in your ears."

Maybe that's why she complains about *Sklyar* far less than I do. "I told him. I knew he wasn't fucking listening, but I thought, to hell with him. It's ridiculous to have a boss that insensitive."

"Look, I don't have to tell you what Grams would say about this, Viv. You already know that."

Kavia said the same thing, didn't she? She told me that I need to work out which ideas can become reality, and which can never be. I tell Wendy as much.

"Sounds like a smart cookie."

I tell Wendy what happened with the train when Kavia told me not to take it. It took this long to tell her because of all the details regarding "my little problem," this is the most difficult to push into my framework of reality. Now I feel ready for the kind of significance Wendy will attach to this. She is the only person I know who would actually *expect* this type of prophecy; she once signed up for Intro to Soul Portal Painting—and not for the jokes.

"I know; it's powerful stuff," she says, as if we're talking about plastic explosives, or Jack Daniel's.

We forge a plan that would have sounded inane to me mere days ago, but now, frigteningly, makes as much sense as packing an umbrella when the weather predicts showers. I rush off the phone because I'm taking an earlier train to mix things up, to "trick" fate, as Wendy says. We did math and everything.

From the get-go, nothing feels right. I am not ready. But I told Stan I would be in, and there's a cold fear creeping up my ankles, the new realities of my finances—mainly, *how can I possibly afford to pay rent on this apartment all by myself?*

I wipe up half the usual amount of crumbs and tea droplets with a pretty tea towel, and distract myself from the silence by thinking how much time we spent hating and planning to quit my job. I was always reticent about it, but I never looked at it the way Kavia put it. It's that Neptune influence, which informs our capacity to believe in ourselves, to believe in what we don't know about our futures. It's enlightening to assess my personal bullshit ability in these terms.

So the question remains: What exactly am I afraid of? I don't know, but I think, picking up my pace, peeling off my clothes and depositing them into the hamper, I think that losing my job now would be disastrous. Besides the obvious—food, water, fast food, and Belgian chocolate with espresso nibs—what the hell am I going to do home alone all day, anyway? I come from a long line of doers, and since, like twins, this trait seems to skip a generation, I have wound up with genes that do not favor sitting still.

Somewhat mechanically, I shower, and pull on a black stretchy dress. I cannot bother, nor do I have time, to make heads or tails of the makeup lined up on my vanity, speaking an obscure language of bottles and compacts, pencils and brushes. So, back at the sink, I swipe on some lip gloss and say to the greenish image with a stress pimple on its chin, "This is your life now. Deal with it."

Thankfully, Jameson extends me only the slightest nod over his newspaper on my way out. Instead of Grams smacking me on the ass and taking a seat across from Jameson to drink her tea, my rear end goes unsmacked, the chair has been pushed far off so nobody has to see it empty, and I walk to the train station. Outside, it's stunningly bright. I reach inside the zipper pocket of my purse to pull out my iPhone.

*Len.*

He's not the staying type. So what? Why should *I* care? In my ear it's "Angel of the Morning." I've forgotten how much I loved this song. Nearly three weeks after Independence Day, decorations are still strung between the telephone poles along the part of Brighton Beach Avenue that isn't covered by the El subway. In the middle of each pole pair are glimmering white stars, hovering between lengths of red and blue tinsel. For the first time this year I can appreciate how beautifully the street's been transformed. It's just as hard to ignore how Grams loved the Fourth—the Mermaid parade and the hot dog eating competition, the Grucci Brothers fireworks extravaganza, and the fluttering flags hung strong and proud. And who could forget all those boxes of sparklers that never lasted quite long enough for my tastes. "Some things you cherish exactly for that," she tried to tell me, "because they can't last forever." I make my way past all of that to the El, where noises carry farther and echo deeper, and the sun only manages to stream through in skinny slats along the sidewalk. My head fills with Len's songs—a mix of big, moody music I fell immediately in love with. Among the cross-genre stuff that only someone serious about music would know, there are the kind of ballads that wrench your heart out, highlight how fragmented we are in our tiny apartments and cubicles, behind our newspapers and books and hang-ups and fears. All this is mixed in with great old Brooklyn-style house music that's so out of date I can't help but smile when I hear it. The songs come to me as if I'm hearing them through his ears. And I can't help but feel there *was* something between us.

Though I can't afford it, for good measure I palm over an extra dollar along with the fifty cents I usually give to the bearded homeless man in the purple shirt at the stairway at Brighton and Coney Island, the one who seems to live in front of the golden menorah outside the bank. For this, I forgo a chai tea.

I've begun to add my own rules about the way the universe works; helping out the man who adds a surprisingly moving rendition of "America the Beautiful" to my mornings can't be a bad thing.

At the top of the stairs, I swipe my card at the turnstile, but instead of turning to let me through, the thing jams up hard against my stomach.

*"What the?"* I ask and swipe, swipe, swipe as the train, which won't be followed by another until I'm on the one I'm meant to avoid, swishes past, taking my "tricking fate" plan with it.

I call Wendy, to ask her how we might alter the plan. She's not there.

I leave a convoluted message, trying to piece together what happened, but come away sounding like an inscrutable game of Taboo. "Chai tea; missed train; menorah bank."

"Just forget that," I say. "And don't laugh, please. Okay, laugh if you have to. I guess I would laugh if you left that message." I clear my throat. "What I'm trying to say is that I missed the train. How do you think I might rectify this?" I glance around guiltily, covering my mouth as I speak.

I descend the stairs back down to the street, to splurge on a chai from the mustached Russian woman on the corner. I deserve it. My head pokes out to sunlight from the clunky darkness of the station. Instinctively, I turn to the heavens. I'm looking up there for unity and grounding, a place where I haven't missed the train. But the frightening thing about stars is that they disappear all day long, as if they were never there in the first place. It's easy to think your reliance on them isn't any more logical than relying on a God you've been told floats around invisibly—sometimes angry, sometimes wanting people to splash lamb's blood on their doorframes, admonishing shellfish. It comes back to the same thing: believing in something you have to trust your gut about.

The dusky, velveteen-upholstered café is packed beyond precedent. But I wait in line and place my order anyway, drowning in a buttery cloud of baking pastry. I know exactly how much time I have before the next train will arrive, and freaked as I am about having to follow my regular routine, I don't see a way out of it. I can't very well say I didn't go to work because my horoscope told me to stay home. The minutes crawl by, and though no one in her right mind would bother this intimidating barista with a question as insignificant as when her drink might be ready, I do just that.

"When *eet ees* ready. When *d'you* think?" I've got a mind to give her the number of an electrologist I know, but I chew the inside of my mouth and keep quiet.

The train is already approaching with a rattle from above when the uncomfortably hot chai is finally in my hand. I tackle the stairs three at a time, sweating, reaching for my Metrocard to use my free transfer. Only, I can't feel it in the front pocket of my tote, or in the back pocket, or the secret inside pocket. I've lost my card. I scramble to buy a new one with a $20 bill that isn't accepted by the vending machine the first way I force it through, or the second. Only when I'm on the other side of the turnstile and the train is rolling in, do I realize I have left my seventeen dollars of change on the counter of the freaking chai tea place. *I won't be a victim of bad fortune,* I tell myself. I *will* find a way to draft twenty dollars of enjoyment I can't afford from this tea. Even if it kills me.

Still, something like a growl escapes my lips as I shuffle through the train doors behind two old women in matching plastic rain bonnets. I help them into seats, setting their rolling bags down safely in front of them, only to find there is no seat left for me. You don't understand how impossible this is: mine is only the second stop on the train. This has literally never happened to me before.

I'm standing, trying to hold on to a pole, while one of these pole hogs has his fleshy back against it, squashing my hand whenever the train takes the hard turns. I manage to snug my entire arm around the pole when the guy's back lifts during a particularly sharp track shift, and I now have a free hand with which to fold back the little plastic tab on the cover of the tea. Only, it won't fit into the indentation that's been perforated for it.

You'd think after all these years the coffee cup lid makers might have come upon a solution to this. Here I am jamming and jamming, and Mr. Pole Hog comes slamming back on my elbow, sending the burning hot tea sailing up out of my grip and onto my chest.

"Fuck!" I yell. Everyone turns to stare. Mothers holding the hands of saucer-eyed children look horrified, and I can't blame them. In fact, as I look around and see all the kids—about twenty or so of them—I realize this must be a nursery school trip I've walked into, which is why there were no seats.

This must be the glitch my horoscope had predicted, missing the train and getting third-degree burns from a hot beverage because a grown man doesn't understand how to share, only to then soil the air space around a bunch of five-year-olds who spend their days hearing things like "Tell Mommy where you left your *binky*" and "Are you sure you don't have to make a *pooh-pooh*? Let me see your hiney."

Assessing the damage, I realize I am pretty badly burnt. But I'm too embarrassed to do anything about it, and too villainous for anyone else to do something. *I'm a nice person!* I feel like yelling.

I whisper an impotent "Sorry," to the group at large. *Okay, that wasn't* so *bad*. It's all over now anyway, and my prophesy fulfilled, it should be smooth sailing for the rest of the day. Besides, I tell myself, it's really a *good* thing this happened, because kids should learn early on that the world is not always a friendly place.

I might just believe this if one thing after another doesn't go very, very wrong.

I rummage around in my purse for some tissues or a napkin, still trying to balance around the pole. The pole hog is *still* not moving, and now he's clucking his tongue at *me*. I leave my cup on the floor where it fell, planning to trash it when I get off the train at Union Square.

Losing my balance, I squat down and give up on the pole. I close my fist around an old Dunkin' Donuts napkin, from the stores Grams is always stuffing in there "just in case." *In case of a terrorist attack, pull out your Dunkin' Donuts napkins!*

This little blond girl in a tight ponytail comes up to me and gets right in my face. I have no idea where these kids get this kind of gall from. I'm bent conveniently down at her level, and so I can just make out the pattern of the state of Idaho in the freckles on her left cheek as she says, spitting slightly, "You know, it isn't right to *lit-ter.*" She splits it into two emphatic syllables like that, picks up the dripping cup, dangling it dramatically from its lid, the tab of which has astonishingly clicked into place, her ponytail swinging righteously.

I am speechless. This little playtime know-it-all. I swear to God, *I* was that little girl once—before the pizza gang nights and the hours behind binoculars spying for my mother from the terrace. I knew everything, and just . . . just look at me now.

I feel drops on the inside of my wrist; I've let a schoolgirl make me cry. "It isn't nice to be a know-it-all," I say to her, my head shaky.

"Francesca, stay away from that awful girl!" her mother yells, holding out her arms for Francesca to safely return to.

Though I have tons of time until my stop, and there won't be another train for at least twenty minutes, I wait by the doors and get out at the next station.

On the empty platform I sit down on one end of a green flaking bench, thankful to be by myself. My phone gives off a little jingle and I pull it out. I've missed a call, so I run through the rigmarole of voice mail and play back this too-little, too-late advice from Wendy: "You'll just have to be late. There's no other way," she says. William is barking in the background, which means Wendy's trying to leave and he's pulling her back, his giant paws at her pants hem, but I can just about make out her words: "Skip the train you normally take and wait for the next one!" she yells. "William. William!" she trills, so I have to yank the phone away from my ear, and then to me, "Excuse me." I take it from the shuffling sound which follows, that she shoves the phone in her pocket.

Poor William cries until noon when the dog walker shows. This all started when Wendy ended things with Roy. It turns out Roy and William were a match made in heaven, even if Roy and Wendy were more like David Lee Roth and Sammy Hagar. *I know, William. Missing people sucks.*

* * *

I arrive an hour and twenty minutes late at the office. I will not go into the details of the rest of my journey, but suffice it to say there were four police officers with varying ideas of graciousness, as well as one incredibly hairy young man in handcuffs and a pretty Mexican girl who now has no date for the "summer fair." I gave her my phone number and my Metrocard—it was all I could think of, before I realized I had no money with which to buy a new one.

Grams would never have allowed me to leave the house as ill-prepared as I was today. She comes from a school of doubling up, wadding up emergency twenties in your kneesocks, wearing no less than three layers, and leaving an extra fifteen minutes *before* fifteen minutes before you were going to leave.

I hear the frantic rhythm of Stan's footsteps as I plop my sopping canvas Earth Lover bag down on my desk. Part of me settles in along with it; it's nice to know something has stayed the same. "Oh, look who decided to stop by!" Stan says, slipping his arms slowly across his chest and tucking his hands in at his sides.

In a flash, I imagine my palm making contact with his left cheek: a great smack, like an expert belly flop from the high dive, that leaves a deep red mark.

The second he crosses the threshold into my cubicle, my radar goes off. Normally I get up and stand at the opening so he can't come in—a thing I have about letting people I despise into my personal space—yet today I let him approach despite the *Bewitched* tic at my nose. Right away I can tell something is very wrong. He's *smiling* and nobody's even mentioned root vegetables or cholesterol-reducing butter spread.

"Oh, hello, Stan," I say, as kindly as possible.

"I hope you are all better now," he says, as if I skinned my knee and took these days off to stick a Band-Aid over it.

Before Stan utters another sentence, a throat-clearing episode erupts from Wendy's cubicle. Oh my God, do I love

Wendy. I can only imagine what she had to go through to escape to the funeral service. Her throat-clearing breaks, followed by a cough that sounds suspiciously like "information silos."

I cough back a laugh. *A laugh!* Maybe, just maybe the day will rebound after all.

Of course Stan doesn't notice any of it. "Vie," he says, "I clearly told you it was imperative for you to return to work on Thursday, otherwise you would be creating information silos by hogging the industry publications you are uniquely subscribed to and relied upon to disseminate."

Bile rises in my throat. I look at him, and maybe for the first time realize something that strikes me as important: this is laughable. And it's my fault. I don't have to be here. I have lots of experience, and I could be writing for tons of different publications; I could have been writing the book I've been planning forever.

My breath runs hot, and the heat seeps through my body. Instead of saying, "Right; information silos," the way I normally would, I close my eyes, exhausted and frustrated, and say, "And I told *you* I wouldn't be back until today. My grandmother died, Stan. I had to sit shiva. God says so."

*"I'll show you where you can stick your 'information silos.'"* I hear Wendy cough out the beats over the cubicle wall.

Stan may or may not have heard what I said; it's never clear. "I don't know who you think you are, Vie," he either continues or retorts. He's being pretty threatening, coming a little too close for comfort, right in my face. "But you'd better keep your eyes open. I had to override your password and go through your e-mail to disperse the content you deprived everyone of, and I didn't like what I saw in there."

"You *what*?"

"I dispersed the e-mails you were hoarding."

"You went through my e-mails?"

"Do not cross me in front of the department, Vie," Stan warns me.

"It's Viv!" I yell.

As if by magic, he's actually, definitely, heard me. I recognize such raw outrage on his face that for a second I glance down at my hand in fear I really have smacked him after all. A hush rolls through the office the way it does in teen-movie classroom scenes—when the popular boy dumps the girl from the wrong side of the tracks to save his reputation.

"Viv! Viv! Viv! What is so difficult about that?" I shout. But I know I'm really yelling at myself.

"Well, Viv," he says, "I can't babysit all of our employees." I have never seen Stan this fired up before. I can only imagine what he's seen; there are so many e-mails making fun of him that I have set up several folders dividing them by topic so I can easily refer to them when I one day want to use them for villain traits: there's "Stan, facial contortions," "Stan, description of things jammed in teeth," and "Stan, many uses of information silos" among (fifteen) others.

A twitch pulses at the right side of his jaw.

"You're right. It shouldn't be this difficult," he says.

Just like that it's over. He turns and walks away.

"That's not what I said," I whisper.

Wendy comes around. The sight of my best friend at my doorway, her hand at her boyish hip, is so much like all the other times she's come into my cubicle, I'm thrown. A few stray surface strands of her ginger hair catch the light in all kinds of pretty ways. All business, her dramatic hairstyle is striking; it's her most attractive feature. She looks at me with her rich brown eyes, perfectly outlined in a maroon she says is really in now. This friend of mine envelops me in the tightest hug, just the right kind, and I do my part to avoid her eye, so we don't go crying.

"Well, I guess our five-year study has finally yielded unmistakable results," she says. "What we suspected on Nine/Eleven when he wouldn't let us go home, and again on Halloween, when he came in dressed as himself, has been proven one hundred percent true: Stan *is* an asshole."

"I probably shouldn't have been so sloppy with those e-mails," I mumble.

"Fuck him," she says, disappearing so we can both scramble up some normalcy.

I switch on my computer, fall into my chair and try to work. It feels sort of normal. I don't have to disseminate my newsletters since my privacy has already been invaded under the guise of doing exactly that, and I can't even bring myself to look at them. How much could I possibly have missed in the fast-paced world of deli kiosks and appetizing platter design? I've had a lot of experience with shiva doilies, anyway.

I open a blank document, save it with tomorrow's date as the file name, and get started reviewing the bank of raw stories and tips that have come in over the past few days. I could do this in my sleep. I don't even need to talk with these people half the time to fill in the details; I barely need to read the responses they write in our questionnaire. I already *know* exactly what everyone is going to say.

Q: What's the goal of this product?

A: To leverage our brand equity and expand the variety of the line.

New associate stories always have the same two quotes: One from the hiring manager: "I am very happy to have Buddy as part of the Green Grocer team, and look forward to his contributions," says Manager Homogeneous; and one from the new hire: "I'm very excited [thrilled/ecstatic/filled with enthusiasm/brimming with joy and elation(!)] to join the Shop Rite [Stop&Shop/Waldbaum's/Foodtown] team, and I look forward to lots of success!" says Shiny-Faced Hiree. The only amusing bits are the language errors the international employees make in their careful, formal English. Like: "I am overjoyed and most ready to touch your team," and "Working you is a dream come true."

Come to think of it, I also have a file on these. Stan *wouldn't.* I'm not spending another minute worrying over this.

But the thing is, Stan *would.* He absolutely would go through my e-mails, pick out all the ones that might be incriminating, and get me into trouble.

I manage to get my mind back onto work, though. I write two articles on new food product launches: a line of fancy fresh peanut butters with extras like chocolate chunks or Nutella, and a cool line of frozen veggie mixes with international inspirations. Then I call to interview a business manager in perishables over at Yum Foods in Arizona. They've got a new Italian sausage line they're importing from Sardinia.

As I'm dialing out the number from memory, I get that same sensation: *I can't bring myself to care about this stuff anymore. And I don't have to.* It's the same place it was before, but I'm looking at it all different now, like Julia Roberts at the end of *Pretty Woman.* At least I'm not a prostitute who's become accustomed to Giorgio Armani.

Haven't I had enough change for the moment? I ask myself this question, and am confounded to find myself instinctively consulting the G Man again, probably to prove once and for all he is of no help whatsoever. I am met with nothing but silence. Of course.

Jim at Yum Foods, whom I often check in with, picks up.

"What's new with you, Viv?" he asks with real warmth, as if it would truly thrill him to hear.

"I'm fine," I lie, thankful the news hasn't reached him. "You?"

Jim says, "Yeah, big news this week, huh?" and I say, "*Hooo* yeah," rolling my eyes. It's probably a new hybrid onion or Pampers packaging featuring the latest Pixar character doing a poop. Jim starts into a complicated story about a mouse in his basement, who may or may not be speaking Spanish to his five-year-old son, and my eyes glaze over.

Suddenly, I feel a chill and stop wrapping the rubber band around my pencil. There's someone behind me.

Stan. He's standing in here again, and this time he's with the big boss, Terrence Comegy.

"I'm so sorry to hear about that, Jim," I say. "Listen, I'm sorry to cut you off, but I've got another meeting I have to get to." A meeting with the devil, that is. I take my time hanging up.

My tension eases slightly when I see a nice flower arrangement in Terrence's hands. Jews don't really do flower arrangements for deaths, but that's okay; it's got all these really nice lilies and violets, tucked along loosely with bunches of wildflowers; Grams would absolutely love it. I feel the lump form in my throat as I reach out for it, but at the very least my tears and I agree on this: we do not cry in front of Stan. "That's really nice of you, Terrence," I say, standing, closing my hands around the twig basket they're packed in.

Terrence pulls the arrangement back into the crook of his arm with a start. "Actually these are for Margaret Reilly; she just got engaged."

"Oh," I say, thrown. "Well, then, what can I do for you?" I'd like to move this along.

"Viv," Terrence says.

"Yes," I say, slowly. Despite the signals (the correct name, for one), it doesn't occur to me that something bad is going to happen now. I've settled into the fact that I'm not ready for change right now; my horoscope was exactly right. And I've decided that snug in this upholstered, absurdly bland nest of sorts—personalized to the extent possible, with my Mardi Gras beads, photo booth shots of me pulling bunny ears behind Wendy's head, my Smurfette figurine—here, I can experience my grieving quite comfortably.

Terrence doesn't speak right away, so I fix my gaze on the shawl I've got draped over the wall I share with Wendy. It's Grams's shawl. It's from the fifties and has one tiny pearl knotted onto every fringe. I force myself to look away from it and back toward Terrence, since I am unable to look completely at Stan after this morning's display. Terrence has unkind features—they are all brittle angles, pointy ears, and small unwelcoming eyes.

"We're going to have to let you go," Terrence says, using the flower arrangement as a barrier between us. It's the only sign he's nervous or uncomfortable delivering this news. He looks directly at me, as if following guidelines out of *How to Win Friends and Influence People*.

When he's through, the words hang in the silence of the entire office listening behind their cubicle walls.

I'm gobsmacked, looking around for the person who's going to hop out and say, "You've been *Punked*!"

Wendy comes around the cubicle wall, bless her heart. But she's no Ashton Kutcher.

"I sat shiva for three days, and now I'm fired because for *one day* people didn't hear from us that green peppers have gone up fifty cents a barrel?" I hear my words in a slight delay, like on a bad telephone connection. I know I'm digging myself in deeper, but I can't help it. It's as if Terrence is responsible for everything that's happened. He's here for me to hurl all the blame at. I needn't worry over tears; I'm too furious for those. I can't get enough of the sound of my own screaming. "You think anyone cares whether diet soda actually contains .0002 milligrams of real sugar, after all? They don't! They couldn't give a crap. As a matter of fact, *I* couldn't give a crap." I stop talking abruptly, as if someone turned off the sound, when it occurs to me—with Wendy standing there, a hand clamped over her gaping mouth—that this *could* be a joke.

Surely those flowers aren't for Margaret Reilly; who would marry a woman with twenty-eight photos of her cockatoo pinned up in her cubicle? It's a bloody red herring is what that basket is. Margaret Reilly—*engaged,* for crying out loud. It's the most subtle, thoughtful joke to spike up my spirits. I bet Wendy put the whole thing together. It's good. Real good. Getting fired for sitting shiva! They really had me.

I turn my "you zany gal" gaze to Wendy and say her name like it's a question: *"Wendy?"* When she wrinkles her brow in a really concerned gesture, shaking her head quickly, tightly, I elbow her.

"Okay. Good one. I've got it. You guys are spectacular. I don't deserve it, really." I look back to Terrence.

He hugs the arrangement in tighter. He's not smiling.

I look back to Wendy, who's shaking her head furiously now.

My throat throbs.

"This inappropriate levity," says Stan, with a grin he's trying to suppress, "this is why you're being let go, Viv. You see, the industry *just might* care that two of the largest supermarket chains in the world—Fresh and Delicious—have merged to create a megachain that promises to alter the landscape of the entire industry as we know it, with unique shipping and manufacturing channels, and ninety percent private-label sales. And they *just might* care that we missed the story after taking their money year after year on the promise to keep them ahead of the curve. They *just might* care that the reason they could lose out on billions, be ridiculed and yelled at by investors and CEOs and employees who depend on their shares to send their kids to college, is merely because it was in *your* mailbox and you didn't show up when you were supposed to." His voice does not have any inflection to it whatsoever the whole time he's saying this, except for when he repeats the words "just might." The effect is powerful. I feel like something once retrieved out of our bathtub drain when it was plugged up—hairy and coarse, crude, something that makes people gag.

The one day I don't disperse my newsletter information. Seven years in which absolutely nothing important whatsoever happens, seven years of painstakingly informing the supermarket and food manufacturing industries of a new low-density soy peptoid, three exciting flavors of smoked bacon, and a breathrough foil bag for chips that increases shelf life by five measly days. And yesterday, of all days, an actual important thing—in fact, the biggest thing to happen to supermarkets since (literally) sliced bread—happens, and I fucking miss it. I would fire me, too.

But Stan isn't satisfied with the fact that I'm fired. He wants more. "You know," he says, trying to maintain an air of innocence, of remorse, as if he wasn't thrilled to death to be rid of me. "I was willing to overlook the unauthorized personal day . . ."

I clap my hand over my own gaping mouth now. Look, I'll be honest. I may not have truly had my heart in this job. But I did the best *I* could under those conditions; I stayed late, always got the facts straight, maintained strong contacts and a sense of curiosity to the extent it was possible for me to do so about jarred herring products and hydroponic arugula. But Stan, he's way out of line here. He never met me even an eighth of the way. I came up with that special issue idea for functional foods, created a proposal with focus group feedback, an article index, artwork, even twenty-five interested advertisers, and he never even looked at it. The janitor showed it to me when he pulled it out of the trash the very day I gave it to Stan.

"—and the inappropriate e-mail folder collection, which unfortunately I *had* to forward to HR, under our tolerance and ethics policies. But missing the biggest story of the last two decades—this is just the last straw, I'm afraid." Stan loses himself and actually lets a smile escape.

I regard Wendy with crazy eyes, hoping she'll hold me back somehow, and she comes over to my side of the cube and puts her hand on my shoulder. I know she's empathizing with me right now, imagining what it would have been like if Stan had fired *her* when she was in these very shoes.

Just like that, I'm unemployed. I always thought that when I left here it would be in a great ticker tape parade that would begin with the words, "Get stuffed," yelled through a megaphone, and end with me walking around the office passing out invitations to my book launch—even to Stan; maybe *especially* to Stan.

"You'll have to pack your things immediately," Stan says.

"I'm sorry," Terrence says, partially covering his mouth so it seems he's hiding something, likely the truth, before both of them hightail it from my cubicle, toward Margaret Reilly, and out of my life forever.

# 18.

♈ ♉ ♊ ♋ ♌ ♍ ♎ ♏

*It is a fine thing to begin, but it is a much greater thing to begin again after what you worked for has been taken from you.*

—Elie Wiesel

So I *wind* up walking around Union Square holding a file box haphazardly filled with all that stuff I thought earlier might comfort me. Now they look pathetic and depressing, meaningless, the way packed things can on their way out. At least I've got a memory stick of condemning character traits and English as a second language errors. But none of it looks very funny from here.

No, no, I shouldn't say that; they're *all* still funny, but I am in no state of mind to appreciate quality wit. And the tacky van Gogh sunflower-topped pencil Wendy brought me back from Provence keeps tumbling out, and that's not helping things. "I'll call you later," she said, on my way out. She felt the flower with two fingers. "I know you're not ready to hear this right now, but really, this is for the best."

"You're right. I'm not ready to hear that right now," I said.

In this human jungle that would pass for a park only in Manhattan, I walk by the animal rights activists yelling, "Adopt, rescue, love forever." I feel for the poor tabby kitten missing an eye, for the dog in a plaster cast, even the featherless chirping parakeet, who's got the worst shot of all at being adopted. We're in the same boat. Unwanted, unfound, uncertain. Somebody should ship me off to East Timor or Somalia to see what suffering is *really* like. At least my mother isn't here anymore. She's the absolute worst person in these kinds of situations. She's a cauldron of "I told you so's" bubbling over like crazy. But at least that part goes quick. She's unable to focus on anyone more than a couple of minutes before starting in on the dramas of her own tormented "biblical, really" life. My mother thinks she's Moses, but with PMS and a degree in the Arts of the Rococo Period.

I keep staring toward Seventeenth Street, wishing there weren't another ninety-two hours before my appointment with Kavia. There's no plan forming, no desperate scramble through the contacts list. I make my way to Kavia's studio, or hoax den for the feeble-minded, fired, and featherless parakeet sympathizers. Whichever way you choose to look at it.

I let the box drop to the stoop and ring the bell.

"You cannot come early," she says, before a sound escapes my gaping mouth.

"But—"

"No but! You think I sit around waiting for you all week? Your appointment in four days. You wait. Good for you." I'm not sure, because of that inscrutable tone, if she means *it's good for you,* or *bad luck, buddy.*

Just as she says that, a trim man in linen pants sidles up next to me.

"Come up, Martin," she says—speaking now in perfect syntax, cheery as Rainbow Brite at a unicorn convention.

Martin lifts a shoulder in a helpless, amused shrug, as if to say, "Hey, what can we do? We need her."

I snub him. Though I am exactly like Martin, I don't want to be. I just don't want to be. Holding the box bottom, which is beginning to fall apart, I make my way back to the park. The box on my lap, I take a seat next to the bench I was on earlier. My original place is now taken by two Japanese girls in striped kneesocks and stubby pigtails. They are talking so loudly and with such speed, I only hope I can absorb some of their energy. Instead, I lose track of the content of their conversation and it fades to background noise.

There's this ridiculous idea I need to confess: I've been holding on to it ever since my father died, and my mother left, and I was old enough to think in such terms. I thought I had a deal with The Big Man—that nothing bad would happen to me again. That, in essence, I was "done." When I should have died in a car accident, I walked away with the tiniest of scratches. When the planes hit the World Trade Center, I was supposed to be there for a whole grains conference—but Grams was sick and I couldn't make it. Bad things just don't happen to me. I'm the lucky one, the one people rub up against before exams and annual physicals. This fearful girl desperate for her astrologer just isn't me. But I have no idea where else to go.

One of the Japanese girls has picked up a cell phone call and the other one is picking at her cuticles. She mouths something to the other girl, and to me it looks like "Give up."

Some people might take this as a sign.

Regardless of how compelling the idea of giving up altogether may be, I know that isn't me. I look around to see the whole park has been transformed. I'm thrilled to see life around me—children pull their mothers away from feral squirrels; the man who can contort his face has his lips twisted up around his nose like a rosebud. I can smell steamy week-old hot dogs a few feet away, and four guys about my age walk past gobbling down falafel from Rainbow, which is just around the corner. Their hands grip shiny foil packets, their ties slung—like summer itself—over their shoulders.

I imagine life welcoming me back like a line of semiformally attired second cousins, great-aunts, and uncles once removed, on a bar mitzvah conga line. "Come on in!" says Aunt Zelda, opening the chain warmly, just for me.

One of the guys with the falafel laughs so hard, he spits out a mouthful of Israeli salad. These half-chewed dices of tomato and purple onion strengthen me enough to stand and get the hell out of here. *"Coming, Aunt Zelda!"*

I smile at him nervously.

He turns my way in the self-conscious way these boys with their clever brand of geekiness that's sexy only in New York City, do. But when we make contact, he gives me an odd look.

I may be having a moment, but I'm also holding a box with a giant nylon sunflower tickling at my chin.

My iPhone rings. I half expect it to be the conga-crazy Aunt Zelda herself.

"Hey there," says Len, surprising me from a number I don't recognize.

His voice is a balm.

"Look," he says. "It's true what I said. You can't rely on me." For a few beats he leaves it at that. The reverberation, the sunflower tickling, the boy looking back at me from far down the footpath; it all makes the statement seem unreal, difficult to swallow as a big, fish-foody vitamin tablet. Still, the silence goes on longer than I'd expect, so I store my breath, squirrel it away, like the last nut in all the forests of all the worlds, because you just never know.

When he continues, I choke on the exhale. "I'm sorry the timing is so bad, but it's the truth about me," he says, the words orderly, soldiers in formation, as if this restraint was precisely what he was rounding up in the pause. "I'm shit at women. But in this case, it actually *was* about Bruce. It was a funeral and I had no right to even be thinking this, but the truth is I didn't like seeing you with him."

"I get it," I say, though I don't, exactly. Still, it's a confession of sorts, an address for issues that have formerly been stuffed in envelopes with no destination, no postage, no hope of getting anywhere at all.

An ambulance screams by, blowing my cover: why am I outside at 4 p.m. instead of at the office? I am just beginning to understand why, but I'm not quite ready to admit it. Besides, I'd like to stay on track with this conversation, which seemed like it was maybe, possibly, trying to wend its way around to the fact that the idea of me and Bruce makes Len jealous, that he might have issues to work out, but wants to try anyway.

"How come you're not at work?"

"Oh, I have to drop something off with one of our contacts."

"Cool," he says, with no trace of skepticism, which, suprisingly, makes me feel instantly like crap. Who would lie to this guy?

"So, what was it you were saying?" I ask.

"Yeah, about that, listen, I . . ." There's a pause; it's long enough to become obvious he's already said more than he'd planned.

Even the ember of the spark of the possibility that he might consider maybe forgiving me and giving it a go makes my palms sweat.

"I've got to go." It's not what I'd hoped he'd say.

Now an ambulance goes off on his side. Only his sounds like it's approaching. I feel a tingle of intuition: he's at the hospital. "Is he all—?"

Len answers my question before I have a chance to get it out: "Dad's got an appointment. It's a scheduled one, so don't worry. See you around, okay?"

"Yeah," I say, more relieved than I probably should be. The thing is, it's a light. At the end of the dingy, moldy tunnel—a motherfucking light. Not an invitation, I note, not a promise or even a hint of one, but a light, nonetheless.

I take my box to the falafel place, order Grams's special with extra tahini and tomato, and inform the restaurant at large that "there isn't nearly enough tahini and tomato" the second I bite into it.

No one's there but the owner, and he says, "Come here, Shishkabob, let me give you some more."

*Shiskabob?* He also gives me an extra generous helping of banana peppers that I didn't even ask for. I smile, and we have a nice conversation about the rising price of onions and pita breads, while I try not to belch from the Pepsi I've been sipping through a straw. When I'm on the sidewalk again, thinking over our special New York moment, the kind of intense connection only the most anonymous city in the world can offer up, rare as a shooting star, he waves me a spider-leg good-bye, and I feel, as the lights behind the rainbow go out, that everything will once again be okay.

I wake shaking in the dark in the middle of the night, the green neon clock numbers casting an alien shadow on the wall, and I just can't remember how I ever had a thought like that.

"I don't even *have* an Aunt Zelda," I say to the empty apartment. My words echo back like an indisputable fact. I screw my eyes tight, and wait for that courage, that feeling of forgiveness, acceptance, to wash over me once more.

But there isn't anything. I've been dreaming about that last minute, when I deserted Grams to freak out on the toilet bowl. Sure, sure. People do crazy things when they don't want to face losing someone they love. But it's as if this guilt is tied to a larger issue: that I never trusted myself enough to really become my own person the way she always wanted me to. I never got there for her, and the pathetic job I did escorting her into the World to Come was merely the final letdown.

# 19.

♈ ♉ ♊ ♋ ♌ ♍ ♎ ♏

Main Entry: [1]**um•brel•la**
Pronunciation: \ˌəm-ˈbre-lə, *especially Southern* ˈəm-ˌ\
Function: *noun*
Etymology: Italian *ombrella*, modification of Latin *umbella*, diminutive of *umbra*
Date: 1611
**1** : a collapsible shade for protection against weather consisting of fabric stretched over hinged ribs radiating from a central pole; *especially* : a small one for carrying in the hand
**2** : the bell-shaped or saucer-shaped largely gelatinous structure that forms the chief part of the body of most jellyfishes
**3** : something which provides protection: as **a** : defensive air cover (as over a battlefront) **b** : a heavy barrage
**4** : something which covers or embraces a broad range of elements or factors

"*You need to* feel sorry for yourself a little," Wendy says the following day over the telephone. She meant to come over but William wasn't standing for it. She said he pulled the "oh, no, you don't, sister; this is *my* hour and you're not taking it away" bark, so loudly that the neighbors complained as soon as she closed the door.

Beyond the terrace railing, it's as clear a day as I've ever seen. A perfectly straight line of white is stretched across the sky's midline, like a length of celestial tape, concealing those stars back there in a Broadway backdrop of a clear sky.

"Feel sorry for myself?"

Through the screen door, I can hear the faint hum of the television. I have it tuned to truTV, with barely a whisper of sound, as if listening the same way she had might lure Grams back.

"Yeah, that's what it means. Let's go through it again. 'Today Pisces will feel the effects of life's recent events. It's best to give in and let yourself recover. It's been awhile. Daily advice: Don't leave the house. Let others come to you.'" She reads this off as if it's a clue in *The Da Vinci Code,* something she found in a vault whose account number is the Fibonacci sequence.

"Where does that say I should feel sorry for myself?" I ask.

"Read between the lines, Viv. There's a little wiggle room between your mother's antics and Atlas taking the world on his back, you know. Sit around. Pout. Feel lousy."

"Who's this Lousy, anyway?" I try for a joke.

"You're not even *trying* to feel like crap. Come on. I know you've got it in you. You've got a lifetime of shit you can start pitying yourself about. Your mom sucks; Grams is dead; you got fired; your boyfriend dumped you; you screwed things up with the best guy you've ever met."

"Oh, so *you're* Lousy. Nice to meet you. Since when is *your* life a bed of roses?" I say.

"Well, I didn't want to tell you this right now, but maybe

this'll be just the thing to tip you over into misery. I just had a great review with Terrence, and he said they may be making some structural changes that could turn out in my favor."

"Why would I be happy for you having to stay at *Skylar* under the burden of success?"

"Um, we are in a global crisis here," she says, after a long pause.

"Listen, if you ever tell me that you actually like your job there, then *that* will be a reason to dive headfirst into the River Pity and take a nice swim, but no global crisis is going to do it. Sorry, but you must have mistaken me for someone with a sense of community. I only look after myself. You should know that by now."

"Stop trying to make the world smile, and go have a good cry. Look what happened the last time you didn't listen to your horoscope. If you'd have done the right thing and told Bruce to shove it, then it might be a half-naked guy telling you this right now."

"Somehow I don't think Len's the horoscope type," I say.

"Really?" She asks this like it's something she'd never considered before. Could someone possibly *not* believe nature is a mirror through which we can see our futures? She doesn't wait for an answer. "Listen, all I'm saying is, whip out the *Steel Magnolias* and *Terms of Endearment* and get really, really, fucking depressed. Do you hear me?"

"Fine," I say, and hang up like an indignant teenager.

As soon as the quiet regains its position, I regret rushing off the phone. I lie down and really try to get into feeling like shit for what must be a good chunk of time. I skim over all the really sad parts of *Jane Eyre*—where they lock her in the closet and when she comes back to find Mr. Rochester in a wheelchair. *Mission accomplished,* I think. I get up, check the clock and find it's only been five minutes.

Look, I tell myself in the mirror, you're going to feel like shit, and you're going to like it. I rearrange the shoes swimming around the bottom of my closet. I clear out the

Tupperware at the top of the kitchen pantry and nestle all the bottoms underneath the tops. I throw out the pieces that have either no top or no bottom.

I come across Grams's favorite Tupperware, the bright red one that I should throw out but don't, though I once washed the lid in the dishwasher and melted it into a mega Twizzler. I root through the hall closet for a pair of pliers and start yanking at the thing, trying to straighten it out. I whack it with a hammer, jam a screwdriver across the inside to stretch it. It snaps right back, the lost member of the Plastic Man family.

There are long spurts of time—fifteen, even twenty minutes—during which I look through photos with no plans to do anything productive whatsoever. But before I know it, I'm organizing those into nice piles to mail out to cousins, aunts, uncles, and to pass out to friends in the building, zipping them into plastic baggies, tucking them in envelopes, and writing out funny captions on the borders in marker. I print "The Year of The Caftan" under one of Grams and Mrs. Regan wearing huge sunglasses and identical Indian cotton caftans, except Grams's is a bright lime green and Mrs. Regan's is pink. A person could go blind staring at them for too long. Just when I'm feeling completely hopeless about feeling completely hopeless, something funny happens: I throw myself into it with all the gusto of the summer's first belly flop.

I lose the urge to shower. I forget to eat. When I do pull the fridge door open, around dark, there are Mrs. Kaufman's unappetizing meals waiting for me. I fork them—ice cold and gelatinized—into my mouth, coax the bites down, telling myself it's a test of survival. There are skinny women in Tribeca who are starving. I pull Grams's muumuu back over my head. Slowly punching one arm out at a time, I sniff its stale musk like a free sample of a good perfume. I imagine it's a hug, a joke, a lamb chop with mint jelly on my special *Peanuts* characters plate. I sob into her pillow and take to chewing at its wet surface like a nine-week-old beagle. At some point I fall asleep with Shirley MacLaine's *Out on a Limb,* which Kavia gave to me, draped over my forehead like a hot towel. The last thing I read is that "ninety-nine percent of reality is invisible." *So true,* I think, *so fucking true.*

In this manner, the next two days stretch out in spurts long and short; time rubber-bands. For the most part I'm reading through Kavia's stack of books, in Grams's orange corduroy easy chair with my knees hiked up under the housecoat. With the far-reaching content and an armchair traveler's spirit, I can nearly convince myself I'm going somewhere. I have no underwear on. In my mind, I keep hearing the one thing I remember my mother being adamant to teach me: "It's good for you to *breathe* down there." *I'm breathing, Mom, I'm breathing like I've just finished the goddamn marathon.*

I call Wendy when something in my reading strikes me as really interesting. "It doesn't sound like you're feeling very sorry for yourself," is what she says. "It sounds like you're being *constructive.*" She handles the word like it's someone else's booger. Every now and again I look out at the spectacular view of the boats that Grams and I never took, and then, when they leave without us yet again, I'm looking at nothing at all. If I turn my head the other way, I can see the Brooklyn and Manhattan bridges, the New York City Etch A Sketch skyline beyond. It's a spectacular view, which always looks to me like it popped up out of nowhere, no matter how many times I see it. I have half a mind to paint its remarkable angles and curves out on the lawn with the Seacoast Watercolor Society. Only I'm not the one who paints well enough even to merit a hook in our bathroom.

But, overlaid on that Mondrian sky, I see the final hospital room scene played over and over again, like that horrible tape in *The Ring.* It all seems to come back to that one moment. I just can't make peace with the way things turned out.

How could I have deserted Grams that way? She encouraged strength; if you didn't know better you'd think she made her living that way, getting commissions when she signed someone up. Even when I was a young girl, she told me I had it in my blood, just the way I had a taste for the creamy onions in pickled herring. I only had to learn to harness it. But I ignored her and concentrated on shaping my mashed sweet potatoes into mountains, river valleys, the parking garage at Caesar's Bay Bazaar.

"Most girls your age can't even manage to match their socks," she said, while I tuned her out, imagining a spiced raisin was a Cadillac, another a Volkswagen Beetle. "You should be proud." I got very good at ignoring her. And at sculpting my food. I learned to create a Barbie Dream House from chicken leg bones. Beneath its splintery peaked roof, with a corkscrew pasta chimney and asparagus turrets, I could imagine a lovely life, with glossy hair, and parents, and pink high heels. And if I was hungry, or lonely, or feeling like I needed to watch *Beaches* just one more time, I could always just eat my way out.

When I gaze long enough, the window and the scene beyond transform into a kind of movie, our greatest hits—there we are building sandcastles, and eating the original Nathan's hot dogs at Coney Island; we're going into Manhattan for a musical matinee, or to Washington Square Park to complain about how homogenized it's become. I'm crying and she's soothing me; she's crying and I'm soothing her. And I'm so glad we have each other, even if I didn't realize just how happy until right now.

Too often, I laugh out loud and say, deadpan, things like, "I will survive; as long as I know how to love I know I'll stay alive," to our fern, who is starting to think I am both a fabulous writer and a spectacular liar. I can tell by the confounded arc of his leaves.

The doorbell rings a lot. Each time, I'm thrilled for the interruption. Any more of this self-pity, and I might actually *turn into* my mother. I've already got her toes.

I can always hear who's on the other side of the door before they knock. They travel in packs: it's Mrs. Kaufman and Jameson and Mrs. Regan, and then so many Russian women in navy eyeliner, uttering incomprehensible syllables that, to me, sound like *shiksa, shiksa.* And I want to say, *But I'm Jewish even if I don't believe.* But I don't.

Instead, I dizzy myself trying to count up the gold rings on their meaty hands, and how many heavy casseroles they've heaped into the fridge, yanking out shelves and vegetable drawers to fit it all in. They leave in one big, sad group.

In the sixth grade, once our tenuous bond had snapped, Shelly Wasserman the Bully threatened to pull my hair and pointed at the four Incredibly Mature Girls behind her. "They're going to do your arm and leg hairs," she said, and ran her tongue over her teeth. I wasn't taking chances. They weren't messing around and they couldn't care less about my abandonment issues—they'd already thrown in the towel on their own. They couldn't even spell it. I hightailed it home under the excuse of a toothache. When Grams opened the door, she had the coiled phone cord from the kitchen stretched straight. She held a finger to her lips for me to stay quiet and told the principal she was bringing me to the dentist on Avenue Q straight away.

It was this important link—Grams the Security Blanket—that I forgot at Union Square Park when I thought I could do it all on my own. Sure, I *can* match my socks, but I'm not wearing any, am I? I haven't even got a pair of panties on. The truth is, I can't even bring myself to do undergarments, never mind strength.

"What's the worst that could happen?" Grams would ask. It has a different, eerie ring now. "You'll get through if you tell yourself you will." I want so badly to believe this is true. When she was here, at least if I couldn't wrap my mind around it, the thought always hung there, like a strip of fly tape. Without her, the tape's got no sticky side. The bugs land on it for a quick rest and buzz right back to business, eating away at whatever they like, sucking, biting, injecting their poison like one of the Passover plagues.

A couple of times, there's a knock at the door, but no voice. I dart up out of the chair, hoping it's Len, with his masculine comforts, but it isn't. It's a mystery visitor, vanished before I can catch him. No footsteps down the stairwell, no puff of air from the elevator shaft. This person, whom I eventually chose to believe is Len and only Len, leaves ironic parting gifts. Once a book entitled *Fresh Air.* Ha ha, I think. Very funny. Well, Jackie Mason, some of us are afraid of relationships and some people allow their horoscopes to frighten them into being a shut-in. At least we both know who we are.

Another time he leaves a red-and-white-striped umbrella looped over our doorknob by its wooden handle. I glance to Len's door, nearly sure it's him speaking to me in inanimate objects, wishing I could just go knock and ask. But I'm letting things come to me, I'm letting things come to *me,* I'm *letting* things come to me, and so I hold back from knocking, telling myself it *might not* be him. There may be no such thing as intuition. Maybe what we can't see simply does not exist.

It seems very nice outside. I wouldn't *need* an umbrella out there. I imagine we are playing an intricate game of riddles and try to work his out. I pull out the big dictionary and page through to "umbrella." It's clever alright. I'll give him that. I pop open the pantry and reach for a couple of cans of creamed corn for the next round. "They stack it up in bomb shelters with Kool Aid," Grams used to say. "It lasts forever." I ring and run.

# 20.

♈ ♉ ♊ ♋ ♌ ♍ ♎ ♏

*There came a time when the risk to remain tight in the bud was more painful than the risk it took to blossom.*

—Anaïs Nin

All *night I've* dreamt of those goosepimply images in Kavia's book: planets hovering overhead absurdly out of scale and within touching distance. While I slept, I revisited ancient pharaohs carved with open arms over the universe, kings, queens. Somehow I understood that I was part of all of it, even if gum kept my sneaker stuck to the pavement. Galaxies spun around me, changing so quickly—day to night and back again, the wind of it on my face like an oscillating fan, the seasons rushing through in a single day. I lost my balance on something Grams had asked me in "the tone" to put away several times and went free-falling. Only, the fall was fantastic. It was the best part of all, as if the entire universe was mine and I'd stumbled upon a way to get at it. I could float at will—picking tulips in Holland, lunching in Provence, drinking a quick pilsner in Germany after a steamy jog along the rings of Saturn. My iPhone played out my very own theme song while key moments of my life flashed on hyper speed. I sat with an open book, dragging my finger across the ephemeris boxes, scratching my head at logarithms. I'm struggling, scrambling to predict what will come next, but I'm too late. I've only just got the book and I don't know where to find anything at all, can't make out the symbols.

I wake up sweaty, already running late for my appointment with Kavia. I look down at my clammy body to see Shirley MacLaine's coppery lipstick bright and shimmery on her paperback book cover, which is lying open on my stomach. I must leave right now if I don't want to miss my appointment.

My armpits are wet inside the giant housecoat armholes, and the back is stuck to me in large spots as I run, walk, run to the station and slip through the train doors sideways just as they're closing. I glance at the people trying not to notice me, my stench, or my housecoat, and immediately I regret not risking the extra few minutes to change.

At the other end, I run my hands over the station's long hallway of memorial white subway tiles, and emerge from the fluorescent lighting into striking sunshine. At the north end of the park there's a skateboarding event going on. The teenagers glide back and forth, doing Flamingos and Beanplants, and I think of Bruce. My head shakes like a disappointed mom's. I don't miss him at all.

I walk quickly, feeling stupid as hell. These teenaged boys aren't too shy to laugh at me as they roll past. "Hey, I think my grandmother has that dress!" one guy in a black T-shirt calls out.

He should be so lucky.

I don't hate them so much as wish I *were* them. They look so confident. They must be Capricorns.

At the sight of the neon pigeon light, I expect to feel something; recognition, or safety. But I don't. I'm panicked, actually, and angry, and a little hungry, too. Sure, there's that wonderful sense of being part of a celestial community, that idea that maybe there's a map to guide me. But there's a darker side, too. A side that the orderly, independent parts of me aren't too keen on. Why should this woman have so much power over me? Why should the stars say that *my* life will be one plagued with loss? That I should spend the day at home and let Len take the reins? And why, most important of all, does it all appear to be true?

Kavia doesn't answer right away, and my chest swims with anxiety. I try again, and when there is no response, I sink down onto the concrete steps. I am desperate for her. She's a rope I'm clutching, my hand wrapped around it like I'm dangling from a helicopter.

I don't know what I'll do if she doesn't answer. I buzz and buzz, as if pressing harder will do the trick. "Hello!" I yell, leaning into the sun-warmed steel speaker. "Kavia, it's Viv! Remember me? Viv, the one with Scorpio in her chart!" You can't imagine how deeply I am embarrassing myself.

I've torn off the only two nails I had left by the time the buzzer at last screams in response. My heart beating triple time, I push the door until it unlatches and make my way in giant three-at-a-time steps up to Kavia. Relief jiggles through me, in spurts, as if on an intravenous drip. This is an addiction: I've seen enough Oprah to recognize it. And the thing to do with addiction is to cut it off cold turkey. I'll just tell Kavia it's bullshit, it's all bullshit, scrape my way back to independence, and call it a day. Tomorrow will be that much better. In a month's time I'll have a shiny abstinence chip to work through my fingers and will be practiced at saying, "My name is Viv; I'm an astroholic."

Kavia's door is held open by a bronze pyramid doorstop. There is music playing on a cheap boom box on the windowsill, the type of new age, wordless tracks played in trendy spas and pretentious yoga studios. It's a tick too loud as I make my way over the threshold. She's not immediately apparent, but right away I can tell something is different here. It's darker, for one thing. And what dim light there is is purple, which is, embarrassingly, my favorite color. My affinity is a holdover from the days when oily stickers and slam books established my sense of aesthetics. My chest's rhythm takes on the cadence of sleep. I won't be leaving. I certainly won't be swearing off Kavia anytime soon.

She makes her way from the back through a beaded curtain with the perfect amount of crystal-on-crystal tinkling. Her hair is secured back into a pretty, if enormous, bun today, and she's got a multicolored caftan on that even I—in my muumuu—think might be overdoing it a bit.

Still, I smile at the sight of her.

"You're back," she says. The sound of her voice soothes me. I realize I have been waiting for it.

"Yes," I say, adopting her serious tone.

"I pulled some more books for you to read," she says, and hands me a stack.

I beam.

The topmost is fabric bound, with another fascinating orb on the cover—the glyphs on the outer rim, the sun and the planets floating over the more central pieces. I can now pick out my own sign, drawn here with two intricate fish, not exact opposites; instead, the one facing right is perfectly horizontal, nestled inside the bottommost curve of the glyph, while the topmost fish, facing left, has his mouth darted up, ready; his tail is flexed, like a dog's—poised to spring. *It looks so important, and it's me.* Flipping through the pages, I see the same information I read on the Internet: Being the last sign, Pisces is the most complex in the zodiac, a culmination of all the signs that came before it. I can't help it; this information puffs my chest, straightens my shoulders. My body is accelerated, I feel a bump of blood flow beneath my eye; my toe taps. I just know that Kavia has what I need. I'm done fighting. If I have to be dependent, trusting, in order to get to know myself, well then, that's what I have to do.

"So," she says, sitting down in a chair and gesturing me toward the empty one opposite, covered in lovely purple velvet. I sit down slowly, trying to savor every second of the consolation I feel here. I pull the chair forward by its curved arms until my knees tuck under the table. Kavia opens an enormous leather-bound volume from the bottom of the stack and flips through its gilt-edged pages. I run my fingers along the silky lengths of the tablecloth fringes.

"You are having a rushed, confused day already," she says.

I want to crawl up onto her lap and wrap my arms around her neck. It's as much as I can manage to nod my head up and down. I'm so ready for her to save me. "Kavia," I say.

"Yes?"

"Everything you've told me, everything that has been predicted about me, has come to pass."

"Of course."

"Of course. You say that like you've helped me study and I scored one hundred on my spelling test."

"So?" She shrugs one shoulder. "You listen, you do okay."

"Well, it's more than that. It's this amazing gift, like it says in that *Astrology Workbook* you gave me, it says, it says—" I flip open the book I've been holding on my lap. I've stuck in one of those Save the Animals bookmarks of Grams to keep the place. But she puts a hand over the page. "Shah," she says. "I know."

I shake my head, press my lips tight. But I need to explain the rest. "To some it's kind of a big deal, all of this meaning and direction, sense of belonging. But the fact that I need you, need this advice to get there, well, I feel like I've lost my independence and I can't make my *own* way anymore. And I, well . . . I always thought I made my own way. And now, I need this. I'm frightened, and I don't like that. But when I don't listen—"

"Shah," Kavia says again. I close my eyes to the wonderful sound of this word, this incredible syllable. "Hey listen, there is no shame in needing help. That is what the planets are there for. I sensed you didn't want to believe. But what you have to understand is that since the beginning of time, people have been relying on astrology. Since man could look up to the stars he wondered why they were there. And there are reasons that are beyond our comprehension, my dear Viv. How do the fish know which way the tide turns? This is the moon's mysterious working. How do the seasons know to change? All of this is the working of the universe. It is there for all of us. We're all tied in to it—we are the microcosm, nature the macrocosm. We exist together. Like crops and tides, we, too, exist in cycles. Astrology gives us a guide to what those cycles are. It's a misconception about astrology; people think it's the stars that force change, but it's not. They are just a map of what we'll do next. It's a reflection; they change, we change—all connected, you see? Without it, we are blind."

I shake my head.

Kavia pulls a cookie from her pocket and eats it in one snappy German shepherd bite, without offering any to me. Not *so* connected, huh?

"Consider this," she says, wiping crumbs away with the back of her palm. "Maybe what you mistook for independence wasn't *really* independence at all. Maybe the real independence is knowing all of your options and exercising whatever controls you have in order to navigate through them. If it was good enough for Queen Elizabeth the First, sister, it's good enough for you."

Bring on the sun beams through the clouds. Cue the "I'm Going to Disneyland" track. I'm done feeling ashamed. Sure, it's crazy, but, so is a staunch opposition to public health care. And at least *this* is working. Baseball players pull on manky old "lucky underwear" before a big game—is this any different, except that, again, it really, really works? *Listen, sister, if astrology is good enough for Queen Elizabeth the First, it's good enough for you.*

"We start with some more of your birth chart. It's important to understand where you come from, so that you can know where it is you are going," she says. "Today we talk about the aspects most important to *you,* Viv—and the nuances of emotions and behaviors we have built up over the years to protect ourselves from these aspects. Because, you see, it doesn't matter what you are if you can't make a go of it, if you can't work what you've got with what the world gives you."

My head darts back like she hit me. When someone identifies your problem, when they've fingered through that ginormous *Grey's Anatomy*, checked a couple of options, and realized that you had all the symptoms of one problem only, and voilà! You are not having headaches because you suffer from macular degeneration, but because you have . . . TMJ disorder! They give you a quick treatment plan and you're done. After years of floundering, this is a wonderful thing.

"The word *horoscope* literally translates to 'the view of the hour.' From the Greek," Kavia says. "To explore these challenges, we look to where the *planets* were, the particular view from exactly where you were at your birth. These locations are identified in terms of the twelve fixed houses, each of which represents a personality trait. Everyone's chart contains each of them. It's complicated, but this means each of us is capable of every kind of experience there is to have. The planets on your chart are a map of how things appeared from earth, from Brooklyn, New York, where you were born at 9 a.m. on February 25, 1979. On this map of what we see, the sun moves across the skies. The zodiac follows this pathway. The planets themselves are life; the zodiac signs are symbols of that life, a way to express the difficult-to-name peculiarities of the force as it occurs with each planet. The houses are the synthesis of these—they are the most nuanced and complex because they indicate the true way we experience and express all of this in our everyday lives."

I have to follow very carefully, tune out the jackhammering outside, the screech of brakes, but it makes sense. I've been looking at the junk closet of my life for years and years, peeking in when it all looks in danger of tumbling out into the hallway, but each time, I've no idea how to organize and classify these problems; where even there is something I might identify from the mass of it—a safe place to begin, an old double dutch rope, a pack of pickup sticks I might throw in the trash. I'm not sure of what I'll see in there, now that I know how to look, but it's becoming clear that I've got to sort it out or I'll soon be buried in the rubble.

"Some houses are stronger in our charts than others. And it is in these concentrations that we can identify how to harness, in a practical way, what will work uniquely for us, this energy pattern only we are born with. The first of these is the most significant: we call this your rising sign. And this, Viv, is what dictates the way your personality will manifest itself in this world." Kavia looks at me as if she really knows me. "This is about figuring out how to be accepted in family, in the world. It represents the central challenge we have to overcome in this life. I personally think this is the most important element of all. You master this—identify your biggest problem, *and* the way to work with it—and you'll be able to tackle your challenges, all your challenges, in a way that really works for you." She holds my gaze long enough that it's awkward. She doesn't seem to mind, but I have to look away.

I cover my mouth with a fist like I need to clear my throat, though I sense there isn't a point to acting.

"As soon as you're born, it's all set out, completely etched forever. Since your birth time was at the edge of your ascendent, if you'd been born just seconds later, you would have had a different rising sign altogether; a different challenge to master. It all comes down, in essence, to that one moment. Your entire chart is filtered through this aspect. How you overcome this challenge can change everything. It's got all your potential.

"And in this very important first house, *your* chart shows Taurus at fourteen degrees. This tells me that you are harmonious, loyal, affectionate. You're not big on risks. This is because Venus, ruler of Taurus, is the ruling planet in your chart: your main focus is love, beauty, ease of living, graciousness, and charm. You can be highly diplomatic and friendly, tactful, but you can fall into laziness and self-indulgence, too. You are tempted by anything pleasurable. But you are practical and realistic, too. These attributes can be at odds. So what do you do? It is vital that you explore how negatively your emotions can affect you if *you* let them. If you don't, you'll stick with people who are terrible for you merely because you get stuck in the routine. You want to feel comfortable *now,* and when you focus so narrowly, you'll never come to the real problems, and therefore, the real solutions."

When someone breaks down the solution you have been hunting down for three-quarters of your life to a bunch of simple steps—like some cub scout would use to build a fire without matches—it's stunning.

She explains the other planets influencing my houses: The second house is concerned with values and security. My security is based on emotional details, determined by Gemini, which is ruled by the planet Mercury. "You are very concerned with having a comfortable environment. In your third house is the way you relate to your siblings or close relatives, but not parents. Your expression and writings are also concerns addressed here; expressing yourself that way is important to your sense of being."

Each word punches to my gut. *Hello, Viv, nice to meet you.*

"The fourth house is all about your sense of home, your parents—in particular, your mother, and with the moon here, too, your home is unbelievably important to your connection with her; you make your home a place that can give you the security you lack from her. Probably, you collect things that have sentimental value to you, always trying to create a place that reminds you of the people you love, and of the love you need that maybe you haven't been given."

*Do not cry, Vivian. Not in front of a woman who's likely to pass you a tissue from the back of her hairdo.*

"The next significant house for you is your seventh, which

is the house of love and close relationships; what you've got here is Scorpio, ruled by Pluto, and this gives you more topsy-turvy times in relationships than you'd like; you attract strong people who love you but might get incredibly jealous; you may need time to work out why you think you need people, and why you need to be accepted and loved by them so deeply to feel okay about yourself."

All the while she's speaking she's holding my gaze. I don't feel awkward anymore. I'm locked into it; it's carrying me, like a father with a sleeping child slung over his shoulder.

I clear my throat. I'm not above a skeptic's thrill at her being wrong about at least one thing. I tell her, sure, she's right about every single one of those things, but not about this guy I was supposed to fall in love with, how that's turned out all bad.

"We'll see about that," she says, her eyebrows arched in challenge. "Now, have you got his birthday?"

I try to seem nonchalant, like I haven't memorized it. I pull out a scrap of paper and squint like I'm trying to make out my handwriting. "Umm, I think it says, *hmmm,* what *does* that say? Oh, I think it's Oct-ob-er 30th. No, it's the 31st, yup, nineteen seventy-three, at 10:27 p.m."

Kavia squeezes her eyes like she's seen the entire Rogers and Hammerstein library, and she isn't buying *this* act. Still, she pulls out another chart and starts to scribble what she reads on the ephemeris. "A Scorpio with Scorpio rising. Oh boy. Danger, excitement, enormous potential for sexual gratification. If you double-cross this guy, you could be in some serious trouble. He's intense, intense, intense. But these men are not committers; you'll have a hard time getting them to stick around. They're patient and driven by power—real pulling-the-strings power that they can and *will* use. A natural leader, a Scorpio with Scorpio rising, is never intimidated even if he's been through hell and back. You will not be able to ignore this man. He has a presence that can overwhelm. You'll love him or hate him. But he can be private as hell, and this will most likely be his downfall. A rising in Scorpio means he has to learn to confront control from others in order to live life fully, and this goes doubly for his parents. Once this is accomplished, he can put these hang-ups behind him; he will be altered for all time. But it is not an easy feat."

*Len.* I look to Kavia with my heart racing. "But it's too late. I've already ruined things with him. I mean, since then we've exchanged pantry items and accessories, but I don't think we'll be getting much past this. If only I'd heard all this before. Then maybe I wouldn't have—" Oh, what's the use? I didn't, and so I did.

"I made the mistake of letting my ex, Bruce, back in—and Len saw this."

I didn't need Kavia to tell me that this would be next to impossible to correct with someone like Len. "But listen, Vivian," she softens the blow. "It's not too late. You do exactly what I say, and you'll get him back."

It takes a moment to realize that whats wrong with that sentence is that she used my full name, the one my mother and nobody else does. "Why did you call me that?" I ask.

"Isn't it your name? It's lovely."

"But I don't like it."

"Maybe get to know it again. It's time."

This is when she hands me a glittery gold star—which looks like a kindergartner might have cut it out. I recognize it immediately: Martin was holding it when I tried to get Kavia to see me again.

"What's this?" I ask, sensing something important in my possession, feeling proud as a Brownie getting a pat on the beanie and a nifty patch for mastering square dancing.

"This is a gold star."

I anchor my lip with my tooth to keep myself from being condescending. I need this woman. I rethink my tack and ask, in what I hope to be a patient, inquisitive tone, "What does it *mean*?"

"It's your frequent reading card. With this you get ten

percent off your daily guidance sessions, and your tenth full session will be free." She pulls out a star-shaped hole punch from another pocket and clicks once, the way they do at manicurists' or cafés. A few glitter flakes shake free. Even astrologers need marketing plans.

"Wouldn't this be my second session?"

She grunts, but punches me out a second star with a noisy click all the same. "Now, you come in for your mini sessions at eight twenty-five every morning. You get five minutes, and not a second more. This is fifteen dollars—payable at the beginning of the session."

"Can't you do it a little later?" I ask.

"It's good for you to wake up early. You have no job, right? You need routine, get back into the city, figure things out. No 'make a deal.' You take it or leave it."

"I'll take it," I say, *"but I won't like it."* The words come out before I have the chance to stop them.

Her eyes dart up. She smites me with them but then the edges of her mouth curl into a smile. "I knew you had it in you."

This exchange is a balm. *The cycle . . . Len. Richter, Grams.* I see us all floating around, like the planets, or those enchanting symbols, not unsure and impotent, as I picture us normally, but deliberate, with purpose, heralded along the natural order of things on a roller-coaster path, tick, tick, ticking, and racing along a predestined pattern. It seems none of us can go wrong.

"Now, back to where we left off. The houses. The ninth house encompasses learning, books, and publishing. It's also to do with long-distance travel and your personal philosophy; and here I see some interesting things: you have trouble leaving your home because it represents so much pleasure to you, but if you combine travel with something professional, this would be a fantastic fit for you. A move might address your yearning for philosophical knowledge and challenge the part of you that doesn't like to accept that people might disagree with your beliefs." Move? Away from Seacoast? It's never occurred to me. But there's a whole world out there where ibises roam, spice markets hawk pungent twiggy things, where women wear severely angled European hairstyles. There is a great big world; all those cruise ships we watched drift off beyond the defunct parachute ride at Coney Island. But they went farther than that. This is the thing I hadn't put together. They went way, way past the Cyclone and the hot dog vendors and the blue cotton candy, to places where people have never even heard of the Cyclone, maybe have never heard of cotton candy.

"The tenth house relates to your ambitions and your need to find a place in the world. In this house is your response to authority and your ability to *be* authoritative, to handle power." She stops her scribbling and looks up at me.

I don't feel like talking about my job. The more I think of the whole thing, I become the bad guy, and Stan turns into, if not a hero, a very insightful idiot savant.

"You don't have a father, do you?"

Oh. I didn't realize we were going there. Instead of using the phrase "I'd rather get a root canal," I'm going to start saying, "I'd rather face the truth about myself." I'm done being clever, so I just shake my head.

"This is important to think about, or I wouldn't bring it up: Why do you want to be successful? Is it for you, or to make up for some attention you missed out on, dear, when your father was busy working all those hours before you lost him?"

She moves on like this—pointing out the most specific problems I've always grappled with—as if they're merely matters of fact like anything else. Yogurt has less fat than ice cream. Whole-grain bread is better for you than that fantastic Italian bread that comes out warm and crusty by the supermarket deli counter. An entire lifetime of behavior modification was a waste of energy. No biggie.

My fists are gripped so tightly, I see a tiny stream of blood trickle down the inside of my wrist. I had no idea I was this resistant. Have I always been this way? What the hell am I so afraid of? As if I'm doing so well the way I've been handling things up till now. I cradle that wrist so I don't drip blood on Grams's housecoat.

"You barely have any Aries at all, which is ruled by Mars, and I think maybe you would have benefited from a little of Mars's aggression; because the truth is, you are very, very brave and strong, too, but you don't know it."

There are prickles at the back of my neck. *It says I'm strong?* I *so* want this to be true I can taste it, gritty on my tongue. "Where does it say that?" I ask, incredulous.

"Right there," she says, pointing to a number, a squiggle, which I can't much discern from the other numbers and squiggles. She looks once more to the clock. This gesture tells me I'm going to have to trust her because she has other things to do today.

"You are a survivor; where others would not make it through, you will. I know it is difficult to see these things about yourself, because this is another trait of yours, Pisces—you do not trust yourself; you always want to be 'the other' whatever, wherever that may be."

This is too much. I'm glad it's coming to a close because it's just too much.

"Now," says Kavia, smacking the book shut. "You talk to me about your loss. Quickly. We have five minutes left. You were not ready to talk with me about it last time. But today, you are."

I'm not sure where that zany Geppetto is hiding, but someone operates my brain and mouth, starting at the beginning, sharing everything about how my grandmother raised me and about our enormous friendship, the way I lashed out at her for things that were never her fault, and the way she tried to tell me some of these things Kavia had, but how I never listened. I say things I didn't know I knew: tell Kavia Grams didn't say these things in a language I understood. It was her own language, and she tried to use it to lift me up, while she loved me enough for everyone who was gone. But I never understood what she meant. I just took the comforting, a kitten enjoying the moment before trotting off to bat a jingly ball. But never *did* anything about it, really. I tell her how despicable I was at the end, looked away from what was happening because I'd run so long and now I had nowhere else to go, no one who might look away while I ran off and batted jingly balls instead of living.



Kavia didn't get the jingly ball thing. This isn't her idea of symbolism. "A dog, maybe, a dog who runs off to chew one of those Denta Bones that make their teeth fresh. *This* makes sense. But a kitten batting a jingly bell? No. This doesn't work."

"I said a ball. It's a ball."

"Still."

"Can we move on?" I say. "I've only got two minutes left."

"Actually it's one minute. That clock is slow," she says, folding her hands over the closed book as if she's already gone.

I speak quickly. I'm age eleven, throwing a fit on Gram's kitchen floor, my fists at her ankles and calves. "Stop lying," I shout. "Because my mother *is* coming back, and don't you say she isn't. You don't know her. She always says you don't understand her at all."

"I'm sure she does," Grams had said, blinking her eyes like she was trying to remove sand stuck in them.

My mind moves along. I'm making excuses for why Bruce isn't around. I want to bring Kavia up to speed on all of it, fill in the gaps until that moment when I'm pretending the hematologist is a television actress instead of a hematologist, while Grams died alone—

"Time's up."

My face rushes with blood. It makes me a little dizzy.

We rise together—me and Kavia and all those unspeakable images, the click, puff, click, of them trying to rescuscitate Grams with the paddles, the tink of a stethoscope against the bedrail.

"Okay," I say.

"Forgive yourself. You're not going to change the ending. And that is just what she wanted from you. You said it yourself. She wanted you to forgive yourself, but she couldn't speak your language. If *this* is your language, you might still miss it if you don't listen."

I nod, palm over the money, and wait for a great, furry forgiveness to unfold from my heart and wrap itself around me. But it doesn't. The door screeches shut. The hallway is harshly lit. My footfalls echo on the steel; it's old and empty and like its own world, the way metal stairwells in Manhattan can be.

Down two flights, my fingers skim something rough along the handrail. It's just a sticker. But it says, "Save the tatas." And it is here, on this scuffed stair, in this worn hallway in dire need of a paint job, that something lifts. Just like that, the fight dissipates. I feel it lift up, like the steam from my mother's soup pot facials, from my fingernails, the tips of my ears. Kavia's right. I feel real forgiveness; and it feels very much like a warm, humid day after a cold stint—uncomfortable, but in the most spectacular, special way.

I forgive myself. Around me, the forgiveness has gone light and feathery, it caresses my wet eyes like kisses, and dances over me in delicious smooches that send me skipping down the stairwell, which I note, rounding the last sunken, scuffed flight, is actually quite beautiful in its way. It feels solid, like it will be around forever. How could I have not noticed before? It's a gem of ornate moldings and tiny lions flashing sharp, perfectly sculpted teeth. It is absolutely stunning.

# 21.

♈ ♉ ♊ ♋ ♌ ♍ ♎ ♏

*If you don't get lost, there's a chance you may never be found.*

—Common proverb

Seeing *Kavia so* early means I get up just a bit later than when I used to get ready for work, but enough that I have to sort out a new routine: there's a different National Public Radio announcer at this time; his name's Simon Stockholm, and he has a pleasant, deep voice that soothes me during my morning tea. My mystery someone left me some fancy gourmet granola and fresh mangoes, bananas, and mandarins yesterday. I'm still choosing, as I crunch down, to believe this someone was Len, continuing our game. I decide to return the favor. I look around and can't think of a single thing to give him. The game is like Kavia; it makes me look at ordinary things in a whole new way. There's a lot more to a carrot scraper than you might first assume.

And so I've been eating this granola—rather than the plain

bran flakes Grams and I ate every day for two decades—and I'm cutting up little bits of the fruit to toss on top, listening to Simon Stockholm diplomatically field callers' creative theories on global warming. The fruit is new. We never did fruit before 9:30 because it gave Grams indigestion. I got used to not having it. On the record she didn't officially mind if I ate it, but she'd make this little squeak, like a puppy who wants out of his pen, every time I bit into a berry or a stone fruit. So the next time we went to the fruit store I said, "Don't buy any for breakfast. I don't feel like it." She raised one eyebrow and scrunched up the side of her mouth, but didn't argue. She made my favorite for dinner that night, even though sloppy joes gave her "a" heartburn. It's all the onions, she used to say.

The fruit with granola is nice. On these mornings, before I know it, I'm on the train, and just as quickly, in the city. Things never went this fast when I was going to work. It's amazing how time can stretch when it feels like it.

It's a little strange that everyone's off to their jobs except for me. But I dress normally now. I've relegated the housecoat to home use only. And the lobby. And the delicatessen. But that was just once. And it was a half-sour-pickle emergency. Wendy and I agreed: if I actually wanted something this badly, finally, it was a good thing, and I was right to run like the wind, to pick out the crunchiest ones swimming around in the barrel.

I've met Wendy for coffee a few times. *Start letting people in, but don't push, Kavia says, and what you want will come to you.* She shoves me out the door, and not gently either, at five minutes exactly.

The thing is, she could kick me out with a steel-toed boot and it wouldn't matter: everything she advises works, makes me dig just that much deeper. Every word I read about my rising sign, my moon, my sun, my midheaven—it all illuminates things just that much more, and I feel free to wend my way through life's challenges with minimum collateral. It's a gift in layers of delicate tissue, which I take care to unwrap so I can reuse it when I need to.

On one of these mornings, a particularly hot one everyone's talking about, I leave my copy of *The Astrology Bible* at Len's door, ring the bell, and round down the stairs to greet the day. I was on the fence about it, but I figured, if it's a little kooky, then that's who I am. I'm going to be myself when it counts. And I think, Grams would be proud. I came across this saying about irony once, which I think perfectly sums up the idea of learning something a person dedicated their life to teaching you, only after they've gone: "Humor brings insight and tolerance. Irony brings a deeper and less friendly understanding." The truth hurts, Grams was fond of saying. It certainly does.

The second I get on the train I backtrack; maybe I didn't have to be quite so much myself.

But that's the thing about this new faith. It's different. If the other one I'd had most of my life was a safe maroon, this one is candy apple red, that shade of lipstick I'm always afraid to wear. My taste for optimism, I found in one of Kavia's books, is a strength of Taurus ascendant, my rising sign: we trust things to work out in the end. Coming across this passage didn't exactly give me my optimism back, but it sure as hell reminded me to listen for its song, to turn up the volume, and tell everyone in the room to shut the hell up so I could hear.

On cue, when I get back from Manhattan that afternoon, there is a knock at the door. On the other side, holding a worn paperback collection of Ralph Waldo Emerson's verse, is Len. After not seeing him for a few days, the sight of him is a little stunning. That smile and the wet eyes and the slight creases, that power boldly Riverdancing beneath the surface. I feel that same sting: I've screwed up something significant. Only now I've also got a nugget of that Viv faith back: It's possible that everything might still work out okay.

"Poetry, huh?" I give him a look like I wouldn't peg him for it. Especially that macrocosm kind of thing, we *are* the puddle in the mud, the muddy water in the stream—all of that.

"It's my dad's. And besides, I thought we were doing wacky stuff."

I screw up my face.

"You don't really believe that astrology crap, do you?"

"Me? No," I say before I can think about it. I cross all eight fingers behind my back and stick the thumbs in the middles.

"And I think it was that goddarned faith that had me so shocked when things didn't work out all right," I tell Wendy over lattes, after another Kavia session, feeling insightful. "I really thought I'd gotten through in that hospital bathroom. I really thought God said, 'Okay, Vivian, you've had enough crap. I'll give you a pass here. But come back to temple. It's been sixteen years.' And I would have. I really would have. At least on the High Holy Days. And Tu Bishvat. I've always liked Tu Bishvat."

"Is that the one with the little huts and those nuts you shake around?"

"No, that's Sukkhot," I say. "And they're not nuts that you shake around. You're getting that confused with dancing the hokey-pokey at your bat mitzvah. That's when you shook around all the nuts."

We laugh.

"Well really, though, it's amazing, what you've been realizing." she says. "I'll tell you what. If you look past the grief, the worst loss you could endure, the fact that your mother's an ass, and this staggering style you've cultivated here, you actually look great—it's something new, something inside, something really, really good."

"Thanks," I say, "But let's not get carried away. I'm no Eliza Doolittle."

"Look, don't take this the wrong way," Wendy says. "But maybe get some younger friends. Ones who might not get an Eliza Doolittle reference, maybe someone who knows who

John Mayer is. I'd even settle for one who might recognize a Madonna song. One of the old ones like 'Material Girl' or 'Holiday.' That would be good enough."

I want to say I've got one, and that I think John Mayer is overrated. I want to say that the one I've got probably thinks John Mayer is overrated too, and that I know this before I have to ask, and that this One I've mentioned has dewy eyes and a way of gripping his hand around your shoulder when he's having an orgasm that might take me ten years or so to bend my mind around. But I don't "have" him, really. And I don't talk like that anyway. Not out loud. Not even when Wendy walks me through each and every "move" of her sex life. Not even when she goes, "Oh, and there was this move with his tongue," and I fake-vomit and beg her to stop. Maybe especially not then.

Instead I say, "Well, let's not get carried away. I'm onto myself. I'm throwing myself in this new life view just because it feels good, right?" I look to her searchingly.

"Why shouldn't you get carried away?" Wendy says, and slurps the dregs of her latté.

A woman in a shocking hat with a foam owl on an actual tree branch along the brim turns around and shakes her head at Wendy. The woman turns back and Wendy gives the finger to her backside. "I say get carried away, go nuts, see where it takes your mind. Set sailing like, like, a, a—" I know what she's doing. She's baiting me to be creative, to get back into the swing of things.

"Like that plastic bag in *American Beauty,*" I say, and roll my eyes.

"You've still got it," she says, smacking the table as if she's the authority on this, Commissioner of Creative. The silverware rattles. The woman she gave the finger to turns around again, curling her lips.

"What? What?" Wendy says and waves her head in the way that she knows makes me laugh; her *Montel Williams Show* impression from a dozen years ago, the one of the girl whose sister was a hoochie.

The woman blanches white and turns around.

"She must have missed that episode," Wendy says. She turns her attention back to me with a sigh. "About what we were saying, don't let anyone tell you different."

"Look, if you're gay and falling in love with me," I say, "you can just tell me. I won't look at you any differently. You're not my type, but I won't judge you."

She gives me the finger. "Talk about not being someone's type. You don't even have boobs."

Len holds out a bag stained through with grease spots. "I brought you some Roll N Roaster," he says. Kavia's prediction is proving accurate once again. His gesture is just my style: instead of asking a lot of questions, he comes bearing junk food. *Say it with French fries,* I always say. *Say it with cabbage knishes.*

I open the door and wave him inside.

But he shakes his head.

I swallow hard, surprised at the many stories I fall through to reach the depths of this rejection. I guess that's what I was saying about optimism. If you hope for the best sometimes you get let down.

He shifts his head in a gesture of listening, his ear toward the hi-fi, where Kavia's tape is still introducing me to my life.

"What's that?" he asks.

"Nothing. Just a . . . something . . . you know."

He looks skeptical.

I don't want to get into this with him again. I tell myself it won't matter if we have different views. You don't have to share identical interests. He might like, I don't know, zucchini, or something. And that's fine. He can have his zucchini. I'll even cook it for him. It doesn't mean I have to eat it myself.

"A 'something,' huh?" He slips his hands down into his pockets. I remember what it felt like under there, and my finger twitches against my thigh.

He's so Scorpio; he's never going to buy it. He's not even

going to buy into the fact that he's a Scorpio. If he looked at his sign in that book at all, he probably said, "Nope, don't recognize any of this. It's all bullshit."

I think I see a hint of that fantastic smile, like maybe he finds me amusingly charming instead of nutty.

This is not a guy who would believe any little star in the sky's got a thing to do with him. He's an island, Hawaii, or Australia, or Tristan da Cunha. Somewhere that costs a fortune and six days to get to.

But I'm me. And I want to show him he's not an island. Not really. That way Kavia explained him, it makes a lot of sense. It makes sense that he'd only shut right off if I forced things. He needs to realize for himself. Which is fine with me. In fact, I might, *ahem,* know someone a little like that myself. Besides, the other side of this all the time thing of his is one I kind of like. It's sexy. It balances me. He's great for me in the role of Logical Rock Number One. I may even fire Number Two. He would just be redundant. If I wound up with someone like myself, or Wendy, that nut bag, we could easily wind up on a commune weaving wall hangings from hemp.

Only, as soon as I recognize this, he catches my eye and retracts his levity. No inappropriate levity here. I'm back to being the girl who fucked and then fucked up.

*If you double-cross this guy, you could be in some serious trouble.*

His light goes out in an instant. No Hanukkah oil miracle today, sir. I feel a pinch in my heart.

"Come on in," I say, trying for casual.

"The food's just for you," he says.

I'm shattered. I nod as if I get it.

Still, there are firefly pulses in the air between us. A pattern so beautiful it can only be that artsy Mother Nature's.

He hesitates, cocks his head to the side, opens his mouth as if he's going to say something, then doesn't.

Instead, he turns, takes the few steps to his own door and reaches for the knob.

A rubbery undulation drops from my chest to my kneecaps. "Wait!" I nearly yell.

"What?" he says, turning halfway back.

"Um, thanks." Behind my back, I pinch my arm.

Len shakes his head, turns to his door, and just when I think he's gone, he spins around and says, "I almost forgot. My dad wants to know if you're going to watch *Lost* with us tonight."

*Oh?* "Sure," I gulp, and without knowing I'm about to, coyly dangle my foot, pointing my toe in his direction.

And then he's gone.

I close the door and do a dance with complex fist syncopations behind it. I drop the food on the table as if it's tainted. I say, the way we do before eating anything "bad" in this house, "Like I would eat *that junk.*" And then I gobble it down right out of the bag, standing, hunched over it, with one foot propped on my chair. I don't even bother with ketchup. Grams keeps the bottle in the fridge and I hate it cold anyhow.

*So take it out,* she says in my head.

I get as far as opening the door and lifting the bottle out of its place between the nail polish and the orange juice. But then I let it slide back in. *Not yet,* I say. *Not just yet.*

I shower for *Lost,* telling myself I'm only doing it because I want to spare "Officer" Richter the stench—he isn't a well man, after all. But the truth is I *feel like* taking a shower, and I stay in long enough to prune my fingers, let the hot water work over my shoulder blades and lower back. Preening in front of the mirror, I hook my thumbs over my waistband, straighten out my posture. I switch from my high school gym shorts to a pair of jeans that sits my butt high and round. Look, I'm no saint. I flick my hair, give myself a sideward glance, and gather my things to go.

When I arrive, my hair is wet, and waving out from behind my ears. I'm in a black tank top and standing like a Robin Red Breast who's really hard up.

Len opens the door before I knock. My fist hovers inches from the door.

"Hey," he says. There's so much kindness in it, I wonder how mad he can really be.

I shuffle inside in my flip-flops, holding a big bowl of popcorn loaded up with butter, the way the three of us—Grams, Richter, and me—always eat it. I'm not telling anyone about the tears that dripped over the bowl; I lasted until I mixed the salt and butter around with the spoon; Grams always yanked the spoon from me and told me I didn't mix it good enough. She claimed she wound up with bites that had no salt. It was the last package, so I had to bring it anyhow.

Grams is sharply absent as I walk inside gripping the bowl—you see, she always held the bowl, and yelled, "This place is a wreck, you schlub! Why don't you spring for a cleaning lady already?" And Richter would say, "Why don't you make an honest man of me and then clean it *for* me?" All the while I would pretend this didn't make me want to puke. Sometimes I wouldn't pretend.

I try my grandmother's speaking part, but only get out "This place is a—" before I see that Richter is in one of those hospital beds, where the couch normally is. Meanwhile, the couch is pushed over along the wall, perpendicular, so that Len and I have to squeeze through to get by.

I can't bring myself to look at Len. He's instantly cast in a different light. It's unbelievable that he could think of me at all. And all this time I'm worrying he hasn't come over because he was mad. I'm a freaking idiot. "Nice redecorating you've done!" It's the best version of something Grams would say that I can muster; but as sarcastic as I can be as a solo act, I've always been the straight man of our duo. She's just that good. It's becoming obvious that a straight man ain't nothing without his lead.

Richter appreciates the effort, offers a smile, and tries a zinger of his own. "Well, we did as much as the company deserves." His voice is weak and trails off at the end. Spittle has pooled up at the side of his mouth; the sight of it could break your heart. More seriously, he continues: "I've been in the hospital. I'm sure Len told you—God knows he's sweet on you . . ."

*He is?* Hope rises up, up, sings the loudest warble, I half expect the guys to cover their ears. Amid the worry and grief around us, it's a phoenix from the ashes. "What happened?" I ask, trying to appear as if I hadn't heard that last bit. I avoid Len in my flush.

"Eh, my ticker. It was tired or something."

"Actually, he had a heart attack and then had to have bypass surgery—not a great thing for someone already going through chemo. Apparently he's eating badly."

I try to hide the popcorn behind my back. Len lowers his chin and eyes, shaking his head. He's got a 3D optical illusion smile you can only see if you know how to look. "Hand over the popcorn, Viv," he says, grabs it, and disappears into the kitchen. If you look really hard, a sub smile has taken hold. This is the gem in the arsenal of smiles; it floats, most often undetected, right under the surface, but can do a shitload of damage.

"Jeez," I say conspiratorially to Richter when Len is out of sight.

"Can't blame the kid for being worried about losing me; I've never been much of a father to him, and he's probably afraid it's too late now. I guess he's right." Richter looks so dejected my stomach flips.

I lean over him, grab his hand. "Now you listen to me; it is *never* too late." We lock eyes; I see the hesitation in his. The gist of his thoughts comes across loud and clear: "Oh, come on, everyone says that but it's not true," his look says. But something rolls out over this; it looks like acceptance, and finally, something like determination. He nods his head sternly. Len emerges again. He's poured me out a tiny bowl of the popcorn, and in two other identical bowls he's given himself and his father veggie chips.

I reach for the remote, turn the channel selector to ABC, and sit down. Len sits as far away from me as he can. I can only assume Richter got Len's feelings all wrong. Maybe he *was* sweet on me, but cozying up to another man on the same morning you woke up with Man A in your bed isn't exactly the stuff of fairy tales. *Let him come to you.* I say it like a mantra and try to lose myself in the show.

*Lost* is as nail-biting, as excruciatingly unrevealing as ever, but I can't seem to muster as much interest. I keep finding myself thinking, *these are just actors. I just saw this guy in the Coco Chanel movie.* Still, twice I have a mind to give Grams a "really well done" about a plot thread she had correctly predicted. Each time, Richter darts me a sideward glance. A dull ache thuds at my rib cage when he does.

Things have certainly changed since the last episode we watched together. There are fewer survivors on the island, and fewer survivors here; and Richter can't make it through the entire episode. A bit after the halfway mark he's snoring—a painful-sounding, rapid wheeze. He can't be doing very well. He looks ashier; gray. He hasn't got a lick of whatever hair he'd had on his head, and what I can see of his feet don't look very promising in the circulation department.

I look over to Len. I have to say something. It's all I can do not to reach out to him and close the distance between us, be there for him as he was for me. But this is not the way to help him. Before Kavia, I would have done just what I'd want done for me. But that just isn't right for everyone. I'd want nothing more than to fall into his chest and not get up for a couple of weeks. On top of that, I'm supposed to be letting things come to me.

"So," I say, my head bobbing in and out like a rooster's. It's the best I can do. I don't exactly know the language in these parts.

"So," Len mimics. Something in his eyes holds back.

"What are the doctors saying about your dad?"

"It's an up and down thing. He's old to be going through

the chemo; and beyond that, he's old to have the surgery they just performed. They've already said we shouldn't get too excited about any upturns in his appearance; the overall picture isn't going to improve. That's why they let him come home when he kept insisting. He's only got so long." Len's trying so hard to look strong, like he's talking about the plot of the show we're watching, that all I can think is how much I want to grab his hand, have him allow me to provide this tiny comfort.

He looks at the space between my nose and mouth, and then to where our hands are nearly touching on the sofa cushion, and finally to my eyes, like he wants me to do exactly this: to touch him. My breath catches; I want to.

Just when I don't think I can stand it another second, his fingers walk over to mine, grab hold, squeezing my knuckles together. I want this to go on and on. He reaches around and grazes my other hand, traces his palm up to my shoulder, and around, until we're locked in an embrace. He allows me to hug him back, my hand gripped all the way around him, as tight as I can. His breath in my ear is too much. I turn my face to meet his and it seems he is about to kiss me. For an agonizing couple of seconds we are frozen nearly lip to lip. And then he turns away. Abruptly, he stands.

I feel like someone has socked me in the stomach.

He's cordial when he shows me out, promises to stop by. We use plastic grins and excessive head shakes and pretend it isn't awkward. There's a lot of "let me get your bowl," and "don't forget your keys." We try to act like we don't want to get out of the other's sight as quickly as possible.

At home, I open Grams's bedroom door. I stand at the doorway, not quite wanting to go inside. From this view, I look at all of her pretty things—her silk slippers, her gently worn willow baskets for hairclips and brooches, the pillows she embroidered with delicate French knots. I would give anything to see her at her dressing table right now, rubbing Lubriderm into her elbows, calling me in to see how dry my elbows are, and *noodging* me to put some on myself. I close the door.

As I lay down to sleep, I think of the words I said to Richter: *It's never too late.* I wonder where I found this pearl, where I got off acting like I knew anything at all. I hope there is some truth to it. In the meanwhile, I clamp my headphones in place and pull the blankets over my head. I pull out the squat red notebook, and with the very same pastel pink flashlight I used to read by as a little angry girl who couldn't sleep, I start writing what I hope will be my very first novel.

# 22.

♈ ♉ ♊ ♋ ♌ ♍ ♎ ♏

*The object of art is to give life a shape.*

—Jean Anouilh (1910–1987)

I *don't hear Len's* knock until there's a lull between songs. When I do, I toss the covers off of my head, and yank out the earbuds with a start. I tiptoe to the door, hopeful, and a little shaky.

"Hello?" I ask, and squint to make him out through the peephole. He looks a little more tired and a little more disheveled than he did earlier.

"Vivian?" he whispers through the door.

"Why'd you call me that?" I whisper back.

"I heard your mom do it. I liked it."

"Well don't," I say.

"I'll call you what I like," he says.

"Really?"

"Really." He says. "Now let me in."

He doesn't have to ask twice. I undo the latches and chains

and hold the door open for him. He steps inside and closes the door behind him, working through the locks I *still* have trouble with like it's nothing at all.

"I'll say this," he says, reaching for his throat, rubbing his hand as if loosening a tie. "I don't think I'm good for you right now, but I can't help it." He looks at my lips. Before I know it, his lips are where his eyes were. I'm hurtling through space. There go Jupiter and Neptune, Saturn and Uranus. It's a rush, and at the same time, completely still, silent, the world asleep—everyone except the two of us. He pulls away and smooths my hair out of my face. He looks down at me from behind those dark lashes, from somewhere far, far away, the 1,500 light-years to the Orion nebula. Somewhere deep in there is the real Len, and I hope to see him. He gives me the briefest flash, if only just to show me he's the only one who can get there, and he kisses me softly on the forehead. "I'll see you tomorrow," he says.

I write one more thing in the notebook before calling it a night:

*This shit fucking works.*

# 23.

♈ ♉ ♊ ♋ ♌ ♍ ♎ ♏

*Hope is the thing with feathers*
*That perches in the soul,*
*And sings the tune without the words,*
*And never stops at all . . .*

—Emily Dickinson

*After that, the* days fly by, each one slightly better than the next. I go to Kavia, get my advice, walk out feeling hopeful, the hole where Grams used to be gaining slightly softer edges, a bit of dirt kicking in here and there. If no less treacherous to negotiate, each day proves less of an extreme drop when I fall—and I do. But Kavia's giving me better tools: a hard hat, a walking stick, a really stretchy bungee cord.

I'm getting used to the feeling of loss, living with it like a bum leg that will always mark me, but won't stop me ballroom dancing. I do exactly what Kavia says; I mark with a green star, on our Seacoast Terrace calendar on the fridge, each day of this month that Kavia had given me advice that turned out to be completely accurate. Even Len couldn't argue with odds like that.

I count ten and stand back in wonder. It all started with the train accident. And then there was letting Len come to me, and the time she said Len will find the right moment to make a move, and he wound up once again—if not back where he was—kissing me in a way that said he would like to be. And on it goes.

Today, the sixteenth of August, it turns out, is supposed to be "a good day for letting go of excess baggage, relationships, things we no longer need." Kavia didn't have the full five minutes for me, I think, because this is all she said, but she swears that was all there was. I decide, looking at my luck, all marked up that way, to trust her. She has certainly earned it. And besides, it was almost as if I sensed this would be on the charts for today. It's like I've tuned in to the universe a tiny bit, and this, in turn, has sharpened my internal view.

I flip to the first empty page in my notebook, sipping a strong black coffee at my desk. After two sentences, I turn to the next page. And the next. And the next time I need to find a new page, there isn't one left.

I've filled up a notebook that's about three inches thick. And it's one of those *college ruled* ones Grams never wanted me to get because they are so much pricier. I think where I am in the plot of the book and realize I'm about halfway done.

I decide to take a walk to buy another book and some nice fresh pens. I pull a hooded sweatshirt over my tank top. Downstairs, I turn the corner toward the lobby, the clean rushing of the waterfall in my ear, and I'm stopped dead in my tracks. It's Bruce. He's an artifact from another time—his perfect hair and manicured hands resting casually on Jameson's desk.

"Viv," he says.

Jameson tries to act like he's not paying attention.

"Bruce." I stand straighter. I feel strong; I feel absolutely nothing for him but burnt up.

"Let's take a walk."

"Let's," I say, realizing that I want, I *need* to tell him how he's failed me. To Jameson, who's not pretending anymore, but stretching his eyes into giant saucers and must be thinking if he'd had Grams's daily gossip updates he would know what this was all about, to him I say, "I won't be long, not long at all."

Bruce's brow rumples slightly. I'm not going to pretend it doesn't feel good.

It's spectacular outside; I'm more aware of it than normal. The breeze is just right—soft and comfortable—and my ponytail picks up slightly along a gust. The clouds are a few cottony strands I can see right through, like freshly spun wool. People are out in force, walking, running, wheeling their upright shopping carts full of woven shopping bags.

We make our way to the boardwalk. Bruce says, "I'm just going to put it out there, Viv. I want you back." He stops, turns me toward him, feels for my hands. It's as many words as I've ever heard him string together. Now that I've got the cushion of emotional distance, I can appreciate the effort. I feel myself soften toward him, the anger spilling out like air from an untied balloon.

"Oh, Bruce," I say. "You never wanted me. And the truth is, I never wanted you. I only wanted you to want me. I thought that was important. But now I know the truth—it isn't what's important at all."

"Don't say that. Don't get all deep on me. It's black and white. I want you back."

A husband and wife walk by, their hands swinging; the husband's wheeling a little boy in one of those light collapsible strollers; a thicket of white hair pokes out from a miniature Yankees cap.

"You hurt me Bruce, but it's my own fault—I let you do it. I never stood up for myself. I just clung to whatever we had way past its expiration date because God forbid I do anything like my mother. I wanted to stay put. I've got no one to blame for that but myself and I'm completely okay with that. You don't want me. And even if you do—I don't want you." I didn't know most of this until I say it, but it's true.

"You know, you're different," he says, still holding my hands. "I don't know what it is, but you have really changed. You look spectacular."

"I'm in love," I say, and know that's true, too. *I'm in love.* I want him to know because it's important. He should know what it really is. And how to recognize it when it comes his way. The thoughts sail off on the breeze, and up, out toward Unus Mundus, or the World to Come, or merely to a pair of gnats performing aerobatic tricks a few inches above our heads. We walk the boardwalk until Brighton Twentieth and then turn back.

I leave Bruce with a quick kiss on the cheek. "Good luck!" I yell. "Life can be really *carp-y.*" He never appreciated the old *Skylar* fish jokes, always complained how annoying they were.

I really couldn't give a carp.

I need to turn my misfortune into opportunity. That's what Kavia said this morning. *Today is the day for it; there's only a small window,* she warned.

I print this out and hang it on the fridge, next to the calendar, and head out onto the terrace, where I've gotten into the habit of thinking these predictions and insights over with my coffee. I used to do this with work tasks—see what I needed to do for the day—when I got to work. But now I see how short-sighted I've been, living in one tiny day of tasks at a time instead of looking at the whole picture of my life. No wonder I never left that job. I was too busy pretending to be wrapped up in ordering Post-it flags to notice the Mack truck rushing at me. The trick is, if you know this about yourself, you can make an effort not to let it go on so long—not to wait until you're fired from your job, or you lock yourself in a bathroom while your grandmother is dying.

Morning's a good time to do this mental inventory. Everything looks better in the daylight. You can see yourself in the boughs of the branches, in the curl of a wave, and figure things out a little more clearly. As I sit on our glider, I look out at the day—another day so clear it's hard to believe it's real. It's as if the water and the sky are one continuous mass; there is nothing at all reflected in the water. No boats disturb its surface.

I lean back, enjoy the coffee. On a whim, I bought it yesterday. Grams couldn't drink it because it gave her heart palpitations. Like the fruit, she pulled The Face every time I drank it, so I stopped. I never could take The Face first thing in the morning. Yesterday I was walking down the street in Manhattan and I smelled this fantastic aroma; it turned out there was a brand-new "coffee boutique." It sounded so pretentious that I had to go in. I was sold. I bought some wonderful beans I couldn't afford, which they ground up right there for me in an old Italian crank grinder. I also went in for some cardamom pods—which is apparently how they drink it in Arab countries. It struck me as romantic. It's these little nuances of newness that are getting me up and out these days.

This morning, I brought a bag for Wendy. After my Kavia session, I told her all about the history of the coffee, which I'd gone to the library to research, and she said, "Wow, that actually sounded like the Viv I know. I don't want to get ahead of myself here, but I think you might actually survive." If I do, I have Kavia to thank for it.

I'm sitting there, thinking about Kavia's words about today, and I'm actually *smiling.* Something good is about to happen. It's a wonderful, powerful idea—the kind I used to walk around with all the time. It's so great to have it again. I smile back a few tears in expectation of what it might be. I'm surprised to find how easily I embrace the thought of feeling good; maybe it's like riding a bicycle—you never really forget how to do it.

While I sit, the sky darkens rapidly to a dense gray, clouds thicken like egg whites beaten for a napoleon. In minutes, they cover all the Manhattan buildings across, and most of the Manhattan Bridge. The Brooklyn Bridge disappears completely.

I sip my coffee, I watch the cars along the avenue, beyond our long entry and parking lot, until the weather completely blocks the view. After that, I shift my view with disdain to the new buildings across the way, thinking of how it looked here in the old days of penny Swedish fish and animal cracker boxes on a string. Back then Grams and Mrs. Kaufman used to take me to the beach club, which stood in the very footprint of those buildings, where we'd splash around in the pool and slurp Italian ices from fluted paper cups—squishing out the last dregs. We'd stay for the big band music after sunset. One of those summers I begged to dye my hair blue, to match Mrs. Kaufman's. Grams kept telling me that was rude, Mrs. Kaufman thought her hair was white.

I've got to remind her about that, I think. And that's when I remember: Mrs. Kaufman's son is a literary agent. My eyes bulge at how close an opportunity lay all this time. Just like that, I know what Kavia's prediction was all about: today I'm going to suck up my pride and ask Mrs. Kaufman to pass the first couple of chapters to him. The draft is rough, and certainly not ready for anything near publishing, but I know he'll give me an honest opinion. He's a good guy. Besides, this way, Mrs. Kaufman gets to do something to make me feel better *and* gets some new gossip to pass around, which she can then act as if she hasn't. Everyone wins. Early evening, when the sun has sunk low enough to set a purple haze over the sky, I get a hankering for macaroni and cheese. I make a box with tinned milk, which is all we have. It doesn't taste so good. I go to bed early.

"A good day ahead; when the time is right, give Len a little taste—nothing too much. You'll think of just the right creative way with the appearance of the new moon." Kavia hands me this on a slip of paper and slams the door in my face.

I knock with the side of my fist. "Hey, what about punching my gold star?" I yell through the door.

She opens up once more with the hole punch in her hand, clicks it along the side of the star, and closes the door without another word. I guess when you have ESP you don't have to rely so much on customer service.

I head home, make my coffee, and sit out on the terrace, thinking over Kavia's paper slip. It does feel like the right time for action. I lose myself in three pigeons on the neighboring terrace—the one on the non-Richter side. One is pulling little bits of something from the feathers of the other two. I know immediately this is a grandmother pigeon. This is the kind of thing grandmothers do—take care of all the crap.

"Hey there," I hear from the next terrace over.

I turn to see Len. He's fully clothed and in need of a shave, which seems off-kilter for him. He's wearing beat-up khakis and a navy T-shirt with an orange neckline. The sight of him is so welcome, my eyes go slightly damp. I overcompensate with a smile.

There are green patches beneath his eyes. Right away I can tell how drained he is. His smile can't make it a five full seconds. I happen to know what it's like when someone you love is dying and you don't want to talk about it.

"Hey," I say, cocking my head to the side. "Would you like some coffee?" I ask, raising my mug.

He nods, and blinks in a way that's more of a brief nap for tired eyes. "Yes," he says. "That would be wonderful."

"Come around," I say, and wave him over. We both walk through our apartments and meet at my front door.

His hands wends its way to the back of my neck. And there he gives a little tug. I feel like I'm in a really great yoga meditation, or completely stoned.

"Can I make a suggestion?" he says as we trace our way over to the kitchen, my neck burning where he has just slid his hand away.

"What's that?" I ask, trying to sound nonchalant, though my reaction to his touch was anything but. I pour out the coffees, stir in sugar and milk.

"I think you should drop the muumuu," he says. In this stormy afternoon dim, his eyes look even wetter, deeper.

Where does he get off? Even while I explore my rage, I see down hundreds, thousands of miles, the kind of distance you won't be able to see for thirty-five years, to yet another layer of Len, one he's not hiding at this moment. I wonder if he knows he's shown it to me. I sense he doesn't do anything accidentally. *We'll get back there,* I think.

"It's a *housecoat,*" I say in defense. It doesn't sound convincing even to me.

"Oh. I didn't realize it was a *housecoat,*" Len teases.

"Well, it is." I'm not giving in on this, and I hope the look in my eyes tells him to drop it. But for some reason I say more. "And not that it's any of your business, but I actually just put this back on. I wore *jeans* before to Kavia." I say "jeans" like it's this amazing new feat I've tackled.

"Well, whatever it is, it's not good for you," he says, insinuating that he knows why I'm wearing it, and this reason of mine doesn't make it okay. "And what the heck is a Kavia?"

"I don't see how it's your business," I say, knowing he's right. "And Kavia is a person, and I don't see how that's your business, either."

"You don't?" he asks, looking up from the napkin holder he's just fixed—the one Grams and I have been temporarily rebalancing the broken piece of each time we've slipped a napkin out for the last ten years. His eyes are unfair. They unlevel the playing field. They say a lot of things his words don't—like right now, they're saying, *I know what I'm talking about, and I get you and you know it, only this kind of thing is really hard for me;* I'm trying to say back *I know you get me, so come on, let's not let this opportunity go to waste, but I'm not ready to give up the damned muumuu, okay?!* But my eyes just don't talk that way. I'm probably saying something closer to *I have something stuck in my eye.*

I don't answer because obviously there's no answer that won't open a Price Club-sized can of worms. Frankly, I don't think either of us is up for it. I sit down on the back of the chair, the way Grams always yelled at me for, and I stare him down.

When our second pot of water is boiled, I fix the coffees in the French press, the aroma from the two steamy cups wending its way around us. I close my eyes and sniff. "Mmmmmm," I say.

Len's head is shaking when I open my eyes and bring the mugs to the table. "What?" I ask.

"You just—you are such a real person. You appreciate things like *coffee*. That's just the kind of thing that keeps bringing me back here even though I know I'm the last thing you need right now." He takes a sip and refocuses his eyes, a gesture that clearly says the topic's done; he's said enough.

On the radio is this show I've started listening to in the afternoons, *Book Talk*. I get a little frisson, like maybe I could be on there talking about my book one day; I can see myself clearly, sitting at an old-fashioned microphone wearing a purple silky dress with a long necklace. It's such a foreign, confident person's thought for me, my head jolts back in shock.

"What?" he asks this time.

"Nothing," I say. I'm certainly not ready to share that crazy thought with anyone. Merely *having* it is strange enough for now.

Len shakes his head back and forth as if I've amused him, and he slips his hand over mine; I get shivers as he grazes my skin and finally settles his fingertips at my wrist. *A good day,* I think, I'm trying to work over the second half, the part about humanitarianism. It's nice, thinking of people I can help, rather than of myself. I've done way too much of that lately.

And like that, we sit in our own thoughts, stiff but undeniably connected, while we silently finish our coffees, listening to the radio program, but not hearing much above the buzz of our attraction.

There's something that needs to happen and I know what it is. Kavia's words weave themselves into the clearest plan; it's a little startling.

Len's face starts to transform, the smile makes that translucent appearance as we continue the stare-down. "See something you like?" he asks, breaking the silence.

I turn away, face the window so it's easier to answer.

"Yes, I do, as a matter of fact," I say.

He doesn't answer exactly, just sort of groans, and I can hear his breath a little louder as he approaches. I don't merely surprise *him,* I also surprise myself. I slowly lift the muumuu up over my hips, then over my chest, shoulders, and finally let it drop to the floor beside me.

His breath audibly catches in his throat.

My eyes close in pleasure as his hands trace the curves of my sides, then my breasts, before traveling down my hips. I'm leaning against the window so I won't fall over. His cheek fits in the cutout of my neck and shoulder.

On tiptoes, I bend at the knees, pick the housecoat up and pull it over my head, letting it slink back down over my body, before I step away. He bites his lip in a way that underlines Kavia's genius. I dress before anything more can happen.

The next day, there's someone waiting for Kavia in the hallway when I get there. He's about nine feet tall and shaved completely bald, with three earrings along his left eyebrow.

The telephone will bring good fortune, Kavia tells me. She rushes me out, and yanks him in. Just as I get back to the apartment to work this all over out on the terrace, my iPhone rings.

"Viv? You up? It's Wendy."

I see us, whispering into our extensions on opposite sides of the cubicle wall. I get a pang. I miss working with people—especially her. I am surprised by this thought, but it's true. "Lemme guess," I say, feeling unusually silly, "A cucumber disaster?"

"You are so out of the loop, that was three days ago!" she says.

"Bad pork?"

"Yesterday."

"You've finally gone cuckoo for Cocoa Puffs?"

"That's not even perishables; it's dry goods. How are you?"

"I'm . . ." I struggle for a second with what to say—at present things seem like a delicate balancing act, a yarn sculpture that hasn't been secured, everything hovering, hovering, all the pieces are there, set up, but it's not quite all worked out. I wipe my eye with the heel of my palm. "I'm okay."

"Well, hold onto your seat," she says. "I've got news."

"*Wellllllll?* Don't make me sit here all day. What is it?" I sink into my chair by the television, look away from Grams's chair, and prop my skinny pillow up against the back before leaning all the way into it.

"I was promoted to Stan's position."

My toes curl up, my shoulders jump; I nearly drop the phone. "And you're this happy about it?"

"Well, yeah."

"But what about 'we don't give a *carp* about this job' and we hope we don't get promoted and actually have to care about it?"

"Can I be honest with you?"

"I hope so. I mean, I've seen you wet your pants. If you can't be honest with a person who's seen you wet your pants, you're in for a long haul." I'm joking because I'm shocked. I grab for the water glass I left out this morning, wonder if this is long enough for bacteria to form, and then take a sip to soothe my throat, which has suddenly gone dry.

"I, I really, well, I really *like* this job, this field, this publication even. I only ever acted like I didn't because I knew you were always meant for more, that you would never be satisfied covering seasonal deli displays for the rest of your life. I was embarrassed because the truth is, I *am* satisfied with it. Sometimes I even dream about deli displays, and ham hocks, and artisanal Gorgonzola. And once there was this dream with organic cauliflower and Stew, in public relations, but I guess that was something different."

I'm floored. And not just about the Stew part. My hand is frozen, holding the water glass inches from my mouth. I haven't swallowed the bit I've sipped; it's just pooled in there, like rain in a pothole.

"Please say something, Viv. Your respect is so important to me."

I'm not ready to comment on the shock part of this, so I make another joke. "Stew? But he goes to lunch with Stan sometimes, doesn't he?"

"Look, that's not the important bit and you know it. And besides, it was just a dream with Stew. I don't really like him. I mean, I kissed him once in the supply closet, but it was very late, and someone brought in ouzo. But that was ages ago."

I speak, forgetting the water, splashing it out down my chin and over my chest. "I just can't believe *you* were pretending for *my* benefit." All those years of following everyone else's cues, of not trusting myself. Was it possible *everyone* thought themselves as big a phony as I did myself?

"But you're so strong, so ambitious, of course I did. I stayed up nights for weeks thinking of those fish puns. You do it without trying."

Just when you think you've got it, life can shock the shit out of you. Before I hang up with Wendy, I've got a freelance gig—writing about perishables for as long as I'd like to. Sure, it's no dream—but the novel is, and for the first time in my life, I'm really working on that part. Who knows how long that will take, though? And in the meanwhile, this is a practical way to have some security, too. She's the whole department now that Stan's been promoted to advertising chief, so he can work closely with the advertisers, whom the publication is at risk of losing to budget constraints. Terrence is on a completely different publication, the one for the Kosher Only market, and now they want Wendy freelancing out the work; because of the economy it's a way to cut corners.

"Just promise me," she says, "you'll write your book. You'd be doing the world a huge disservice if you didn't." There's a long pause, and then she says, "Following your passion—that's what it's all *a-trout.*"

"Now that wasn't off the cuff?" I ask.

"Took me twenty-five minutes last night . . . did it right after I watched *Friends.*"

"Well, what do you know," I say.

"Nobody knows shit, darling. The sooner you realize that, the better off you'll be. Nobody knows fucking *carp.* That's one you can bet your *bass* on."

"That one? I never heard that one about the bass before," I try.

"Hey, whaddya freaking know? That one actually was spontaneous. There you go: all you can expect is the unexpected. Now, I'm too important to be spending all this time with a piddling freelancer like you, you're a dime a dozen, so let me go perfect my Stan walk already, will ya?"

On Thursday, Kavia is still in her bathrobe when I arrive. Her hair is hidden beneath a towel twisted into a turban, and a fair amount of water is leaking out around her neck. She makes no reference to this at all. Who am I to comment on professionalism? I've been carrying around a glittered gold star. "Look for a humanitarian effort to sink your teeth into; Unus Mundus, one world," she said, and pushed her chair out, ushering me to the door with no excuse whatsoever. I don't argue when she makes a brushing gesture as if I'm a toast crumb on a tabletop, because I know exactly what I'm going to do. I saw an ad on a board in the subway station and it flashes in my mind now. It was something Grams and I were going to do, but never got the chance.

"Hey, Jameson," I say, for the first time since everything happened. I come back down with one of the cardamom coffees and we have our very first post-Grams chat on the way out. "Wait one second," he says when I place the cups on his small desk, next to the olive green house phone that's been here longer than me. Jameson disappears into the supply room, quick as I've ever seen him move, while I watch the door for him. He comes back carrying a brand-new chair: a tall ladderback with a leopard print seat, Grams's favorite pattern. "Something new, something her," he says. I sit in it, feeling like a queen.

"Anytime you want to come down and bring me one of these coffees, I'd sure appreciate it," he says. This is code for we can try to have a little sort of relationship of our own; it won't be nearly the same, not even close, but we'll do the best we can without her.

"Of course," I say, and run into the mailroom before Jameson can see me sob. The mailman's in the middle of distributing everything. I thank him for bringing all the freaking mail. In return I receive a deep sigh, followed by a thoughtful, single-note laugh. I take the elevator up to our floor, marveling at just how much mail there is in my hand. I can't bear to look through it, but I notice all the envelopes are the same size and color and the top one says *Coney Island Hospital* on the left-hand corner. I shove them into my purse, trying not to worry over them, and when the doors slide open, I pass right by our door and ring Richter's bell.

“I think we should,” is what I come out with when Len opens the door.

“ ‘Should,’ what?”

“Take your dad out. We should take him to Manhattan, to see a show.”

Len’s eyes size me up big time. *What the heck are you up to?* they’re saying. He doesn’t move them around so much as stir the ideas swimming beneath. This man has an effect on me. The smile takes over, and this time, stays planted.

“To see a show?” he asks.

“Yeah, I was thinking *The Lion King.*”

*“The Lion King?”*

“I see you’ve mastered mimicry. Maybe next you’ll move onto solid foods.” I’m being sarcastic, but my body is not co-operating. I shift my weight onto my left leg and my other toe darts around the carpet.

Len drags a hand over his chest. He doesn’t have to say “ouch” like everyone else. His look says it all. I’m stuck on that hand, on the notch out of his middle finger, when he throws me off guard by being serious.

“You’re just full of surprises,” he says. He reaches out, grabs for my wrists—each one between his thumb and forefinger. He’s looking at me real close, our faces only a couple of inches apart. His mouth opens like he’s going to say something. But he closes it and smiles for real.

“Are you afraid you’ll like it?” I tease. I cannot tell you how good it is to be close to him. I pick apart and feast on the smells—his shampoo, soap, cologne. I can remember just exactly why I slept with this man only a few hours after I met him.

“Well, I was actually just thinking how we could all use a little *Lion King* at the moment, couldn’t we?” he says, making fun of me a little.

“Sure you were,” I say.

“Just to prove it, I’ll get the tickets,” he says, caressing my wrists before sliding his hands away. We discuss the details, and decide to use the computer at my place to pick the best seats available for tomorrow's show—through those outrageously overpriced brokers. There's no more physical contact, but I feel as if I've been touched everywhere.

Len's just clicked our sale through, and we're waiting for the confirmation page to print.

"Hey," I say.

He turns, slowly.

I don't speak; can't, now that I have one last shot.

"What?" he asks. I'm tempted to say something about what's happened between us, to lose my patience and push too hard.

I lose myself in his eyes for a moment, and then shake my head. I'm going to do things right. The phone rings, helping me to shift gears. Len hears my mother's voice over the answering machine. He can probably read the shock on my face because he starts to gather his credit card and grab for the printer paper that hasn't quite come through all the way yet, and motions toward the door.

"Should I go?" he says, picking up on my tension.

"Nah." I shake my head.

On the machine, my mother is off and running. It's the first time she's returned one of my calls since she left after the shiva. "Vivian, I am going to need you to take Grams's money out of the bank for me. This ice cream thing is really coming together, and all I need is the cash to get it to the next level. This is it, it really is." I can only imagine how she spent the money she got hocking Grams's lovely jewelry. "I can feel it in my bones," she continues. I hate the earnestness in her tone. "The fact that I can actually come up with the money at just the right time is a sign that this was meant to be."

My throat lumps and thickens. There isn't a lot of money,

and it's mine just as much as Grams's. My name's on the bank account. It doesn't belong to my mother; Grams went over this more times than I can remember. This is the money that some parent would have left for me if they had thought of it. Your mom will claw through all my jewelry first chance she gets, and that'll be worth more than you know, Viv.



Bless his heart, Len's acting like he can't hear it, clearing away our mugs and rinsing them at the sink. It's ten thousand dollars, this money my mother is talking about, and it's meant to sit there for me in case of an emergency. And there's a reason my grandmother didn't leave it for my mother, because she'd waste it on exactly this kind of ridiculous scheme.

Still, I feel an ache in the arch of my foot, and this ache can mean only one thing: my mother still has power over me. No matter what happens, I can never let go of the idea that maybe, one day, she'll come around and be a real mother to me. I think of her leaning over my father's casket—shaking and sobbing silently after her voice has worn out—and I feel just like I did then: like a giant, awful burden on someone who was never meant to handle this kind of thing on her own. I could have made things easier if I'd really wanted her to stay, I could have scored better grades, not thrown her boyfriend's jeans out the front door. And I can only imagine how much more pointed those feelings are inside her now that Grams is gone. I'm the only one left to blame.

I'm cold and tingly with a mix of anger, nerves, resentment, and duty.

When the message clicks to an end, Len and I are silent. The ancient tape rewinds.

"That's embarrassing." I say exactly what I'm thinking.

"Don't be embarrassed," Len says. "Do you want my advice?" he asks.

"Sure," I say, politely but unsure. I start to walk him through the details, and I realize I'm actually comfortable talking to him about something so personal, more than comfortable—I'm glad he's there to discuss it. I've never talked about anything like this with a guy, with anyone other than Grams and Wendy, and Kavia recently. I was loath to let a vulnerable part of myself show.

I get through the long, winding, full-of-asides-with-asides-of-their-own version of my life, and end it at the morning of the funeral. It's the first reference we've made to our night together, and there's a strange pause following it—during which I fear for what else I might not remember.

"I don't think this is what you want to hear," he says, "but you need to take control of the situation."

"That's easy for you to say. You're a Scorpio ascendant," I say without realizing how silly that must sound, how much of an obsessed freak I must sound like. I might as well have been twirling my hair around my finger and talking about my crush on Kirk Cameron. "I mean, you seem like you are," I backpedal, and then, realizing that didn't come out a whole lot better, I try once more: "I mean, that's what my friend Kavia said." *Oh fuck*.

Len's just standing, his chin tucked back like he's anticipating I won't be making sense anytime soon.

I snap my eyes shut, as if my lids could actually hide me behind them. I pin my hopes on the possibility that he'll give me a pass, and move on.

When I open them Len's got that fabulous smile turned all the way up. *The submarine has surfaced! Watch out!* His eyes are glittering, laughing at me, but glittering all the same. "Please don't tell me you put stock in that B.S."

I try to give no reaction at all.

Mercifully, he continues on his original tack. "What I mean is, you have to stand up to your mother, the way your grandmother said. You've got to tell her where things stand. You owe it to your grandmother to do it."

I nod my head. This is exactly what I feared. Part of me has always thought that was true, that standing up to her was the only way, but part of me isn't so sure: and *that* is why I have never stood up to her all these years. Part of me thinks my mother requires a special kind of patience and handling, a kind maybe only I understand, and that yelling at her or putting her in her place will merely drive her farther away from me than she's been keeping herself all this time. So, what I normally do is nothing. Which, honestly, hasn't worked so well, either. "Thanks," I say, feeling I've shared as deeply as I'm capable of for the moment.

"Hey, I'm gonna go tell my dad about our trip tomorrow," he says, cradling the back of my head again as he stands. In the frenzy of his fingertips, I can barely remember what we were talking about.

He reminds me, halfway out the door. "Promise me one thing, though."

"What?" I ask.

"Just don't do *nothing*. Time goes by way faster than you can imagine."

Boy don't I know it. I nod my head tightly, press my lips together. I wish that *he* didn't have to know it. But maybe that's what brought us together in the first place . . . one thing leads to another and then to another, and without the same string of events, who knows if we'd ever have even crossed paths. *Unus Mundus,* I think, truly thankful, and maybe, *maybe*—on the verge of some understanding.

His head twists back my way; he sees me out of the corner of his eye. "You do believe all of that horoscope stuff. Don't you?"

Blinky, I cross my fingers behind my back, swallow hard, and do too much head shaking. "Of course not!" I say in a tone I don't even recognize. "That's for teenagers in love with Kirk Cameron."

"Right," he says, inspecting me in a very thorough way for someone who's only able to see me from the periphery of his vision field. "Hey, I don't think anyone's been in love with Kirk Cameron for some time."

"Speak for yourself, buddy," I say.

"Don't change the subject. Look, I get it. You're a little crunchy. Maybe it's part of why you're so nice. Maybe it's part of your charm."

"Stop. It's not. There's no charm! There's no astrology obsession!" I smack the air to prove the point.

"Well, just in case there is, I wanted to show you something."

He reaches behind his back, underneath his T-shirt. He pulls out a small hard cover book. *The Collected Works of Emily Dickinson.* It's the exact same edition Grams bought me back in college. I started looking at it last night.

"What's this? Are you into poetry?"

"Me?" He makes like I've kicked him in the groin. "Never. You wanna know yourself? Join the military, run a marathon. Push yourself to the limit. That's the only way I know. But I'm sensing that you might be into it. Plus, I hear from Mrs. Kaufman that you're writing a book. If anyone knows how to turn self-reflection into art, it's this chick."

"I thought you weren't into it."

"I'm not," he says.

"You're funny," I say.

He ignores this point. "So, I went to that little used-book store—it's quite charming. I'm not sure if you've ever been there, but it seems right up your alley, it's an old dreamy kind of a place. Something from another time."

I certainly know the place. I can't even count how many rainy afternoons Grams and I spent there, rifling through the messy shelves.

"I thought, if you're going to insist on metaphysical crystals and chants and things, you might as well explore another aspect of it. Here's something I think you'll really like. Another way of expressing things."

I hug it to myself.

"I guess you like it," he says.

"Nah, I hug all books. It's something I do."

"I thought you're meant to hug trees. Maybe I've got it wrong."

"Honestly, I have this book. It's one of my favorite things. And I think the fact that you bought it for me is great. The exact same edition and everything."

"Maybe it shows that we're more alike than you think. Just not in the ways of sanity. You're all by yourself there." Only, he doesn't mean this. He puts his hand at the back of my head and looks at me like he might never leave me alone again.

I shove him out the door before collapsing to the floor on the other side of it.

# 24.

♈ ♉ ♊ ♋ ♌ ♍ ♎ ♏

*The very idea of a bird is a symbol and a suggestion to the poet. A bird seems to be at the top of the scale, so vehement and intense his life. . . . The beautiful vagabonds, endowed with every grace, masters of all climes, and knowing no bounds—how many human aspirations are realised in their free, holiday-lives—and how many suggestions to the poet in their flight and song!*

—JOHN BURROUGHS *(1837–1921)*, *BIRDS AND POETS*

T*he next morning,* after listening to my new radio program, writing a couple of pages of my book, and sharing coffee with Jameson, I take the train to Kavia's for a full one-hour appointment. Thankful for the time she has to give me today, I tell her about my mother's call. I've thought about it all night, and then all morning after she called again at two. I couldn't sleep for more than fifteen minutes at a pop.

"This, Viv, is the lesson of your rising sign, it is what I told you. You are more in tune with the needs of others than your mother is. And because of this, you have the more rewarding relationships, like the one with your grandmother—but the burden of it is, that you have to be patient with those, like your mother, who cannot catch up with you, those who don't get it. What you should do for now is ignore her completely. Let her spin her wheels about this, and then she'll give up."

For the first time since coming to seek her advice, I get a sinking feeling in my gut that there might be more complexity to the situation than Kavia has lent it. I shake it off; the woman's got a perfect scorecard. And I certainly don't. *My* gut feelings never gets me further than Roll N Roaster.

There are two messages from my mother on the machine when I get home. I erase them and meet Len and Richter and head off to see *The Lion King*. We have such a wonderful time, I feel even more tied to following Kavia's lead: she's right again.

On our *Lion King* excursion, it feels like a journey to a different country, if not a different planet altogether. Len is driving Richter and me in his Land Rover, across the Manhattan Bridge, listening to Richter's favorite singer, Buddy Holly. My hair is wet and clean and I derive a simple pleasure from this.

I'm not going to lie. Richter doesn't look good. In fact, when I first saw him, waiting in a wheelchair in front of his door, I had to try very hard to look cheerful. Sitting in the backseat now, I remember what Len said about the peaks and valleys being insignificant, that his father is not going to get better. It's impossible not to draw parallels here, so once they've been stretched along my mind and I have to step over them with every thought and sensation, I try to coexist with them. It's the best I can do. *People die,* I tell myself. *It has nothing to do with you.* Already, the fear of failing Richter in some major way has entered my head. I care about these guys. I think they might care about me.

We have the windows open. The sea air feels wonderful as it

whips my hair back from my face. I'm unfamiliar with the rockabilly beats sailing through the speakers, and yet I find my head easily, surprisingly, swinging to the melancholy riffs in a way that's completely new and yet comfortably natural at the same time. My heart squeezes around the haunting steel guitar—it reminds me of that sad, sad *plink* of a ukulele.

Every so often, I notice Len noticing me in the rearview. Maybe, even when you screw things up terribly, some things that are meant to be will just *be*. Everything feels so right at this exact moment, I can't help but feel that must be true. The music builds in momentum. By the time the third track is at its crescendo, we're merging onto the Belt Parkway toward the city, and I'm something close to sublime.

At around the time the Belt turns into the BQE, Len carefully hands me the CD cover—the exchange is not exactly all business, but there's no flirty finger-grazing, either—and when I bring it before me, I look deeply into Holly's eyes. They are extraordinarily kind, soft and intense, sort of like Len's. His iconic glasses solidify his aura, as if we have to see through them to see into Buddy. *Are we one world, Buddy?*

It hits me; the music is familiar because Len loaded it into my iPhone. The songs must have become part of my consciousness. I wonder which one of them up there in the front seats exposed the other to Buddy.

"This music is fantastic," I say, squeezing myself up between the two front seats. I pull my hair back into an elastic, feeling queerly female as the two of them watch me—Len in the rearview and Richter cranking back from the passenger seat. Secured, my ponytail swings back and forth, jolly of its own accord. Richter's mouth rises into Len's half-smile. My heart thuds. They are father and son. And Richter might die before they make things right between them.

"Buddy?" Richter says, with the enormous emphasis on both syllables the way only New York Jews of a certain age can manage. And then he gives me my answer, watching me now in the visor mirror. "It's good, isn't it? You know, we were the same age; both wore the same glasses; both extraordinarily handsome in an unassuming way."

I smile and notice in the rearview Len tries to pin his down with a tooth. Richter continues. "I went to Lubbock, where he lived, for my second honeymoon. It's where Len was conceived. But I guess that's where the similarity ends; I never did anything with my life before . . ." He leaves the idea lingering there, but we all know where it ends.

What can I, of all people, possibly have to say that might be of any merit to a man who married and lost two women, whose heart feeds on this kind of music, who has a terminal illness, who's ushered thousands of children safely across the street, and as thanks for it all, bore the honor of being called "Officer" Richter for twenty some-odd years?

Nothing comes to mind. And if it came to Len's, he's not saying.

Richter continues, filling the awkward gap. "So many mishaps and eerie coincidences about who was gonna be on that little plane Buddy crashed in, that—Beechcraft Bonanza was what they called it. Supposed to be Buddy and his backup band, Allsup, and Waylon Jennings, but it was the Big Bopper—you kids know him, don't you? He's the one who asked Jennings for his seat, 'cause he wasn't feeling all that good. And Carl Bunch was supposed to be on the flight, but he was in the hospital with—of all things—frostbite, because of the tour bus's bum heater!"

He's so animated, it's almost possible to rewind to what he used to look like. *Len's father!* I remember suddenly the generous, full-sized candy bars he handed out on Halloween when I was a child. I should have appreciated him more, drawn him pictures of princesses with cone hats. Lord knows I made enough to go around. To think of all those dinners he must have eaten alone while Grams and I were right next door.

"Ritchie Valens and Allsup flipped a coin for the fourth seat, but Allsup lost. Unbelievable how that plane crashed—just a few minutes after it took off, around one a.m. The owner found it a few hours later just eight miles from the airport where it took off. The three musicians were thrown from the wreckage; they all died on impact."

I get the sensation of hairs pricking up on the back of my neck. It's inexplicable, the way you can connect so deeply to a work of art, and then you realize that the person who created it is dead. Also, there's Richter, explaining this with such tenacity it's impossible to think that he, too, will be lost to us soon enough. When we die, where do our passions go? *Unus Mundus,* I think, and this time I'm not being sarcastic, *this* time, I picture a mist of energy swirling endlessly, meshing, drifting apart, like fairy dust, or powdered sugar riding along a breeze. I see Grams, and even my mother.

"But would you believe the craziest part was that the story was overshadowed by another plane crash that happened on the exact same day? In New York City, American Airlines Flight 320 crashed en route to LaGuardia Airport, killing sixty-five people. What a coincidence! Don McLean called it the Day the Music Died."

I can't help it. The first thing I think when I hear the word *coincidence* is *synchronicity,* and then I think, clear as day, that those things happened on the same day because of what the stars said would happen. I think of that and I am so freaked out that cold creeps into my chest and sits there, though it must be 89 degrees. I'm hearing the music, the traffic zooming by, but nothing's registering. It's just eerie, whooshing through my ears.

Len hasn't said much—come to think of it, he hasn't said *anything* since we got in the car. The parts of his face I can see in the side view and the rearview look closed off; that smile is nowhere to be seen. It reminds me of the way he was on the night we watched *Lost*. It's as if he's set his features to a default mode and can't find the button to reposition them. There must be incredible tension between the two of them. Now I think of it, I don't think I've even seen either of them speak directly to the other at all.

Soon enough, we're rounding the base of the BQE, by the bridge, and there's the Manhattan skyline, looking too close to be real, same as always. According to the liner sheets, Buddy's "Blue Days, Black Nights" accompanies our journey across the bridge, and I can't help but see the city entirely differently under its spell. It has a timelessness that I've always sensed but couldn't quite articulate. It's like the symbols of astrology, I think. Can art do the same thing as astrology? Can it show you things in a way you wouldn't have thought of, or might have thought of but couldn't quite name? I couldn't tell this for certain, but I gather Len and Richter experience it the same austere way.

We drive up Broadway, and the traffic thickens; car horns and screeching brakes wend into a noise landscape, as do screaming sirens and music from rolled-down car windows.

We pull up to the theater, and before I have a chance to open my door, Len's got it for me. He opens Richter's door after he helps me out, and then goes around the back to get the wheelchair. The idea of him unfolding this contraption sends a tightness squeezing around my throat. We are all wondering, in one shade or another, how anything can ever be the same again. Things have grown heavier, taken on a soaked weight.

Richter is quiet as he allows Len to guide him into the seat. I look away.

"Here are your tickets," Len says to me when he's through, and not, I notice, to his father, who must know he's been relegated to child status; he might think he deserves it. "You two go sit down; I checked, they have an elevator to get Dad to his seat. I'm going to park the car." His eyes hold mine; there is so much he's not saying.

Sex aside, we have toed across that line into shared terrain; we were strangers, but now what we are to each other has a life force of its own—it's stretched and twisted up the regular course of time, done crazy things to minutes and hours and days, so that it appears we've known each other always. And thanks to what I've learned about Scorpios, about human nature, really, I won't lose this once-in-a-lifetime opportunity.

The thing about Len and Richter is that they need each other but can't quite figure out how to capitalize on it, how to navigate the barricades. I'm beginning to see how life can quickly extend out in this way, if you aren't careful, with close, but not quite complete, connections piling up like old newspaper sections you promise yourself you'll get around to reading.

We watch Len climb back into the car and then roll our way up the ramp.

We smush inside the elevator with an usher. "He's never going to forgive me," Richter says. The irony of his status is not lost on me: he spent decades safely crossing people from one corner to the next, and now he's helpless, stuck in the middle of a road with no clear path to get across.

"That's not true," I say, though I can't help but feel relief the second we've parted ways from Len.

The elevator comes to a smooth stop. The door slides open, into its secret pocket, and out of the blue, a bird—*a freaking pigeon*—flies right into the car with us. "What the—?" the young usher exclaims, swatting at it.

It's amazing, beautiful. The oily iridescent blue feathers on its head glimmer in the soft elevator light. I can't help but think this is happening just for my benefit, like the bird's a court jester and I'm a queen. I recognize this scene: the same thing happened on the boardwalk the day I sat watching the waves with Len. A rush of warmth soothes my neck, my face. There *is* a plan. This squawking bird is trying to tell us that things *do* happen for a reason.

Richter's equally astounded. "Beautiful," he says, "stunning." And it is. We watch, heads tipped, as the speckled bird flaps furiously. The usher swats at it with both hands, jumping a little so the car bounces.

Images of Grams pervade my mind—I see her, feel her, smell her Jean Naté—in the most concrete way, and then she marches on, down the hallway of our building, through the door to the incinerator. She's gone, but I've managed to hold on to a little piece of her, the tag from her blouse, an automatic teller receipt—not her exactly, but something at least still warm from her touch.

The doors close and we're stuck in there, ascending above our stop. As if possessed, the usher will not leave this bird be. My hand is on Richter's shoulder, and I'm squeezing. His fingers shoot up to my arm and squeeze me right back. I have half a mind to lean over and bear-hug him. Has he seen Grams, too?

"Goddammit!" the pink-skinned usher yells, punching at the air.

"Don't say that about God," Richter says, shocking the two of us.

The usher stops suddenly, as if realizing he's fighting a losing battle. The click of wings furiously flapping sounds flauntingly alive. Richter's hand squeezes a little tighter. The usher pushes the button for our floor again and the bird is zigzagging over our heads. We reach our floor and the door slides open again. The usher, redder even than seconds earlier, fixes his slight eyebrows in sturdy concentration. He can't help himself; he takes another swing. This sends the bird out; she soars through the doors, up, up into the far reaches of the domed lobby ceiling beyond. The bird stretches her wings wide—wider than I've seen any measly pigeon do before—and flies swiftly back our way, the quick motions lending her a fuzzy appearance. In her beak, she grabs the usher's little monkey hat, and flies down and out of sight.

Richter and I exchange glances, and I can tell you this: he is thinking the exact thing I am.

In the aftermath there is confusion. Running after his hat, the usher forgets us completely, and I roll Richter over to our seats without assistance.

"Wow," Richter says. It's the most either of us can bring ourselves to say.

Less easily than Len had outside, I support Richter as he rises from the chair and, probably too quickly to feel good, sinks into the end seat. The maneuver is humbling for both parties—helping like he's a child a guy who isn't used to help. But whatever we exchanged in that elevator eases the awkwardness. This is territory where I have failed and my chest tingles with that, but I've made peace with this for the most part. And so I quickly regain perspective, refocus on Richter: I was incorrect; it isn't anything like being a child. The equal transmission of tenderness, the surrendering of ego, it's subtle and unspoken, but inherent to the whole thing; and this makes me think there is hope for this father and son after all.

In the buzz of possibility, I am emboldened. "Hey," I say, "I don't know what happened between the two of you; I don't know your reasons, or whether Len even knows them, but you should just yell at each other really loud, with a ton of fist wagging, and then forgive each other. Let it go. You both wear that tough exterior, but it's what you both want. It's not just for you. It's for him, too. What he'll get from you is worth showing your cards; worth it in spades. He might act like he doesn't, but he needs it, too." I leave out the Scorpio ascendant jargon, the Pluto Ruler bit. It doesn't seem as important as what it represents: that Len has to go through an intense process in order to heal. But that he's getting there. "I can tell," is as much as I say to this point.

I grab for Richter's hand when a couple of tears spill down his cheek. I recognize his look—he's fighting against things that are so obvious spelled out this way, there's nothing you can do but throw yourself into the blazing truth of them.

Len emerges through the doorway, just a few feet away. "Don't say anything," Richter says. "You don't know what I've done." Shame and guilt rim his eyes like kohl.

I nod my head as Len makes his way across the patterned, hushed red carpet toward us. He has the look of a guy with the entire weight of the world on his shoulders. He sits in the seat we've left open for him, right in between Richter and me. "What'd I miss?" he says, looking down at the *Playbill* I hand him.

Richter and I exchange looks, but in the end I say, "Nothing really." The bird was something just for Richter and me.

The lights dim, and in seconds, the theater goes black. I recognize this frisson of excitement as a show is about to begin, recall Grams squeezing my hand in expectation. I gulp in the air of history, of people who've sat in this very seat for decades, loosening the stuffing, working down the shape on the sides, many of them probably long gone. I plan to enjoy this for both of us, for all of us. A crazy thought pops into my head, but I know it's true. I'm going to enjoy this for my mother, too.

The curtains begin their smooth, swift ascent just as the bird makes its return; her wings perfectly poised, she soars across the stage, and drops the miniature red usher's hat directly onto it with a rushing sound—air, amplified under the microphones—and then, without so much as a glance, she flies off. A little actor boy dressed in a brilliant lion headdress, painted in brown and orange streaks over his body, runs out to thunderous applause and laughter. He grabs the funny hat from the wooden stage, takes hold of its elastic chin strap, and tucks the thing under his arm, all business, as he runs toward stage left.

And then out of nowhere, it seems, he remembers where he is, stops suddenly, and turns a quick back flip, tumbling high and higher still.

The sloped seating area erupts in applause; sharp whistles are blown. The boy's smile is the shamelessly proud kind that only children can manage. Richter's eyes meet mine. I wag my head sternly. *We are all going to be okay* is what I'm trying to say; I'm so sure of it, I can taste it, delicious, soothing, like fresh potato latkes slipped from the frying pan.

Suddenly it's all business again. The performance-to-audience illusion is safely restored, and the stage is bathed in rich blue light. The color is rich and powerful. My heart races; the space floods with dancers. They scatter, splendidly costumed in authentic animal patterns; antelope and lion masks balance on the dancers' heads, chiffon flutters from hands to waists like delicate sets of wings, headdresses and tribal insignias painted on bare skin enchant. Movement, rhythm, pacing, it all builds in my chest and pulses through my limbs. A single voice from the stage sings out, startles me so I push back into my seat; Len's arm has extended back there and I jump forward when my back makes contact with it.

I can't make out which body the voice belongs to down there, but it's strong as hell, warbling a single word, stretched out, shaping the sounds like bubbles through a very special wand, long and haunting, glittering and pure. The word is African, and I don't know it, but I get the sense of it clear as day, it's life and power—a symbol language, like those on the ecliptic Kavia pointed out to me. I'm wholly immersed, and the story hasn't even begun.

Throughout the entire first half I carefully hover an inch or two from Len's arm, which hasn't moved away, but hasn't made a move toward me, either. People are so moved by the production, they constantly break into applause, which spreads from one person to the next in increasing volume and intensity.

I hadn't realized how the musical score of this production is so deeply ingrained into our social consciousness. I mean, I've Hakuna Matata'd with the best of 'em, but from the very first song, "The Circle of Life," I'm so affected, it's no use trying to stop the sniffling. In fact, for once, I don't want to. It is such a beautiful song, packed with so much simple truth, that I can't help but believe everything happening is the most natural thing in the world, that we are, the four of us—Richter and Len, Grams and me—on different spokes of the Circle, and that it *will* all somehow be okay. I sit back, Len's hand now on my shoulder as if it had been waiting for just this exact realization to throw me back: Unus Mundus, the Circle, a Song, a philosophy, a religion, whatever works to grind your issues down and shove them into something you recognize: a sausage! A hamburger! A meatball!

I was meant to come here today. We all were.

The scene unfolding before me is so powerful, its ups and downs send my eyes and chest swirling. I float along its incredible movement, and I am completely, utterly swept away. I forget myself and lean back completely slack; I feel Len's forearm tense and then relax.

It's a story of a father and son, of having to cut your way through dangerous territory; it's the story of avoiding and then eventually becoming an adult—ready or not—and it's the story of loss, death, love, and making peace with your lot in life.

By the time the curtain sails down for intermission, Len's hand is back on his own mahogany armrest, and we've all got our heads buried in *Playbill,* trying to conceal our red faces and glassy eyes.

"This is fantastic," Richter says, facing the wondrous height of the ceiling. His face tilts just the slightest bit toward his son, though his son won't quite look at him. This I'm counting as progress.

"I absolutely love it," I echo the sentiment.

"It's pretty good, I guess," Len says, a sort of tough-guy joke. His shoulder lifts in a little shrug. "Alright, who needs a soda?" he asks, maybe having revealed too much.

He stands. My arm tingles. We've been sitting in such close proximity, experiencing the music, the dancing, the colors, the emotions, and something has passed through the tiny patches of skin where our bodies met—our elbows, knees, my shoulder, his fingers. The contact removed, breath comes easier. More natural.

"He's warming up," I say when Len is out of earshot.

"You think so?" Richter asks. He so wholeheartedly wants to believe me. "I don't know."

"The two of you are more alike than you think," I say. "You both want to be stoic. You want to be the rock, the mensch, and that is a wonderful thing, but it isn't always practical.

Sometimes you have to risk everyone's security, even your own, to let people in, to rely on someone in a way that brings you close."

Richter shakes his head to indicate he understands. "I'm a Scorpio," he says, shrugging. "We're bullheaded."

I nod my head. "I know," I say, and smile. I reach over and hug him. It feels really good.

Len smuggles in our sodas, charms the usher out of her scolding look with a smile, and heroically quenches our thirst.

Richter wraps both shaky hands around his enormous novelty *Lion King* cup, looks directly at his son, and says, "Thanks. That's wonderful."

"I love soda, but he never lets me drink it," Richter says to me.

My chest numbs over. I get it. It's only a Coke six times larger than Len's and my regular Simba-topped ones with crazy straws bobbing in them, and not exactly the same thing as a son declaring his dedication to reviving a dead relationship with his deteriorating father. But, in a rudimentary, quite promising way, it is *exactly* that.

I think Len might cave and ruin the moment; it looks like he has something snarky to say. It is clear from the way one side of his mouth turns up, the way his eye crinkles. But he smooths it all out, goes blank. I sit at the edge of my seat. *This is it; they are going to speak.* It's so close I can taste it.

Len takes a sip, his lips over the crazy straw, his nose close to Simba's, and Richter and I lose it: we're laughing hysterically, wet eyes, loud wails.

"What?" Len asks, but we don't answer. We just keep laughing until he gets caught up in the wave and laughs, too.

My nose prickles when I catch it: Len's gorgeous smile, directed first at me and then swinging behind my shoulder to his father, where it stays until it turns into a soft, forgiving grimace.

It was so quick you could have missed it. After, Len leans forward over his soda, as if there's an indecipherable code printed down the side of his cup. The lights dim twice and we direct our eyes toward the stage. I'm all the more hungry for a happy ending for this poor lion now that our own journey has begun. Simba finds his own unique way, and it's so deeply satisfying; despite all odds, he finds love—a different kind of love than he had with his father. Not a replacement—never that. And finally, he finds the courage to accept his place in the world.

I'm not dumb: I know this is merely a Broadway show with a specific Broadway rhetoric—good and evil, lofty symbols of right and wrong, and spick-and-span happy endings that we reach in two and a half hours, allowing for fifteen minutes' intermission. However, after the conclusion, I am left knowing this, too: I have begun to build a new life, not trying to replace Grams, not even battling jungle animals or saving anyone's life, but significant all the same: drinking coffee, putting on clothes, trying to write, trying to salvage my chance at the real kind of love, the true thing, with Len.

Len's hand inches close to mine again; we are sharing the slender wooden armrest and there's merely a millimeter between his fingertips and my thumb. I can feel his warmth, the rush of blood beneath the skin, before his fingers grip mine.

Simba assumes his role as king, and we cheer with no self-consciousness at all, like tourists, like the children we once were, always wanted to be. I hoot with the sea of people, completely unrestrained, not Viv Sklar-Singleton, but guest in a party of three, an audience member, a Brooklynite, a New Yorker, an American, a human being, a living thing, a part of the universe. That's what good art can do.

If he weren't wearing one himself, I would blush when Len notices my tremulous grin. We catch each other in a glance, which burns behind my eyelids like the sun after I've stared too long. We turn back to the cast, who bow to the unrelenting clapping, the satisfied roar of applause, yet again. Someone throws a rose, which lands at Simba's feet. He bends down, exuberant, springy as ice cold Jell-O. He holds the rose in his mouth, and jumps another backflip. He lands perfectly, lightly on his feet, and thrusts his hands in the air like Mary Lou Retton. "Thank you," he mouths to the audience, with the kind of poise, the kind of peace we all aspire to.

We eat dinner at a place down in Little Italy where Len knows the owner and all the wait staff from back when he was a child. All three of us are a little giddy, overtired. I see us reflected in the mirror lining the wall and I can't help but think how much we look like a family, slurping our pasta and laughing a little too loudly. I allow myself the fantasy and position us around a browned, seasoned Thanksgiving turkey, mounds of side dishes dotting the table like in a Stove Top ad.

On the way home, Richter falls asleep and I get the oddest feeling I've imagined it all; the two of them haven't made any headway, Len and I are not okay, and I am no better off than the day Grams died. That is ridiculous, I tell myself. I'm just tired; it's the latest I've been out in weeks.

Len and I don't talk; we don't want to wake Richter. When we climb out back at Seacoast, I open Richter's door while Len heaves the wheelchair from the back. We have a sort of rhythm after three goes at this. My heart drops when I notice Richter has wet himself. *It's the circle of life,* I tell myself, *the circle of life.* But this seems so much more *can't get there from here,* that it's hard to overlook.

His father now passed out and urine-soaked, Len can, and does, look at him straight-on. He stares and stares, as if at a curiosity at a carnival, and then, finally, he pulls me tight next to him. He squeezes me into his side with such force, like he wants to find something in me—the strength to ride this forgiveness for the long haul. I want to give it to him.

A great breath rises up from the very bottom of his rib cage; it rocks us both slightly, like a gentle wave. I can sense the streams of our breath merge into one. He turns, and I can feel a warm cloud at the side of my face. It is more powerful than a kiss. If I didn't know for certain before, I want to go screaming it from the terrace now: I love this man. And this man I love is standing on the edge of a cliff, the same cliff I have spent most of my life peering over. I search for his hand, and I close my fingers around it tightly.

There's a clip-clop along the walkway. It's Lluba Sobiesky, an off-the-boat Russian from 5K. She approaches nonchalantly, her chin higher than her giant alligator high heels.

Len hinges the door gently closed to conceal his father.

She calls out to us, "Rachel Valmay's cat *seek.* Is *keed-knee.*" As Lluba says this, her fingers squeeze in a gesture I'm not sure is appropriate to *keed-knees*, or in any social situation, for that matter. She starts to click past us in her backless shoes.

Len hasn't had the experience I have with these Russian accents. "Her cat is a Sikh and bit a kid's knee?" he asks, scrunched up.

"She's sick," I say. "She's sick and has a bad kidney."

*"Ooooooh,"* he says, working out the syllables with his index finger.

We laugh. It's such a treat.

Lluba turns back, like she forgot something. But she keeps on walking. "You donate in mailroom," she says. "Big cans."

"I'm not even going to touch that one," Len says.

Lluba continues alongside the manicured hedge, which she reaches out to grab handfuls of, picking them apart and dropping them in a trail all the way to the avenue.

At home, there's another message from my mother on the answering machine. I try to sleep, but I can't. It's too quiet and I'm restless—feeling it's time to go on to the next phase of my life but not sure what that is. Curious, I go downstairs to the mailroom. Sure enough, there is a huge sign posted over the boxes on our side, with a picture of the damned black-and-white-spotted cat in its pink rhinestone collar, asking for donations to be put in a giant Folgers Crystals can that Rachel must have got at the Price Club in Bensonhurst. The residents have moved on from grieving for Grams to campaigning for a *keed-knee* for a cat, the same way that last February, they stopped campaigning against the pigeon-feeding Mrs.

Sigmund—apparently to blame for every drop of poo on every terrace on the building's façade—as soon as the management increased the price of a washing machine cycle from seventy-five cents to a buck. This is the kind of population I'm dealing with.

"Nothing's too small," it says in perfectly straight print, which I could pick up out of a line-up. It's Mrs. Kaufman's. Someone I can't identify penciled in a thought balloon sprouting from the cat's tiny pink mouth. Inside is a puffy-lettered "mewwwwwwwwwwwwwwwwwwwwwwl."

I have a mind to give $10,000 to that cat and call it a day. In the meanwhile, I dig a twenty out of Grams's little purse and fold it in half, stuff it down inside the slit in the plastic top.

Back upstairs, I make lists of the contacts I have so I can make calls for my first assignment with Wendy the Big Boss Woman tomorrow. Now that my mother's calls have stopped disturbing the quiet, I am sort of wishing she *would* call, daring her to test me, to push me to the point of no return just to see what I'll do. I'm as curious as anyone else. But she doesn't ring.

In the dim light of the barely rising sun, I coax my snarled hair into a rubber band, tie it loose down at the base of my skull. I yank the muumuu over my head and pull on a pair of leggings, the elastic snapping around my thinning waist. Peeking into the hush of my grandmother's room, I open her closet and pull the light chain, finger through her neatly rehung garments on motley unmatched hangers collected over the years from clothing stores and dry cleaners, until I find what I want: the purple sweater I bought her for her seventieth birthday. We laughed and laughed. She knew how I felt about purple, and I knew she hated it. She wore it, but only so she could say, "God, this is the world's ugliest sweater." I'd introduce her down the street like a circus act, "Ladies and Gentlemen, step up and check out the senior citizen in the world's ugliest sweater!" God, I miss her.

I pull it over my head, close my eyes, and let her scent hug me. I don't know how much time passes before I'm ripped from the delicate portal of peace I had managed to slip into. It's the doorbell.

"Coming!" I yell, pulling the sweater over my head. I replace it with the muumuu, run out of the bedroom and around the corner to tackle the length of the hallway. I fling myself toward the door like a person who's got something to hide.

# 25.

♈ ♉ ♊ ♋ ♌ ♍ ♎ ♏

*The irony of love is that it guarantees some degree of anger, fear and criticism.*

—Harold H. Bloomfield

It's Len. I peep shamelessly through the hole, exploring in a way I wouldn't dare if he could see me. He looks sleepy, huggable, like someone in an ad for fabric softener. He's in sleep-worn shorts and a white undershirt that's slightly torn at the neckline. Given his normal edge, his impenetrable prophylactic exterior, this pajamas intimacy gets me right in the chest. The panicked rhythm there begins to slow. It's been a long night, and I am reminded by the sight of him exactly why he is the only thing I want.

"You gonna stop checking me out through the peephole and just let me in already?"

I bang my head on the broken cuckoo clock next to the door when I pull back with a start. "Ow," I say.

I hear him breathe a round of clipped chuckles as I click

the four locks open, slide and drop the chain, and watch it dangle for a second too long. Something is about to change.

When I swing the door open, it's as if the thing unfolds in slow motion. There's the Len I saw through the peephole, but now I can smell him and *feel* him—cold and hot and kinetic, a miracle of physics.

He doesn't speak.

This throws me. "What?" I ask, suddenly self-conscious.

He either hasn't heard me or has chosen not to answer.

The air between us changes, thickens like a really nice gravy. There are those eyes, and they are the wettest I've seen them, and they seem to go on and on and on—all the way through to the floaty silhouette I picture as his soul—a haystack sketch by Monet. My hand fidgets inside the pocket of the housecoat.

Len shakes his head back and forth; a smile floats briefly across his features.

"What?" I say again, trying to sound irritated this time.

"I told you that wasn't right," he says. His voice is heavy with sleep around the edges. His tongue slips to the corner of his mouth; my heart beats faster. "You need to get rid of the housecoat."

"So what are you going to do about it?" I taunt, my hands at my hips. I'm all instinct; I might lead myself directly into the mouth of a shark, a wildebeest.

"I didn't want to have to do this," he says, and lifts me up, one arm beneath my shoulders and the other under my knees. I have dreamed of being carried this way, felt ashamed at how wonderful I imagined it, scared little me carried off to safety—nothing but an indulgent dream at a weak moment. But it *is* everything I imagined.

He carries me down the hallway to my bedroom, our eyes glued. He kicks the door open with a toe, slowly, like he's done this zillions of times. Len sits me down on my bed real gently, and begins to open the buttons on the muumuu painfully slowly. I jump whenever I feel his fingers through the flimsy cotton. After three are undone, my skin is quivering.

He leans in for a kiss. Vertigo dizzies me; I find myself meeting him halfway, my head swirling. Just as our lips are a centimeter apart, Len pulls back; his eyes survey me as if to say he is, and has been, in control of this no matter what I may think, that here is one place he can have some control, and that he needs me to give it to him. *Of course, of course. Anything,* I think.



I can't help it, the holding back makes me want him more—the prolonged desire, the chance to be there for him the way I want to be, to help him like I couldn't yesterday, like I couldn't help Grams or myself, the idea that I've worked out how to make contact with someone, to really, really connect.

We're rough, cords pulled tight, determined. I'm sitting there, completely exposed, my back an exaggerated arch, the housecoat sleeves still hooked at my elbows and the length of it bunched around the back of me, like spilled milk with gaudy flowers swimming in it.

Len stands me up with a hand at my underarm and another at the opposite elbow. He slips the muumuu all the way off, letting it drop to the floor, a few of the snaps clinking on the cold vinyl tiles between my bed and the Oriental rug. I look down; it's fallen nearly straight, laying stiff, with the arms out, a starched sculpture of a muumuu. I imagine Grams created the sculpture. Though she was crap at painting, she is wonderful in this medium, this metaphysical language of muumuus.

He tips my head up toward him, with my chin in the crook between his thumb and index finger. My hand he places beneath the hem of his T-shirt. When my fingers make contact, I feel his smooth skin shudder; I am powerful too, he is telling me. He looks at me as my hand travels down, below the waist of his shorts. He gives out a moan, his mouth on my ear. The sound of him echoes there. I'm struck by the exquisite vitality. *We are alive.*

It's pure intuition—where our lips, tongues, bodies press, the way they lean in and know each other; we're not gentle, instead we take and steal, looters with television sets, DVD players. We'll take what we can, my fingers in his mouth, his lower half pressing, our hipbones scraping. There's nothing else. His hand spreads wide, gently lands on the base of my throat; it's weightless there. Len pulls away from my lips and takes me in, his eyes focused where his fingers rest, seeing something there that I haven't, perhaps can't. He leans in and drops tiny kisses, light as anything, in the space above his hand. When he finds my eyes, he comes at me with more ferocity. I shock myself and meet him with the same; I feel it racing, pulsing behind my lids. Our eyes open and then close in synchronicity; we are shut inside this beautiful, terribly beautiful, place.

"Do you know that Counting Crows song?" I ask Len afterward, our bodies so tightly intertwined it's impossible to tell where one of us ends and the other begins. Our scents are strong, the heavy fug of our sex hangs in the air. "The one that goes—"

" 'What brings me down is love; I can never get enough.'" He finishes it, the too-daring thing I was about to say. I've hung myself out there for anything to happen to me.

"Just wondering," I say as a cover-up.

"Yeah, I thought so." He rests his hand at the curve of my hip and looks at it for a long time. If he's yanking in all his hang-ups from the hang-up line, then so will I.

We do it again, somehow even better. I don't ask where Richter is. If he wants to tell me, he will. After, we both nod off a little. I wake at some point later, before falling back to sleep. I'm amazed: Kavia has changed my life. Dare I even think where I might have wound up if I had never stumbled upon that neon pigeon? But I did find her, and here I am. Leave well enough alone," Grams always said.

I fall asleep—tired, still with a long road ahead of me, but happy, confident I've got the galaxy trailing behind me, gently nudging me in this direction. I dream of peace, of that place

Jews believe we are all looking forward to, the End of Days. My grandmother is there; she's trying to tell me something, but I can't make it out. We're on a cruise ship—one of those we've seen out the window—and the wind is howling something awful. It sounds like she's saying, "Drink the bear," but that can't be right, I keep thinking, working the syllable beats out on my fingertips the way Len did with Lluba Sobiesky.

The phone wakes us at seven thirty. "Vivian, don't you think I deserve this after a lifetime of suffering?" my mother says, nearly yelling, sending the ancient answering machine into a sharp feedback.

Len's lids stretch, but they don't open. He gives me that. I watch his eyes roll around under there, glad I can't see what they're saying. Now the sun is up and I'm not so brave. I want to explain how things aren't as bad as they look, how this is all part of my long-term plan, and things will work out with my mother if I just wait. My lips twitch, but nothing comes out.

"Vivian? Can you hear me?" she's yelling. I can see her cheeks reddening, the way they do, in concentrated circles, like Raggedy Ann's.

*Can I?* I'm so busy trying to ignore her, I can barely bring myself to listen to what she's actually saying. I'm angry and hurt and disgusted, but I still don't know what I want to do.

She hangs up and a disappointed silence fills my room. All that pushing Len to do the right thing with his dad, and I look like I haven't got a leg to stand on. Am I just planning, once again, to wait so long that my decision is made for me?

The shrill ring pierces through the dim morning light once again, and this time I shoot up and over Len to grab it, to stop the ringing. I cannot tell you what makes me say hello instead of simply hanging up. It probably has something to do with shame: doing nothing is not a plan. It goes so deeply against everything I believe in, and yet for years and years this is exactly the way I have handled my mother. I want to tell her off, the way that Grams, Wendy, and Len would all suggest, though lately, more than ever, something tells me there's simply more to it that I haven't worked out. But whatever the consequences, I feel one thing quite clearly: it's time, at least, to face her.

I'm in the kitchen, where we keep our phone, and I'm talking as low as possible, still I know that any conversation in any part of the apartment can be heard from any room.

My mother's off and running, saying all the things she's said before, now more angry, self-righteous, and with more "Vivian's" jammed in wherever she can fit them.

"My name is Viv," I say.

She doesn't pay this a lick of attention. She's going on about mothers and daughters and how there isn't anything that can break a tie like that between them, and how dare I? I want to smack her.

*"Mmm-hmmm,"* I mumble when she's through. She puts the phone down onto a table top with a tinny thud; I imagine an old corded phone like ours, as a muffled conversation with God-knows-who ensues. I smart from the intimacy I overhear in her tight whispers; this person has my mother in a way I, who doesn't even know what her phone looks like, never will—whether or not I stumble upon the right mix of coping with her. I get a glimmer of insight; it's this irrational desire to have her that way—that way this person has her—which makes objective, logical advice feel so far off the mark. This is my *mother.*

Len and I had left the TV on before falling into bed, and as she continues to strategize with whatever-his-name-is, I crane my head around to see what's on. It's still on mute, and there's an episode of *Law & Order* playing, which seems all the more intense because the content of the heated exchange on the screen is anyone's guess. Maybe the fear of the unknown is scarier than the actual consequences. Maybe living with the fact that we don't have any control whatsoever is the real trick.

My mother is still talking with her boyfriend; I hear some numbers—two thousand, four thousand—and then it's incomprehensible. My memory stretches back to something Grams said once, when Mom didn't show up for my twelfth birthday. I was in my pretty green velvet dress with the lacy collar. It had been expensive and I'd picked it just to see how much Grams loved me; I felt terrible as she unfolded the bills and counted out the change at the register, but I let her buy it, enjoyed the power I had over someone, power I'd never have over my mother. I wore it at the table, with Wendy and a few school friends I don't speak with anymore. It became clear that my mother wasn't going to show; still I refused to allow anyone to eat until she came.

My grandmother pulled me inside her bedroom, sat down on the bed, pulled me into the triangle nook her geometric print dress made between her legs, and took both of my hands in hers, firmly. "Listen, you are only twelve, but you are smart." Her words sent warm puffs of air onto my face and I liked the familiar feel of that, even if her breath smelled like tuna fish. "Can I be honest with you?" she had asked.

I nodded my head slowly, once, the way I had a habit of doing back then; I'd seen a girl do it in a Hitchcock mystery once and I thought it had a clever look to it.

"Your mother is not coming."

I stared Grams down. Back then I blamed her for everything. Sometimes she took it, sometimes she told me fresh little girls get rounded up and taken to a place with no My Little Ponies and no candy cigarettes, only lots of clothes to fold up and put away, forever and ever. "Sure you're nice to your mother—nicer than you are to me, and that's okay, I get it—but what good is being nice to her if it eats you up? You can yell at her, you know. Let's you and I call her up. You yell at her, and then we go and have a wonderful party, because you'll feel so much better."

I didn't do it. What if she'd been thinking of coming back for me and this ruined it? What if I made her feel so bad that she could never face me again? My grandmother was exasperated. I sobbed into her bedspread. When she shuttled me back out to the party, I sat dejected while she shoved ice cream and presents under my face.

Here I am now, still sitting the same way, waiting; hoping that if I'm pleasant enough, she'll come around; taking care not to further damage her fragile ego and send her away for good. Doing nothing has always been my answer with her, but I'm sensing the expiration date on that tactic has finally come to pass. It's so obvious that I can taste it—bitter and crisp, like burnt garlic bread. Just as quickly, it's gone. That glimmer of what I might do has been eclipsed, and in its place are Kavia's words: *Ignore her*. And along with her words is a grave fear. Holding my breath, I hang up the phone. I don't notice that the power has gone off until I look at the television screen, which has gone completely black.

As quietly as I can, I hinge the fuse box open and flip all the switches back and forth, hoping against logic this might just jump-start the system and that this has nothing to do with the bills I've been ignoring for the last few months. I go back to bed, praying Len will ignore the whole thing the way I ignored my mother, that he hasn't noticed about the electricity since the lights in my bedroom were off to begin with. It's dim yet, and I step over him to the part of the bed next to the wall, where I'd been sleeping. The sheets are cold, and I snuggle the summer blanket over my shoulders, close my eyes. Len's quiet and so I relax, breathe. I am doing my best to ignore the sinking feeling in my chest, and silence is exactly what I need to achieve this goal.

"Viv," Len says in the dark.

"Yes?" I answer, hesitant.

"You never talked with your mother, did you?"

"Not exactly."

"And by 'not exactly,' you mean you've completely ignored her, haven't you?"

"No, I just picked up the phone, didn't I?" I don't know if my anger is appropriately directed, or whether it should be more evenly distributed between myself and my mother, but in the moment that sort of logic hasn't made itself available.

*"Mmmm-hmmm,"* he says. "And what's going on with the electricity?"

"I don't know what you mean."

He reaches up, pushes in the switch on my bedside lamp. Nothing happens. He turns, blinky, his mouth scrunched on one side.

"Must be a burnt bulb," I say, shrugging my shoulders. I get up to go to the bathroom, to figure out just where in that enormous pile the electric bill might be, and I flick the switch, forgetting I can't turn the light on. When the hollow click produces nothing he shakes his head.

"Now why is it dark in the bathroom, too, do you think?" he asks.

"I don't know," I lie.

"Okay," he says, in a tone that is anything but. "What is going on here?"

"Nothing," I say. I don't want to be the kind of person who can't take care of things. I don't want to be my mother.

"It's not nothing. Listen, I don't want you to lie to me. There's nothing to be embarrassed about. You're not going to get a prize for keeping your problems a secret until they explode and you're lost in the wreckage. Believe me, I've been there," he says, with surprising openness. "All you're going to get with that kind of thinking is a headstone that says 'Lost in the Wreckage.' Now, you haven't decided what to do with your mother, have you? And that's why you haven't gone through that mountain of bills, because you're afraid they will sway your decision, that they will indicate you should not give your mom the money. Because after the hospital bills and all of that, there won't be a cent left. Am I right?"

All I can think is that I don't need to answer to him, don't need to defend my judgments to *anyone* (especially when I'm feeling so unsure of them myself), and I'm definitely not going to answer to someone who thinks he has to control everything just because it's in his Scorpio rising nature to do so. I snap before I know it. It's so much like what I used to do to Grams from time to time, I'm thrown. "That's what Kavia—who is not a thing, who is not my ass, but who is, yes, my *astrologer*—told me to do; she said I should ignore my mother." I slap my hand over my mouth. *Fuck. Shit. Fucking shit.* I cannot believe I've said this out loud to a person who the other day wore a T-shirt emblazoned with the words *Hope is not a method.*

"Your *astrologer* told you to do it. We're back on this. Maybe I shouldn't have encouraged you." He drops his head in his hands. Let me tell you, he doesn't need to say another word. His tone betrays his antipathy. Still, he *does* go on. "Can't you think for yourself?"

"Of course I *can,* but you don't understand. Everything she said is helping me to think for myself. Like your poetry book did. It's hard to explain, but she's teaching me how to handle myself. And besides, everything she advises works out so well—it worked out perfectly with you, and—"

"With *me*? You think that's why we're together? Because that charlatan told you when to call me? Did she tell you to fuck me, too?"

I wince. It looks like he's about to apologize, and then he stops, as if he's putting together all the pieces and getting further enraged at the image he's assembling.

I can only imagine how bad it looks.

"What kind of things did she tell you, exactly?"

I look at him and know I can't lie, especially when my own reservations have begun to creep in. But I *can* mumble. I've always been good at that. "Well, she told me to *letyoupullstrings*." I say these words low and strung together, with my hand over my mouth, so they're barely decipherable. But he gets it.

His eyes say terrible, ugly things. I wish he'd speak. Anything would be better than this.

His brows dart up in another realization. "Did she give you the idea to take us to the musical?"

It looks so bad when he puts it like that. While it was happening, it was just like using a roadmap when you're lost, tracing your finger over the right path to get you where you have every right to be, but this way he's making it seem sinister, manipulative, dishonest. I know this isn't an accurate reflection at all, but I can't find the words to convey that, so I just nod my head up and down, squeeze my mouth.

"So, let me get this straight," he says, sitting up, bridging the distance between us. "You allowed our relationship to fall into the hands of some wack-a-doodle?"

I can't have Len be right. I can't have Kavia be wrong. The very idea that everything I've learned is crap makes me feel so isolated, so defensive, so right back where I started, that I can only attack. Why I act so impulsively with Len when I've sat on my feelings for my mother for decades, I have no idea. But the words are out the gate and running before I know it. "You just think that everyone should do exactly what you say, that you have to control everything, because you're overcompensating for your dad abandoning you; that's your Scorpio ascendant. I have to do whatever you say, but it doesn't work in reverse, does it? You think it's easy tiptoeing around you, waiting for you, trying to read your mind so I don't push too hard on what we both know you want, because if I do, I'll lose you?"

Len's jaw squares off; his eyes go dark. The truth hurts—especially when you're not ready to hear it. Double especially when it arrives in a package you want to prove is a load of horse shit. *Triple* especially when you're trying to trust someone and let yourself be a little vulnerable for the first time in your life—and that someone comes and throws it all in your face like a complete asshole.

Len shakes his head and grimaces, as if he's just realized that sticking around here with me was as big a mistake as he'd originally imagined it would be. "I should have known," he says.

"Len . . ." But what are the words? "Should have known what?"

"Not to trust you. How can I be in love with someone who can't even think for herself, who goes to some charlatan to figure out what to eat for dinner?"

I'm so prickly and frightened myself I can't even begin to consider apologizing. He's dead wrong. I have to disprove him and it's all I can concentrate on. "She's not a charlatan! Who uses that word, anyway? *Charlatan!* Ha! What is this, seventeen ninety-five? Listen, Laura Ingalls Wilder, if she's so wrong, then how can you explain me wanting to do things again? Taking showers, wearing normal clothes, smiling, helping you?" I'm shaking; I can feel my shoulders tremble against the wall once I stop shouting. My throat is shredded.

"It's called acceptance, Viv, and it's not magical; it's just a natural progression of grief, just like your denial that Grams could be gone was a normal first reaction. That's why I let you tell me she was in Florida. I indulged you . . . I don't see you listening to everything I tell you to do. In fact, I don't think you've listened to *anything* I've said, and all *I* want to do is help you. This Kavia, on the other hand, she's just preying on someone who's clearly desperate. That's what these charlatans do. And about helping me—do me a favor: don't."

He's up and pulling his pants on, and all I can say is, "Again with the charlatans? Jesus Christ. At least you could be a little original!"

Len pulls his shirt over his head, his bottom lip anchored by his teeth. He shoves his wallet into his back pocket and picks up his keys with a scrape. "And by the way, *Little House on the Prairie* took place in the mid–eighteen hundreds."

Anger wins out. "Yeah, well, you know what I think? I think that hope *is* a method, except for people who are broken. How long is it going to take you to realize that you don't have forever to fix things with your dad? Buying him an obnoxiously large soft drink topped with a lion head is *not* enough. Do you hear me?" I'm right in his face, poking his ribs. I don't think I've showed this kind of aggression in my life. "I may not know the exact date of a freaking television series, I may not have all the answers, but I do know this: You do *not* have forever to make things up! And that is a freaking *fact*!" I'm still in his face, screaming, shaking like crazy. I'm angry at everyone I've ever been angry at. I'm back where I started, furious at myself, too. I'm back on that hospital toilet, and it feels like everything I've learned since then is a pile of crap.

"You don't have forever—that's exactly what I told *you*! What does it take to get through to you? If it doesn't come with charts and pretty pictures Vivian's not listening, folks! So don't even try." He looks like he's going to say something else, but his jaw hangs midair for a second and then snaps shut.

"Look who's talking!" I scream, loud enough so Richter can probably hear, if he's even in there; as if Len could bring himself to tell me even that much. I grab a couch cushion, a cute embroidered one, and squeeze the crap out of it, so I won't throw something.

He shakes his head in a way that makes my stomach cramp. He gently opens and then closes the front door behind him and leaves me in a sting of quiet.

I throw the pillow at the door once he's disappeared behind it. "Maybe you should listen to your own advice," I sneer, picking up the pillow and slinking down to the ground, my back against the sofa arm.

The last thing he says comes at me, muffled, through the door. It's layered over the sounds of him working the lock on his own door. "You think you know everything, don't you, Vivian?"

As I hear his front door swish shut methodically behind him, I whisper to the empty room, "No, that's just the problem, Len. I don't know shit. And for the last freaking time, it's Viv."

In my room, which is filling with morning light, I lie down where Len slept, but as soon as I've settled into the blankets, I throw them back. There'll be no more sleep today. "I don't know shit," I say.

I pace the hallway a few times and then stop in front of a

framed photo halfway down the hall, by the kitchen entryway. The photo is of me, and it's from a work event; I never understood why Grams framed it. In it I'm wearing a blouse I always pass over in the closet until all the ones I like better are dirty. But now I see; it's a Viv with places to go and important things to do, one with a marked-up phone extension list pinned to her cubicle wall. It's a girl with the potential to overcome her past and embrace all the gifts she has—not merely *act* like she has and make a joke about whitefish.

*It's Vivian.* This thought comes to me the way a boogie board tied to your wrist does in the wake of a showy speedboat: with a smash to the *kepi.* I used to love my name. As a child I'd go around asking everyone their names, and weigh them out against mine. I always liked mine better. I learned to write it in twelve languages, and did so in every color pen. I worked out the lines and curves of it from sticker sheets, had it airbrushed onto T-shirts, strung in beads on the laces of my sneakers, woven onto hair clips. *My name is Vivian.*

I look at this Vivian straight in the eye, and I imagine she's trying to tell me, with a pen through her hair and a file folder snugged in the crook of her arm, *You're stronger than you know.* But she can tell I don't believe her, that she's just wasting her time with me, someone who can't work a slightly funky blouse from the Village that her friend talked her into.

I take the photo from its hook and turn it facedown on the bookshelf. I don't know who this Vivian thinks she is. I'm not sure I ever will.

# 26.

♈ ♉ ♊ ♋ ♌ ♍ ♎ ♏

*There is a feeling of near reverence for astrological knowledge and, some years ago, I decided to investigate it. I placed an announcement in the press:*

*ABSOLUTELY FREE!*
*Your ultra-personal horoscope*
*A 10-PAGE DOCUMENT*
*Benefit from a unique experiment*
*Send name, address, date and*
*Place of birth to: ASTRAL ELECTRONIC.*

*To the first 150 who replied, I sent the same psychological analysis—a true interpretation by an authentic astrologer of the horoscope of a person who had actually existed. It belonged, in fact, to a celebrated French criminal, Dr Petiot, who had murdered over fifty people during the Second World War, although neither the astrologer nor "my" clients knew his identity.*

*I received a dozen enthusiastic letters of acknowledgment. Ninety per cent thought that the portrait was very true and expressed their personal difficulties well, while for 80 per cent this favourable judement was shared by family and friends. Psychologists have taught that we all tend to see a mirror of ourselves in the horoscope; but it is still disquieting that these people should find a resemblance in a profile drawn to fit only one individual—a murderer.*

—MICHEL GAUQUELIN, *TRUTH ABOUT ASTROLOGY*

"Vivian"—*my mother's* voice pierces the air of the apartment—"you will not ignore me. Believe me. I will not let you ignore me." She hangs up and the hairs on my neck stand on edge.

Before the train even crosses the bridge, I know something is different. I've been eagerly awaiting this long session with Kavia all week and now I would rather be anywhere else. It's as if I know, I sense, that she is going to say something I don't want to hear. She'll say I have to face my mother now, that Len is right.

All I want to do is have her tell me how to make up with Len, and yet I know how much he would hate this. I don't know what to do.

I'm trembling by the time I mount the stairs at Kavia's, working my glittery gold star over and under my fingers. At the second landing, the same one where I'd admired the beauty of this stairwell, my frequent reader star slices my thumb right open, releasing a fresh line of blood.

As she punches the last hole, I see I've nearly rubbed all the glitter off; it's encrusted in the weave of my tote bag. I sprinkle it wherever I go, like a trail of bread crumbs, or cheap glitter that won't stay put.

"This one's free, right?" I ask.

"No, next one," she says.

This is not what she said. I tell her as much. Her I can yell at.

"Between me and you, who is the one who knows where things stand?"

I don't like this. Not one bit. "That's not very nice," I say.

*"Hmmmph,"* she says, tossing off one of her signature shrugs. This woman doesn't care about anything. How many times have I excused the way she looks at her watch, throws me out when I'm supposed to be having a session, slips me a paper in place of giving me a drop of her time? If I had as slight a conscience as she does, I could probably be president.

"Now, we talk about this week. Mercury will retrograde; you must wait until it turns direct on the last day of the month to sign contracts, to purchase electrical equipment, to begin new jobs." Kavia has a green palor, like she's very, very ill, or turning into the Wicked Witch of the West.

"Retrograde?" I ask.

"It means that from where we stand, from Earth, the planet appears to stop or rotate backward for a little while; and this can create quite a disturbance. If your life has been moving forward, feeling more orderly, now it will be chaos and disorder.

"There is a Mars-Saturn conjunction, an excruciating planetary combination, in your house of relations. Expect aggression, arguments, sadness, and pain. Relationships will be problematic in every way imaginable. Consider this: maybe it's the wrong time to be in a relationship. Uranus and Mars are opposed and this can create major clashes between you and a partner."

I don't have to tell you that I've gone numb, completely numb. I don't want to hear this; I won't hear this. She's speaking and I really want to go over and jab the stop button on her tape recorder and pretend that I haven't heard a word she's said. I'll just go back to not doing anything about anything and acting like that's the way I like it. And everyone will be happy. Except for me. And everyone who cares about me.

I don't even notice that I've let the tissue drop from my finger, don't even feel the blood pooling and sliding down my wrist.

Neither does Kavia. She's got the most peculiar expression on her face, as if she's daring me to disagree with what she's said, almost as if she wants me to. But I don't have the slightest idea whether it is a challenge or a threat. She clears her throat as if she's going to pick up where she left off.

"Wait, wait, just wait a minute," I say. "What about Len? Remember him? How does this all jibe with 'the young man who's going to be important in my life'?" I'm angry as hell. I've listened to everything she said, and now *this*?

"Look, I said he was important, but I never said that you would be with him forever. Some people are just meant for a certain time; they come into our lives and then, once they've served their purpose, they go." Kavia shifts in her chair, blinks twice, hugely. "A relationship is going to dissolve. It says it right here." Whatever makeup she had on yesterday makes a shadow underneath her otherwise unlined eyes today, like an errant swipe of charcoal on an artist, or Courtney Love. "Now let's talk about what is happening at this moment. The most important thing right now, you remember, that we talked about, is the progressed lunar return, which you are going through. It throws everything in your life into a tailspin. It will bring you through a great transition. Your life may seem unrecognizable when it's through. But you have to remember that these returns always leave you with a gift for your troubles, they get you somewhere you needed to be. Try to remember this, through the pain . . . because they *are* painful, there's no getting around that. It's all part of the cycle, you understand. Keep this in mind: this Scorpio rising, this man, his purpose in your life is nearly through. This was something just for now, you understand."

She stops speaking and claps the book shut. Apparently, that's all it says. Dust rises in a cloud from the pages. It settles all around us and I start to cough. When I can breathe again—with no offer of water, or pat on the back—I speak up. "This can't be right, Kavia." I want to tell her about the argument I had with Len, but I'm afraid she will only take this as proof of her point.

"*Whatchu* mean?" she asks, her brows knitting tightly.

"I mean I've met someone wonderful, and I've done everything you said, and it worked perfectly, and I'm actually *happy,* and on the train over, I've just decided that I have to stop pushing him away." I know I don't need to tell her even this much. I hear Len's words, and I don't agree with him, but some of it seems to make a little bit of sense. I think back to some of my own thoughts over the last couple of days: Kavia's take on my mother felt too neat and tidy, the way she's become less and less willing to give her time, less and less pressed to act like she cares, like our sessions are nothing more than a means to pay her rent. Some of the things Len said actually make *a lot* of sense: the natural progression of grief, the idea that I was lost and desperate for someone to show me the way. But, that's just it: *I am* desperate. And even if Len might be right, he might be wrong. And I just don't know if that's a risk I'm willing to take. If I haven't been able to navigate the relatively calm waters of the last couple of weeks—with their simple pattern of coffee and talk radio, writing and watching the seagulls and the weather—then what kind of disaster am I headed for with a progressed lunar return coming to a head? I try one last desperate attempt to have her tell me she's read things wrong, that I *should* be with Len, after all. "He feels so right, though."

"Everyone, like your Len, is wonderful in the beginning," she says.

"How can you say that? Astrologers are not supposed to tell you what to do. It says so right on that tape you gave me."

*"Hmmmph,"* she says.

If I never hear that syllable again, it will be too soon. I cringe, waiting for her to change her mind. But I should have known better.

"Don't listen to me. I forgot how well you've been doing on your own," she says. She pulls out a nail file and begins to saw the thing back and forth over four nails at once—like a career secretary on a personal call.

Now, it's one thing to think that myself, but to hear her say it makes me defensive. "It's not easy when you lose the one person you love most in the world! It's not easy, you know!"

She gives me silence just long enough to feel stupid for stating the obvious, the one thing that everyone—not just me—has to endure in their lives. And then she says, "Why don't you take a good look at yourself and figure out what it is you're looking for? You don't need any reading to tell you that. It's plain psychology, my dear. Plain psychology. Eighty dollars." She holds out her palm, and with the other pulls her rolled-up schedule book out of the space between her bosoms to show she's moved on.

I can't believe what she's saying, but I can't do this on my own, either. "You know, I really thought you were going to help me here. Len said this was a bunch of crap, that you were a charlatan. And I had a huge fight with him about it and called him bad names, like Laura Ingalls Wilder. But I wonder if I was mistaken," I say, pulling some money out of the little red leather pouch. "You know, we still have ten minutes left. Apparently things aren't as black-and-white as I thought they were."

She appears to be turned off. She sticks her nose in the date book and swishes her big mouth left and right.

I count out the cash, feeling degraded, disabused, all the bad adjectives that start with D. "In fact, I don't know what I was thinking at all coming here. Your sign is a pigeon! A freaking pigeon. Don't you know that nobody likes pigeons? Maybe you should change it to something strong, like an eagle, or a lion! Did you ever think of that?" Suddenly, Kavia is the object of all of my rage. I hate the way she counts the money, slowly, licking her thumb. The only sign she gives that she's hearing me at all is a slight flutter of her eyelashes, as if a fly has zoomed too close.

This throws me further into the fiery pit. "I mean, who's buying all of this junk about us being connected? About everything happening the way it has for centuries? About each of us affecting the other? *Me*—intuitive, belonging to a larger, meaningful framework of life? Please. And worst of all—that all of"—I wave my hand indicating the crap storm of my life—"*this* is a freaking lesson I'm supposed to be learning. Why me? What about everyone else? Len was right! It's an idea for pathetic losers that have nowhere else to turn!" The last word comes out in a croak. My throat is raw. I've said every single word that Len said to me, but I don't believe it. More than anything, I want to throw myself at Kavia's feet and just grab on. I don't care where she drags me. I just don't want to leave here alone. I cannot make myself forget all the comfort I've felt here, that fantastic sense of direction and safety; I can't go back to gumping around on my own, blindfolded and banging into sharp edges all the time. My chest inflates and then deflates so fast; my line of vision ripples along its rhythm. I might pass out.

*If you're so safe, why is there blood all over your hand?* The thought crosses my mind.

Kavia dips the cash into her hip pocket, retrieves the emery board, and starts filing away at the other hand in slow, hypnotic motions. Tiny flecks of nail dust settle in the air around us, and I'm just standing there. I'm still holding onto the purse, and the sight of fingers pulling the zipper closed is such a déjà vu—I've watched Grams do that so many times—a chill reverberates from my belly. I see the kernel of something important in the image of us laid one on top of the other, doing the same things, but differently. I file it for later. I'm too exposed now. I need to get out of here.

I turn to go, but then stop, spin around, grab the pile of books. They've helped. They've inspired me and taught me to see the world differently, the way the best books can, and I'm not giving that up.

Avoiding Kavia's gaze, which I can feel on my back, I head for the door. Just as I'm turning the knob, she speaks.

"You know, you're right. Nothing is black-and-white. I'll tell you this: ornithologically speaking, pigeons and those beautiful doves everyone's gaga for are actually interchangeable. They are the same species. And in the New Testament, the very symbol of the Holy Spirit is none other than . . ." She pauses for dramatic effect, which given the full weight of what she's saying, isn't really necessary, "The dove."

I have no reply.

"And the Hebrews, well, they used the dove for sacrifice. In fact doves were the only bird that could be used in a sacrifice—something that gives its life for the greater good of everyone else." She didn't mean to, or maybe she did. But those words finally make everything clear.

"So?" I spit the word out. I'm tired. I'm Goldie Hawn in *Private Benjamin*. I wanna go out to lunch, I wanna go to Bloomingdale's. I'm sick of walking around in the rain with a heavy pack. Just when I think I've figured things out, they change on me, and I'm sick of trying to keep up.

"So, life is very much about how you look at things. They do not always fit neatly into the boxes you'd like them to. You want me to be everything to you, to be your perfect savior. You want me to be God. But I'm not, have never said I am. I merely read what's already there and translate it for you. And I'm a little psychic. But whatever it says there, *you* need to decide for yourself what this life is about. If you want to ignore your fate and let life smack you around, all *will-nill*, that's your prerogative."

"It's '*willy-nilly*,'" I hiss, and spin on my heel to go. I shove her own word back in her face: "*Hmmmph*," I say, and snap my head to the side. And I'm gone. Back in the world once again, nothing the way I left it.

For three days and three nights it rains. It rains sideways and diagonally, and so hard that someone has to come and string a tarp over the roof because Alina and Sergey Bakhvalova in the penthouse were getting a leak on their marble countertop and threatening to sue.

I don't call Len or knock on his door, and Len doesn't call or knock on my door. I have to get my Richter updates from Mrs. Kaufman, who got them from Jeanine Myer, who accidentally listened through the wall of her living room with a glass cup.

It is on the second day, when I have no more work to do on my *Skylar* articles (tear 'n' share breads, a new hire at Wegmans, and one on a gluten-free chip targeted at Tri-State Area cats with a taste for tortillas), that I remember something important. I think of the way I'd felt when Kavia first inducted me into her esoteric language of symbols and articulate personality classifications. I remember how amazingly simple it had all seemed, how miraculous a solution its concise, easy-to-follow steps appeared.

The thing I realize now is, like most things, it's not all that clear if you really look into it. You see, even in the relatively simple world of the tinder fungus, things aren't always what they seem. That's just not realistic. Life is complicated and messy and there isn't always an obvious way through.

I should just walk away from here and never look back. So I won't have faith. Who *does* these days? Life isn't a T-shirt slogan. Not even a really good one like "Life sucks and then you die."

# 27.

♈ ♉ ♊ ♋ ♌ ♍ ♎ ♏

*We shall not cease from exploration*
*And the end of all our exploring*
*Will be to arrive where we started*
*And know the place for the first time.*

—T. S. Eliot, "Little Gidding";
Number 4 of *Four Quartets*

M*y cell phone* rings. It's Len. I don't dare pick it up. I haven't got a clue what I'll say.

I've got a good guess what Len would say though. He once told me a story about a Texan who thought a mint-flavored toothpick from a steakhouse in Tennessee had been bringing him good luck. He took the toothpick with him everywhere. Prior to this, the man had been trying to make money in real estate but had never made a good investment. The first time he stuck that toothpick in his mouth, he bought a little desert piece in Las Vegas, and boom—the place exploded, values went through the roof. Now he's one of the biggest landowners in Sin City. "Thing is," Len said, "guy's brother wanted to make a point; switched out the toothpick for one from the supermarket, and the guy never noticed. Lucky charms are all about what you believe them to be. The guy didn't need the toothpick to be successful; he just thought he did, because by coincidence, he had it when things started turning around. Now, there's something to be said about the power of positive thinking, I'll give you that. But I wouldn't take it any further than there."

This story gets me thinking about my own magic talismans. I grab Grams's little red purse and tuck it into an old yellow raincoat we've been sharing for at least two decades. I've got somewhere to go.

I step off the train sure of exactly where I'm headed. This isn't the best neighborhood, but I'm not worried. This place is mine, the way we each have a stake in everything under the sun. At the park entrance, I walk directly to the ticket line for the Cyclone. I don't stop for cotton candy or a Nathan's frank.

It's nearly noon on a weekday and there's barely anyone here. In the wrong light, it could look depressing. I remember how fabulous this place used to be, how I used to beg for another go at that roller coaster, and now it's so worn out.

I only have to wait ten minutes to get on, and while I do, I recall many of my favorite factoids about the Cyclone. I look up, to the 2,640 feet of track, the first drop at 85 feet, its 60-degree angle. I take in the six turns, the 12 drops, the 18 crossovers, 27 elevation changes, 16 changes in direction. Grams was a fan, maybe because we could see it from our window, and maybe because she was here when it was built, remembered seeing it rise from nothing. Or maybe it was simply because we loved it—together.

By the time I climb into the third car something has shifted in me. Like the lever with which the man is operating this glorious piece of machinery, this piece of history really, I have switched over. *I get it.* It's a subtle shift in understanding, and I can look at it through the eyes of astrology, or through Emerson's poetry. I can see it in psychology, metaphysics, the Talmud—anything that speaks to me. Life doesn't go along "will-nill" in order to jibe with my particular way of doing things. And I have to learn to adjust. But, and this is a big but—it's not for my benefit alone. When we understand and make peace with ourselves, we're better people, happy ones, who live up to our potential, bake yummy treats that make peoples' days, teach bratty kids to be patient rather than satiating them the easy way. We're the best we can be, and guess what? The world's a better place for it. You don't need to go changing your name and hiding out. You have to adjust. It just takes some of us longer than others to really get it.

The hot wind has picked up, and I hear it in my ear like a towel being flapped out for line drying. I gulp; you see, this roller coaster Yoda of mine nearly didn't make it. The neighborhood had become plagued by riots and crime. In 1969 the ride was condemned—the symbol of so much hope, was considered too dangerous and left deserted, a mass of rotting wood and rusting steel. And yet, here it is.

Sooner than I'm ready, we're rising. As we head up the enormous hill, I can just see my bedroom window, in miniature, beyond. Grams and I once hung a pink swath of fabric there for exactly this purpose. The fabric in the window, the tiniest sliver, that I have to squint to see, looks frozen in time. I'd completely forgotten it was there. It's survived, like a fossil or a cockroach. I'm here, the plastic of the seat warm through the flimsy material of the housecoat. And there's my home, my place.

I grab the rail tightly and imagine myself absorbing the strength I'm riding. We, both of us, had no idea what we were in for. And, chart or no chart, I've got to figure out how to deal with that myself. Anyone can tell you, but doing it, well, that's a different thing altogether, isn't it? In 1972, after all those hardships, the aquarium wanted to tear this roller coaster down. But by then enough people were in love with the Cyclone, they wouldn't have it. A campaign was struck, and against all odds, Save the Cyclone reopened Astroland Park. The ride raked in $125,000 its first weekend. *This* is a survivor. I, too, have this kind of strength, somewhere inside. I feel it building, like a brush fire, or the ingredients on a submarine sandwich. And maybe, just maybe, being open to what life may bring is a strength all its own.

The Parks Department's and U.S. flags wave like brigade colors at the peak, auspicious. When we ascend higher, closer, I feel the familiar ache to reach out and touch them. I raise my hand, exhilarated, a child again, and after a lifetime of trying, my fingertips actually make contact.

We straighten out as we crest the peak, the iconic Cyclone sign to our right. For this moment we, every last passenger—wherever we've come from, wherever we'll go—are part of this unstoppable force, this champion of time and space and energy; I hold my breath, prepare for the terrible rip of vertigo, the intestinal rise, in the best way we can for such a thing. The man to the front of me, with his longish hair and his Hawaiian shirt, turns to show me he feels it too, he's bracing himself as best he can.

We sit, still, for an achingly long second, lingering at the top of the world. A few fluffy clouds appear to be in reach on either side. Someone yells prematurely; the rest of us laugh, nervous, terrified, thrilled. The first car hits the tipping point and we're shooting down; there's a silent pause during which our adrenaline takes over, and then there's nothing but marvelous screaming, ringing in my ears, deafening, numbing, invigorating. When strands of my hair catch at the corner of my mouth, I realize I'm smiling from ear to ear.

The ride goes quickly after that, the wind whipping through the sleeves of the housecoat as we rush over the jumble of crossovers, the smaller drops, the jerky twists; in all the world there's nothing but this fantastic propulsion.

I remember something I'd forgotten about that day when

Shelly Wasserman threatened to pull my hair. Grams said, "Now you listen to me. Don't you let anyone push you around." She emphasized the words with jabs of her finger. "They'll only push you around if they think they can. They'll only push you around if *you* think they can. You're a wonderful woman, Viv. You take after me, and you are a wonderful woman." She was shaking me by the shoulders and her eyes were locked into mine. We were so close our noses touched.

We pull into the station alongside the red, blue, and white bubble print of the Cyclone sign. The blue haphazardly painted bench, the aqua and white weave of the plastic fence coated in grit—it's all exactly as it has always been. With a shiver, I feel that sensation of her nose on mine. I stretch my memory back to get the details right: I didn't think they *should* push me around, but I didn't know that the reason was because I was just as good as everyone else. I only wanted to fit in. Now I get what Grams was trying to shake into my shoulders that way: just because my mother didn't want me didn't mean I wasn't worth wanting. Just because I have my own way of doing things doesn't mean it isn't a vital, important way, that someone else who took the time might happen to like. Maybe they wouldn't, but that doesn't make it any less vital. It just makes it mine.

When my feet descend to the red concrete, I know—as clearly as I knew my complete fear before—that I've taken some of that inexorable force with me. It's mine now, and I feel it spread down my spine in spectacular trembles.

I go home with a plan. I know exactly what I'm going to do.

# 28.

♈ ♉ ♊ ♋ ♌ ♍ ♎ ♏

> *We will find what kind of behavior we must develop in order to gain acceptance into our family, and into our world. Each rising sign has specific lessons that need to be learned. When those traits are owned, and integrated into the personality, the rest of the chart can find its way out into the world, and express itself with true integrity.*
>
> —Eileen Grimes, "Rising Signs R Us: Aren't They?"

*The universe decides* to test my new understanding of flexibility as quickly as I settle on it. I take the walk home from Coney Island, though no one in their right mind would walk this dangerous route. If my grandmother were here, she'd kill me. I like to think I have an open mind to what people consider "bad neighborhoods," but the truth is, you don't want to know how many girls get mugged over this way. Astroland was good to me, though, and I see this walk as a gesture, a way to give it something back—it's the solidarity I wasn't able to muster back in the hospital room.

Eventually the neighborhood changes, and the boarded-up stores give way to pricey Russian cafés marked by indecipherable chalkboards full of specials. I step inside one for a coffee, point to the white porcelain cup on my table to indicate what I'd like, and watch the late-afternoon sky interact with the ocean for a while. I forget, sometimes, how stunning this scene can be when there aren't millions of people milling around speaking too loudly and baring plump body parts.

The seagulls are silent, soaring in grand gestures, loop-the-looping over one another in an intricate choreography. I'm not sure how long I sit there, trying not to feel like one part of a party of two, trying to forge my new identity. I think, *This is beautiful, but there's more. And I'd like to see it.*

I leave five dollars on the table and walk the remaining distance to my building. That earlier breeze has mounted, and it seems to be pulling the storm out of here. In minutes, the trees along the streets running perpendicular to the boardwalk are rushing in a softer, familiar sound of summer afternoons. I'm listening, open to everything the universe wants to tell me.

By the time I round the corner and approach the parking lot, making my way toward the main lobby, I have flip-flopped three times—call Len, don't call Len. Either way, I am definitely pulling the ketchup out of the fridge. And that's when I see it. My mother's beat-up old Celica, the hard diagonal of the trunk she once slammed my thumb in accidentally. It throbs at the sight.

"I gather you've seen her car," Jameson says from behind his desk. He touches my hand, a tender surprise. I watch his old, wrinkled fingers, the eraser pink of his neat fingernails clamping around my comparably tiny hand.

"Is it that obvious?" I ask, still watching his cocoa hands around mine.

"Listen to me, and you listen to me good," he says, surprising me, forcing my eyes to his. "Your grandmother did not take crap from that woman, and don't you take crap from her. You remember that there are people here who really care about you. Don't need to be no blood relative to love you, Viv. But you have to love yourself."

He jerks my hand pointedly. And when I lower my head in understanding, he eases his grip slowly, stands, and turns to the window. "Good," he says to the setting sun. That's Grams's point of view he's reflected, not necessarily my own. But I think that's okay.

I don't think anything in the elevator. It's as if my head is completely full and one extra thought will knock out the delicate dynamic it's all balancing on. At our floor, I pause before Len's door. He's in there, and he is something I want. Along a road of waking and working it all out endlessly, often trudgingly, like something out of a Cormack McCarthy novel, there is a person on the other side of that door who makes me want to jump out of bed and figure it all out. That's got to mean something.

I ball my hand up to knock, but inches from the surface it stops short. I let it drop to my side.

My mother's left the door unlocked, which gets me twisting every lock, only to find I've just locked it again instead. She doesn't get up to help though these locks make a racket.

When I finally swing the door open, both the television and the radio are blaring. The electricity is back on. Maybe it was just a blackout, after all, or an error. Who knows? I know one thing for certain: my mother sure as hell didn't pay the bill. I'm not asking questions.

I come upon her napping on Grams's bed. There are pillows strewn all over the floor, though there's a perfectly good basket at the foot of the bed, which she knows is there for this purpose. The blankets are so rumpled, it reminds me of a crime scene on *L.A. Law.* I taste sickness, sour, at the back of my throat.

She doesn't notice me at first, and I steal this time to look at her. I practice soundless sentences at my lips: "I am angry with you. I have never forgiven you for abandoning me, for continuing to abandon me. I tell you this with the understanding that you aren't going to change, and that—" I know what I want to say, but I don't have the right words.

My mother wakes in a sort of fit, her small fists shaking, her head tossing, until her eyes roll back and her lids part suddenly. She starts when she sees me.

I enjoy the notion that I've frightened her.

"Vivian," she says. This woman is the queen of black-and-white, for her, right now, this voice of an enemy she's using is an honest portrayal of how she feels about me.

Another piece pops into place: this is not the same woman I fantasize about holding hands with along the boardwalk. This is someone I don't know, haven't for some time. She always does this, I realize; morphs into someone so far from the woman in my head that I don't even recognize her.

This woman can't take being told off; you can see it all over her face. A good telling-off might make me feel better for a moment or two, but it would be the death of her. She's half-dead already, and she doesn't even know. She doesn't have this kind of awareness; it's people like me who have to shoulder the burden of that type of thing. It's a burden, but a gift, too. Even that shameful menstrual cycle, the one I endure like a plague—if we make it to the end of it, in return we get the ability to create life. If you look at it that way, like Kavia's pigeons, even the most repugnant things can have spectacular beauty.

My chest opens up as the two images of my mother—the one in my head and the actual one—layer over each other, like those tracing papers in the expensive coloring books I used to grovel for at the five-and-dime.

"Sit," my mother says, patting the bedspread next to her.

I kick off my shoes and lower myself slowly to the mattress, with an aching hesitation; here is another place now relegated to the post-Grams part of my life. Tears wash right through me, though this is the last person I'd want to cry in front of.

"Oh, Vivian, what's the use in crying? Now *I'm* the one who should be crying! No parents, a daughter who won't even answer the telephone. I had to come all the way here, I was worried sick about you."

*No you weren't.*

"Do you have any idea how difficult this has been on me?"

*Fuck you.* I shake my head, close my eyes. I can't help it. I may see things more clearly, but I will always want her love. I will *always* want her love, even if she'll never show me a speck of it.

She throws herself back onto a pillow, inflating it at either side of her face. "I just wish there was something I could *do* for you," she says. My chest hollows out. In some sense, she truly believes she can't, that there isn't anything she can give me—like Richter used to think with Len.

She turns, props herself up on an elbow, as if she's completely forgotten what she had said, or as if she'd never said it in the first place. "Vivian, we have to talk."

My belly flip-flops.

"I want to spend some time with you," she says, her head rocking up and down with each word, her emphasis like a schoolteacher's. "I want to make up for lost time. I want to make things right."

This is so much like my dreams I am stunned into silence. The words soothe me like a lullaby. Was I wrong to believe she'd never come around? Look, if I have to adjust, like I just said, I will. I'll bend myself into knots for this. Still, I feel shy, all this attention, this special treatment. My cheeks heat. "Really?" I say.

She smiles tightly for an answer. "Why don't you go take a shower and I'll bring you out for a nice dinner, something Italian. I'll drive to Bay Ridge."

I don't dare speak. I nod my head in tiny jerks.

The shower is cold; she's running the sink in the kitchen the whole time I'm in there, washing out her panty hose, using up all the hot water. I tell myself she just doesn't know about the way the water works here. It's okay. It doesn't mean anything. But the cold water makes me hyper alert, directs my thoughts into a fine, sharp point. If it seems too good to be true, it probably is. It's fine to be sympathetic to your mother; you are the only person in the world who can be this to her. But she is going to use you. Just watch the hell out.

She chooses a slick restaurant decorated with modular furnishing on wheels, one which I have never been to before, have never even heard of. My mother always kept up with things like that.

As the waitress with crinkly curly hair struts us to a table by a window, I indulge myself with the thought, if only for a second, that maybe my mother *is* coming back. After all these years, just *maybe,* she finally wants me. *Stop,* I tell myself. *Remember what you have learned, finally.*

But the fantasies mount quicker than I can restrain them. I'm caught up in the hip environment of this place she's picked for us. My head bobs to the jazzy old music, which seems just right. My heart skips a beat as my mother gently squeezes my arm.

I catch sight of myself in the mirror, and I think I look different, better, like someone who means something. Is it my mother who's done this to me? I feel the sun on my shoulder as I sit in the chair my mother left vacant for me, the worst of the two—the one facing the wall, rather than the restaurant. I do what I've always done: I make excuses. Perhaps she thought this one more to my liking, as if she would know something like that about me.

A girl in barrettes walks by wheeling a baby doll in a pink sling stroller. Her mother is behind her, picking up everything that falls out of the stroller along the way. My mother watches for a second. I watch her watching.

"Remember how much you loved that baby doll of yours? You were absolutely obsessed."

I guess that's one way to remember it.

"So," she says, clamping her hands together over the plastic-coated menu. Her rings bang. "Isn't this nice, just us two girls, together?" Her smile is gigantic.

I nod my head.

"Should we share an appetizer? What do you like? Calamari? Bruschetta?" She pronounces the hard C in bruschetta, as if she is fluent in Italian, speaks it around the house.

"Sure," I say. "I like everything." But I don't. I don't like calamari, and I have been allergic to tomatoes since I was eleven. But I won't say so. Of the two, she thankfully opts for the calamari, and orders, at her own suggestion, two pasta dishes—one in garlic and oil, and the other in heavy cream with mushrooms—for us to share. They seem like the chicest dishes and they are both from the specials list. It will be entirely too much food.

I still don't have much of an appetite. I wonder at hers. In fact, she looks great. Her skin is shiny, catching the light from the overhead chandelier in all the right places: at her cheek apples and forehead, the tip of her nose. She always looks radiant, as if life is irrelevant in this regard. She'd never be caught dead in a muumuu with no makeup on. She's wearing a printed blousy dress, belted up with a macramé scarf that hangs long. My mother is elegant, I think proudly. I wish I had worn something nicer than a black tank top and faded black pants with flats. I wish I had thought to apply some eyeliner.

The calamari comes out on a glazed red plate; she loads up the serving spoon and slides a few crispy rings onto my plate, skidding them to the rim, like jacks, which we used to play on the wooden floor of her bedroom closet when Dad was alive. She always won, with a lot of fist cheering. I never got past threesies. But I always cheered; I'd get caught in her energy and punch the air, turn tumblesaults right into the rows of her high heels. The sight of the oily trails the squid has left turns my stomach. Still, I fork one with a loud clink on the plate before me, force it down with a big gulp of water.

She wants to talk about the economy, too loudly, and with a lot of hand gestures. She wants people to overhear how intelligent and tuned in she is. She's read about body language. She knows the hand gestures are a sign of intelligence. She thinks Brooklyn people are unsophisticated and she wants to show them what they can become if they ever leave. Which most of them won't. *We like it here!* I used to think, when she'd slander the discount tchotchke shops Grams and I had a habit of touring on Sundays when they reopened after Shabbat. "All junk, made in China, made in Taiwan. How can you stand it?" she said. "Taiwan is *in* China," Grams said and winked at me. "Yeah," I wanted to say. But I didn't.

Now she's chopping one hand into the palm of the other. "Everyone's saying we need a change. Now that this Obama is in office, they say, we'll all be back in the clear. I think maybe that's not true. I think we'll be in it for a long time. Everyone will be looking to feel good with simple, thrifty treats—things that remind them of a better time." She's rehearsed this; it's clear as day. The layers flip-flop—she's the one in my mind, the real one, the one in my mind, and then finally, truly, she's the real one. I force down another flaky ring and try to rework my view. I want so badly for her not to be here just for the money.

To her credit, she leads the talk in a slightly different, more poignant direction, an attempt, I assume, to appear less obvious. I try one last time to swallow her words.

"It seems to me like the beginning of the end," she says, baring her palms in a gesture of honesty. "Just when you thought you knew where things stood, what things you could count on, it up and changes on you. Where do you suppose we can go from here, Vivian?" The problem with studying body language is, if you boast about how you've mastered it, no one can know when to actually believe you.

I am so aware that I am not going to hear the answer I want that I reach for a joke. "To Froishe's?" I try. But as soon as it's out, I know she won't get it, because she's missed all the good stuff.

My mother starts to cry.

"I don't know what you mean by that, Vivian, but I'll tell you this: it isn't funny. It isn't funny at all." At the thought of the funeral, her makeup breaks down in a matter of seconds; it's navy and pink mud and it runs down the side of her nose and streaks across her cheek. It amazes me, how she hoards grief. I push my chair back and rush over to her, I cradle her from behind, whisper, *"Shaaah,"* and think of all the times Grams did this for me when my mother had done something unspeakable or, worse, nothing at all. Grams did it for me; I do it for my mother—right or wrong, this is just the way things are, and will always be, between us.

For a while my mother holds her shoulders tense, but eventually she relaxes, sighs. I feel good knowing I'm comforting her a little; maybe it's irrational, but this feeling is something I get to keep, that no one can take away from me, drive away with, forget to call back about or show up with. She shakes her shoulders, an indication she's had enough. My mother only likes to be touched just so much.

And at that moment it makes sense to me. While she's trying to con me out of ten thousand dollars, my mother has inadvertently handed me over the missing link. She isn't part of my life every day, but I am and will always be a part of *her,* and the world, and everything. And no matter what she does, she cannot change this fact.

Cradling her wineglass, using it as a barrier between us, she speaks.

"Now, Vivian, about that money. We're going to the bank tomorrow morning, right when it opens, so I can get back."

It doesn't matter that I was expecting them, her words are a hot iron pressed over every inch of my body. But the pain makes everything clear. It's as if I've finally got the right eyeglass prescription—and I can see that other image was just a floater, a trick of the eye.

This is it: I have to forgive her. This was what was hiding between "tell her to fuck off" and "sure, whatever you say

Mommy." It's the only thing that will work for me. I have to forgive her, and then I have to find a way to let go of the anger. I'm not getting anywhere swimming back and forth from it like a raft in a lake. It's a very frail sort of love, but it's the only one we will ever share. It's not the world that's been against me all this time, it's that I refused to appreciate the way the world worked; I couldn't wait to see what was around the corner, I had to know, or I wasn't budging. Doing nothing is a choice, and I'm not choosing that anymore.

Before we leave the restaurant, I tell her that I want her to know that I have been very angry at her all these years for leaving me, but that I forgive her, that I know that in a way—though she didn't intend it—I am a better person for Grams's raising me, and that I am okay; I have made peace with everything and I love her very, very much. I tell her we will split the money. "I will not give you a cent more," I say carefully, slowly, so she will not question me, "and I don't ever want to speak about it again."

My mother is silent, probably more stung than sympathetic—which is to be expected—but she's wrapping her mind around how much this has cost me. She doesn't say anything, doesn't envelop me in a dramatic embrace or apologize. She purses her lips and nods her head tightly. Her eyes don't tear; they merely glass for a second, so I'll never be sure whether it was the light in her eye or a real, true display of emotion for me. But it's the most I'll get. Amazingly, it is enough.

After that, my mother shakes it all off, like a winter coat, and takes to finishing off the pasta, slurping and chomping like a teenage boy, talking about the kind of fresh ingredients she'll be using in the ice cream—boysenberries and elder flowers, lavender and honey—and I get a little appetite myself. I swirl some papardelle ribbons and fat ziti tubes onto my fork. My mother has excellent taste in food; I've never tasted pasta this fresh in my life. I swallow without chewing.

"That's vulgar," my mother says, twisting up her mouth. "This is why you need to leave Brooklyn. Get some manners."

She's right. Not about the manners—Mrs. Kaufman is the head of the Emily Post Club, and I don't know many residences that have something like that. But the other part's true enough. It's time to go.



The following day, when my mother drives away five thousand dollars richer, I clean the house from top to bottom, box up all the things I never liked. There are maybe five things that fit in this category, and they look insignificant in their cardboard home: a velvet painting of a sad-faced girl, a figurine of an angry-looking Chinese spear-fisherman with a Fu Manchu, that photo of me in my cubicle, a too-shabby driftwood bowl that sheds bark over the carpet, and all the dried flowers—which I always told Grams were bad Feng Shui. *"Uuchhhhh,"* she'd say, "feng shui this," and she'd stick out her generous butt. "When I'm dead," she used to say, "you can do whatever you like."

"I guess you were right," I say, shaking my head as I fold over the box flaps, because this is the kind of zinger she would appreciate. I reach my hand inside, pull out the Chinaman once more, and shake it. *"Uuchhhhh,"* I say, real loud, so I know she'll hear. I run to the fridge and yank the ketchup out, once and for all. *"Uuchhhhh,"* I say. "Double *uuchhhhh.*"

I clean the entire apartment. I start by the door and just keep going—picking up, throwing out. I've forgotten how simply therapeutic the smell of bleach, Pine-Sol, Lysol, the blue of Windex, and the squeak of paper towel on a mirror can be. I dock the iPhone into Len's nifty speakers and let the music penetrate the experience.

When the smells become too concentrated, I open all the windows, starting in the living room. I just keep going, forcing one ancient window lock after another, lifting the sticky frames as high as they'll rise. I open Grams's door and slowly, thoughtfully, open her windows. Her sheer gold embroidered curtains billow out with a start and then roll, undulating with the breeze. I stand by her dresser, and watch this for a few moments—the Cyclone in the distance, the parachute ride, the beach, the bridges, the new buildings. This little corner of the earth is all I've ever known. The cruise ships are out in number today—there are at least five of them, and I feel a tug, a sense of their adventure.

My foot wobbles and I knock against the dresser. One of her owl bookends falls over and the three books she'd had standing in between topple over the side. I lean down to pick them up: *The Collected Works of Emily Dickinson, Pride and Prejudice,* and the third—the third I don't recognize. I lift it, inspect its Indian print fabric cover. It's a journal, and it's never been used. I flip through the pages, let them breeze across my face. A note card drops out. This is one of the pretty cards I picked out for her birthday a few years back: *Sandra Sklar* is printed in capital letters at the top in pale peach relief. She'd written the card out to me.

*Dearest Viv, there is a story I heard today, at the doctor's office, and I wanted to share it with you before I forget. That cute doctor I'm always noodging you to go out with told me. He's Jewish, you know. You could do worse than a Jewish doctor. So, the story he told me goes like this: The Jewish sages say there is a bone in the neck, called the luz bone, which unlike the rest of the body, does not ever decompose when we are buried. This bone insures that at the End of Days, when we are all reunited, that God will have something with which to re-create life—a starting point, like I leave with my knitting, since I always screw up.*

*Now, this is a wonderful thing to look forward to, but we must not forget that this afterlife is not the main point. The main point is earth, your life here: this is the center of God's attentions and the center of all that is in the universe. The point is that this second life is a life* after *life. When we die, or when it feels like part of us has died, we always have this to look forward to, but we must never lose sight of what we have here, on earth. No matter how painful it can be—and no one's saying any different; it can freaking hurt, and don't you know it, my little girl, my wonderful little girl with all the fish jokes, who brightens my life every day and doesn't eat fruit before nine a.m., because it gives me a heartburn, and never has a coffee because her old Grams will get palpitations—this life* is *a blessing. Is it terrible for me to say that sometimes I am thankful for having had the chance to raise you, to have you raise me, to have you be my closest friend? I wish it hadn't been this way for you, but all the same I am more thankful, feel more blessed than I can say, my beautiful Viv, my Vivian. My wish, in return for all you have given to me, my wish for you is that you find, finally, a way to tighten your fist around the gifts you* do *have. It sometimes takes a long time to identify them when you've been screwed around as much as you have been. But as you have always been a gift to me, I know I have been the same to you—even when you were being a pain in the* tuchus, *I always knew how much you loved me, my dear girl. It's those we feel most secure with whom we allow ourselves to be unkind too when we need to know they'll stick around no matter what. And so, now I want you to enjoy all the other gifts in THIS life. I will see you in the next one, kiddo. And I won't be letting you get away with any crap like "sincerly" either. Might I also say something else? I would never, and I mean never, be able to say goodbye to you. I'd run away screaming, rather than face it. And so I don't want you beating yourself up for the way you handle things. I'm sick. I'm going to die. But I will always know how much you love me. I want to say thank you, for taking care of me, and for letting me take care of you. Thank you for being my granddaughter, and my daughter, and my best friend, and for being yourself, Bubbala, because there is no one like you. And don't you forget it.*

*Until we meet again, I hope this gift will inspire you to follow your destiny. Please use it to tell the world the wonderful, maybe painful, stories you have been gathering throughout your life. Once you've worked it all out, you'll understand that this is what art is all about.*

*Love always,*
*Grams*

There is a receipt in the notebook. She bought it right when she was diagnosed. She went directly from the doctor's office to the stationery store—the out-of-the-way, pricey one we only go to for special occasions. She took the bus there, and she picked out this journal for me, wrote this card out when someone told her she was going to die.

Wouldn't you know it, though? I had to figure it all out for myself. I *am* a Taurus rising, after all.

After I clean the entire apartment, dust each cherished tchotchke, wash, dry, and replace each dish, I safely slide my box to the top of Grams's closet, and then carefully fold and pile her clothing—except for a few pieces I can't bear to part with—and bag them up for Goodwill. I rearrange the sofa and chairs the way *I* always said looked better, and finally, I gather my laundry and bring it down to the laundry room. It's on the first floor, around the way from Jameson's desk, and when he says, "How are you?" I say, "I'm okay, actually." And I mean it.

I separate the colors and the whites—one garment after another is mine, and mine alone. But at the very bottom is a white undershirt; it's Len's.

# 29.

♈ ♉ ♊ ♋ ♌ ♍ ♎ ♏

*The mourners take a walk around the block, as a way of taking a first step back into the world. There are those who suggest that the soul of the deceased abides with the mourners. The soul is there to comfort the family. This first walk is for the mourners to escort the soul out of the house, indicating that they are going to be all right.*

—Rabbi Tom Louchheim

A*fter I've cleaned* every single thing I can think of—including the cans and bottles in the kitchen—I tackle the mail. It's frightening. I'll be negotiating payment plans for the rest of my life. When I get to the electric bill stack, all six of the letters, I can't help but think of that awful argument with Len. That huge argument, just to have the damned lights come on right after he left!

I flip to the most recent bill, slice it open with Grams's mother-of-pearl letter opener. It's addressed to "Mr. and Mrs.

Len Richter." It's the oddest thing. First I think it must be a mistake, just mailed to the wrong apartment. Then I look at the date of the last payment. It's the same day we had the fight; the same day the lights went off and then, *miraculously,* on. I slice open the other bills, to match up the amounts. They are the same. This *is* my bill. *Len paid it.* All I want in the entire world is to feel his hair in my fingers, to say his name over and over at his ear, to hold on and never let go. Except to go to the bathroom. Or to have my hair cut.

All I know is that the tug toward Len is so strong, I can't question it, no matter what the stars might have to say about it. What more do we ever have to work with than that? I love him. I have to face the risks involved.

I can hear the television inside his apartment. It's too loud and the wall vibrates with the baseball announcer's words. Knuckles tight, I knock on Len's door three times, loudly. I clear my throat. I'm nervous. What if I've put him off by not answering his calls? What if he's had too much time to mull over our argument and can never forgive me? What if he's back in California, and sorry, Charlie, but he told me he wasn't to be trusted right from the beginning?

He doesn't answer. But I have an idea.

I take the elevator down. At the tenth floor, Lluba Sobiesky gets in. "*Dey* cure Rachel's kitty cat." She inspects her purple manicure as she says it. "She all be-*tter* now."

It doesn't take long for the car service driver to arrive. It's the same Russian guy my mother was flirting with on the day of Grams's funeral.

"Don't I know you?" he asks. He's leering into the rear-view, checking me out a little too intensely for my taste.

"I don't think so," I say.

"Oh come. What's your name?"

I'll be spending at least an hour with this guy, all the way to Manhattan and back, and so I decide to be pleasant. "I'm Vivian," I say. "Vivian."

“Vivian? Beautiful name, this ‘Vivian.’”

“Yes, it is. Isn’t it?” I say.

The ride goes quickly. We make all the lights, miss all the traffic. Even Midtown has cleared the way for us. We stop in front of the Minskoff Theatre. I run inside, beneath the *Lion King* marquee, prepared to beg someone to let me in to buy one of those obnoxiously large Simba Cokes. I’ve got a story with a boss’s bratty kid all worked out.

The first person I see is that usher, the one whose hat was pinched by the pigeon. He looks at me oddly. It’s a day for Vivian making impressions, let me tell you. Because he looks at me and he says, “You’re the girl with the dad in the wheelchair, right? I thought about you a lot. Here I was supposed to help you take your dad safely to his seat, and what did I do? I run off and chase a freaking pigeon like a real tool. I’m sorry. I really am. Hey, what can I do you for?”

In two minutes, I’m back in the cab, the cubes clinking in my obnoxiously large Mufasa Coke.

Back at Len’s door, I ring and run.

I can’t see him through the peephole. I can’t see the reaction on his face when he sees the cup. I wait with bated breath, my ear to a glass, the same way Mrs. Hirsch is doing, in the apartment on Len’s other side.

There’s a knock on my door.

“Yes?” I say.

There’s no answer. I pry the door open but nobody’s there.

I look down. It looks like a miniature of the planets. Each one is skewered through a metal arm, which can be turned. It’s old, maybe from the ’60s, all done in pop colors. It’s awesome.

Len comes out. He’s freshly cologned and in an ancient Mets T-shirt and jeans. “Hey, you know what?” he says, walking over. He doesn’t look at me, but crouches down.

“What?” I ask.

“A lot of people look at the world in two tones. Black and white. But really, it’s not like that, you see. Really it’s got all these colors, like you see here: blue, and red, Day-Glo orange, and green."

I smile, gaze, dazzled as before, maybe more so. "You think there's actually a tempera blue planet, do you?"

"Sure. Why can't there be? You know what? There's this book somebody left at my door the other day—I don't want you to go getting jealous or anything, but I think I have a secret admirer. And this hot chick—"

"How do you know she's hot?"

"A guy knows this kind of thing."

"Is that so?"

"Yes, it's so. Now can I get back to the point I'm trying to make here?"

"Of course," I say.

We look at each other.

He continues. "Well, take something real obvious. Like how the earth is round. Everyone knows that, right?"

"Right," I say. I'm locked into his eyes. And I'm not being polite.

"Well, actually, if you look at it from space, Earth is slightly pear-shaped."

"That's fascinating," I say. "And sexy. It's definitely a little sexy."

We lean in, slow, millimeter by millimeter.

"You think that's sexy?" he says. And we're there again. In that kiss place of ours, spinning, traveling light-years along comets, asteroids, and Saturn's rings.

He stands and pulls me up by both hands. But instead of making his way to my apartment, his toe points toward his own.

I should have known. What did I think, that everything would just be okay—*will-nill*?

His hands are hooked over his belt. "I've got some stuff to do in there," he says, indicating his doorway with his chin.

When he leaves, I wonder if I'll ever see him again. If I've learned anything at all, it's that the world isn't necessarily ready just because you happen to be.

I put the kettle on and there's a knock at the door.

I run to let him in.

It's Wendy. "Oh, it's only you," I whisper.

"Boy, I'm honored," she says.

"Sssssh!" I whisper back and yank her inside and all the way into the kitchen with my finger over my lips.

"What the fuck are we being so quiet about?"

"Nothing," I say.

"Nothing," she mimics and lets out a sigh.

As Wendy sits on the back of the seat I normally sit on the back of, I fix us tea. My mouth is tight, stretched into a sort of concealing smile, and I know this is not working. She doesn't say anything, so I continue.

"So what does Kavia say about all of this 'nothing'?" she asks.

"Sugar?" I ask, though I know she likes her tea black, strong.

"Viv?"

"Listen, I don't want to hear what a giant mistake this is, but I've decided, I don't want a road map, don't need to do what everyone thinks I should do. I'm just going to . . . trust myself." I wince, pull my face away, bracing for how much her opinion is going to hurt. This is a girl who won't eat breakfast without reading her own tea leaves first.

She's quiet, chewing on the inside of her cheek.

She lets out a huge breath, flapping her lips. "I hate to be the one to tell you this, Viv. I really do."

"Okay, give it to me. Just get it over with please."

"I think—I *think*—possibly, you're actually going to survive all of this. I wasn't sure there for a while, but now I see it. You're definitely going to be okay. Maybe more than okay."

"Thanks, you're a peach." I croak. "Remind me to sign you up for cheering up the cancer kids."

"Don't thank me yet. The bad news for all the strong people in this world is that once you survive, you'll have to deal with an unrelenting amount of shit until the day you die. Just ask those cancer kids; they all think I'm a hoot, anyway. They love my impression of broccoli."

I forgot, she actually has worked with the cancer kids. Her picture was on the front page of *Skylar.* She was being broccoli, her cheeks puffed out and her hair all matted up, her arms limp at her sides. The kids were cracking up. Another thing I had missed for Bruce, some kind of Nintendo convention at the Javitz Center.

"Is there a bright side?" I ask.

"Sure. You got me, don't you?" She does the broccoli.

"About that," I say. "How are you set for long-distance calling packages?"

She steps back, takes a good look at me. "Something's different," she says. "I'm the one who leaves *you.* Now you'd better tell me what's going on." She's smoothing down her hair and looking me up and down.

I shrug, grimace.

"You got laid, didn't you?"

"Do you always have to be so crass?"

"Yes. Yes, I always have to be crass. Or is it obnoxious I always have to be? I can't remember which. So it's Len, isn't it? You know Hirsch has got her glass up against the wall. I'll tell you, it's a sad day when you have to rely on that kind of operation to tell you about your very own best friend."

"Well, *you* look wonderful, absolutely wonderful," I say to her, changing the subject. It really is true. She's glowing like that last, conspicuous string of Christmas lights in March.

"Fine. You like depriving your best friend of all the fun parts. You keep me around for the body odor stage and the fast food binges and the funerals. But you just go on right ahead and keep all the sexy stuff for yourself. I'm just glad it's not Bruce. Besides, I don't need your sexy stuff anyway. I'm in love," she says, shrugging. "All that makeup I spend my paychecks on and all I needed to do was find a skinny Japanese guy to fall in love with."

"Who, who is it? Someone you met in Japan? Is it the guy with the left-pointing thingy? Is it that guy?"

"Which one? Oh no, not him. It's the one with the Woody Allen thing. The one who made me watch *Annie Hall* all the time. What can I say? He must have a fetish for neurotic Jews. It works out for me, so I'm not complaining."

"Well there you go, how come you didn't tell me?"

She swings her palms up in surrender. "Whoa, whoa. I didn't think it was a good time to tell you my life was finally falling together perfectly right when yours was falling to crap."

"Well, that's very gallant of you," I say. "But I guess if you *really* wanted to be a good friend, you'd have said no to the promotion, and told the love of your life to fuck off."

She socks me in the arm. "Whadda you have to do to get a refill around here?"

Len knocks at the door.

I dart the death look at Wendy.

"How's everything?" I say.

"Okay," he says. "It's okay."

I breathe.

"I'm Wendy, Viv's boss. And you must be Len," she says, before I get the chance, walking over to him. To my excruciating discomfort, she adds "Viv's boyfriend."

"A pleasure to meet you," Len says. He doesn't even flinch.

"She's not technically my boss," I say, trying to steer away from any awkwardness.

"Let's not get technical," Wendy says. "So, Mr. Tall Dark and Handsome, I was just telling Viv that we're going to Lundy's with Lai, my Japanese boyfriend with a Jew fetish, and my parents tomorrow night. And we want you to come."

Len and I exchange quick looks; I shrug—it's an apology for Wendy's crazy talk, which even I know is an acquired taste, and for her assuming he wants to be my boyfriend. I start to apologize for him.

"I'm there," he says. "I never miss the chance to meet a real Japanese boyfriend."

"He's not half bad, is he?" Wendy says, kisses me, and heads for the door. "Adios, people, adios."

" 'Officer' Richter!" Wendy yells before she's even closed the door. She's probably the only girl in the world who could get away with using the air quotes to his face.

He laughs and holds out his arms to her. "Great to see you, gorgeous," he says from his wheelchair, right inside his door frame. "You look fabulous."

Len and I lean out my own open door.

"I'm in love," she says, shrugging, this now apparently her tag phrase.

I don't know if it's wishful thinking or whether Len's eyes truly do sweep in my direction when she says it.

To temper my discomfort, I say, "I'm having a commemorative T-shirt printed."

"You can do better than that," Wendy says.

Richter, in his wobbly voice, bests us all: "How about getting a tattoo on your ass?"

"See, Viv, that's how it's done," Wendy says. "And she fancies herself a writer, this one," she says, tossing her head back in my direction.

Before we part ways, Richter promises to come, too, though he looks so terrible, I sense there is some untruth to this. I want to ask, but these Scorpios don't want to talk about it unless they bring it up, and that's a fact.

# 30.

♈ ♉ ♊ ♋ ♌ ♍ ♎ ♏

*When we are no longer able to change a situation, we are challenged to change ourselves.*

—Victor Frankl

A*t the last* minute, just when I'm packing my purse to leave for Lundy's, Len knocks on my door. He can't come, he says. His dad's not up to it.

Richter wheels himself to their doorway, the same way he did yesterday. "He's going. Over my dead body he's not going."

Len doesn't turn around. He says to me, "He can't stay alone."

"I'm not staying alone. You can tell the *pischer,* I'm not staying alone. Rachel Valmay jumped at the chance to spend the night. She's always had the hots for me."

It takes obvious effort for Len to keep from smiling.

I was really looking forward to Len and Richter having another go at wrapping that old bandage over their wound. I think even Len seemed hopeful.

Len is quiet in the elevator and in the Range Rover on the way over. When the valet takes the keys and Len passes him a ten, he must have made up his mind about something because he springs to life. Lundy's is as grand and over-the-top as it's always been.

"Whatcha thinking?" I ask, as we make our way inside. My head tilts to the side. I'm jubilant.

"You ready to meet the Japanese boyfriend?" Len asks as he holds the door open for me.

"Ready as I'll ever be," I say and cluck my tongue.

"Your friend is something else," he says as he spots her across the room.

"You don't know the half of it," I say, just as she nods at me, and pushes back her seat at the best table in the house—the one with the picture-window view of the water. When she stands it frames her like a movie poster. Her parents are dressed the same way I always remember them—in frumpy, intellectual clothing that says they're too evolved to care. Mrs. Berk's big brown eyes—the exact same eyes she passed on to her daughter—are not overshadowed by her blousy floral top. The Berks, and our entire table, are far more casual than the other diners. People overdress to come to Lundy's, trying to conjure up a Brooklyn that, sadly, no longer exists.

Legend has it that this place used to seat up to 2,800 people, all of whom waited two weeks to preen around their booked tables and feel glamorous, even if Scotch tape was holding their hemlines up. They brought out their molting furs and their threadbare top hats to remember exactly why it was they came to America in the first place. They ate enough shellfish to bring on a nasty case of gout, and gobbled down the famous flaky biscuits, warm and with perfect shell-shaped butter pats melting inside. This was the place where Grams was asked for her hand in marriage. I could tell you exactly what she wore, where she sat, and what the fish of the day was. She told stories about Lundy's that made up the backdrop of my own daydreams about what love was supposed to be—mink stole, cigarette holder, and all.

Len is in black pants with a faint blue check ghost-patterned over them, and a crisp white shirt with the top button undone. It's a slim, classic cut and it really suits him. His shoes are shined, and I swear, even this insignificant detail is novel to me. Len ties his shoes! Len wears a work shirt! Len goes to a fancy restaurant! I'm as silly as a children's book, but I guess Grams left that part of love out. Or maybe there are some bits you just have to learn on your own.

"Viv!" Wendy's parents stand as one solid unit. I am not proud of the fact that their solidarity has always pained me in a deep, envious way, though I am so happy for them. But today I don't react with anything but joy at the sight of them. Grams and I had that—and more. What I feel now is proud of this wonderful family I've known for most of my life. I see that what I want more than anything is to make this kind of family for myself—to raise children so confident they can say anything to anyone, the way my dear, dear friend can.

I embrace them one at a time, at each stop making the necessary introductions.

"A pleasure to meet you," Len says, one after the other. He's so formal. There are many things I have yet to learn about him. Mrs. Berk gives me a nod of approval over his shoulder.

Wendy introduces her Japanese boyfriend, Lai, who is quite charming. He has delicate skin—almost translucent, with a pristine, creamy texture—which looks magnificent against Wendy's olive complexion. His eyes are gray, heathered, with intricate variation.

"Viv," he says, standing and embracing me. "I feel like I know you already. I'm sorry about Grams. I hear she was quite a woman."

"Don't be so proper with Viv," Wendy says. "She's likely to start a folder on you."

I grit my teeth at her. No one knows what she means but everyone laughs in the nervous way first meetings tend to foster.

"Thanks, Lai. She was, is, quite a woman," I say. I wonder which anecdotes Wendy shared; I think, in a way, Grams is being dispersed throughout the world, like those fluffy dandelion seed pods—blown around the globe: Unus Mundus.

Dinner goes smoothly. Everyone seems to hit it off. It feels almost as if I am introducing Len in the same important way that Wendy is debuting Lai. It feels like a family dinner, a reunion. There are the proper measures of warmth and nostalgia and overeating.

"Did you know that Lundy began by selling clams out of a pushcart?" Len asks the group at large, over chocolate mousse and fruit pies. "Amazing how a guy can pick up on the pulse of an entire borough, thousands of people from all over the world, and create something with so much relevance—out of a clam cart. That's the kind of thing most of us can only dream of achieving."

"I know what you mean," Mr. Berk says. "When I started teaching, I thought I'd change the whole world, revolutionize the way people thought about life." He shakes his head, spins his wineglass by the stem. "But I didn't."

"Don't say that," his wife argues. To us she says, "You wouldn't believe how many students wrote him over the years, how many still write. 'You were a wonderful teacher,' they say; '*Catcher in the Rye* is still my favorite book because of you,' they say; 'I bought it for my kid,' they write. And that's really something."

We all nod our agreement.

The check arrives and the Berks won't let anyone so much as look at it. We all wave our credit cards around halfheartedly, but it's only a show. The Berks take pride in the fact that they've scrimped over the years, made enough to buy Wendy and her friends a fancy dinner replete with chocolate mousse if they want to. We don't take that away from them.

After the check is settled, I go to the ladies room. Returning around the back corrider I see our table—dozens of feet away. My energy drains as I take in the gathering. Grams is missing. *Grams is missing, and life must go on.* Though I have the urge to curl up on Len's lap, I straighten up, square off my shoulders, and make my way back to the table.

When I settle into my seat someone's phone starts to vibrate. We all laugh as one at a time we take a turn reaching inside pockets and dipping in purses to see whose phone is buzzing. First Lai, then Wendy, Mr. and then Mrs. Berk, myself. Len is last. I don't like the feeling I have at this realization.

He must not either, because he stares at his phone—a slim silver thing; not a fancy iPhone like mine—for several seconds before picking it up.

"Who is it?" I ask, growing worried.

"It's my dad," he says.

" 'Officer' Richter?" Wendy asks, too smiley, giddy from the easy attraction of the gathering, from the energy of a really good time. She does the air quotes.

Len's lips tighten, the skin around his mouth blanches; he's staring at his own hand on the water glass. He flashes a smile for Wendy's benefit and answers the call.

My jaw locks up; something is wrong.

"I'll be right there," he says into the phone, and rises.

"Excuse me," Len says, manages a polite smile, and walks toward the door looking smaller than I've ever seen him. Silverware tinkles against china plates; busboys saunter by less purposefully than they ought to look. Something in my head pounds.

I funnel in the confused looks. To Wendy's apologetic shrug I shake my head, toss a palm—she shouldn't worry. But I wobble out of my seat, rubbery, obviously worried myself, and offer quick thanks and greetings before I rush to catch up with Len.

"Okay, okay," he's saying; he seems to be in a loop where only a few key words apply. "I'll be there."

"I'm coming," I say. I don't know where. But I feel power, faith. And I want to give it all to Len.

# 31.

♈ ♉ ♊ ♋ ♌ ♍ ♎ ♏

*The biggest disease today is not leprosy or tuberculosis, but rather the feeling of being unwanted.*

—Mother Teresa

L*en has clammed* up. He's driving, his cheek a tight knot. The street lamps and stoplights whiz past like something interplanetary. We're traveling somewhere far off—somewhere neither of us wants to go.

Five minutes later, I realize one of us isn't going. We're taking the turnoff to our building.

"What are you doing?" I say, like we've been married for a couple dozen years.

"I'm dropping you off," he says, his eyes straight ahead, as if he knows they'll give too much away.

I don't want to say the wrong thing. Look how I handled things in his position, and Grams and I didn't have any "issues" between us to work out. I flip the pages of my emotional thesaurus, reticent, searching for the kind of careful, soothing vocabulary that simply does not exist. I know that this isn't a guy who leans on people. This is a guy who stands real strong while everyone piles up to lean against him. Letting a woman he's just starting out with serve as armchair, or even armrest, that's just unheard-of. Add in the part about how twice, just as he was close, I've let him down, and I might be the last person on earth this Scorpio of Scorpios would let behind the curtain now. And I can't say I blame him. All the same, I want to wrap my arms around his neck, like one of those rearview-mirror koalas, and never let go. If only life were as simple as it is for synthetic wildlife tchotchkes.

"Yeah, okay," is all I come up with. Nothing's black-and-white, someone told me earlier.

Even those koalas are made in China, probably in sweat-shops full of little children inhaling petrochemicals that cause early-onset leukemia.

I get out of the car and watch him drive away, around the back of the building. I say to his receding taillights what I never could to his face: "Let me be there for you."

And then he's gone. On a bench outside is Rachel Valmay; she's petting her cat, who's hiding, jiggly in her purse, mewling.

"I thought you were with 'Officer' Richter," I say, the air quotes too deeply engrained to go without, even at a time like this.

"He made me leave the hospital. Said a woman shouldn't see a man this way. Said he wanted to watch my backside wiggle out of the room while he could still enjoy it." She stares far off, to the new buildings, to the death of the old beach club. "I did my best, but it's been many years since I wiggled."

"I know," I say, sitting down next to her, right where my old cell phone met its demise.

"And it's a lot of pressure to be the last wiggle for a dying man."

"I know," I say again, an image in my mind of a stoic Richter holding himself up on the bedrails, trying for a last laugh, wanting to be remembered that way. We both shake our heads. No matter how much experience you have with it, no one knows what to say when death comes around. It's always awkward, like a blind date, or a visit to the OB-GYN.

"He was in so much pain; I could see it in the way he was clenching his jaw, but he kept saying that he was fine. He didn't want me to call Len and tell him. 'My son's got a great girl,' he kept saying. 'My son's got a great girl.'" Every few seconds, a mewl emerges from the puff poking through the zip-top bag. "Shah, shah," she says, to the beat of long, slow strokes with the flat of her palm. The miraculously cured cat heeds, as if all that jostling was just to make sure that Rachel was nearby.

"Don't be silly," Rachel Valmay says, apropos of nothing, her hand inside the cat bag, moving more rapidly now.

"Excuse me?" I ask.

"Go to him. Just go. I was married for fifty years. I know men like these Richters. They think they want to be heroes, they just want to run around sticking Band-Aids on everyone, and they mean to, they really do. But they need women like us to show them they sometimes need Band-Aids, too."

We sink a little deeper into the mesh-coated steel bench outside the entrance, a replacement that was part of last year's renovation. We're right by the old Seacoast Terrace sign, its elegant aqua and chrome steel letters cropping out of the grass like a retro-modern take on a pruned hedge. I used to scale the S when my mother and I would come to visit. "S is for Sandra," my mother used to say, her smile resplendent. We'd pick the dandelions, which are still growing around the base.

I reach down and pick one. With the fragrant, velvety head at my nose, I breathe in deeply, and laugh.

"What?" Rachel Valmay says.

"Nothing," I say.

*"Hmmmph,"* she says, and gives the cat a scratch under its neck.

My mother used to rub the dandelions on my nose, let the

golden color dye my skin. And then she'd hold up her silver compact so I could see. I'd giggle—amazed. Such a simple thing as that. I haven't thought of that in so long.

I pull the long stem through my fingers, weave it over and under, over and under, finally tucking its oniony stem behind my ear. I can't remember the last time I had a good memory involving my mother. It is such a relief *not* to be angry at her for a change.

We watch the sun tuck down behind the buildings. Rachel reaches into the bag with one hand and pulls the cat out, like a rabbit from a hat. She puts it on my lap. "Here," she says.

The cat is fluffy for something so old. I'm a bit surprised at the warmth the little thing gives off. It stares at me, blinky, its head cocked in consideration. Up close, its pink nose looks more like marble—veins of brown and cream running through. It squeals a meek meow, its long tongue curls out, and deciding I'm okay, it snuggles its little head into my neck. It is very, very cute. And it feels wonderful to be a source of comfort for the thing.

Rachel Valmay nods her head up and down in enormous strokes. One side of her mouth pinches in a smirk. "I know, I know," she says. "The cat is freaking wonderful; she's really something." The "freaking" thing really caught on a few years back.

I go back to petting. The cat is caught up in bliss. Its eyes are closed and it's rubbing up against me in a trance. I realize, for the first time, that I have no idea what this cat's real name is. We've been calling it Rachel Valmay's Cat around here since she brought it home. I ask.

"Ira," she says, searching my face for a reaction to this, to her naming her cat after her husband. Probably she's heard the rumors.

"That's a lovely name," I say.

"Well, it's a girl." She shrugs, as if there's nothing that can be done about it now.

"Still," I say. My smile creeps out, bringing Rachel Valmay's with it. Soon, we're in hysterics. There's tears, snorting, the whole shebang.

She retrieves Leonard, as if she can't bear to be separated from her any longer. "How do you like that, Leonard? Shall we get you a sex change, like those transvestites in *La Cage aux Folles*?" Rachel asks the cat in a baby voice, standing it on her lap, waving it by its cotton ball–white rib cage, arms splayed, like it's dancing.

Then Rachel closes her eyes, snuggling the fluffball into her chest, the way mothers do with infants. Rachel Valmay's face is as peaceful as I've ever seen it. *Everyone needs something,* I think. Whether it's mystical, metaphysical, or just plain adorable, we all need something to keep us believing.

I walk Rachel Valmay up to her apartment while I wait for the car service to arrive.

# 32.

♈ ♉ ♊ ♋ ♌ ♍ ♎ ♏

Lost Illusions *is the undisclosed title of every novel.*

—André Maurois

*The automatic door* at the hospital is broken, zooming back and forth like crazy. I watch the rhythm from the bench while I try to work out whether showing up is brilliant or just plain nuts. By the time I make up my mind that I'll never know, I manage to slip right through like a pro. On the third floor, I find the room easily. I know the schematic here—the rooms are laid out identically. The only difference is the sound of the cries, whether the patient gets regular or soy milk with their matzo ball soup and green Jell-O. When I get to Richter's room, I hear them talking—father and son. My throat thickens.

I duck my head in, the room is only half lit. The other bed, the one closer to the window, is empty. In a flash I see myself as my character, the one in my book, and I think something surprising: She looks pretty brave to me.

I eye the en suite: *Just dare me.* But there's no point. I'm not that girl who hides in bathrooms anymore. There was a fork in the road, and she took one and I took the other. We made a deal beforehand, and I'm not going back for her.

Richter is completely deflated, a plastic bag that's been stomped on, driven over, splashed with mud; but he is remarkably calm. You see this kind of calm only once in someone's life.

I take one dip into Len's eyes and know I'm on eerily familiar territory. We may be different in many ways, but we're not so different.

"Dad," he says. I am relieved and shocked to see, with my own eyes, Len address his father. He approaches the bedside, his hand gentle over the bedrail. "You've got a visitor." Len puts his other arm around me. It's not the same way as before. It hasn't got any of the oomph. Even like this, my skin reacts; there are electron storms, molecule collisions.

Len lets both of us go and lowers the rail. He sits me down in the awkward, backward way people sit alongside patients in hospital beds. I take the posture in the usual way—half afraid to squash something or pull out a plug, legs dangling uncertainly.

Richter doesn't speak immediately. It's just as well. I need a second to catch my breath. I can't help but reach back; it's so vivid I feel I've been transported to that terrible day. It takes all I've got to send the screaming voice in my head away, to quiet the words: "CAN YOU HEAR ME, MS. SKLAR?" "CAN YOU STAY WITH US, MS. SKLAR?" I'm not so angry about the *Ms.* part now. I feel the terror I wasn't able to on that day. It's a knife point in my belly. It doesn't go; even when nausea barrels over it. I clutch my stomach.

"Are you okay?" Len asks when he sees my face, the quick repositioning of my hand.

"Of course. I'm just glad to be with my two boys." When I say it, I know it's true. I wish I could have years and years with these two—share holidays and birthdays and French fries. They are wonderful together, and I think, maybe, finally, they see it. Probably it's breaking their hearts. "You're both so wonderful," I say, though it must sound strange. They are both silent, exchanging looks, tight grimaces.

"Son," Richter says, his lids fluttering. This grounds me, brings me back. It's too formal. But he hasn't had the time to try out names: Len, Junior, Lenny, Kid, My Kid. He reaches out a hand. Len accepts. Richter gasps.

"Dad," Len says, looking his father in the eye before his eyes squeeze close, a trickle sliding down his nose before sailing down into the whiteness of his nice collared shirt.

"Oh, oh, your eyes are just like your mother's when you look at me." From the wobble of his words, the set of his jaw, I can tell it must be the first time Len spoke directly to Richter. "I just want to say, I want to say—" He chokes on tears, bites back whatever's rising.

I hold my stance though a vicious wave of nausea has done its best to knock me down. My belly reprimands me. The nausea trails rapidly down my abdomen. I swallow it down. I'm not going anywhere near that bathroom.

"You don't have to, Dad," Len says now, flounders to show his dad he gets it. The corners of his mouth twitch. I'm met with an image of the first time I saw Len, out on the balcony, how upset he appeared at the idea of his father being alone.

I am half standing, fidgety on my left, but strong—where Len and I are holding hands—on my right. The three of us form a chain. We are connected; there is no denying that now. When Richter dies and things are tough one far-off day—there's not enough money or one of us falls ill—we'll have this image: a people chain, half on and half off a hospital bed, lumpy and smelly and all the things you could ever need.

"No, that's where you're wrong, Len. I do have to do this. It's the most important thing of all. And I want Viv to hear. She's important to us." He looks at me, and my nose burns, pride swells in my chest—I'm embarrassed by how proud I feel.

I sit down again, all the way now, alongside Richter's leg.

"Now, I know I fucked up. I know that. I've known it for as long as I can recall. And it's too late to fix what I've broken. I know that, too. I took the coward's way out."

Len's face is completely still, he's holding it like a fragile piece of china that could crack into a million pieces. He squeezes my hand and love jolts right through it.

"I know now that none of this is a fair excuse. You have to be brave, and you have to learn to do what you have to do, to work around your weaknesses. But it can take a person awhile to learn that. And I'm not using that as an excuse. I was dead wrong. And I was the kinda guy, nobody could tell me anything. I think maybe you got some of that from me, Len. I want you to hear this. At least I can give you this."

Let me tell you, the most magical thing happens when Richter says this. Len's fantastic smile peeks through—not the entire smile, you understand, but enough to see that there is hope. Richter notices it, and his own face reflects the exact same smile—genetic evidence of the connection, emotional evidence. It's extraordinary.

Richter steels himself; his fist grasps the edge of a pillow, his head steadies against the faux wood headboard. "I loved you; I loved your mother. I couldn't believe that a loser like me had gotten so lucky. And I *was* a loser." His nose twitches and his eyes are instantly drenched. He waves away the cup of water Len holds out. He swallows down some spit. Richter doesn't believe he deserves his son's love. He is wrong, of course.

"I was a gambler. I'd go to the underground spots on Kings Highway and blow my paycheck before I even brought it home. I had nothing to contribute to you and your lovely mother; there was nowhere good you would have gone under my direction. I know now that this was cowardice. I should have challenged myself, forced myself onto the straight and narrow, sacrificed, for you, for Maria. But I wasn't that insightful. So I took the easy way out—made it so that neither of you would want anything to do with me."

Len is quiet. His gaze shifts to the floor. He's avoiding my face. I think he wants my advice but can't bring himself to look. The second he does, I'll know he wants me to tell him it's okay to forgive.

The thing is, a wise woman once told me that you get what you get; there's no use in his trying to change things now. "Yes, it would have been better if you had tried—maybe," I say. I look at Len while I speak. "But in the end, maybe you would have gone down a bad path and Len would have grown to hate you, would have become someone he himself hated. You don't know. You can't. What you have is the way it has already happened. You can't worry yourself with what that bitch next door has. You have what you have," I say, the familiarity of the words like a punch in the stomach. She's here. Once again with Richter, my grandmother is here. Just like when the bird flew into the elevator, and she just whispered this in my ear: *You had it wrong; your mother did know you were better off with me.*

Len reaches down and holds his father for a long, long while, his hand squeezing mine all the time. When he stands he turns to me. "Thanks for wanting to do the right thing for me," Len tells me, exploring this strange vocabulary of emotion the way I once watched fish through a snorkel mask in Orlando—with an equal mix of terror and reverence. He turns back to Richter, wild-eyed, as if he's seeing him for the first time. He looks back at me, grabs my face in both of his hands.

There are moments when things do seem to fall into a larger plan. This is what goes through my head when bile rises and I'm forced to run into the en suite, knowing I won't be able to swallow it back down this time.

Leave it to me to interrupt the most important scene in Len's and Richter's lives. I can do nothing to stop the deluge. I press the door shut and kneel right in front of the toilet—and my guts surge up from what feels like every crevice of my body. The last time I was this sick was from the Bad Salmon Experience of 1997. Grams was sick, too. We spent my entire Christmas vacation in bed watching old films on television. Funny how that turned into a good memory.

"Don't come in; don't come in," I say when Len knocks. But there is no lock on the door and Len isn't a good listener. He's at my shoulders, passing me tissues and pressing a cold, wet towel to the back of my neck.

I can hear Richter from the bed. "Is she okay? What's going on? I bet she's pregnant."

It turns out the doctors might put money on the same thing, because they order a pregnancy test among several other options—including food poisoning and botulism screens. Len and I exchange inscrutable looks; there's so much going on it's all we can do to try and fit this into the schematic. What can I say? Like Ford possibly going out of business, like the idea of a twenty-first-century economic depression, it doesn't seem real when the impossible becomes reality. Me, making a family of my own? I fill out the forms as if they are about someone else.

Richter shakes his head tightly. Now they've sprouted, his tears are on free fall. Frankness prevails when there isn't time for anything else. "A baby is a treasure," he says. "Make sure you treat it like a treasure." His chest and shoulders are heaving the way you never want to see on a grown man.

"We haven't heard back yet, Dad," Len says.

"Don't tell me. I know."

We shrug. You can't argue with these old people. This, I know.

Instead, I make my way to the bed and nestle against Richter's shoulder. I rest my head in the crook of his neck the way Leonard did to me earlier. His breathing calms and I'm strong as I've ever been. I'm that Astroland girl, the chorus concert girl, the ten-year-old who could run all the way down nineteen floors and back up like it was nothing.

"You're a good girl," Richter says. "The best."

Later, when Richter is sleeping and Len is outside talking with the doctor, I consider this: without Richter, there would be no Len. Without Grams, I would not have lived in Seacoast. Without my mother being the way she is, my father dying . . . it goes on and on, and I can see the lines reaching out across the greatest of distances—through time and space and life. Yes, we are connected. And maybe I could have looked out and seen this moment on a star chart, on an intricate table filled with directions and know-it-all logarithms. But then again—one turn down a different avenue, and maybe I wouldn't be here at all. And maybe, just maybe, that is the very reason why it's so special that I am.

I'm on the verge of making sense of it, and yet maybe I'm just getting to the next level, where things will be just that much more complicated and I'll realize I didn't know a damned thing. And for once, that's okay.

Len comes back. I sit up and he holds my other hand, the one that isn't in Richter's. And amazingly, with Len's hand, Richter's hand, this grounding in human contact, in life, I'm okay not knowing which way I'm going. I'm okay with myself. *Thank God,* I find myself thinking, with enormous relief, before I realize precisely what I've just thought, and where I'm thinking it. A massive wave of strength bolts through; my muscles tense, my feet anchor themselves into the earth.

And then the nausea is back.

We won't get the tests back until tomorrow. Meanwhile, Len and Richter seem to enjoy treating me like a fragile piece of ancient pottery. It's something they can easily agree on. And so I don't argue when they send me home for the night. Besides, they are tired, and Len, I think, wants to take the ride with me back to the building, wants to be someone besides the man whose father is dying—if only for a moment. We ride with all the windows open and Buddy Holly playing so softly we can barely hear it. He holds my belly the whole time, his thumb working up and down beneath the material of my shirt.

When he drives away, I stand with Jameson and imagine I can hear Len's car all the way down Coney Island Avenue.

"The season's changing," Jameson says.

It's the second time I've heard this. I root around in my tote bag. I wrote something for Jameson while Richter was asleep. I hand him the paper, folded into a tight square.

"What's this?" he asks.

"Something I wrote for you."

"Well, that is very Sandra of you," he says.

"Thank you," I say. "Thank you very much."

There are five tin trays stacked outside Len's door. They are Mrs. Kaufman's, clearly. I'm at the foot of the toilet in seconds just thinking of what's in them.

Right after that I shower, looking down at my belly the way I used to look at the phone when I wanted my mother to call: desperately wanting, and cursing my helplessness. There is a child in there or there isn't; the child would be everything I want it to be, or it wouldn't. I can only do the part that I can do, and the rest is out of my hands. I say out loud, just in case, my neck cranked toward my abdomen: "That is the way life goes, little one."

There are two messages on the answering machine. They are both from Wendy. "Lai and I love you. We just want you to know that." She says the same thing both times, like maybe she forgot she'd done it the first time. At the end of each, William barks identically in the background.

Back at the hospital the following day, in a minute alone with Richter, I ask him what the view is like from that side. He says it's a lot easier than the view from where I'm sitting. We—on this end—won't know what we lost, he says, but you, you'll see it all too clearly. And you'll have to go on knowing that one day it will happen to you, too. "I am terrified to death for you. Ignore the pun," he says, bumping me with his arm, his poked, taped, and blood-crusted arm.

"So, knowing that, what would you say to me if you could say anything?" I ask.

"I'd say get me a corned beef sandwich, please." His face is as straight as I've ever seen. "And don't forget the mustard."

And so I turn to go.

I'm right at the door when he calls me back. "And I'd also tell you that you and Len are in love. I'm old enough and I've lost my chance at it enough to recognize the real thing when I see it."

I turn back and nod.

"Don't just nod your head," he says. "Make sure you don't fuck it up."

"I won't," I promise. I mean it. "I won't fuck it up." I get shy at the swear word once it's out.

Richter smiles and looks like he's trying not to cry.

Instead of going to the Super A Kosher Takeaway around the block, I decide to pass up all the joke opportunities about what exactly is so super about that "A," and take the long walk down to the best deli in Brooklyn. I know every item on the neon menu above the counter by heart. I'm met with a glimpse of recognition from the cashier—a woman with maroon hair and glasses dangling on a chain over her generous chest.

When I return with my warm bag, the hospital doors are broken again. This time there's a computer paper sign adhered to the glass with a piece of masking tape; it's printed neatly, thoughtfully, in earnest caps: BROKEN; NO ENTRY. GO AROUND TO SIDE DOOR.

In the hospital lobby, President Obama speaks of the GFC—a crisis so big it's got its own acronym—via a television hanging from a steel arm off the ceiling. Things are finally looking up, is the sense of it. Then again, the attacks in Mumbai remind us of the value of life itself, he says. He wants us to have hope. Above all, this is what he wants.

A stout man in an official Giants track suit yells at the television: "Soon enough we will all have nothing."

"Don't say that," I say, without pausing or looking at him.

"Don't bury your head in the sand," he yells.

There's a flashback clip on the television. It's from before the election: a huge crowd of Obama supporters marches in front of the Washington Monument, the ring of flags waves above them on a breeze. One person holds a sign that reads, "He'll bring us better days."

"You can't predict the future," I say to the man, his belly peeking out below the hem of his zip jacket. "Right now is all we have."

The elevator doors close between us. I recall a phrase from a DOS computer game my dad and I used to play: "You can't get there from here," it said from time to time in that ancient green on black type, when you'd corner yourself by the 69-eyed Dornbeast or the creepy Hangman. Dad used to love that prompt. He'd squeeze his lips and shake his head as if he'd found something important in it.

Somewhere in that there's great irony: when he was killed in a motorcycle accident he'd been lost; always he was getting lost. If I happened to be with him for the ride, he'd use that phrase a lot, and laugh. He'd say, "You can't get there from here," with the twang the computer voice used. He'd lose hours and hours and my mother would chew her cuticles until pinheads of blood sprouted around her nail beds. This time he'd nearly made it back. He was just about to get over for our exit when he swerved to stop, trying to avoid two girls in a convertible. His body slid for twenty-two feet, the coroner's report said. I walked that distance with a pedometer forty-seven times in my senior year of high school. My grandmother took me to a therapist in Park Slope with hair curling out of his nose. After five minutes of his referring to "your late father" and "your absent mother" like character roles to be filled in a play, I got up, met my grandmother in the waiting room, and told her I wasn't going back there anymore.

I didn't want to face those things. I wanted to see if a swing could go all the way around. I wanted to brush the tails on my Little Pony until the waves came out. I wrapped myself in optimism and considered myself lucky. But there's a middle ground, that hairy therapist was trying to show me. And that's where most of us have to live if we want get "there" from here.



When I get to the room, swinging the paper bag by its folded-over top, Len's at the window and Richter is already dead.

"But he wanted a corned beef sandwich," I whisper.

"No, no. He wanted you to go *get him* a corned beef sandwich." Len's still at the window, but motions for me to come and fit myself in under his arm. It's a spot I'm starting to grow fond of.

"He told me he wanted that to be his last memory of you," Len says. "He said he wanted to go thinking of how we'd soon all be sitting, eating a nice corned beef sandwich."

"Anticipation," I say.

"Some sideshow-freak types call it faith," Len says.

"I guess sometimes it really does work in mysterious ways," I say. "It's not just for bearded ladies and mermen after all."

"We're going to be okay," Len says, seriously, like he's convincing himself.

"How do you know?" I turn my head against his shirt. My cheek brushes against the buttons. I keep from crying because that is what he is trying to do himself.

"Because we love each other."

"We do?" I ask.

"We do," he says, and looks at me for a long, long while before kissing me.

He's right, of course. I take the hand he extends, a prayer answered perhaps, and we face the unknown. Loss descends on the room like a deflating parachute.

"We do," I whisper.

His other hand moves to my belly. "You know, I've been thinking about you," he says.

"You have?" I pull back, look up at him, strangely peaceful.

"Yeah. I do that sometimes. I'm thinking nobody knows a thing. We're all scrambling for the answers. That's the big secret, Viv: the big secret is that *you've* known it all along, while we've all been too damned afraid to face it."

We stand there—he turns me to look at Richter. I take in his closed eyes, the settled lines of his leathery face. His jaw is slack, his eyebrows natural. "Peace is a corned beef sandwich," I say.

We're quiet with that for a moment.

"The test is back," Len says, finally.

"Oh yeah?" I ask, the paper bag crinkling in my hand as my sensations ratchet up.

"Yup," he says.

"Well, what did it say?"

"It said you are about to get acquainted with the business end of a diaper genie." And then—for happiness, or sadness, or both—he finally lets go, sobs great wails into my shoulder.

I'm going to have a baby. With Len. I'm going to be a mother. Someone, some little boy or girl, will look up one day and call me Mom, Ma when they're being whiny, Mommy when they are sad; they'll love me unconditionally before I have a chance to make all the mistakes I certainly will. It will be up to me to make sure they love me, make sure they know how much I love them, after that. Before I can squeeze the thought back, I think of my mother, of how this would be one of those times I'd want her to say something warm and comforting, the kind of thing I've come up with for her dozens of times—"Oh, Vivian, I'm so happy for you. You'll be a wonderful mother." But she won't. She just loves me in her way, and I have no choice but to accept that, insufficient as it feels at the moment. Life is good and bad; life is about getting ready to eat a corned beef sandwich. And I'm going to count my blessings, keep my faith.

"Hungry?" I ask, waving the bag up to Len's face.

"Yeah," he says. "Yeah. Let's go eat that bad boy. I hope

you remembered the mustard," he says, scooching me around and toward the door, both of us taking one last lingering look at his father.

"I did," I say. "If there's one thing I'm good at, it's knowing what people want."

We're outside the hospital. The door has been fixed.

"Let me guess? It's your rising sign that gives you that, right?"

I don't answer. Instead I say, pointing up to the sky. "Hey, you see that bull up there? That's you and your dad."

I work out some calculations, sprinkle in some wishful thinking. "Our child will be born in March, so that makes her sign—"

Len's hand claps over my mouth for what will most likely *not* be the last time. "Why don't we just try to take things as they come—just for a little while, okay?"

I nod my head. I couldn't have said it better myself.

# 33.

♈ ♉ ♊ ♋ ♌ ♍ ♎ ♏

*In three words I can sum up everything I've learned about life. It goes on.*

—Robert Frost

"We're *throwing the* housecoat in the ocean," I say to Len when we're awake again, watery-eyed and disheveled. "Get dressed."

He cranes his neck back. "Just when I've grown fond of it."

"There's no accounting for taste," I say. "I'll get something you like better. I promise."

"Deal," he says. "I know you usually save your stockings for funerals, but I really like all those straps and lace."

And so we go, turning left on the ground floor, to the back exit nearest the beach. We descend the steps where the surf crawls up to the sand—just beyond that same bench where we sat on that first day: with the pigeon or the dove, whichever way you prefer to look at it. Len holds my hand and recites, imperfectly, a beautiful Jewish prayer I remember from Hebrew School.

*Modeh ani lefanecha melech chai v'kayam sh'he'chezarta bi nishmati b'chemlah, rabba emunatecha.*

I've lost the exact meaning years ago. But I know the sense of it. *Thanks a million, God, for restoring my soul, for my faith.*

What I always loved about the prayer was the simplicity of its imagery. I saw my faith as a pretty painted box, which the bearded Big Guy hands back to me, covering my hands in his large, warm ones.

The image blurs and I get the sense that these are just words. They could be anything: a poem by e. e. cummings, Wordsworth, anyone; it's faith if you believe it. Faith is Len; *this* is something to believe in, something real, something I can actually put my hands on, isn't it? I look into his eyes, deep down, and hold my nose to his so I can't see straight. I kiss him like I want to show God exactly what I'm doing.

We each hold onto a side of the housecoat. Len counts to three and we let it go. The air gets inside, puffing the snapped thing up like a Macy's parade float. A swift wind sends it sailing up, nearly vertical, like an apparition. Len squeezes both of my hands in one of his. My heart freezes, feels as if it has stopped beating; seconds stretch out long and thick. Finally, the dress goes horizontal, and then deflates in an instant, landing on the water's surface, where it coasts toward the cafés and then, turning, out toward the distant sun.

We sit on the bench and watch it for a long while. The mood shifts. It's lost a good two hundred pounds. We try to top each other with tall tales. The dress is off conceiving illegitimate children, picking up prostitutes, opening Al Capone's vault.

"That dress has led a full Life, Viv," Len says. He hooks an arm over my shoulder. "You shouldn't feel sad; you shouldn't be sad at all. You did your best to share the dress with the world. And you were very generous and brave about it. There comes a day where we all have to say goodbye to our dresses.

You can ask my mom all about it when we are living in San Francisco. That is, if you would like to do that."

He slipped it in there like he already knew the answer. "I would love to," I say.

"Maybe we'll meet the dress there. But maybe we won't."

I sock him in the arm because he's getting a little carried away.

"Enough with the dress already," I say.

He ignores me completely. "Now you've let it off into the world on its own, and who knows where it will go, what kind of trouble it will get in? I'll tell you one thing, though. I for one won't forget the good times I had with you and that dress anytime soon."

"Okay, continue," I say.

He winks. "But I won't worry over it. For us, there'll be plenty more dresses. There will always, always be dresses for us, right, little baby Richter?" He pats my belly, which is just the slightest bit stretched, the slightest bit crampy, and wonderfully, wonderfully alive.

"What if we want to give her my name?" I say, again picturing a daughter. "Do you want Mommy's name? Do you want Mommy Vivian's name?" I ask. We exchange a look, the kind that shows you know just what the other person's thinking. It's funny, and it's sad, and it's symbolic, too. And most of all, it feels really, really good.

As we turn off the boardwalk and down the steps leading back to Seacoast, I have the strangest feeling in my chest. Maybe God *was* there. Maybe, just maybe, he's been there all along.

Then again, maybe it's indigestion from all that fruit before nine thirty.

# Author's Note

Throughout history, man has looked up and seen the stars. It is no surprise really that we've been trying to attribute meaning to them ever since. For my part, after making a remarkable new acquaintance, I've often been partial to inquiring, "What's your sign?" But for ego's sake, I feel compelled to excuse myself: "I know it's crazy, but sometimes I believe in *that stuff.*" Likewise, when my horoscope had something good to proffer, I might hang it on my corkboard; while if there was an unpleasant prediction, I'd write it off as bull honky. When I introduce myself as a Pisces, it's because as an artist, I'm a *real Pisces,* but when someone warns me against a new laptop purchase during Mercury retrograde, I probably won't listen—until it inexplicably goes berserk and someone astrologically inclined tosses out an "I told you so."

To me, astrology had always been a bit of a fascination to flirt with when it's convenient to do so. It's often the topic of conversations with close friends, and I have to admit it's remarkable, this affinity I have for befriending Scorpios and Libras. Reading through the attributions of Pisces, and of my rising sign, Taurus, I cannot deny that the experience is like reading a map of myself. Though I can go years without a peek, there have been times in my life that I religiously followed my sign: daily, monthly, yearly. I have one dear, dear friend in the beauty industry who makes it her business to remember the signs of all of her clients (who always become her dear friends) and carefully reads through their charts and horoscopes each month and whenever new people come into their lives. I can tell you, she was certainly right about everything she told me about my husband (she's a big fan, even though his Pisces sign isn't ideal for me).

I fondly recall a trip with two of my closest friends in Northern California—during dramatic life changes for the three of us. We spent hours reading from books I was studying to research this novel, filling out online questionnaires to get our charts read, amazed at the insight the stars offered about our personal challenges and what the future might bring. Looking back, I wonder how much of our intense absorption had to do with a desperate search for hope, an assurance that we would make the right decisions.

One suspicion my research has confirmed for me is this: there is no way to deny that we are all connected. And it's not just the people who mean the most to me in the world who prove that—my sister, my brother, "Cousin" Kevin, my absolutely world class friends—both in America and Oz—like Julie and Courtney, Mimosa and Debora, and of course Roger and Minnie, and my Australian family, The Nobles. It's often the strangers who get tossed in your path just when you need them, the person whom *you* help out, only to find your own issues serendipitously illuminated in the process, the love of a pet, the guy at the shoe shine place who turned my miserable day sunny all those years ago. And if we each remember this, try to treat one another with this connection and potential in mind, think how much nicer a place the world could be.

Throughout the years, I've heard both negative and supportive opinions about the celestial arts, but I had no idea, until researching this book, just how polarizing the topic of astrology has been, and continues to be. It appears to be a favorite enemy of religion, though its history is interwoven with nearly every faith you can think of, and an enemy of reason, too, though scientists, like the fascinating Michel Gauquelin (1928–91), have proven certain of its dictums to be fact, thousands of times over. In 1975, a group of 192 scientists published a condemnation of astrology in *The Humanist,* and were publicly ridiculed from their own soapbox when they tried to stage a coup against astrology, but hypocritically, offered absolutely no scientific evidence as to why it should be discredited. The worst offense I've come across is one common in all areas of thought, and across all nations and times: being afraid of what we can't understand. Most often, it is the fear of the unknown that causes this kind of impassioned crusade against new ideas—how funny that this is the very reason people look to the stars in the first place.

One thing is for certain. Whether you believe it or not, the language of astrology is some of the most articulate and soul-searching around, ditto its symbol language: a picture says a thousand words, after all.

There is certainly nothing to be lost by investigating the ideas considered at great lengths in the science, just as there is nothing to be lost in dipping your toe into psychology, natural sciences, sociology, anthropology, or history. In fact, as an artist, or a citizen of the world, the benefit of new experience, exposure to different ways of seeing the world, or to new opinions on familiar experience is priceless. If the job of an artist is, as Shakespeare so eloquently put it, "to hold a mirror up to life," then we will certainly be that much better at our jobs the more we know about it. On the other hand, the more we realize we don't know, often, the better we are at asking the right questions, and exploring the ever-increasing complexities of it.

I like to believe that there will always remain some forces out there that we'll never understand—a charm or magic that somehow connects us all—that swings our existence into a new light, a richer meaning, and if that gets my goat, well, then, I'm going to stick with it . . . until the next time I don't like what my horoscope has to say. I am a Pisces with a Capricorn medium coeli, after all.

I'd like to hear your thoughts on the matter. Please e-mail

me (*daniella@daniellabrodsky.com*) to let me know it's all crap, or just to tell me your sign, or how you've managed your way through a particularly rough Saturn return of your own.

With caring and sharing (as *my* Grams used to write),
Daniella

# Acknowledgments

Vivian is a character who owes much thanks all around. To my editor, Abby Zidle, who is a dream come true. She could teach the world how it's done. To my sister: thank you, thank you, thank you; your husband isn't too bad, either. Of course, Rye Bread is the apple of my eye, and "Cousin" Kevin thanks as always for being who you are and doing what you do; nobody does it better. Thank you to the love of my life, Rog-*ah* (Australian for Roger), who has shown me that this magical kind of true love I've always questioned the existence of actually exists, and for showing me that when you find it, your entire life blossoms. Through him, I have been blessed with so many new friends—The Howses and the Colmers, the Reynoldses, the fabulous Mr. McNichol, and many many more. It was on one beautiful morning at the coast that one of these new friends, Deanne, a friend I'm pretty sure I was *meant* to meet, helped me to refocus this novel with her fantastically unique perspective.

At the top of the list, thank you to *my* Grams, Grandma Sylvia, who is the true inspiration for this story, and for my entire way of being. There is no way to put into words how much I miss you; we once said we were soul mates and the more time I clock, the more I believe that to be true. I hope this book illuminates how much you've given to everyone who knew you. It has been a great pleasure to spend this time with you again. And no, I *still* don't want to order the salmon burger. I think it's gross. And it smells like cat food. Most of all, thank you for being the kind of person I can come right out and say that to.

## Reading Group Guide

# *Vivian Rising*

Daniella Brodsky

## Summary

In so many ways, Viv's life is in a holding pattern that she can't or won't change. When her beloved grandmother dies, Viv appears to have lost the glue that's held her together, and her faith gives out completely. As she searches for something to believe in again, Viv finds hope in a most unlikely place: with Kavia, an alarmingly perceptive astrologer. Viv is skeptical, but under Kavia's guidance Viv begins to process her grief and rebalance her life. Every prediction Kavia makes seems to speak directly to Viv's life—even the one about meeting Len, who quickly becomes Viv's greatest source of security and comfort. But just as she settles into his arms—and into his heart—Kavia insists a relationship with him is dangerous. The stars haven't steered her wrong yet, but Viv has a choice to make: follow the path written in the stars, or trust herself to write her own story?

## For Discussion

1. What do you learn about Viv in the first scene of the novel? How do her thoughts contrast with her lack of physical action? What do you think prevents her from leaving the hospital bathroom? What does this tell you about the ways in which Viv is held back in her life?

2. In what way does Grams's death force Viv to "relearn the world" (pg. 105)? Why is the pigeon an appropriate symbol for Viv's experience? Why do you think it takes a tragedy for Viv to make positive changes in her life?

3. Viv's astrologer, Kavia, is a strong-willed older woman. Do you think Viv sees Kavia as a substitute mother figure? Is her decision to trust Kavia a rational one, given the astrologer's eerie insight, or is this choice more a result of Viv's emotional frailty? Why is it ultimately important for Viv to see Kavia as she truly is?

4. How is the reading of Viv's rising sign supported by what you learn about Viv's personality throughout the novel? How does astrology help Viv learn about herself, forgive herself, and become stronger? Do you believe that her reading was specific to her time and place of birth, as Kavia says, or does it hold universal truth, helpful to anyone?

5. Kavia advises Viv, "You master this—identify your biggest problem, and the way to work with it—and you'll be able to tackle your challenges, all your challenges in a way that really works for you" (pg. 180). What do you think is Viv's biggest problem? How does resolving it make everything else in her life easier?

6. Why do you think Viv hangs onto the “one in my head” version of her mother, when all evidence points to “the real one”? Viv ultimately decides to give her mother half of the money in Grams’ account. Would you have done the same?

7. Discuss the title, *Vivian Rising*. Who has risen by the end of the novel? Why does Viv refuse to be called Vivian at first? What is the significance of Vivian acknowledging her given name?

8. Why is Len so angry when he learns that Viv has been consulting an astrologer? Is he right when he says that she “can’t even think for herself” (pg. 256)? Why does Viv need horoscopes to come to decisions? What is preventing her from being in control of her own life?

9. Viv was born into an atheist household but raised in the Jewish faith. She turns to astrology when her belief in God falters. Why do you think Viv continues to reach out and seek a deeper meaning to her life, even after a crisis of faith? Does she use astrology as a spiritual guide or as a crutch? In what ways is choosing to forsake Kavia’s advice for a future with Len a true leap of faith?

10. Listening to Buddy Holly, Viv wonders, “Can art do just the same thing as astrology” (pg. 232)? What do you think are the similarities between art and astrology? Can appreciating art lead to understanding yourself? What about reading horoscopes?

11. When Viv’s ready to leave Kavia for the last time she decides to take the pile of books with her. “They’ve helped. They’ve inspired me and taught me to see the world differently the way the best books can and I’m not giving that up” (pg. 265). What books have inspired you? Can a book be great without offering such influence?

12. Chapter 32 opens with the quote, "Lost Illusion is the undisclosed title of every novel." How does "Lost Illusion" relate to *Vivian Rising*? Discuss this quote in the context of other book club picks.

## A Conversation with Daniella Brodsky

**What inspired you to write *Vivian Rising*?**
*Vivian Rising* began to take shape a year after the death of my best friend and grandmother, Sylvia. When I was once again head-on with the blank screen, there appeared a woman named Viv, locked in an ensuite bathroom, faced with the terrifying prospect of losing the one person who'd always cared for her. She had her own unique circumstances and sensibilities, but we shared our grief and the seemingly unanswerable question: "now what?" As the novel unfolded, it became an ode to the grieving process that at one point or another we all go through. Along with a gigantic thanks to the influence and support a grandparent can be, my wish is that the novel provides a flicker of promise—that the hopeful place we emerged from can once again be ours if we learn to adjust to the inevitable realities of loss and change.

**Do you follow astrology yourself?**
I have a cautious romantic's relationship with astrology. I will always remain in awe of the uncanny specifics of readings, especially in a fully detailed chart and will never cease to think, "How the heck does that work?" It boggles my mind to imagine the world so interconnected as astrology deems it, but as science continues to study events and causation, it appears undeniable. Just look at global warming! At times I have entered into embarrassingly dedicated consideration of my chart and horoscope, and as a benefit, I've enjoyed enlightening discussions and thought patterns. I'm not sure I would list it

on my resume, but I always walk away from astrology knowing something more about myself, or with a new perspective on a situation. However, I sometimes find the more negative readings can color my outlook, and in those cases I wonder about the power of suggestion for starting out a month, or a day, on the wrong foot.

**Viv is a New York native, a journalist and by the end of *Vivian Rising*, a novelist. How closely do you identify with Viv?**

Novelists should always identify with their heroes. If you love them, others will love them, too. I write about real, important conflicts people are faced with in life. The incidentals of their lives aren't what makes them sympathetic. There are plenty of journalists and New Yorkers I would never be able to identify with. So why did I give Viv the familiars of a journalist's life and a setting in Brighton Beach? Good question: I made her an artist afraid or otherwise unready to face up to her calling because I am obsessed with this idea of what makes an artist, of this idea people always have that "things happen for a reason," and that artists must face brutal lives to understand pain. I recall an agent telling me before I got married that she was afraid I'd be too happy and lose my inspiration. This has always stuck with me. I consider my creative output during wonderful and painful periods—I think both offer their own unique experience that adds texture to fiction. I have interviewed dozens of artists and I never cease to be amazed at the unique ways in which they take the world in, process it, and present it to us in a way no one else in the world could do. I also believe artists have an important role in recording life. These questions are some I expand on in my new novel.

Why Brighton? This is something I knew I wanted to do the second Viv showed up on my computer screen trapped in a bathroom: I wanted to pay homage to this "Old Brooklyn" that is almost on its way to extinction. This lifestyle is so unique to this place and these people who immigrated to America before and during World War II—many of whom have already passed on. As I cleaned my grandmother's apartment out with my cousin—heartbreaking business—I had this strong sensation that I wanted to preserve this world we were packing up and throwing out. It was a place so special I wanted to share it with the world. Viv's is my grandmother's apartment; this is her floor tile, her fruit store, her view of the Manhattan skyline and the Atlantic.

**Many of your novels deal with upheavals that force your protagonists to learn more about themselves. Have you experienced similar situations in your own life?**
I wouldn't share this with just anyone, but people who love books so much they want to know more about what's behind them are just the kind of people I would want to share this with. When I was in the fifth grade my father suffered a massive stroke. He died four years later from complications of this. I cannot begin to write about the terror I experienced during those years. I don't believe we ever get over such fear and loss. They inform every aspect of our development—our sense of security, our confidence, our outlooks. In some way or another, I always revisit this idea of how experience shapes us. I'm told, "write a story with the title *Princess of Park Avenue*," and what do I do but find my heroine's life has been stunted by an inability to get over a love who was terrible for her? I believe I will always be riddled by this concept, but lucky for me, this is the subtext of every story ever told—we are never divorced from our history, no matter how we try to shake it. Just ask Madonna.

**You write very lovingly of Brooklyn. How do you think place informs your writing?**
I first learned the power of a writer changing environs when I left New York City for rural Connecticut several years ago. It was such a fertile time for my imagination—driving, seeing

how pumpkins grow on vines, not in a box at the corner bodega, deciding whether it's safe to tiptoe past twelve deer on the way to my car. Currently, I'm living in Australia, and I have never been more inspired . . . every day offers a new experience, and as I've said, this is the most nourishing food for a creative mind.

Because of my new home, I've been thinking more and more about what place does as a story element, too. I believe it can be extremely important; for instance, could *Le Divorce* take place anywhere but in Paris? But it can be irrelevant, too, if a story relegates setting to the background and concentrates on universal experiences instead. One thing is for certain about changing your environment, though: it certainly forces you to think outside your own experiences.

**In *Vivian Rising*, you've created a warm community of spirited seniors. Have you been inspired by older family members or friends?**

I often tell people they better watch out or I might steal their mother or grandmother when they aren't looking. I "collect" these people because I am drawn to them in a way I don't fully understand myself. I've been told I have an "old soul." I think, in a way, this may be true. I remember, several years before my grandmother passed, telling a friend, "I'd better prepare myself; my best friend is in her eighties." Like a smoker, I casually recognized the danger, but my heart wasn't in it. My grandmother really got me. I'm not so sure you get more than one of those people in your life.

**Are there any authors who have been inspirational to your work? Do you have any suggestions for future book club picks?**

I have so many favorite authors, and the list keeps growing—both in name and in genre. I owe a great deal to all of them because they inspire me and create a "best practice" guide for me so that I don't get lazy and always aspire to be better.

These include, but certainly are not limited to: Lorrie Moore, John Cheever, Dorothy Templeton, Kazuo Ishiguro, and Doris Lessing's short fiction. Mona Simpson's *Anywhere But Here* and Janet Fitch's *White Oleander* have kept me company over so many reads the pages look antique. I tend to reread lots of classics, too. My husband has completely different reading tastes to me, but I respect his own writing and world view so deeply that I eat up the books he gives me. This has certainly had a profound effect on widening my perspective, interests, and even my style: some of those are Marcus Aurelius's *Meditations*, *The Road* by Cormac McCarthy, and *Shantaram* by Gregory David Roberts.

**How does your writing process as a freelance journalist differ from the process of focusing on a novel? Do you prefer one or the other?**

I eat, breathe, and live fiction writing. It never feels like work. Even on the worst deadline, in the middle of my holiday, I still get a high and a satisfaction from the seemingly infinite layers of mastery on offer if only you stick at it. On the other hand, I loathe, procrastinate, and feel boxed in by most of the non-fiction lifestyle journalism I have done—though I worked tirelessly to score the assignments. Fiction is a natural fit for me because it's organic and in many ways unrestrained—completely the product of creative expression, whereas magazine articles most often have a specific unbending thesis that must be upheld, no matter how messy and malleable the actual truth is. My mind naturally repels this clean, categorized, black and white version of anything, though I fought it for many years to pay the bills and to prove to myself that I could. The only kind of periodical writing I would like to do now is of the interview, opinion, or personal essay variety, however, any time I try to write about myself I am hopeless at taking myself seriously, and the effort flops right on the page. I will not give up, though. One day I will be able to give myself the same reverence I do my characters. Hopefully.

**Can you tell us about any upcoming projects?**
I am working on a novel about a woman with an unconventional, powerful, yet painful relationship with her mother. It is in many ways about the sort of artist's experience I mentioned above as well as the universal questions about how love can shape us. I am also working on a novel about a woman's strange and dangerous dip into self-discovery and alcoholism after a divorce. In the non-fiction realm, I am compiling a book of inspiration for writers, artists, and artful people.

**Do you have any advice for aspiring writers?**
I have *tons* (such as don't overuse italics: look, I haven't used them at all, so now I've gotten you to believe I have something very important to say). Seriously though, in my newest role, I've been teaching novel writing at the Australian National University's continuing education program. This is as rewarding to me as it is for my students because they teach me to look at writing in a logical way that hadn't occurred to me before, and mostly because each person who didn't believe they could write, and then actually does, backs up my theory that a little encouragement goes a long way.

## Enhance Your Book Club

1. Viv finds it helpful to read her horoscope in the morning, then take inventory of the day ahead. Try it out for a week. Check your horoscope daily, keep a journal of your findings, and share your insights with the group.

2. Check out Daniella Brodsky's website for information on her other novels, upcoming projects and events: www.daniellabrodsky.com

3. For more information on astrology and other spiritual belief systems, check out www.Beliefnet.com. While you're there, take the BeliefOMatic quiz and see what tradition your beliefs are most connected to.